FESTIVAL OF FEAR

Recent Titles by Graham Masterton available from Severn House

Anthologies

FACES OF FEAR
FEELINGS OF FEAR
FORTNIGHT OF FEAR
FLIGHTS OF FEAR
FESTIVAL OF FEAR

The Jim Rook Series

ROOK
THE TERROR
TOOTH AND CLAW
SNOWMAN
SWIMMER
DARKROOM
DEMON'S DOOR

The Sissy Sawyer Series

TOUCHY AND FEELY
THE PAINTED MAN

Novels

BASILISK
BLIND PANIC
CHAOS THEORY
DESCENDANT
DOORKEEPERS
EDGEWISE
FIRE SPIRIT
GENIUS
GHOST MUSIC
HIDDEN WORLD
HOLY TERROR
HOUSE OF BONES
MANITOU BLOOD
THE NINTH NIGHTMARE
PETRIFIED
UNSPEAKABLE

FESTIVAL OF FEAR

Graham Masterton

This first world edition published 2012
in Great Britain and in the USA by
SEVERN HOUSE PUBLISHERS LTD of
9–15 High Street, Sutton, Surrey, England, SM1 1DF.

British Library Cataloguing in Publication Data

Masterton, Graham.
Festival of fear.
1. Horror tales, English.
I. Title
823.9'2-dc23

ISBN-13: 978-0-7278-6408-6 (cased)

For Maria Wiktoria Raczkowska,
with thanks for everything.
Who needs more vinegar, anyway?

All Severn House titles are printed on acid-free paper.

Severn House Publishers support The Forest Stewardship Council [FSC], the leading international forest certification organisation. All our titles that are printed on Greenpeace-approved FSC-certified paper carry the FSC logo.

Typeset by Palimpsest Book Production Ltd.,
Falkirk, Stirlingshire, Scotland.
Printed and bound in Great Britain by
MPG Books Ltd., Bodmin, Cornwall.

Contents

The Press

Few people shed any tears when Padraic Rossa died at the age of eighty-nine, even his publishers, because he hadn't produced a book that was either comprehensible or commercial since the mid-1970s, and he was probably the most cantankerous man that Irish letters had ever known. Even Brendan O'Neill, who was loved by authors everywhere for his emollient reviews in the *Cork Examiner*, had called Rossa 'a foul temper on legs.'

Rossa's last work, *All Hallows' Eve*, was published in 1997 and was little more than a splenetic rant about the way in which the Irish had allowed the rest of the world to turn a sacred Celtic ritual dating back to the fifth century into a 'cash cow for the makers of plastic pumpkins and Hallmark Cards. It was one thing to turn our folk music into fiddle-de-dee for the tourist trade, and our magical beliefs into garden gnomes. But by allowing the commercialization of Halloween we have dragged the souls of our dead ancestors out of the eternal shadows and hung them up in the common light of the marketplace for every inquisitive passer-by to finger.'

When it was published two weeks before Halloween, Rossa's book was widely excoriated in the book pages of the *Irish Times* and several other newspapers and magazines for being 'a saliva-spraying welter of Celtic superstition and Druidic mumbo-jumbo, by a man who seems to believe that "fun" is a notifiable disease.'

You no doubt remember, though, that five of the reviewers who gave Rossa such critical notices disappeared on the night of All Hallows' Eve, and no trace of them was ever found. There was a lengthy investigation by the Garda Síochána, during which Rossa was questioned several times, but he made no comment about their vanishing, except to say that they had probably got what they deserved. Nervous jokes were made in the press about 'the curse of Padraic Rossa' and stories were told in Henchy's Bar that he had summoned up Satan to drag his critics down to hell, their way lit by embers, in turnip lanterns.

After he died, Rossa's huge Victorian house on the steep hill overlooking the River Lee in Montenotte came up for auction almost immediately, since there were bills to be settled and Rossa's books hadn't made any decent money in decades. The coal bill alone hadn't been paid for six and a half years.

I was called up by *Irish Property* to write a feature about the house and I went up there one slick, wet Thursday morning with John McGrorty, who was to take the photographs. John was a very humorous fellow with a head of hair like a bunch of spring carrots and a taste for ginger tweed jackets.

We parked in Lovers' Walk and John took a selection of pictures of the outside. The house was a four-story building in the Gothic style, painted pale green, with dark green window-frames, as tall as a cliff. I think 'forbidding' would be your word for it. It stood on the brow of the hill with the river far below, and from the steep back garden you could see all of Cork City and all the way beyond to the drizzly grey-green hills.

We rang the doorbell at the glass front porch and a young woman from the auctioneers came to answer it. A large, yellowish slug was clinging halfway up the window and John touched it with the tip of his cigarette so that it shriveled and dropped on to the flagstones.

'You're a sadist,' I told him.

The young woman from the auctioneers was pretty enough, with a short brown bob and a pale heart-shaped face and sea-green eyes and rimless glasses. 'My name's Fionnula,' she said, holding out her hand.

'I'm John,' said John, 'and this is Michael. Do you know what "Fionnula" means in Swahili?'

Fionnula shook her head.

'It means "bespectacled beauty from the auctioneers".'

'Oh, yes,' she said, 'and do you know what "John" means in Urdu? It means "red-headed chancer in a clashing orange coat".'

'Well, girl, you give as good as you get,' John told her. 'Are you going to be conducting us on a tour of these delightfully gloomy premises, then?'

The hallway was vast. Over a marble fireplace hung a dark oil portrait of Padraic Rossa himself, clutching his lapels as if he were trying to tear them off his jacket. He had a blocky-looking head, and he looked more like a bare-knuckle boxer than a writer.

'He was a sour-tempered man and no mistake,' said Fionnula. 'I met him only the once. I came up here to make a valuation but he wouldn't let me into the house. He said that he wouldn't be dealing with an empty-headed young girl who knew nothing of the Celtic tradition.'

She showed us the drawing room with its heavy velvet curtains and its strange paintings of pale men and women, peering out of the darkness with luminous eyes. Some of them had beaks like owls, while others had foxes' claws instead of hands.

'You could well believe that Rossa was a close friend of his Satanic Majesty, now couldn't you?' said John. The flashes from his camera seemed to make the people in the paintings jump, as if for a split second he had brought them to life.

We toured the bedrooms. The ceilings were damp, and in some places the wallpaper was hanging down. In Rossa's own bedroom, the mattress on the four-poster bed had a dark stain in the middle of it, and there was an overwhelming smell of urine and death.

At last we came back downstairs to take a look at the dining room. At the far end of the room stood a huge mahogany cupboard, with carved pillars and bunches of grapes, which must have been used for storing china. In Ireland we would call a cupboard like this a press.

'That is a massive piece of joinery and no mistake,' said John, taking pictures of it. Its finial touched the ceiling, and it had a wide drawer underneath with handles in the shape of demons' faces, with rings through their noses.

Fionnula turned the key in the lock and opened up the press so that we could look inside. It was completely empty, but it was unexpectedly large inside, almost three times as deep as it looked from the outside. It had that sour, vinegary smell of old cupboards that have been closed up for years.

'You could almost live in this,' said John. 'In fact I think it's bigger than my flat. And look . . . what's that written on the back?'

The back of the press was covered in lettering, faded black, with some gilded capitals. It looked like Gaelic.

'We'll have a picture of this,' said John. 'Here, bespectacled beauty from the auctioneers, do you think you could hold my light for me?'

He helped Fionnula to climb up into the press, and then he climbed in after her. He handed her his electronic strobe light and started to take pictures of the lettering at the back. 'Now I recognize some of the words here,' he said. '*Beó duine d'éis a anma* . . . that means "a man may live after his death".'

He peered at the lettering even more closely. 'This is some kind of Celtic incantation . . . a summoning-up of dead souls. It must be connected with Rossa's book on All Hallows' Eve.'

As his fingers traced the words, however, I heard an extraordinary noise. A slow, mechanical ticking, like a very loud clock, but punctuated by the clicking of levers and tumblers, and the flat *donk* sound of expanding springs.

'What the hell's that?' asked John, turning around. But before any of us could do anything, the huge doors to the press swung silently shut, and locked themselves, trapping John and Fionnula inside.

'Will you open the effing doors, Michael?' shouted John. 'This isn't a joke!'

'For God's sake, let us out!' said Fionnula. She sounded panicky already. 'I can't stand enclosed spaces!'

I turned the key, but the doors wouldn't budge. I went to the sideboard and pulled open the drawers. One of them was full of tarnished cutlery, so I took out a dinner knife and tried to pry the doors open with that. They still refused to open. Both John and Fionnula were hammering and kicking on them, but they were so solid that they didn't even shake.

It was then that I heard two more sounds. A high-pitched squeaking, like a screw turning, and then a sliding noise.

'John!' I shouted. 'John, are you all right? I'm going into the garden, see if I can find a shovel or a pick or something!'

But John yelled, 'The ceiling! The ceiling's coming down!'

'What?'

'The ceiling's coming down! It's going to crush us!'

The squeaking went on and on. I ran into the rainy garden and came back with an iron fence-post, and I beat at those doors until the fence-post almost bent double. John and Fionnula were both screaming and then I heard something break, and John crying out in agony. '*Oh Mary Mother of God save us*! *Oh Mary Mother of God forgive me*!'

After that there was nothing but a slow complicated crunching.

I stood outside the press with my eyes filled with tears, trembling with shock. Eventually the squeaking stopped, and then I heard ratchets and cogs, and the doors to the press slowly opened themselves. Inside, there was nothing at all. No John, no Fionnula.

For a moment I couldn't understand what had happened to them. But then I saw blood dripping from the edge of the drawer at the bottom of the press. I took hold of the demon's-head handles and slowly pulled it open.

If you have never seen human beings compressed until they are less than an inch thick, it is almost impossible to describe them to you. The most horrible thing is their faces, which look like pink rubber Halloween masks, with scarlet lips, and empty, liquid eyes.

But John and Fionnula's bodies weren't the only remains in the drawer. Underneath them were the crushed remains of several other people, their skin as papery and desiccated as wasps' nests.

I could only guess how Padraic Rossa had persuaded his critics to step into his cupboard. Perhaps he had pretended to be conciliatory, and invited them up to his house to explain the mysteries of Halloween to them. Then perhaps he had suggested that they examine the Celtic incantations at close quarters. Whatever had happened, he had made sure that they, too, had a very bad press.

The Burgers of Calais

I never cared for northern parts and I never much cared for eastern parts neither, because I hate the cold and I don't have any time for those bluff, ruddy-faced people who live there, with their rugged, plaid coats and their Timberland boots and their way of whacking you on the back when you least expect it, like whacking you on the back is supposed to be some kind of friendly gesture or something.

I don't like what goes on there, neither. Everybody behaves so cheerful and folksy but believe me that folksiness hides some real grisly secrets that would turn your blood to iced gazpacho.

You can guess, then, that I was distinctly unamused when I was driving back home early last October from Presque Isle, Maine, and my beloved '71 Mercury Marquis dropped her entire engine on the highway like a cow giving birth.

The only reason I had driven all the way to Presque Isle, Maine, was to lay to rest my old Army buddy Dean Brunswick III (may God forgive him for what he did in Colonel Wrightman's cigar box). I couldn't wait to get back south, but now I found myself stuck a half-mile away from Calais, Maine, population 4,003 and one of the most northernmost, easternmost, back-whackingest towns you could ever have waking nightmares about.

Calais is locally pronounced 'CAL-us' and believe me a callous is exactly what it is – a hard, corny little spot on the right elbow of America. Especially when you have an engineless, uninsured automobile and a maxed-out Visa card and only $226 in your billfold and no friends or relations back home who can afford to send you more than a cheery hello.

I left my beloved Mercury tilted up on the leafy embankment by the side of US Route One South and walked into town. I never cared a whole lot for walking, mainly because my weight has kind of edged up a little since I left the Army in '86, due to a pathological lack of restraint when it comes to filé gumbo and Cajun spiced chicken with lots of crunchy bits and mustard-barbecued spare ribs and key lime pies. My landlady Rita Personage says that when she first saw me she thought that Orson Welles had risen from the dead, and I must say I do have quite a line in flappy, white, double-breasted sport coats, not to mention a few wide-brimmed white hats. Though, not all of those are in prime condition since I lost my job with the Louisiana Restaurant Association, which was a heinous political fix involving some of the shadier elements in the East Baton Rouge catering community and also possibly the fact that I was on the less balletic side of 290 pounds.

It was a piercing bright day. The sky was blue like ink and the trees were all turning gold and red and crispy brown. Calais is one of those neat New England towns with white clapboard houses and churches with spires and cheery people waving to each other as they drive up and down the streets at two and a half miles per hour.

By the time I reached North and Main I was sweating like a cheese and severely in need of a beer. There was a *whip, whip, whoop* behind me and it was a police patrol car. I stopped and the officer put down his window. He had mirror sunglasses and a sandy moustache that looked as if he kept his nail brush on his upper lip. And freckles. You know the type.

'Wasn't speeding, was I, officer?'

He took off his sunglasses. He didn't smile. He didn't even blink. He said, 'You look like a man with a problem, sir.'

'I know. I've been on Redu-Quick for over six months now and I haven't lost a pound.'

That really cracked him up, not. 'You in need of some assistance?' he asked me.

'Well, my car suffered a minor mechanical fault a ways back there and I was going into town to see if I could get anybody to fix it.'

'That your clapped-out, saddle-bronze Marquis out on Route One?'

'That's the one. Nothing that a few minutes in the crusher couldn't solve.'

'Want to show me some ID?'

'Sure.' I handed him my driver's license and my identity card from the restaurant association. He peered at them, and for some reason actually *sniffed* them.

'John Henry Dauphin, Choctaw Drive, East Baton Rouge. You're a long way from home, Mr Dauphin.'

'I've just buried one of my old Army buddies up in Presque Isle.'

'And you *drove* all the way up here?'

'Sure, it's only one thousand nine hundred and sixty miles. It's a pretty fascinating drive, if you don't have any drying paint that needs watching.'

'Louisiana Restaurant Association . . . that's who you work for?'

'That's right,' I lied. Well, he didn't have to know that I was out of a job. 'I'm a restaurant hygiene consultant. Hey – bet you never guessed that I was in the food business.'

'OK . . . the best thing you can do is call into Lyle's Autos down at the other end of Main Street, get your vehicle towed off the highway as soon as possible. If you require a place to stay I can recommend the Calais Motor Inn.'

'Thank you. I may stay for a while. Looks like a nice town. Very . . . well swept.'

'It is,' he said, as if he were warning me to make sure that it stayed that way. He handed back my ID and drove off at the mandatory snail's pace.

Lyle's Autos was actually run by a stocky man called Nils Guttormsen. He had a gray crew-cut and a permanently surprised face like a chipmunk going through the sound barrier backward. He charged me a mere sixty-five dollars for towing my car into his workshop, which was only slightly more than a quarter of everything I had in the world, and he estimated that he could put the engine back into it for less than $785, which was about $784 more than it was actually worth.

'How long will it take, Nils?'

'Well, John, you need it urgent?'

'Not really, Nils . . . I thought I might stick around town for a while. So – you know – why don't you take your own sweet time?'

'OK, John. I have to get transmission parts from Bangor. I could have it ready, say Tuesday?'

'Good deal, Nils. Take longer if you want. Make it the Tuesday after next. Or even the Tuesday after that.'

'You'll be wanting a car while I'm working on yours, John.'

'Will I, Nils? No, I don't think so. I could use some exercise, believe me.'

'It's entirely up to you, John. But I've got a couple of nifty Toyotas to rent if you change your mind. They look small but there's plenty of room in them. Big enough to carry a sofa.'

'Thanks for the compliment, Nils.'

I hefted my battered old suitcase to the Calais Motor Inn, changing hands every few yards all the way down Main Street. Fortunately the desk accepted my Visa impression without even the hint of hysterical laughter. The Calais Motor Inn was a plain, comfortable motel, with plaid carpets and a shiny bar with tinkly music where I did justice to three bottles of chilled Molson's and a ham and Swiss-cheese triple-decker sandwich on rye with coleslaw and straw fried potatoes, and two helpings of cookie-crunch ice cream to keep my energy levels up.

The waitress was a pretty, snubby-nose woman with cropped blonde hair and a kind of a Swedish look about her.

'Had enough?' she asked me.

'Enough of what? Cookie-crunch ice cream or Calais in general?'

'My name's Velma,' she said.

'John,' I replied, and bobbed up from my leatherette seat to shake her hand.

'Just passing through, John?' she asked me.

'I don't know, Velma . . . I was thinking of sticking around for a while. Where would somebody like me find themselves a job? And don't say the circus.'

'Is that what you do, John?' she asked me.

'What do you mean, Velma?'

'Make jokes about yourself before anybody gets them in?'

'Of course not. Didn't you know that all fat guys have to be funny by federal statute? No, I'm a realist. I know what my relationship is with food and I've learned to live with it.'

'You're a good-looking guy, John, you know that?'

'You can't fool me, Velma. All fat people look the same. If fat people could run faster, they'd all be bank robbers, because nobody can tell them apart.'

'Well, John, if you want a job you can try the want ads in the local paper, *The Quoddy Whirlpool*.'

'The what?'

'The bay here is called the Passamaquoddy, and out by Eastport we've got the Old Sow Whirlpool, which is the biggest whirlpool in the Western hemisphere.'

'I see. Thanks for the warning.'

'You should take a drive around the Quoddy Loop . . . it's beautiful. Fishing quays, lighthouses, lakes. Some good restaurants, too.'

'My car's in the shop right now, Velma. Nothing too serious. Engine fell out.'

'You're welcome to borrow mine, John. It's only a Volkswagen but I don't hardly ever use it.'

I looked up at her and narrowed my eyes. Down in Baton Rouge the folks slide around on a snail's trail of courtesy and Southern charm, but I can't imagine any one of them offering a total stranger the use of their car, especially a total stranger who was liable to ruin the suspension just by sitting in the driver's seat.

'That's very gracious of you, Velma.'

I bought *The Quoddy Whirlpool*. If you were going into hospital for a heart bypass they could give you that paper instead of a general anesthetic. Under 'Help Wanted' somebody was advertising for a 'talented' screen-door repair person and somebody else needed an experienced leaf-blower mechanic and somebody else was looking for a twice-weekly dog-walker for their Presa Canario. Since I happened to know that Presa Canarios stand two feet tall and weigh almost as much as I do, and that two of them notoriously ripped an innocent woman in San Francisco into bloody shreds, I was not wholly motivated to apply for the last of those positions.

In the end I went to the Maine Job Service on Beech Street. A bald guy in a green, zip-up, hand-knitted cardigan sat behind a desk with photographs of his toothy wife on it (presumably the perpetrator of the green, zip-up, hand-knitted cardigan) while I had to hold my hand up all the time to stop the sun from shining in my eyes.

'So . . . what is your field of expertise, Mr Dauphin?'

'Oh, please, call me John. I'm a restaurant hygienist. I have an FSIS qualification from Baton Rouge University and nine years' experience working for the Louisiana Restaurant Association.'

'What brings you up to Calais, Maine, John?'

'I just felt it was time for a radical change of location.' I squinted at the nameplate on his desk. 'Martin.'

'I'm afraid I don't have anything available on quite your level of expertise, John. But I do have one or two catering opportunities.'

'What exactly kind of catering opportunities, Martin?'

'Vittles need a cleaner . . . that's an excellent restaurant, Vittles, one of the premier eateries in town. It's situated in the Calais Motor Inn.'

'Ah.' As a guest of the Calais Motor Inn, I couldn't exactly see myself eating dinner in the restaurant and then carrying my own dishes into the kitchen and washing them up.

'Then Tony's have an opportunity for a breakfast chef.'

'Tony's?'

'Tony's Gourmet Burgers on North Street.'

'I see. What do they pay?'

'They pay more than Burger King or McDonald's. They have outlets all over Maine and New Brunswick, but they're more of a family business. More of a *quality* restaurant, if you know what I mean. I always take my own family to eat there.'

'And is that all you have?'

'I have plenty of opportunities in fishing and associated trades. Do you have any expertise with drift nets?'

'Drift nets? Are you kidding? I spent my whole childhood trawling for pilchards off the coast of Greenland.'

Martin looked across his desk at me, sitting there with my hand raised like I needed to go to the bathroom. When he spoke his voice was very biscuity and dry. 'Why don't you call round at Tony's, John? See if you like the look of it. I'll give Mr Le Renges a call, tell him you're on your way.'

'Thanks, Martin.'

Tony's Gourmet Burgers was one block away from Burger King and two blocks away from McDonald's, on a straight, tree-lined street where the 4x4s rolled past at two and a half miles per hour and everybody waved to each other and whacked each other on the back whenever they could get near enough and you felt like a hidden orchestra was going to strike up the theme to *Providence*.

All the same, Tony's was quite a handsome-looking restaurant with a brick front and brass carriage-lamps outside with flickering artificial flames. A chalkboard proudly proclaimed that this was 'the home of wholesome, hearty food, lovingly prepared in our own kitchens by people who really care.' Inside it was fitted out with dark wood paneling and tables with green, checkered cloths and gilt-framed engravings of whitetail deer, black bear and moose. It was crowded with cheery-looking families, and you certainly couldn't fault it for ambience. Smart, but homely, with none of that wipe-clean feeling you get at McDonald's.

At the rear of the restaurant was a copper bar with an open grill, where a spotty young guy in a green apron and a tall green chef's hat was sizzling hamburgers and steaks.

A red-headed girl in a short green pleated skirt sashayed up to me and gave me a 500-watt smile, complete with teeth braces. 'You prefer a booth or a table, sir?'

'Actually, neither. I have an appointment to see Mr Le Renges.'

'He's right in back . . . why don't you follow me? What name shall I say?'

'John.'

Mr Le Renges was sitting in a blood-red leather chair with a reproduction antique table beside him, on which there was a fax machine, a silver carriage-clock, and a glass of seltzer. He was a bony man of forty-five or so with dyed-black collar-length hair which he had combed with something approaching genius to conceal his dead-white scalp. His nose was sharp and multi-faceted, and his eyes glittered under his overgrown eyebrows like blowflies. He wore a very white open-neck shirt with long 1970s collar-points and a tailored black three-piece suit. I had the feeling that he thought he bore more than a passing resemblance to Al Pacino.

On the paneled wall behind him hung an array of certificates from the Calais Regional Chamber of Commerce and the Maine Restaurant Guide and even one from Les Chevaliers de la Haute Cuisine Canadienne.

'Come in, John,' said Mr Le Renges, in a distinctly French-Canadian accent. 'Sit down, please . . . the couch, perhaps? That chair's a little—'

'A little *little*?'

'I was thinking only of your comfort, John. You see my policy is always to make the people who work for me feel happy and comfortable. I don't have a desk, I never have. A desk is a statement which says that I am more important than you. I am *not* more important. Everybody who works here is of equal importance, and of equal value.'

'You've been reading the McDonald's Bible. Always make your staff feel valued. Then you won't have to pay them so much.'

I could tell that Mr Le Renges didn't quite know if he liked that remark. It was the way he twitched his head, like Data in *Star Trek*. But I could also tell that he was the kind of guy who was anxious that nobody should leave him without fully comprehending what a wonderful human being he was.

He sipped some seltzer and eyed me over the rim of the glass. 'You are perhaps a little *mature* to be seeking work as a burger chef.'

'Mature? I'm positively overripe. But I've been working in the upper echelons of the restaurant trade for so long, I thought it was time that I went back to basics. Got my hands dirty, so to speak.'

'At Tony's Gourmet Burgers, John, our hygiene is second to none.'

'Of course. When I say getting my hands dirty – that's like a metaphor. Food hygiene, that's my specialty. I know everything there is to know about proper cooking times and defrosting and never picking your nose while you're making a Caesar salad.'

'What's your cooking experience, John?'

'I was a cook in the Army. Three times winner of the Fort Polk prize for culinary excellence. It made me very good at home economics. I can make a pound and a half of ground beef stretch between two platoons of infantry and a heavy armored assault force.'

'You're a funny guy, John,' said Mr Le Renges, without the slightest indication that he was amused.

'I'm fat, Tony. Funny goes with the territory.'

'I don't want you to make me laugh, John. I want you to cook burgers. And it's "Mr Le Renges" to you.'

He took me through to the kitchen, which was tiled in dark brown ceramic with stainless-steel counters. Two gawky young kids were using microwave ovens to thaw out frozen hamburger patties and frozen bacon and frozen fried chicken and frozen French fries. 'This is Chip and this is Denzil.'

'How's it going, Chip? Denzil?'

Chip and Denzil stared at me numbly and mumbled, ''Kay, I guess.'

'And this is Letitia.' A frowning, dark-haired girl was painstakingly tearing up iceberg lettuce as if it were as difficult as lacemaking.

'Letitia's one of our *challenged* crew members,' said Mr Le Renges, resting one of his hairy tarantula hands on her shoulder. 'The state of Maine gives us special tax relief to employ the challenged, but even if they didn't I'd still want to have her here. That's the kind of guy I am, John. I've been called to do more than feed people. I've been called to enrich their lives.'

Letitia looked up at me with unfocused aquamarine eyes. She was pretty but she had the expression of a small-town beauty queen who has just been hit on the head by half a brick. Some instinct told me that Tony Le Renges wasn't only using her as an iceberg lettuce tearer.

'We take pride in the supreme quality of our food,' he said. Without any apparent sense of irony he opened a huge freezer at the back of the kitchen and showed me the frozen steaks and the frost-covered envelopes of pre-cooked chili, ready for boiling in the bag. He showed me the freeze-dried vegetables and the frozen corn bread and the dehydrated lobster chowder (just add hot water.) And this was in Maine, where you can practically find fresh lobsters waltzing down the street.

None of this made me weak with shock. Even the best restaurants use a considerable proportion of pre-cooked and prepackaged food, and fast food outlets like McDonald's and Burger King use nothing else. Even their scrambled eggs come dried and pre-scrambled in a packet.

What impressed me was how Mr Le Renges could sell this ordinary, industrialized stuff as 'wholesome, hearty food, lovingly cooked in our own kitchens by people who really care' when most of it was grudgingly thrown together in giant factories by minimum-wage shift-workers who didn't give a rat's ass.

Mr Le Renges must have had an inkling about the way my mind was working.

'You know what our secret is?' he asked me.

'If I'm going to come and cook here, Mr Le Renges, I think it might be a good idea if you told me.'

'We have the best-tasting burgers anywhere, that's our secret. McDonald's and Burger King don't even come *close*. Once you've tasted one of our burgers, you won't want anything else. Here – Kevin – pass me a burger so that John here can try it.'

'That's OK,' I told him. 'I'll take your word for it. I had a sandwich already.'

'No, John, if you're going to work here, I insist.'

'Listen, Mr Le Renges, I'm a professional food hygienist. I know what goes into burgers and that's why I never eat them. Never.'

'What are you suggesting?'

'I'm not suggesting anything. It's just that I know for a fact that a proportion of undesirable material makes its way into ground beef and I don't particularly want to eat it.'

'Undesirable material? What do you mean?'

'Well, *waste products,* if you want me to be blunt about it. Cattle are slaughtered and disemboweled so fast that it makes it inevitable that a certain amount of excrement contaminates the meat.'

'Listen, John, how do you think I compete with McDonald's and Burger King? I make my customers feel as if they're a cut above people who eat at the big fast-food chains. I make them feel as if they're discerning diners.'

'But you're serving up pretty much the same type of food.'

'Of course we are. That's what our customers are used to, that's what they like. But we make it just a little more expensive, and we serve it up like it's something really special. We give them a proper restaurant experience, that's why they come here for birthdays and special occasions.'

'But that must whack up your overheads.'

'What we lose on overheads we gain by sourcing our own foodstuffs.'

'You mean you can buy this stuff cheaper than McDonald's? How do you do that? You don't have a millionth of their buying power.'

'We use farmers' and stockbreeders' cooperatives. Little guys, that the big fast-food chains don't want to do business with. That's why our burgers taste better, and that's why they don't contain anything that you wouldn't want to eat.'

Kevin came over from the grill with a well-charred burger

patty on a plate. His spots were glowing angrily from the heat. Mr Le Renges handed me a fork and said, 'There . . . try it.'

I cut a small piece off and peered at it suspiciously. 'No shit?' I asked him.

'Nothing but one thousand percent protein, I promise you.'

I dry-swallowed, and then I put the morsel in my mouth. I chewed it slowly, trying not to think about the manure-splattered ramps of the slaughterhouses that I had visited around Baton Rouge. Mr Le Renges watched me with those glittering blowfly eyes of his and that didn't make it any more appetizing, either.

But, surprisingly, the burger actually tasted pretty good. It was tender, with just the right amount of crunchiness on the outside, and it was well seasoned with onion and salt and pepper and the tiniest touch of chili, and there was another flavor, too, that really lifted it.

'Cumin?' I asked Mr Le Renges.

'Aha. That would be telling. But you like it, don't you?'

I cut off another piece. 'OK, I have to confess that I do.'

Mr Le Renges whacked me on the back so that I almost choked. 'You see, John? Now you know what I was talking about when I told you that I was called to enrich people's lives. I keep small farmers in business, and at the same time I give the people of Calais a very important community venue with the best food that I can economically serve up. Well, not only Calais. I have Tony's Gourmet Burgers in Old Town and Millinocket and Waterville and I've just opened a new flagship restaurant in St Stephen, over the river in Canada.'

'Well, congratulations,' I coughed. 'When do you want me to start?'

I dreamed that I was sitting by the window of Rocco's restaurant on Drusilla Lane in Baton Rouge, eating a spicy catfish poboy with a cheese fry basket and a side of brown gravy. I had just ordered my bread pudding when the phone rang and the receptionist told me in a clogged-up voice that it was five fifteen in the morning.

'Why are you telling me this?' I asked her.

'You asked for an alarm call, sir. Five fifteen, and it's five fifteen.'

I heaved myself up in bed. Outside my window it was still

totally dark. It was then that I remembered that I was now the *chef de petit dejeuner* at Tony's, and I was supposed to be over on North Street at six a.m. sharp to open up the premises and start getting the bacon griddled and the eggs shirred and the coffee percolating.

I stared at myself in the mirror. 'Why did you do this to yourself?' I asked me.

'Because you're a nit-picking perfectionist who couldn't turn a blind eye to three mouse droppings at the Cajun Queen Restaurant, that's why. And they probably weren't even mouse droppings at all. Just capers.'

'Capers schmapers.'

It was so cold outside that the deserted sidewalks shone like hammered glass. I walked to North Street where Chip had just opened up the restaurant.

'Morning, Chip.'

'Yeah.' He showed me how to switch off the alarm and switch on the lights. Then we went through to the kitchen and he showed me how to heat up the griddle and take out the frozen bacon and the frozen burgers and mix up the 'fresh squeezed' orange juice (just add water.)

We had only been there ten minutes when a young, mousy-haired girl with a pale face and dark circles under her eyes came through the door. 'Hi,' she said. 'I'm Anita. You must be John.'

'Hi, Anita,' I said, wiping my fingers on my green apron and shaking hands. 'How about a cup of coffee before the hordes descend on us?'

'OK, then,' she blinked. From the expression on her face I think she must have thought I said 'whores.'

But they were hordes all right, and once they started coming through that door they didn't stop. By a quarter after seven every booth and every table was crowded with businessmen and postal workers and truckers and even the sandy-haired cop who had first flagged me down as I walked into town. I couldn't believe that these people got up so early. Not only that, they were all so *cheerful*, too, like they couldn't wait to start another day's drudgery. It was all, 'Good morning, Sam! And how are you on this cold and frosty morning!' 'Good morning, Mrs Trent! See *you* wrapped up warm and toasty!' 'Hi, Rick! Great day for the race – the human race!' I mean, please.

They not only looked hearty and talked hearty, they ate hearty, too. For two hours solid I was sizzling bacon and flipping burgers and frying eggs and browning corned-beef hash. Anita was dashing from table to table with juice and coffee and double orders of toast, and it wasn't until eight that a sassy black girl called Oona came in to help her.

Gradually, however, the restaurant began to empty out, with more back-whacking and more cheery goodbyes, until we were left with nobody but two FedEx drivers and an old woman who looked as if she was going to take the next six months to chew her way through two slices of Canadian bacon.

It was then that one of the FedEx drivers put his hand over his mouth and spat into it. He frowned down at what he had found in his burger and showed it to his friend. Then he got up from the table and came over to the grill, his hand cupped over his mouth.

'Broken my darn tooth,' he said.

'How d'you do that?' I asked him.

'Bit into my burger and there was *this* in it.'

He held up a small black object between his finger and thumb.

I took it from him and turned it this way and that. There was no doubt about it, it was a bullet, slightly flattened by impact.

'I'm real sorry,' I said. 'Look, this is my first day here. All I can do is report it to the management and you can have your breakfast on us.'

'I'm going to have to see a darn dentist,' he complained. 'I can't abide the darn dentist. And what if I'd swallowed it? I could of got lead poisoning.'

'I'm sorry. I'll show it to the owner just as soon as he gets here.'

'This'll cost plenty, I bet you. Do you want to take a look?' Before I could stop him he stretched open his mouth and showed me a chipped front incisor and a mouthful of mushed-up hamburger.

Mr Le Renges came in at eleven a.m. Outside it was starting to get windy and his hair had flapped over to one side like a crow's wing. Before I could collar him he dived straight into his office and closed the door, presumably to spend some time rearranging his wayward locks. He came out five minutes later, briskly chafing his hands together like a man eager to get down to business.

'Well, John, how did it go?'

'Pretty good, Mr Le Renges. Place was packed out.'

'Always is. People know a good deal when they see one.'

'Only one problem. A guy found this in his burger.'

I handed him the bullet. He inspected it closely, and then he shook his head.

'That didn't come from one of our burgers, John.'

'I saw him spit it out myself. He broke one of his front teeth.'

'Oldest trick in the book. Guy needs dental work, he comes into a restaurant and pretends he broke his tooth on something he ate. Gets the restaurant to stump up for his dentist's bill.'

'Well, it didn't look that way to me.'

'That's because you're not as well versed in the wiles of dishonest customers as I am. You didn't apologize, I hope?'

'I didn't charge him for his breakfast.'

'You shouldn't have done that, John. That's practically an admission of liability. Well, let's hope the bastard doesn't try to take it any further.'

'Aren't you going to inform the health and safety people?'

'Of course not.'

'What about your suppliers?'

'You know as well as I do that all ground beef is magnetically screened for metal particles.'

'Sure. But this is a bullet and it's made of lead and lead isn't magnetic.'

'They don't *shoot* cows, John.'

'Of course not. But anything could have happened. Maybe some kid took a potshot at it when it was standing in a field, and the bullet was lodged in its muscle.'

'John, every one of our burgers is very carefully sourced from people who are really *evangelical* when it comes to quality meat. There is no way that this bullet came from one of our burgers, and I hope you're prepared to back me up and say that there was absolutely no sign of any bullet in that customer's patty when you grilled it.'

'I didn't actually *see* it, no. But—'

Mr Le Renges dropped the bullet into his wastebasket. 'Attaboy, John. You'll be back here bright and early tomorrow morning, then?'

'Early, yes. Bright? Well, maybe.'

All right, you can call me a hair-splitting go-by-the-book bureaucrat, but the way I see it any job has to be done properly or else it's not worth getting out of bed in the morning to do it, especially if you have to get out of bed at five fifteen. I walked back to the Calais Motor Inn looking for a bite of lunch, and I ordered a fried chicken salad with iceberg lettuce, tomato, bacon bits, Cheddar and mozzarella and home-made croutons, with onion strings and fried pickles on the side. But as comforting as all of this was, I couldn't stop thinking about that bullet and wondering where it had come from. I could understand why Mr Le Renges didn't want to report it to the health and safety inspectors, but why didn't he want to have a hard word with his own supplier?

Velma came up with another beer. 'You're looking serious today, John. I thought you had to be happy by law.'

'Got something on my mind, Velma, that's all.'

She sat down beside me. 'How did the job go?'

'It's an existence. I grill, therefore I am. But something happened today . . . I don't know. It's made me feel kind of uncomfortable.'

'What do you mean, John?'

'It's like having my shorts twisted only it's inside my head. I keep trying to tug it this way and that way and it still feels not quite right.'

'Go on.'

I told her about the bullet and the way in which Mr Le Renges had insisted that he wasn't going to report it.

'Well, that happens. You do get customers who bring in a dead fly and hide it in their salad so they won't have to pay.'

'I know. But, I don't know.'

After a double portion of chocolate ice cream with vanilla-flavored wafers I walked back to Tony's where the lunchtime session was just finishing. 'Mr Le Renges still here?' I asked Oona.

'He went over to St Stephen. He won't be back until six, thank God.'

'You don't like him much, do you?'

'He gives me the heebie-jeebies, if you must know.'

I went through to Mr Le Renges' office. Fortunately, he had left it unlocked. I looked in the wastebasket and the bullet was still there. I picked it out and dropped it into my pocket.

* * *

On my way back to the Calais Motor Inn a big, blue pick-up truck tooted at me. It was Nils Guttormsen from Lyle's Autos, still looking surprised.

'They brought over your transmission parts from Bangor this morning, John. I should have her up and running in a couple of days.'

'That's great news, Nils. No need to break your ass.' Especially since I don't have any money to pay you yet.

I showed the bullet to Velma.

'That's truly weird, isn't it?' she said.

'You're right, Velma. It's weird, but it's not unusual for hamburger meat to be contaminated. In fact, it's more usual than unusual, which is why I never eat hamburgers.'

'I don't know if I want to hear this, John.'

'You should, Velma. See – they used to have federal inspectors in every slaughterhouse, but the Reagan administration wanted to save money, so they allowed the meat-packing industry to take care of its own hygiene procedures. Streamlined Inspection System for Cattle, that's what they call it – SIS-C.'

'I never heard of that, John.'

'Well, Velma, as an ordinary citizen you probably wouldn't have. But the upshot was that when they had no USDA inspectors breathing down their necks, most of the slaughterhouses doubled their line speed, and that meant there was much more risk of contamination. I mean if you can imagine a dead cow hanging up by its heels and a guy cutting its stomach open, and then heaving out its intestines by hand, which they still do, that's a very skilled job, and if a gutter makes one mistake – *floop*! – everything goes everywhere, blood, guts, dirt, manure, and that happens to one in five cattle. Twenty percent.'

'Oh, my God.'

'Oh, it's worse than that, Velma. These days, with SIS-C, meat-packers can get away with processing far more diseased cattle. I've seen cows coming into the slaughterhouse with abscesses and tapeworms and measles. The beef scraps they ship out for hamburgers are all mixed up with manure, hair, insects, metal filings, urine and vomit.'

'You're making me feel nauseous, John. I had a hamburger for supper last night.'

'Make it your last, Velma. It's not just the contamination, it's the quality of the beef they use. Most of the cattle they slaughter for hamburgers are old dairy cattle, because they're cheap and their meat isn't too fatty. But they're full of antibiotics and they've often infected with *E. coli* and salmonella. You take just one hamburger, that's not the meat from a single animal, that's mixed-up meat from dozens or even hundreds of different cows, and it only takes one diseased cow to contaminate thirty-two thousand pounds of ground beef.'

'That's like a horror story, John.'

'You're too right, Velma.'

'But this bullet, John. Where would this bullet come from?'

'That's what I want to know, Velma. I can't take it to the health people because then I'd lose my job and if I lose my job I can't pay for my automobile to be repaired and Nils Guttormsen is going to impound it and I'll never get back to Baton Rouge unless I fucking walk and it's one thousand nine hundred and sixty miles.'

'That far, hunh?'

'That far.'

'Why don't you show it to Eddie Bertilson?'

'What?'

'The bullet. Why don't you show it to Eddie Bertilson. Bertilson's Sporting Guns and Ammo, over on Orchard Street? He'll tell you where it came from.'

'You think so?'

'I know so. He knows everything about guns and ammo. He used to be married to my cousin Patricia.'

'You're a star, Velma. I'll go do that. When I come back, maybe you and I could have some dinner together and then I'll make wild, energetic love to you.'

'No.'

'No?'

'I like you, John, but no.'

'Oh.'

Eddie Bertilson was one of those extreme pain-in-the-ass-like people who note down the tail-fin numbers of military aircraft in Turkey and get themselves arrested for espionage. But I have to admit that he knew everything possible about guns and ammo and when he took a look at that bullet he knew immediately what it was.

He was small and bald with dark-tinted glasses and hair growing out of his ears, and a Grateful Dead T-shirt with greasy finger-wipes on it. He screwed his jeweler's eyeglass into his socket and turned the bullet this way and that.

'Where'd you find this?' he wanted to know.

'Do I have to tell you?'

'No, you don't, because I can tell *you* where you found it. You found it amongst the memorabilia of a Vietnam vet.'

'Did I?' The gun store was small and poky and smelled of oil. There were all kinds of hunting rifles arranged in cabinets behind the counter, not to mention pictures of anything that a visitor to Calais may want to kill: woodcock, ruffed grouse, black duck, mallard, blue-wing and green-wing teal.

'This is a seven point nine two Gewehrpatrone ninety-eight slug which was the standard ammunition of the Maschinengewehr thirty-four machine-gun designed by Louis Stange for the German Army in 1934. After the Second World War it was used by the Czechs, the French, the Israelis and the Biafrans, and a few turned up in Vietnam, stolen from the French.'

'It's a machine-gun bullet?'

'That's right,' said Eddie, dropping it back in the palm of my hand with great satisfaction at his own expertise.

'So you wouldn't use this to kill, say, a cow?'

'No. Unlikely.'

The next morning Chip and I opened the restaurant as usual and by eight a.m. we were packed to the windows. Just before nine a black panel van drew up outside and two guys in white caps and overalls climbed out. They came down the side alley to the kitchen door and knocked.

'Delivery from St Croix Meats,' said one of them. He was a stocky guy with a walrus moustache and a deep diagonal scar across his mouth, as if he had been told to shut up by somebody with a machete.

'Sure,' said Chip, and opened up the freezer for him. He and his pal brought in a dozen cardboard boxes labeled Hamburger Patties.

'Always get your hamburgers from the same company?' I asked Chip.

'St Croix, sure. Mr Le Renges is the owner.'

'Ah.' No wonder Mr Le Renges hadn't wanted to talk to his supplier about the bullet; his supplier was him. I bent my head sideways so that I could read the address: US Route One, Robbinstown.

It was a brilliantly sunny afternoon and the woods around Calais were all golden and crimson and rusty-colored. Velma drove us down US One with Frank and Nancy Sinatra singing *Something Stupid* on the radio.

'I don't know why you're doing this, John. I mean, who cares if somebody found a bullet in their hamburger?'

'*I* care, Velma. Do you think I'm going to be able to live out the rest of my life without finding out how an American cow got hit by a Vietcong machine-gun?'

It took us almost an hour to find St Croix Meats because the building was way in back of an industrial park – a big gray rectangular place with six or seven black panel vans parked outside it and no signs outside. The only reason I knew that we had come to the right place was because I saw Mr Le Renges walking across the yard outside with the biggest, ugliest dog that I had ever seen in my life. I'm not a dog expert but I suddenly realized who had been advertising in *The Quoddy Whirlpool* for somebody to walk their Presa Canario.

'What are you going to do now?' Velma asked me. There was a security guard on the gate and there was no way that a 290-pound man in a flappy white raincoat was going to be able to tippy-toe his way in without being noticed.

Just then, however, I saw the guy with the scar who had delivered our hamburgers that morning. He climbed into one of the black vans, started it up, and maneuvered it out of the yard.

'Follow that van,' I asked Velma.

'What for, John?'

'I want to see where it goes, that's all.'

'This is not much of a date, John.'

'I'll make it up to you, I promise.'

'Dinner and wild energetic love?'

'We could skip the dinner if you're not hungry.'

* * *

We followed the van for nearly two and a half hours, until it began to grow dark. I was baffled by the route it took. First of all it stopped at a small medical center in Pembroke. Then it went to a veterinarian just outside of Mathias. It circled back toward Calais, visiting two small dairy farms, before calling last of all at the rear entrance of Calais Memorial Hospital, back in town.

It wasn't always possible for us to see what was happening, but at one of the dairy farms we saw the van drivers carrying cattle carcasses out of the outbuildings, and at the Memorial Hospital we saw them pushing out large wheeled containers, rather like laundry hampers.

Velma said, 'I have to get back to work now. My shift starts at six.'

'I don't understand this, Velma,' I said. 'They were carrying dead cattle out of those farms, but USDA regulations state that cattle have to be processed no more than two hours after they've been slaughtered. After that time, bacteria multiply so much that they're almost impossible to get rid of.'

'So Mr Le Renges is using rotten beef for his hamburgers?'

'Looks like it. But what else? I can understand rotten beef. Dozens of slaughterhouses use rotten beef. But why did the van call at the hospital? And the veterinarian?'

Velma stopped the car outside the motel and stared at me. 'Oh, you're not serious.'

'I have to take a look inside that meat-packing plant, Velma.'

'You're sure you haven't bitten off more than you can chew?'

'Very apt phrase, Velma.'

My energy levels were beginning to decline again so I treated myself to a fried shrimp sandwich and a couple of Molson's with a small, triangular, diet-sized piece of pecan pie to follow. Then I walked around to the hospital and went to the rear entrance where the van from St Croix Meats had parked. A hospital porter with greasy hair and squinty eyes and glasses was standing out back taking a smoke.

'How's it going, feller?' I asked him.

'OK. Anything I can do for you?'

'Maybe, I've been looking for a friend of mine. Old drinking buddy from way back.'

'Oh, yeah?'

'Somebody told me he's been working around here, driving a van. Said they'd seen him here at the hospital.'

The greasy-haired porter blew smoke out of his nostrils. 'We get vans in and out of here all day.'

'This guy's got a scar, right across his mouth. You couldn't miss him.'

'Oh you mean the guy from BioGlean?'

'BioGlean?'

'Sure. They collect, like, surgical waste, and get rid of it.'

'What's that, "surgical waste"?'

'Well, you know. Somebody has their leg amputated, somebody has their arm cut off. Aborted fetuses, stuff like that. You'd be amazed how much stuff a busy hospital has to get rid of.'

'I thought they incinerated it.'

'They used to, but BioGlean kind of specialize, and I guess it's cheaper than running an incinerator night and day. They even go round auto shops and take bits of bodies out of car wrecks. You don't realize, do you, that the cops won't do it, and that the mechanics don't want to do it, so I guess somebody has to.'

He paused, and then he said, 'What's your name? Next time your buddy calls by, I'll tell him that you were looking for him.'

'Ralph Waldo Emerson. I'm staying at the Chandler House on Chandler.'

'OK . . . Ralph Waldo Emerson. Funny, that. Name kind of rings a bell.'

I borrowed Velma's car and drove back out to Robbinstown. I parked in the shadow of a large computer warehouse. St Croix Meats was surrounded by a high fence topped with razor wire and the front yard was brightly floodlit. A uniformed security guard sat in a small booth by the gate, reading *The Quoddy Whirlpool*. With any luck, it would send him to sleep, and I would be able to walk right past him.

I waited for over an hour, but there didn't seem to be any way for me to sneak inside. All the lights were on, and now and then I saw workers in hard hats and long rubber aprons walking in and out of the building. Maybe this was the time for me to give up trying to play detective and call the police.

The outside temperature was sinking deeper and deeper and

I was beginning to feel cold and cramped in Velma's little Volkswagen. After a while I had to climb out and stretch my legs. I walked as near to the main gate as I could without being seen, and stood next to a skinny maple tree. I felt like an elephant trying to hide behind a lamp post. The security guard was still awake. Maybe he was reading an exciting article about the sudden drop in cod prices.

I had almost decided to call it a night when I heard a car approaching along the road behind me. I managed to hide most of myself behind the tree, and Mr Le Renges drove past, and up to the front gate. At first I thought somebody was sitting in his Lexus with him, but then I realized it was that huge ugly Presa Canario. It looked like a cross between a Great Dane and a hound from hell, and it was bigger than he was. It turned its head and I saw its eyes reflected scarlet. It was like being stared at by Satan, believe me.

The security guard came out to open the gate, and for a moment he and Mr Le Renges chatted to each other, their breath smoking in the frosty evening air. I thought of crouching down and trying to make my way into the slaughterhouse behind Mr Le Renges' car, but there was no chance that I could do it without being spotted.

'Everything OK, Vernon?'

'Silent like the grave, Mr Le Renges.'

'That's what I like to hear, Vernon. How's that daughter of yours, Louise? Got over her autism yet?'

'Not exactly, Mr Le Renges. Doctors say it's going to take some time.'

Mr Le Renges was still talking when one of his big black vans came burbling up the road and stopped behind his Lexus. Its driver waited patiently. After all, Mr Le Renges was the boss. I hesitated for a moment and then I sidestepped out from behind my skinny little tree and circled around the back of the van. There was a wide aluminum step below the rear doors, and two door-handles that I could cling on to.

'You are out of your cotton-picking mind,' I told myself. But, still, I climbed up on to the step, as easy as I could. You don't jump on to the back of a van when you're as heavy as me, not unless you want the driver to bounce up and hit his head on the roof.

Mr Le Renges seemed to go on talking for ever, but at last he gave the security guard a wave and drove forward into the yard, and the van followed him. I pressed myself close to the rear doors, in the hope that I wouldn't be quite so obtrusive, but the security guard went back into his booth and shook open his paper and didn't even glance my way.

A man in a bloodied white coat and a hard hat came out of the slaughterhouse building and opened the car door for Mr Le Renges. They spoke for a moment and then Mr Le Renges went inside the building himself. The man in the bloodied white coat opened the car's passenger door and let his enormous dog jump out. The dog salaciously sniffed at the blood before the man took hold of its leash. He went walking off with it – or, rather, the dog went walking off with him, its claws scrabbling on the blacktop.

I pushed my way in through the side door that I had seen all the cutters and gutters walking in and out of. Inside there was a long corridor with a wet, tiled floor, and then an open door which led to a changing room and a toilet. Rows of white hard-hats were hanging on hooks, as well as rubber aprons and rubber boots. There was an overwhelming smell of stale blood and disinfectant.

Two booted feet were visible underneath the door of the toilet stall, and clouds of cigarette smoke were rising up above it.

'Only two more hours, thank Christ,' said a disembodied voice.

'See the play-off?' I responded, as I took off my raincoat and hung it up.

'Yeah, what a goddamn fiasco. They ought to can that Kershinsky.'

I put on a heavy rubber apron and just about managed to tie it up at the back. Then I sat down and tugged on a pair of boots.

'You going to watch the New Brunswick game?' asked the disembodied voice.

'I don't know. I've got a hot date that day.'

There was a pause, and more smoke rose up, and then the voice said, 'Who *is* that? Is that you, Stemmens?'

I left the changing room without answering. I squeaked back along the corridor in my rubber boots and went through to the main slaughterhouse building.

You don't even want to imagine what it was like in there. A

high, echoing, brightly lit building with a production line clanking and rattling, mincers grinding and roaring, and thirty or forty cutters in aprons and hard hats boning and chopping and trimming. The noise and the stench of blood were overwhelming, and for a moment I just stood there with my hand pressed over my mouth and nose, with that fried shrimp sandwich churning in my stomach as if the shrimp were still alive.

The black vans were backed up to one end of the production line, and men were heaving out the meat that they had been gleaning during the day. They were dumping it straight on to the killing floor where normally the live cattle would be stunned and killed – heaps and heaps of it, a tangle of sagging cattle and human arms and legs, along with glistening strings of intestines and globs of fat and things that looked like run-over dogs and knackered donkeys, except it was all so mixed-up and disgusting that I couldn't be sure what it all was. It was flesh, that was all that mattered. The cutters were boning it and cutting it into scraps, and the scraps were being dumped into giant stainless-steel machines and ground by giant augers into a pale, pink pulp. The pulp was seasoned with salt and pepper and dried onions and spices. Then it was mechanically pressed into patties, and covered with cling wrap, and run through a metal detector, and frozen. All ready to be served up sizzling hot for somebody's breakfast.

'Jesus,' I said, out loud.

'You talking to me?' said a voice right next to me. 'You talking to *me*?'

I turned around. It was Mr Le Renges. He had a look on his face like he'd just walked into a washroom door without opening it.

'What the fuck are *you* doing here?' he demanded.

'I have to cook this stuff, Mr Le Renges. I have to serve it to people. I thought I ought to find out what was in it.'

He didn't say anything at first. He looked to the left and he looked to the right, and it was like he was doing everything he could to control his temper. Eventually he sniffed sharply up his right nostril and said, 'It's all the same. Don't you get that?'

'Excuse me? What's all the same?'

'Meat, wherever it comes from. Human legs are the same as cow's legs, or pig's legs, or goat's legs. For Christ's sake, it's all protein.'

I pointed to a tiny arm protruding from the mess on the production line. 'That's a baby. That's a human baby. That's just *protein*?'

Mr Le Renges rubbed his forehead as if he couldn't understand what I was talking about. 'You ate one of our burgers. You know how good they taste.'

'Look at this stuff!' I shouted at him, and now three or four cutters turned around and began to give me less-than-friendly stares. 'This is shit! This is total and utter shit! You can't feed people on dead cattle and dead babies and amputated legs!'

'Oh, yes?' he challenged me. 'And why the hell not? Do you really think this is any worse than the crap they serve up at all of the franchise restaurants? They serve up diseased dairy cows, full of worms and flukes and all kinds of shit. At least a human leg won't have *E. coli* infection. At least an aborted baby won't be full of steroids.'

'You don't think there's any moral dimension here?' I shouted back. 'Look at this! For Christ's sake! We're talking cannibalism here!'

Mr Le Renges drew back his hair with his hand, and inadvertently exposed his bald patch. 'The major fast-food companies source their meat at the cheapest possible outlets. How do you think I compete? I don't *buy* my meat. The sources I use, they pay me to take the meat away. Hospitals, farms, auto repair shops, abortion clinics. They've all got excess protein they don't know what to do with. So BioGlean comes around and relieves them of everything they don't know how to get rid of, and Tony's Gourmet Burgers recycles it.'

'You're sick, Mr Le Renges.'

'Not sick, John. Not at all. Just practical. You ate human flesh in that piece of hamburger I offered you, and did you suffer any ill effects? No. Of course not. In fact I see Tony's Gourmet Burgers as the pioneers of really decent food.'

While we were talking, the production line had stopped, and a small crowd of cutters and gutters had gathered around us, all carrying cleavers and boning knives.

'You won't get any of these men to say a word against me,' said Mr Le Renges. 'They get paid twice as much as any other slaughterhousemen in Maine; or in any other state, believe me. They don't kill anybody, ever. They simply cut up meat, whatever it is, and they do a damn fine job.'

I walked across to one of the huge stainless steel vats in which the meat was minced into glistening pink gloop. The men began to circle closer, and I was beginning to get seriously concerned that I might end up as pink gloop, too.

'You realize I'm going to have to report this to the police and the USDA,' I warned Mr Le Renges, even though my voice was about two octaves above normal.

'I don't think so,' said Mr Le Renges.

'So what are you going to do? You're going to have me gutted and minced up like the rest of this stuff?'

Mr Le Renges smiled and shook his head; and it was at that moment that the slaughterman who had been talking his dog for a walk came on to the killing floor, with the hell beast still straining at its leash.

'If any of my men were to touch you, John, that would be homicide, wouldn't it? But if Cerberus slipped its collar and went for you – what could I do? He's a very powerful dog, after all. And if I had twenty or thirty eyewitnesses to swear that you provoked him . . .'

The Presa Canario was pulling so hard at its leash that it was practically choking, and its claws were sliding on the bloody metal floor. You never saw such a hideous brindled collection of teeth and muscle in your whole life, and its eyes reflected the light as if it had been caught in a flash photograph.

'Kevin, unclip his collar,' said Mr Le Renges.

'This is not a good idea,' I cautioned him. 'If anything happens to me, I have friends here who know where I am and what I've been doing.'

'Kevin,' Mr Le Renges repeated, unimpressed.

The slaughterman leaned forward and unclipped the Presa Canario's collar. It bounded forward, snarling, and I took a step back until my rear end was pressed against the stainless steel vat. There was no place else to go.

'Now, *kill*!' shouted Mr Le Renges, and stiffly pointed his arm at me.

The dog lowered its head almost to the floor and bunched up its shoulder muscles. Strings of saliva swung from its jowls, and its cock suddenly appeared, red and pointed, as if the idea of tearing my throat out was actually turning it on.

I lifted my left arm to protect myself. I mean, I could live without a left arm, but not without a throat. It was then that I had a sudden flashback. I remembered when I was a kid, when I was thin and runty and terrified of dogs. My father had given me a packet of dog treats to take to school, so that if I was threatened by a dog I could offer it something to appease it. 'Always remember that, kid. Dogs prefer food to children, every time. Food is easier to eat.'

I reached into the vat behind me and scooped out a huge handful of pink gloop. It felt disgusting . . . soft and fatty, and it dripped. I held it toward the Presa Canario and said, 'Here, Cerberus! You want something to eat? Try some of this!'

The dog stared up at me with those red reflective eyes as if I were mad. Its black lips rolled back and it bared its teeth and snarled like a massed chorus of death rattles.

I took a step closer, still holding out the heap of gloop, praying that the dog wouldn't take a bite at it and take off my fingers as well. But the Presa Canario lifted its head and sniffed at the meat with deep suspicion.

'*Kill*, Cerberus, you stupid mutt!' shouted Mr Le Renges.

I took another step toward it, and then another. 'Here, boy. Supper.'

The dog turned its head away. I pushed the gloop closer and closer but it wouldn't take it, didn't even want to sniff it.

I turned to Mr Le Renges. 'There you are . . . even a dog won't eat your burgers.'

Mr Le Renges snatched the dog's leash from the slaughterman. He went up to the animal and whipped it across the snout, once, twice, three times. 'You pathetic disobedient piece of shit!'

Mistake. The dog didn't want to go near me and my handful of gloop, but it was still an attack dog. It let out a bark that was almost a roar and sprang at Mr Le Renges in utter fury. It knocked him back on to the floor and sank its teeth into his forehead. He screamed, and tried to beat it off. But it jerked its head furiously from side to side, and with each jerk it pulled more and more skin away.

Right in front of us, with a noise like somebody trying to rip up a pillowcase, the dog tore his face off, exposing his bloodied, wildly-popping eyes, the soggy black cavity of his nostrils, his grinning lipless teeth.

He was still screaming and gargling when three of the

slaughtermen pulled the dog away. Strong as they were, even they couldn't hold it, and it twisted away from them and trotted off to the other side of the killing floor, with Mr Le Renges' face dangling from its jaws like a slippery latex mask.

I turned to the slaughtermen. They were too shocked to speak. One of them dropped his knife, and then the others did, too, until they rang like bells.

I stayed in Calais long enough for Nils to finish fixing my car and to make a statement to the sandy-haired police officer. The weather was beginning to grow colder and I wanted to get back to the warmth of Louisiana, not to mention the rare beef muffalettas with gravy and onion strings.

Velma lent me the money to pay for my auto repairs and the Calais Motor Inn waived all charges because they said I was so public spirited. I was even on the front page of *The Quoddy Whirlpool.* There was a picture of the mayor whacking me on the back, under the banner headline HAMBURGER HERO.

Velma came out to say goodbye on the morning I left. It was crisp and cold and the leaves were rattling across the parking lot.

'Maybe I should come with you,' she said.

I shook my head. 'You got vision, Velma. You can see the thin man inside me and that's the man you like. But I'm never going to be thin, ever. The poboys call and my stomach always listens.'

The last I saw of her, she was shading her eyes against the sun, and I have to admit that I was sorry to leave her behind. I've never been back to Calais since and I doubt if I ever will. I don't even know if Tony's Gourmet Burgers is still there. If it is, though, and you're tempted to stop in and order one, remember there's always a risk that any burger you buy from Tony Le Renges *is* people.

Anka

'That's all of them?' asked Grace, as Kasia came down the stairs, carrying a bundled-up blanket in her arms.

'The very last one,' said Kasia. She lifted the corner of the blanket to reveal a boy of about three years old, with a white face and bright red lips and curly black hair. His eyes kept rolling upward and off to the left, and his chin was glistening with dribble. This was little Andrzej, who was suffering from cerebral palsy and a heart murmur.

'Thank God for that,' said Grace. 'Now let's hope they knock this terrible place down.'

She took a long look around the hallway: at the faded, olive-green wallpaper and the stringy brown carpet, and the sagging red vinyl couch where visitors were supposed to sit. The windows on either side of the front door were tinted yellow, so that even the air looked as if it were poisoned.

'So many children have suffered here,' said Kasia. 'So much misery. So much sadness.'

'Come on,' said Grace. 'Let's get out of here. It's a long drive to Wrocław.'

'Your husband is coming this evening?'

'He missed his connecting flight to New York, but he'll be here by tomorrow morning. He's bringing Daisy with him.'

'Oh! You will be so pleased to see her!'

Grace smiled, and whispered, 'Yes.' It had been over a month since she had last seen Daisy, and she had missed her so much that she had been tempted more than once to give up the whole project and fly back home to Philadelphia.

But each time she had revisited the twenty-seven children in the Katowice orphanage, she had known that she could never abandon them. Ever since she had first been taken to see them, seven months ago, she had been determined to rescue them.

As Kasia had said, 'These children, they are not unhappy. To be unhappy, you have to know what it is like to be happy, and these children have never been happy, not for one single moment, from the day they were born.'

Last September, as the poplar trees of southern Poland had been turning yellow, Grace had been visiting the industrial city of Katowice to take photographs for a *National Geographic* feature on 'Newly Prosperous Poland.' But on her last evening, at a crowded civic reception at the Hotel Campanile, she had been approached by Kasia Bogucka and Grzegorz Scharf.

Kasia was anorexically thin and very intense, with cropped blonde hair and high angular cheekbones and startlingly violet eyes. Grzegorz was much more reserved. He wore rimless spectacles and a constant frown, and although he couldn't have been older than thirty-five, his hair was receding, and he had a middle-aged tiredness about him, as if he had witnessed more misery than he could bear.

'We work for a charity for disabled childs,' Grzegorz had explained. 'Both physical disabilities, if you understand, and also mental, in the brains.'

'You *must* come with us to see the Cienisty Orphanage,' Kasia had pleaded with her. 'You must take pictures, so that people will know.'

Grace had sympathetically shaken her head. 'I'm sorry. My flight leaves at eleven tomorrow morning. I won't have the time.'

'Then, *please* – why don't you come now?'

It had been well past nine. Grace had been wearing her red cocktail dress and red stiletto heels, and she had already drunk two and a half glasses of champagne. Outside, the night was black and she could see raindrops sparkling on the hotel windows.

'I am beg you,' said Grzegorz. 'These childs, they have no hopes, none at all.'

Even now, she couldn't really explain why she had decided to go. But ten minutes later, she had found herself in the back of a Polonez station wagon with no springs, jolting her way along a rutted road toward the south-eastern outskirts of Katowice. Grzegorz had lit a cigarette, and when he had wound down the window to let out the smoke, the rain had come flying into her face.

After fifteen minutes' driving, they had reached a scrubby, desolate suburb, with only the illuminated sign of a Statoil gas station for a landmark. Off to the right-hand side of the road there was a tall stand of fir trees. Beyond the fir trees, Grace had been able to make out an overgrown garden, with overturned shopping carts in it, and a large square house, with peeling purple stucco on its walls.

Grzegorz had driven up to the front of the house, and parked. It had stopped raining now, but water had still been gurgling down the drainpipes. The three of them had climbed the steps to the front door, but even before Kasia had been able to knock, it had been opened by a plump, round-faced woman with a headscarf and a tight checkered overall. Her eyes had looked like two raisins pushed into unbaked dough.

'Ah, Panna Bogucka,' she had said, as if she hadn't been entirely pleased to see her.

'I hope you don't mind, Weronika. I brought a photographer with me.'

The plump woman had eyed Grace with deep suspicion. 'She is not going to take any pictures of me? What happens here, this is not my fault. I do my best but I have no nurses and you know how little money they give me.'

'Weronika . . . I just want her to take pictures of the children.'

Weronika had clucked in disapproval, but had stepped back to allow them inside. Grace had noticed how worn out her shoes were. The hallway had been dimly illuminated by a chandelier with only two of its six bulbs working, and it had been deeply chilly. It was the smell, though, that had affected Grace the most. Boiled turnips, and damp, and urine-soaked mattresses, and something else – some sweetish, nauseating stench, like rotten poultry.

'The Cienisty Orphanage was first opened after the war,' Kasia had explained. 'In those days there were so many children who had no parents, and nobody to take care of them. But now they use it for children with anything from cystic fibrosis to cerebral palsy to Down's syndrome. What do you call it? A garbage dump, for children that nobody wants.'

'Aren't they given any treatment?' Grace had asked her.

Grzegorz had let out a bitter laugh. 'Treatment? You are meaning *therapy*? There is nobody even to wash them, and to change their clothes, and to give them foods. Nobody even *talks* to them. They are forgot, these childs. They are worse than being orphans. They are worse than dead people.'

As they were talking, a girl of about seven years old had materialized from one of the side rooms, as silent as a memory. She had approached them very cautiously, to stand only three or four feet away, listening. She had been painfully thin, with straight brown hair and huge brown eyes. She had been wearing a black tracksuit that was two sizes too big for her, and soiled red slippers that were almost gray.

She had been clutching a doll. The doll had a white china head, with a wild shock of white hair, but a strange and beautiful face. Most dolls have a blank, witless stare, but this doll looked both serene and knowing – as if she were alive, but far too shrewd to let anybody know.

'What's your name, sweetheart?' Grace had asked the little girl. At the same time, she had lifted her Fuji camera off her shoulder, and removed the lens cap. She had understood at once why Kasia had wanted her to take pictures. There could be no more graphic way to explain what these children were suffering. It had all been there, in the little girl's eyes. The loneliness, the constant hunger, the bewilderment that nobody loved her.

Weronika had tried to put her arm around the little girl's shoulders, but the little girl had twisted herself away.

'This is Gabriela. Say "*dobry wieczór*" to the ladies and the gentleman, Gabriela.'

Grace had hunkered down in front of Gabriela and reached out her hand. 'Good evening, Gabriela. How are you?'

Gabriela had lowered her chin, but had kept on staring at Grace with those enormous dark eyes.

Grace had taken hold of the doll's hand, and shaken it. '*Dobry wieczór*, dolly! And what's *your* name?'

Kasia had asked her the same question in Polish. Gabriela had hesitated for a moment, and then she had whispered, 'Anka.'

'Anka? That's a nice name. Do you think that Anka would mind if I took her picture?'

Again, a long hesitation. Then Gabriela whispered something and Kasia translated. 'Anka does not like to have her picture taken.'

'Oh, really? I thought all pretty little girls like to have their picture taken.'

Gabriela had looked around, as if she had been worried that somebody might overhear what she was whispering. 'My grandmother gave her to me, before she died. My grandmother said that I must keep her close to me, day and night, and especially at night. And I must never let anybody else hold her, and I must never let anybody take her picture.'

Grace had stood up, and laid her hand gently on top of Gabriela's head. 'OK, have it your way. I just thought Anka might enjoy being famous.'

Kasia had said, 'Come and take a look at the other children. They will give you plenty of photo opportunities, I promise you.'

Grace had waved goodbye to Gabriela and Anka, and Gabriela had waved Anka's hand in reply.

'What an odd little girl,' Grace had remarked, as they followed Weronika and Grzegorz down a long, poorly lit corridor.

'She has delusions,' Kasia had told her. 'The last doctor who came here, he diagnosed her as schizophrenic.'

'What kind of delusions?'

'She doesn't believe that she belongs here at all. She believes that she lives on a farm someplace in the country, with her father and mother and her two younger sisters. She says that her father grows turnips, and keeps pigs. She sits in her room most of the day, talking to her sisters, even though she doesn't have any, and never did, so far as anybody can make out.'

'And Anka?'

'I don't know. Maybe she *did* get her from her grandmother. Who knows? But what a strange doll, isn't she? I never saw another doll like that. Beautiful, but strange.'

Kasia had taken her upstairs and led her from room to room. Every room was crowded with cribs, and in each crib there was a thin, hopeless child. Some of them sat staring at nothing at all. Others slept, clinging to their blankets. Many of them rocked endlessly from side to side, or banged their heads against the bars of their cribs. One little boy kept his face covered with his hands, and endlessly grizzled.

Every room was cold, with rough brown blankets pinned up at the windows instead of curtains, so it was always dark.

Grace had tried to stay as detached as she could. She had taken scores of photographs, at least ten of every child. When she had finished, she had followed Kasia back down to the hallway, where Grzegorz and Weronika had been waiting for them.

'Well?' Grzegorz had asked her.

'I don't know what to say,' Grace had told him. She had been very close to tears.

'You will show these to your magazine, yes?'

'I'll do more than that, Grzegorz, I promise you. I'll get these children out of here.'

As she had been about to leave, Gabriela had approached her and tugged repeatedly at her sleeve.

'What is it, Gabriela?'

'She wants you to take her with you,' Kasia had translated.

'I'm sorry, sweetheart. Not this time. But I promise you that I'll come back for you.'

'She says that the witch is coming to get her.'

'The witch?'

'Baba Jaga. She is a witch from Polish legend who is supposed to eat children.'

Grace had taken hold of both of Gabriela's hands, and said, 'There's no witch, Gabriela. Nobody's going to hurt you.'

But Gabriela had held up her doll, and said, 'Anka keeps me safe from Baba Jaga. Every time I have a nightmare about Baba Jaga, I kiss Anka and Anka swallows it up. But now she is full up with so many nightmares and she cannot swallow any more. Next time Baba Jaga comes, Anka will not be able to save me. Baba Jaga will eat me, and spit out my bones, and stick my head on a pole.'

Once this had been translated by Kasia, Grace had shaken her head and smiled. 'Gabriela – nothing like that is going to happen to you. I have to talk to some people in Warsaw about you, and make some arrangements. Do you understand? But when I've done that, I'll come back and take you away from this place.'

Gabriela had looked up at her with pleading eyes. 'Please, you must take me now. I do not want to be eaten.'

Grace had turned to Kasia. 'Can't we take her? She's so upset.'

'It is absolutely not possible, I am afraid,' Kasia had told her. 'Not tonight, anyhow. We have to ask for the proper permissions from the Public Adoption Commission. They are always helpful with healthy children, but with sick children like these – well, there can be very difficult bureaucratic problems. Hundreds of forms to fill out.'

'OK,' Grace had said, with reluctance. But then she had wagged her finger at Gabriela's doll, and said, in a stern voice, 'Anka! You listen to me, Anka, and you listen to me good! You keep Gabriela safe for just a little while longer, OK? Make sure you find the room in your tummy to swallow a few more of her nightmares. We can't have Baba Jaga eating her up, can we?'

Gabriela had said nothing more, but had held Anka close to her, and stared at Grace with such desperation that Grace had said, 'Come on, Kasia. Let's go. This is all too painful.'

As they had left the Cienisty Orphanage, Grace had seen lightning flickering on the horizon, over the factory chimneys of Katowice, and heard the rumbling of distant thunder, like a wartime barrage. She had looked back, and seen Gabriela standing in the open doorway, still staring at her.

Kasia had been right. If the children at the Cienisty Orphanage had been healthy, there would have been no problem at all in finding homes for them. An American couple could adopt a healthy Polish child for less than $7,500. But who was going to take on a ten-year-old girl with Down's syndrome; or a seven-year-old boy with violent epilepsy; or any child with multiple sclerosis?

After more than three months of pleading and cajoling, however, Kasia had found places for all twenty-seven children – with private families, or children's homes, or hospices. It was her tragic photographs that touched most people's hearts. They had been published in *The Philadelphia Inquirer* and *Newsweek* and shown on CBS and NBC nightly news.

She had been able to call Kasia at the end of February to tell her that she was flying over to Poland again, and this time she was going to take the children back to Philadelphia, all twenty-seven of them.

Kasia's voice had sounded very distant. 'I am so sorry, Grace. Now we have only twenty-six.'

'What's happened? Don't tell me that little Andrzej's heart gave out?'

'No . . . it was Gabriela. She disappeared from Cienisty three days ago. We thought that she had run away. She was always talking about going back to find her father and her mother and her two sisters. But early this morning some people were picking mushrooms in the woods nearby, and they found her body.'

'Oh, no! Not Gabriela.'

'The police don't yet know how she died. They say that her body was savaged by animals, dogs maybe, so it is difficult for them to be sure.'

Grace had slowly sat down. Through her kitchen windows, she had seen Daisy building a snowman, with two lumps of barbecue charcoal for eyes and a carrot for a nose and one of Jack's old, khaki fishing hats on top of his head. Daisy was only a little older than Gabriela, but she was rosy cheeked and well fed, with shiny blonde hair. Watching her running around their snowy back yard, in her red woolly hat and her fur-collared coat, Grace had thought of the last time she had seen Gabriela, standing in the front porch of the orphanage in her shabby black tracksuit, with Anka clutched tight in her arms.

'*Please, you must take me now. I do not want to be eaten.*'

Kasia carried little Andrzej out to the waiting bus. It was sunny outside, but very cold, and exhaust fumes floated past the window like departing ghosts. Grace was about to follow her when she thought she heard a noise in one of the bedrooms upstairs – a mewling sound, like a cat, or a very young child in distress.

She went to the bottom of the stairs, and called, 'Hallo? Is anybody there?'

She waited, but there was no reply. The children couldn't understand her. Many of them wouldn't have been able to understand her even if she had spoken to them in fluent Polish. But they always spoke to her, and smiled, and touched her, and called her 'Gracja'.

She had nearly reached the front door, however, when she heard the mewling noise again.

'Hallo?' she repeated. There was still no reply, so she climbed the stairs to the second-floor landing. She had torn down all of the blankets from the bedroom windows, so that sunlight fell across the corridor in a series of shining triangles. She walked slowly past all of the open doors, looking into every one. All she saw was empty cribs and filthy mattresses, and white plastic potties.

She was just about to go back downstairs when the mewling was repeated. It sounded as if it was coming from the bathroom, right at the very end of the corridor. She opened the bathroom door and said, 'Hallo? Is anybody still here?'

The bathroom was cold and silent, with a huge bathtub that

was stained with rust, and old-fashioned faucets with strings of black slime hanging from them. In the far corner, next to the grimy washbasin, there was a dilapidated laundry basket, with a broken lid.

Wrinkling up her nose, Grace picked up the lid and looked inside. There, lying on a tangled heap of soiled pajamas, was Anka, Gabriela's doll, with her wild white hair.

'Anka!' said Grace, lifting her out and straightening her arms and legs. 'Who left you in there, you poor little creature!'

Anka stared back at her, as serene and knowing as ever. The sight of her brought back such a vivid picture of Gabriela that Grace felt her eyes fill up with tears. If only she had listened, when Gabriela had begged her to take her away. Who cared about bureaucracy, and form filling, when the life of a seven-year-old girl was at risk?

'Come on, Anka,' she said. 'At least I can save *you*.'

She carried Anka downstairs. Then she walked out of the front door and closed it behind her. It refused to shut completely, so she opened it again and slammed it hard.

She climbed on to the bus. Kasia and Grzegorz were sitting at the front, next to the driver. Halfway down the aisle sat two young nurses from the children's hospital at Chorzow. Grace had arranged for them to accompany the children all the way to Warsaw, and then for two student nurses from UHP to take care of them while they were being flown back to Philly.

The children themselves were unexcited. Some of them rocked in their seats, as they always rocked, while others stared listlessly out of the windows. None of them had any experience of a day away from the orphanage, so they had no idea of where they might be going or what was going to happen to them.

However, the nurses gave them each a carton of Sokpol cranberry juice, and a Princessa chocolate wafer, and they were so pleased that they chattered and laughed with pleasure and one or two of them even screamed.

Kasia took hold of Grace's hand. 'It is a wonderful thing that you are doing today, Grace.'

Grace looked down at Anka, sitting in her lap. 'I just wish that Gabriela could have been here, too.'

'The police think she ran away,' said Grzegorz. 'They believe she was try to get home to her father and mother.'

'So she died of what? Exposure?'

'They think so,' said Kasia. 'Her body was so badly torn to pieces that it was almost impossible for them to say. They could not find one of her arms.'

'Oh, God. I hope she didn't suffer. She was so frightened that she was going to be eaten by a witch, and look what happened to her. I feel so guilty.'

'It was not your fault, Grace,' Grzegorz told her. 'These childs, they have great luck to be alive at all. Even ordinary childs in Katowice has terrible troubles with the health, because of the pollutement in the air. The steelworks, the factories. The doctors find the heavy metals even inside the unborn babies. Lead, arsenic. We try our best, but we cannot save every one of them.'

Grace lifted up Anka. 'Gabriela said that Anka always kept her safe, didn't she? Anka breathed in all of her nightmares, so that they wouldn't hurt her.'

Kasia tugged Anka's hair, trying to straighten it. 'Many Polish children have nightmares about Baba Jaga. She is *very* scary!'

'I never heard about her before.'

'Well, Baba Jaga lives in the forest, in a wooden hut that runs around on chicken legs. The keyhole to her front door is a human mouth with sharp teeth inside it, and the fence around her hut is made of human bones with a skull on top of every pole, except for one, which is supposed to be for *you*, if you are having a nightmare about her.'

'In that case,' said Grace, 'I think I'll try not to.'

Kasia smiled. 'Baba Jaga is always hungry, and so she is always out searching for food. She flies in and out through the chimney, in a mortar, with a pestle to steer with, and she carries a net for catching children.

'The story goes that the only child who ever managed to escape from Baba Jaga was the daughter of a turnip farmer.'

Grace said, 'The daughter of a turnip farmer? That's what Gabriela believed she was, didn't she?'

Kasia nodded. 'Every time Baba Jaga was about to eat her, the girl said that she would taste much better with turnips, so Baba Jaga took her back to her father's farm to collect a sack full of them. The girl cooked them into a turnip stew, and Baba Jaga ate so much that she fell asleep.

'It was a bitter night in winter, and Baba Jaga slept so long that she was frozen stiff. The girl was able to steal the special key from Baba Jaga's belt and escape.'

'Poor Gabriela,' said Grace. 'If only *she* could have escaped.'

The doll, Anka, continued to stare at her, unblinking, and for a split second Grace could have sworn that she was smiling. But she was only being jiggled by the bus, as they turned off the side road that took them away from the Cienisty Orphanage, and on to the broad S1 highway to Warsaw.

The sun shone, the cumulus clouds blossomed in the sky, and the two young nurses started the children in a clapping song.

'*Kosi kosi lapci, pojedziem do babci*! *Babcia da nam mleczka, a dziadzius pierniczka*! Clap, clap little hands, we will go to grandma's! Granny will give us milk, and grandpa a gingerbread cookie!'

Jack and Daisy were sitting in the second-floor lounge of the Holiday Inn in Warsaw, waiting for her. Jack was looking unshaven and tired, and his dark hair was ruffled, but Grace knew that he had only been back from Tokyo for a day and a half before he had brought Daisy over to Poland.

When she had told him about her determination to rescue the children from the orphanage, Jack had told her that she was mad. 'You're a crazy woman. You're worse than my mother. All *she* did was rescue cats.' But he had supported her right from the very beginning, and never once told her that she was wasting her time. More than that, he had called in favors from senior executives at five different hospitals to whom he sold scanning equipment. He had emailed dozens of his friends and golf partners and he had even taken the junior senator for Pennsylvania, Bob Casey, Jr, for lunch at Vetri's, and canvassed his support, too.

As she came up the stairs, Daisy ran over and flung her arms around her.

'Where *did* you get that baseball cap?' asked Grace. It had a rubber rooster's head on top of it, with wildly staring eyes.

'Daddy brought it back from Japan. He says it's to stop me from running around like a headless chicken.'

Jack took Grace in his arms and kissed her and held her close. 'I've missed you,' he told her. 'How's Project Totally Bananas?'

'The kids are staying overnight at the University Children's Hospital, so that we can give them a last check-up before they leave. They don't have the least idea what's happening to them, but they all seem happy enough.'

Jack said, 'I had a call from NBC before we left home. They want to interview you as soon as you get back – you *and* the kids. You know what the *Inquirer* is calling you? "Amazing Grace". And I agree with them. You *are* amazing.'

'Oh, come on, Jack. Those kids were living in such terrible conditions. They were cold, they were hungry, they weren't being given any medical attention. Anybody would have done the same as me.'

'Whose doll is *that*?' asked Daisy, pointing at Anka.

Grace held her up. 'Her name's Anka. She used to belong to a little girl called Gabriela.'

'What happened to her?'

'Gabriela? I'm afraid she died. She was only about the same age as you.'

Daisy carefully took Anka out of Grace's hand. She pulled Anka's dress straight and brushed back her hair.

'She's *weird*. But she's very pretty, isn't she?'

'Gabriela said that Anka stopped her from having nightmares.'

'Can I look after her? Oh, please! I can take her to school for show-and-tell!'

'I think she needs disinfecting first.'

'But then can I have her? She's *so* cool. She makes Barbie look totally dumb.'

Jack raised his eyebrows, as if he didn't always let Daisy get whatever she wanted. Grace said, 'OK, then. But I want you to remember that this will always be Gabriela's doll, and you're just keeping it for her, in her memory.'

'I will. I promise. Anka and me, we'll say a prayer for Gabriela every night.'

It took over three weeks to place all the children in their various homes and hospitals, but at last Project Totally Bananas was all over, and Grace found that she was free again. Unexpectedly, she felt bereaved, as if the children had been her own, and she had given them up for adoption.

But one evening in the second week of April she received a call from Frank Wells, the picture editor of *Oyster* magazine, who wanted her to go to North Vietnam to shoot travel pictures.

'Just don't bring back a plane-load of Vietnamese orphans, you got me? If you do, *Oyster* isn't going to pay for their air fares.'

'Don't worry, Frank. I think I've done my Mother Teresa bit for one lifetime.'

She poured herself a glass of Chardonnay and switched on David Letterman. She never watched much TV, but Jack was away for three days in San Diego, and the house always seemed so silent without him, especially after Daisy had gone to bed.

She was sitting on the couch, leafing through *Good Housekeeping* and half listening to the TV, when she heard Daisy cry out. It was a strange cry, more like a moan than a shout. It sounded to Grace as if Daisy was so frightened that she couldn't even articulate.

'*Daisy*! *Daisy, what's wrong*?'

She threw aside her magazine and ran up to Daisy's bedroom, which was the first on the left at the top of the stairs. Daisy cried out again, but this time her cry was shrill and piercing.

Grace flung open the bedroom door. It was dark inside, but she was instantly aware that there was something in there – something huge and black that smelled of smoke. Something that shifted and crackled, like breaking branches.

'*Mommy*! *Mommy*! *What is it*? *What is it*? *Mommy, what is it*?'

'Come here, Daisy! Come here, quick!' Grace held out her arms for her and Daisy scrambled off her bed and almost threw herself at her. Grace backed out of the bedroom door and set Daisy down on the landing. Then she reached inside and switched on the light. Daisy was sobbing and she herself was gasping with fright.

She could hardly believe what she saw. In the far corner of the room, as high as the ceiling, stood the figure of a woman dressed in dusty, black sacking. Her hair was stuck up on top of her head with some kind of mud or wax, which made it look like a bundle of twigs, and it was her hair that was making the crackling sound as it brushed against the ceiling.

Her face was long and emaciated, as if it had been stretched, and her skin was jaundiced. Her eyes were huge and red-rimmed, with yellowish pupils. Her mouth was curved downward to reveal a jagged crowd of sharp-pointed teeth.

Her arms were insanely long, and almost reached from one side of the room to the other. Both of them were lifted up high, and her fingers were stretched wide like claws.

'*Jestem głodny*,' she croaked.

'Who are you?' Grace demanded, although her words came out like broken pieces of china. 'How did you get here? Get out!'

'*Jestem głodny*,' the women repeated, more urgently this time, and she beckoned lasciviously toward Daisy, and stuck out the tip of her tongue, which was pointed and slippery-gray, like a snake. Her long chin was covered in black bristles.

It was then that Grace glanced downward, and saw how the woman had materialized. Gabriela's doll Anka was lying on the floor, half hidden by the comforter that hung down from the side of Daisy's bed. Anka's eyes were closed, as they always were when she was laid down on her back. But her mouth was wide open, and thick black smoke was gushing out of it.

The smoke had risen up into the room and twisted itself into the shape of the woman in black sacking. *Like a genie rising out of a lamp*, thought Grace.

She looked up again. She was so frightened that she felt as if her skin was shrinking. The woman was swaying toward them, her claws still lifted, her eyes gleaming. But now Grace understood who she was, and *what* she was – or at least she thought she did. All of the nightmares that Anka had swallowed to protect Gabriela had come pouring out of her, as black and as noxious as burning oil.

It was Baba Jaga, the Polish witch of the woods, the ever-hungry devourer of innocent children.

'*Jestem głodny*,' she rasped, for the third time. 'I am starving, you understand me? I have need to eat.'

Daisy said, '*Mommy*,' but Grace pushed her toward the stairs and said, 'Run, sweetheart! Run! Get out of the house just as fast as you can!'

'No!' screamed Baba Jaga, swaying toward them. 'I must have her! I must suck her bones!'

But Daisy scampered down the stairs, whimpering, and Grace stood her ground. Although her voice was shaking, she managed to say, 'I have plenty of food for you, Baba Jaga. I have so much food you won't feel hungry for another year.'

Baba Jaga's tongue darted out again, and licked her sharpened teeth. 'I do not believe you. You do not want me to eat your girl, that is all. But I *will* eat your girl, I promise you, and I will eat you, too, and I will chew your intestines like pasta.'

She lashed out at Grace, and caught the sleeve of her sweater in her claw. Grace tried to pull herself away, but Baba Jaga drew her closer. Grace turned her face aside, but she could feel the prickle of Baba Jaga's chin hairs against her cheek, and she could smell Baba Jaga's breath. It smelled like the Cienisty Orphanage, of boiled turnips and dirty disinfectant water and rotten chicken. It smelled like children's despair.

'Come with me,' she said. 'Come on. Come with me. I will give you food.'

Baba Jaga's eyes closed. Unlike human beings, her eyelids closed upward. Then they rolled down again, with several fine strings of sticky residue clinging to her lashes.

'Very well,' she agreed. 'But do not try to trick me. The people who have tried to trick me, their skulls surround my hut.'

Slowly, Grace edged her way out on to the landing. Baba Jaga followed her, with her claws still snared in the sleeve of her sweater. Although she was mostly made of black smoke, and appeared to have no legs, she walked with a lurching, complicated limp.

Grace led the way slowly down the stairs to the hallway, and through to the kitchen. For some reason, she had imagined that Baba Jaga would not be reflected in mirrors or windows, like a vampire. But as she crossed the kitchen she could see the witch clearly in the shiny black glass of her oven, and in the windows that looked out over the yard.

She could see herself, too, pale faced, but looking surprisingly calm. *Is that really me*? she thought. *Me, with a real, live witch*?

There was no sign of Daisy anyplace, and Grace prayed that she had left the house and run next door, or even further.

'So where is this feast that you have promised me?' asked Baba Jaga. 'I see no food anywhere, only you!'

'Please, be patient,' said Grace. She led Baba Jaga through to the utility room beside the kitchen, where she kept her washing machine and her tumble dryer, and also her freezer chest.

She switched on the fluorescent light, and then she went over to the freezer chest, unlocked it and lifted the lid. Inside it was heaped with frozen turkeys, frozen chickens, pies and fish and packets of vegetables. Icy vapor poured out of it and sank to the floor.

'This is all for you,' she told Baba Jaga. 'You can eat all of it.'

Baba Jaga stared at the frozen food wide eyed.

'This is for me?'

'Everything. Fish, chickens, pastries. Ducks. Blueberries, too.'

With no more hesitation, Baba Jaga tore her claw away from Grace's sleeve, reached into the freezer, and dragged out a whole frozen pike, which Jack had brought home last year from a fishing trip on Marsh Creek Lake. With a sharp crunch, she bit into it, and tore away half of its body.

Grace said shakily, 'Good? What did I promise you?'

Baba Jaga turned toward her, her mouth filled with chewed-up lumps of frozen fish. She said nothing, but when Grace tried to take a step away from her, she took hold of her sleeve, and pulled her back.

'After cold food, warm food,' she warned her.

Grace raised both of her hands to indicate that she wasn't thinking of going anyplace. Baba Jaga released her again, and started to pull out rib-eye steaks and hamburgers. Grace couldn't believe that she was able to eat them when they were frozen solid, but her teeth bit into them voraciously, and she chewed and swallowed everything – frozen meat and frozen fat and frozen bones, and even the frozen plastic bags they were wrapped in.

At the bottom of the freezer there were four frozen ducks. Baba Jaga reached down and tried to wrench them free, but they were all frozen solidly together, and wedged beneath boxes of frozen pastry.

She tugged and tugged at the ducks, gasping in frustration. She leaned further and further over the side of the freezer chest.

Grace thought, *if this doesn't work, I'm going to be killed, and eaten, and that* will *be a nightmare*. She thought of the horror of Daisy returning home, to find her body ripped apart like Gabriela's had been, in the woods.

But suddenly, Baba Jaga climbed right into the freezer chest, and knelt on top of the pastry and the bags of frozen peas. She grasped the ducks with both hands and pulled at them, cursing and spitting.

She raised her head and said to Grace, 'Find me a knife. And do not think of trying to kill me with it. I cannot be killed by stabbing – or hanging for that matter, *or* poisoning, *or* drowning.'

Grace said, 'OK, I understand.' She turned away, but immediately she turned around again, and took hold of the lid of the freezer chest, and slammed it down, and locked it.

Baba Jaga screeched in fury. She began to beat on the lid with her fists, until dents appeared all over it. Then she kicked at the ends and the sides, and threw herself left and right, again and again, so that Grace was terrified that the whole freezer chest would fall over, and Baba Jaga would be able to crawl out.

'I curse you!' screamed Baba Jaga. 'I curse you a thousand, thousand times over! I curse you so that worms will crawl out of your eyes instead of tears! I curse you so that you will be blind and deaf and your skin will burn like fire! *I curse you*!'

But Grace dragged over one of the kitchen chairs and sat on top of the freezer chest and stayed there, even while Baba Jaga was thumping and banging and rocking it so wildly that it moved halfway across the utility room.

'Gabriela,' she prayed. 'Wherever you are, please help me.'

She hung on and hung on, while Baba Jaga continued to scream and curse. After a few minutes, however, Daisy came into the utility room, carrying Anka. She looked very pale and serious.

'Mommy?' she said. 'I ran next door but there was nobody there and then I got scared that the witch was going to hurt you so I came back.'

'She's locked in here, sweetheart. The witch is locked in here. I just have to keep her here until she freezes.'

Baba Jaga screamed again, and the freezer chest tilted dangerously to one side, but Grace managed to brace one leg against the wall and push it back upright.

After that, the witch was silent. Ten minutes passed, then twenty, then an hour. After an hour had passed, Grace thought she heard a soft crunching noise inside the freezer chest, but that was all.

It was nearly three thirty in the morning before she dared to turn the key and ease open the lid.

The witch was crouched inside, unmoving, and her black sacking dress was thickly coated with sparkling white rime.

'Is she dead?' asked Daisy, peering anxiously over the edge of the freezer chest.

'I don't know. I hope so.'

Very cautiously, Grace reached out and touched the witch's twig-like hair. It was so brittle that three or four strands of it snapped off.

She hesitated, and then she took hold of the witch's bony arm. She twisted it around, and as she did so it cracked, sharply, and broke. She dropped it on to the floor, and it shattered into even more fragments.

Feeling emboldened, she plunged both of her hands into the freezer chest and seized the witch's body. It collapsed, with a crunch, as if it were made of nothing but layers of burned, frozen newspaper. Her skull broke apart, too, and her pelvis, until Grace was left with nothing but a freezer strewn with black ashes.

'I think we've killed her, sweetheart,' she told Daisy, smacking the ash from her hands. 'I think we've gotten rid of her for good and all.'

She closed the lid and locked it, and then she picked up Daisy and carried her back upstairs to her bedroom.

'Can I sleep with you tonight?' Daisy asked her.

'I was going to ask you the same question. But I don't think I want Anka in the room.'

'But she'll be so *lonely*!'

'No, she won't. She can spend the night in your closet, with all of your other dolls.'

'But—'

'No, Daisy. I think she still needs some more disinfecting. The place where I found her . . . well, it was very germy. They had an outbreak of pneumonia, not long ago, and I don't want you to catch *that*.'

She tucked Daisy into her bed and kissed her. 'It's OK. I'll leave the landing light on. And I'll go down and lock the door to the utility room, OK?'

'Tell Anka I'll see her in the morning. Give her a kiss.'

'OK, sweetheart.'

Grace went downstairs. She paused in the kitchen doorway, and then she went through to the utility room. The freezer chest was still firmly locked, and when she rapped her knuckles on top of it, there was no response. She didn't know how she was going to get rid of Baba Jaga's ashes, but she would think about that in the morning.

Meantime, she went through the living room and opened the front door. It was a quiet night, cold and clear, with a three-quarter moon shining through the oaks. She walked across the front lawn, and then across to the other side of the street, where there was nothing but trees and tangles of briars.

She held up Anka in front of her and now she could clearly

see that the doll was giving her a narrow-eyed look of expectancy, as if she were saying, *what are you going to do with me now, Grace*? Maybe that was why Gabriela's grandmother had warned her never to allow anybody to take photographs of Anka. Anybody who saw them would have realized that the doll was capable of changing her expressions, and some superstitious nun might have taken it away from her.

Anka had been Gabriela's only protection against Baba Jaga, but her protection hadn't lasted indefinitely. Anka now had so many nightmares swarming inside her that she was more dangerous to children than a plague-carrying rat.

There were still so many unanswered questions. Why had Baba Jaga killed Gabriela – if it *had* been Baba Jaga who had dragged her into the woods and half eaten her body? Had she done it simply because she was hungry? Or had she done it so that Grace would take her away from Cienisty, inside Anka, and give her the chance to feed on healthy children, instead of the sick and the schizophrenic and the chronically undernourished?

After all, what more innocent way could she have found of getting close to young children, than hiding inside a china doll?

Grace didn't know if any of this could possibly be true. Logically, it was all madness. It was the stuff of fairy stories. But the witch in her freezer was madness, and if there was any trace of Baba Jaga left inside Anka, Grace wasn't going to give her the chance to re-emerge.

'*Dobranoc,* Anka,' she said. Then she swung back her arm and threw the doll into the briars as far as she could.

Over a week later, Mike Ferris came back from his morning walk, let his boxer Ali off the leash, and came through into the kitchen.

'Boy!' he told Margaret, peeling off his windbreaker. 'It's cold enough to freeze a squirrel's nuts off.'

'Mike,' Margaret protested. 'Not in front of Abby.'

Abby, three, was sitting up in her high chair, making a mess with a bowl of cream of wheat. 'Nuts off!' she repeated, and kicked her feet. 'Nuts off!'

'See?' said Margaret. 'Children have an instinct for anything rude.'

'Rude!' Abby repeated. 'Rude!'

'Oh, well, here,' said Mike. 'This will take her mind off it.'

He held up a doll with wild white hair and a white china face. Her ragged gray dress was sodden, but she looked strangely knowing and serene.

'Found her in the woods,' said Mike. 'Or at least Ali snuffled her out. She looks like she could be antique.'

'She's *filthy*.'

'Sure. But you could make her a new dress, couldn't you, and wash her hair for her? Maybe she's worth a few bucks.'

Abby held out both hands for her. 'Dolly!' she cried out. 'I want the dolly!'

'There you are,' said Mike. 'Love at first sight.'

Margaret came over and took the doll out of Mike's hands. She turned her over, and looked under her dress, to see what she was made of. 'Well . . . she's all china. She could be antique. I wonder what she was doing in the woods?'

'*Jestem głodny*,' whispered a voice.

'What did you say?' asked Margaret, turning around.

'I'm starving,' said Mike, picking up an English muffin.

Margaret frowned, and looked around the kitchen again.

'That's strange. I'm sure you said something else.'

Mike came up and kissed her. 'You're imagining things, as usual.'

But while he was kissing her, the doll was staring over her shoulder at Abby, and suddenly her eyes gleamed, as if there were a light inside her. Abby stopped kicking her feet and stared back at her, unblinking, open mouthed, bewildered.

None of her dolls had ever looked at her like that before, as if they were thinking of eating her.

Dog Days

OK, Jack was much better looking than me, but I was funnier than he was, and women love to laugh. That was how I picked up a girl as stunning as Kylie, when Jack was still dating Melanie Wolpert.

Melanie Wolpert might have been a judge's daughter and she might have screamed like Maria Callas whenever she and Jack did the wild thing together, but she had masses of wiry black curls and millions of moles and she thought that *The Matrix* was an art movie. Apart from that, she was a Scientologist and she smelled of vanilla pods.

I met Kylie in the commissary at Cedars-Sinai. We were standing in line with our brown melamine trays, and both of us reached for the last Cobb salad at the same time.

'Go ahead,' I said. 'You have it. Please. I shouldn't eat Cobbs anyhow, I'm allergic.'

She peered into the salad bowl. 'I don't even know what a Cobb is.'

'You're having a Cobb salad for lunch and you don't even know what a Cobb is?'

She shook her head. 'I'm Australian. I've only been here for two weeks.'

Yowza, yowza, yowza, she was amazing. She was tall, nearly as tall as me, with very short, blonde hair, sun bleached and feathery. She had strong cheekbones and a strong jaw and wide, brown eyes the color of Hershey's chocolate. Her lips were full and cushiony, and when she smiled her teeth were dazzling, so that you wanted to lick them with the tip of your tongue, just to feel how clean they were.

She had an amazing figure, too – beachball-breasted, with wide surfer's shoulders, and long, long legs, and those wedge-heeled Greek sandals that tie up with all those complicated strings. I realized almost instantaneously that I was in love.

'Don't worry,' I told her. 'I'll have the Five-Bean Surprise.'

'OK . . .' she said. 'What's the surprise?'

'Well, it's not really a surprise, if you eat that many beans.'

We sat down together in the far corner of the commissary, and I pointed out John G. Dyrbus MD, the proctologist, and Randolph Feinstein MD, who specialized in aggressive kidney tumors, and Jacob Halperin MD, who could take out your prostate gland while he was playing *Nobody Loves You When You're Down And Out* on the harmonica.

'I'm a physiotherapist, myself,' said Kylie. 'Children, mostly, with muscular disorders.'

'Kylie, that's an interesting name.'

'It's Aboriginal. It means "boomerang".'

'You know something?' I told her. 'I don't believe in boomerangs. All that ever happens is, one Aborigine throws a stick, and it hits this other Aborigine right on the bean, so this other Aborigine gets really pissed and throws it back. So the first Aborigine thinks, "that's amazing . . . I throw this stick and five minutes later it comes flying back".'

Kylie laughed. 'You're crazy, you know that?'

And that was how we started going out together. I took her to The Sidewalk Café at Venice Beach and bought her a Georgia O'Keeffe omelet (avocado, bacon, mushrooms and cheese). I took her to Disneyland, and she adored it. She met Minnie, for Christ's sake, and I still have the picture, although it's wrinkled with tears. I took her bopping at The Vanguard and I bought her five kinds of foie gras at Spago. We drove up to see my cousin Sibyl in San Luis Obispo in my '75 Toronado, with the warm wind fluffing our hair, and Sibyl served us chargrilled tuna and showed Kylie how to throw a terracotta pot.

Idyllic days. Especially when we went back to my apartment on Franklin Avenue, cramped and messy as it was, and fell into my bed together, slow motion, with a full moon shining through the open window, and Beethoven's Fifth Piano Concerto tinkling in the background, and Juanita next door clattering saucepans in the sink like a Tijuana percussion band.

For a beautiful girl, Kylie was a strangely clumsy and inexperienced lover, but what she lacked in experience she made up for in strength and energy and appetite. I'll tell you the truth: there were some nights when I almost wished that she'd leave me alone, and give me a couple of hours to get some sleep. Just as my eyelids were dropping, her hand would come crawling across my thigh and start tugging at me, like I was some kind of bell rope, and much as I liked it, I used to wake up in the morning feeling as if I had been expertly beaten up.

I should have counted my blessings. We had been together only eight and a half weeks when the inevitable happened and we ran into Jack.

We were strolling along the beach eating ice-cream cones when I saw him in the near distance coming toward us, with that monstrous mutt of his bounding all around him. Even if you hated his guts, which I didn't, you had to admit that he was a great-looking guy. Tall, with dark, brushed-back hair, a straight, Elvis Presley nose, and intensely blue eyes. He was wearing a black linen shirt, unbuttoned to reveal his gym-toned torso, and knee-length khaki pants.

While he was still out of earshot, I turned to Kylie and said, 'Why don't we go for a latte? There's a great little coffee-house right on the boardwalk here.'

'Oh, do we have to?' she pleaded. 'I just love the ocean so much.'

'I know. The ocean's great, isn't it? So big, so wet. But I'm really jonesing for a latte and the ocean will still be here when we get back.'

'How can you feel like a coffee when you're eating an ice-cream cone?'

'It's the contrast. Cold, hot – hot, cold. I like to surprise my mouth, that's all. I believe in surprising at least one of my organs every single day. Yesterday I surprised my nose.'

'How did you do that?'

'I tried to walk through the balcony door without opening it. But – come on, how about that latte?'

I glanced quickly toward Jack, trying not to make it obvious that I was looking in his direction. I was growing a little panicky now. Apart from Brad Pitt, Jack was the only person in the world I didn't want Kylie to meet.

'Well . . .' she said reluctantly, 'if you're really dying for one . . .'

But then Jack's dog ran into the surf, barking at a trio of seagulls, and Kylie turned and saw it, and said, 'Look! Look at that gorgeous Great Dane! My parents used to have one just like it! Oh, it's so *cute*, don't you think?'

'That dog is bigger than I am. How can you call it *cute*?'

'Oh, it just is. Great Danes are so lovable. They're intelligent, they're obedient, and they're so *noble*. I adore them.'

'Listen,' I said, 'I could really use that latte.'

But I don't think that Kylie was even listening to me. She clapped her hands and called out, 'Here, girl! Here, girl!' and the stupid Great Dane came galloping across the beach toward her, wagging its stupid tail, and then of course Jack recognized me and shouted out, 'Bob!' and ze game vas up.

'Bob! How's it going?'

'You two *know* each other?' asked Kylie, kneeling down in the sand and tugging at the Great Dane's ears with as much enthusiasm as she tugged at my bell rope. 'Oh, you're a beautiful, beautiful girl, aren't you? Oh, yes you are! Oh, yes you are!' God, it was enough to make me bring up my Cap'n Crunch.

'Sure we know each other,' said Jack, hunkering down beside Kylie and patting the Great Dane's flanks. His grin was ridiculously dazzling and his knees were mahogany brown and he even had perfect *toenails*.

'Jack and I were at med school together,' I explained.

'We were the Two Musketeers,' said Jack. I was beginning to wish that he would stop grinning like that. 'Both for one and one for both, that's what Bob always used to say.'

'But – we went our separate ways,' I told her. I chose oncology because I wanted to alleviate human suffering and Jack chose cosmetic surgery because he wanted to elevate women's breasts.'

'You're a cosmetic surgeon?' Kylie asked him, and I could tell by the way she tilted her head on one side that Jack had half won her over already. A dishy cosmetic surgeon with a beautiful dog and mahogany knees. What did it matter if he didn't know any one liners?

'How's Melanie?' I asked him. 'Still as voluptuous as ever?' I gave him a sassy wiggle and winked. Come on – I was fighting for my very existence here.

'Oh, Melanie and I broke up months ago. She met a divorce lawyer. A very rich divorce lawyer.'

'Sorry to hear it.' Jesus – Kylie was even *kissing* that goddamned dog. 'You – ah – who are you dating now?'

'Nobody, right now. It's just me and Sheba, all on our ownsome.'

Kylie stood up. 'Listen,' she said, 'Bob and I were just going for a latte. Why don't you and Sheba join us?'

'I thought you didn't want to go for a latte,' I told her. 'I thought you wanted to stay on the beach.'

Kylie didn't take her eyes off Jack. 'No . . . I think I could fancy a latte. And maybe one of those cinnamon donuts.'

The three of them walked up the beach ahead of me – Jack, Kylie and Sheba – and all I could do was trail along behind them feeling pale and badly dressed and excluded. Thank you, God, I said, looking up to the sky – Ye who giveth with one hand and snatcheth away with the other. Kylie turned around and smiled at me and just as she did so a seagull pooped on my shoulder.

The café was called Better Latte Than Never which I thought was bitterly appropriate. I sat at the table with Jack and Kylie and tried to be witty but I knew that it was no use. They couldn't take their eyes off each other and when I came out of the bathroom after rinsing the seagull splatter from my shirt, I saw that Jack's hand was resting on top of hers, as naturally as if they had been friends all their lives.

'What a great *guy*,' said Kylie, as we drove back along Sunset. 'He's so interesting. You know, not like most of the men you meet.'

'He's multifaceted, I'll give you that. Did he tell you that he knits?'

'No, he didn't! Maybe he could knit me a sweater!'

'I don't think so. He only knits blanket squares. They're not very square, either. I think it's some perceptual weakness he inherited from his mother. Did he tell you that his mother played the glockenspiel? She only knew one tune but it could reduce strong men to tears.'

'You're jealous,' said Kylie. Her eyes were hidden behind large Chanel sunglasses – the same large Chanel sunglasses that *I* had bought for her on Rodeo Drive.

'Jealous? What are you talking about?'

'I can tell when you're jealous because you belittle people. You always make it sound like a joke but it's not.'

'Hey, Jack and I go way back.'

'And you're jealous of him, aren't you? I'll bet you always have been.'

'Me? I'm an oncologist. You think I'm jealous of some tit

doctor? Besides, his breath smells of cheese. That was one thing I always noticed about him, but I never liked to tell him. His girlfriends always used to call him Monterey Jack, but he never figured out why.'

'You're jealous.'

I looked at her acutely, but all I could see was two of my own reflection in her sunglasses, in my crumpled lime-green T-shirt with the damp patch on the shoulder.

'Do I have anything to be jealous *of*, do you think?' I asked her.

At that moment I almost rear-ended a dry-cleaning van and her answer was blotted out by the screaming of tires, so I never heard it.

Of course, I knew what it was. I took her out to 25 Degrees on Thursday evening for hamburgers. We sat in one of the black, leather-upholstered booths, which I thought would be romantic. It's incredible what a reasonably supple person can get up to, in a black, leather-upholstered booth. But she was unusually preoccupied, and she kept fiddling with her fork, around and around, and when our orders eventually arrived, she said, 'I've been thinking, Bob.'

'You've been thinking that you should have ordered the three-cheese sandwich instead of the turkey burger?'

'No, not that.'

'Let me see. You've been thinking that you hate this loose-weave sport coat I'm wearing? No, I don't believe that's it. Aha! *I* know what it is. You've been thinking that you and I should stop seeing each other because Jack has called you and asked you out on a date. A threesome. Him and you and the houndess from hell.'

She looked at me sideways and there was genuine remorse in her eyes. 'I'm sorry.'

'You're sorry because Jack has called you and asked you out on a date, or you're sorry you waited until our food arrived before you told me about it? Because I can't possibly eat a twelve-ounce cheeseburger while my throat is all choked up.'

'I'm just sorry. I didn't mean to hurt you.'

'Nobody ever does, Kylie. Nobody ever does. But I shall have my revenge. Jack may be good looking and he may be able to charm the turkey buzzards out of the trees, but you will very soon discover that Jack suffers from premature ejaculation and because of that, your love-making will last for no more than nanoseconds. Don't ever sneeze when Jack's making love to you, because you might miss it.'

Kylie looked away. 'As a matter of fact, Bob, he's very good. He's tender, and he's creative, and he can keep it up for hours.'

I sat up very straight with my chin tilted upward and I didn't know what to say. I don't know what upset me the most: the fact that she had already gone to bed with him, and that he was obviously better in bed than I was, or the Australian way she said 'tinder' instead of 'tender.'

Eventually, I shuffled my butt sideways out of the booth, and stood up. The waiter came up to me and said, 'Something wrong, sir?'

'Yes. This isn't what I wanted, none of it.'

He frowned, and flipped back his notepad. 'I think you will find that you have everything you asked for, sir.'

I shook my head. It isn't easy to argue when you're trying to stop yourself from crying.

'You're going, sir? Who's going to pay?'

'The lady will pay,' I told him. 'She – ah—'

'Bob,' said Kylie. 'Don't let's end it like this. Please.'

'How else do you want to end it? You want violins? You let me take you out for hamburgers and you'd already gone to bed with him?'

She shook her head.

'Good,' I told her. 'Have a nice life. Jack and you and that bitch of his. Hope he can tell the difference between you.'

I shouldn't have said that, but I had fallen for Kylie in a way that I had never fallen for any girl before. It wasn't only her fabulous looks, and the way that other men swiveled around and stared at her whenever we walked past together, although of course that was part of it. It was her utter simplicity, the way she trusted the world to take care of her, and her genuine surprise when it didn't. It was the way she propped herself up on one elbow when we were lying in bed, and stroked my hair, as if she couldn't believe I was real.

She was magical, in every sense of the word. And that evening, after she had told me that she and I were through, all I could do was creep back to my apartment like a wounded animal and lie with my face buried in her pillow, smelling her perfume.

The phone rang. After a long while, I heaved myself off the bed and answered it.

'Bob? It's Jack.'

'Jack? Not my best friend Jack? Not my old med school buddy? Both for one and one for both?'

'Bob . . . I don't know what to say to you.'

'I have a good idea. You could say, "Bob, I'm going to go to the top story of Century Park East and I'm going to jump off".'

'Please, Bob. Don't joke.'

'Who the fuck is joking? You think I'm joking? I put a curse on you, Jack! I swear to God! You and your fucking Great Dane! I curse you!'

There was a lengthy pause. Eventually, Jack said, 'Can't say I blame you, buddy. Stay well. Don't be a stranger forever.'

I hung up. There was so much I could have said, but most of it would have been obscene, and what was the point?

Six weeks and three days later my curse worked.

It was a Saturday morning and I was driving east on Olympic, on my way to see my friend Dick Paulzner for a game of squash. I pulled up at the intersection of Western Avenue and who should be waiting at the traffic signal right ahead of me but Jack, in his fancy-schmancy Porsche Cayenne SUV. Sitting much too close to him, with her fingers buried in his hair, was Kylie, in a pink baseball cap; and hunched up in the back seat like somebody's Hungarian grandma was Sheba.

My Jeep was burbling away like it always did, on account of a sizeable hole in its muffler, and it wasn't long before Jack checked his rear-view mirror and saw that it was me. He said something to Kylie and Kylie turned around and gave me a little finger-wave.

I ignored her. But then she took off her baseball cap and waved it wildly from side to side, and I could see that she was laughing.

I could go to confession three times a day for the rest of my life and still not be forgiven for what I did next. I saw scarlet. All of the hurt and all of the rejection and all of the anger, they all boiled up inside of me, and I went temporarily mad. That was supposed to have been *my* life, sitting in that SUV in front of me.

That was supposed to have been *my* happiness. Instead of that, I was sitting alone in the vehicle behind, being laughed at by the girl of my dreams.

I pressed my foot down on the gas, and rear-ended the Cayenne with a satisfying *bosh*!

I could see that Jack and Kylie were both jolted, and Sheba was knocked right off her seat and on to the floor.

Jack and Kylie turned around and shouted at me, although I couldn't hear what they were saying. I shrugged, as if I didn't understand what they were shouting for, and then I pressed my foot down on the gas again. There was another *bosh*! and the Cayenne was shoved forward three or four feet.

Now Jack was really mad. He climbed out of the driver's seat and came storming toward me swinging Sheba's metal-studded leash. Just to annoy him one more time, I slammed my foot down and rear-ended the Cayenne again.

This time, though, there was no loud impact. Jack's foot was no longer on the brake pedal and he must have left the Cayenne in neutral. My Jeep barely nudged its rear fender, but it rolled forward another ten or twelve feet, well past the traffic signal.

Without any warning, a huge red Peterbilt semi came bellowing across the intersection and struck the passenger side of the Cayenne. The collision was so devastating that the SUV was pushed all the way across Olympic and on to the sidewalk on the opposite side of the street, demolishing a mailbox.

Even today, I can't recall the noise of that crash. It must have been deafening, but the way I remember it, there was no noise at all, only the silent crumpling of metal and the glittering explosion of glass.

When my hearing suddenly returned, however, I heard the screaming of twenty-two tires on the blacktop, and Jack screaming, too, as if he were trying to drown them out.

I jumped down from my Jeep and ran across the road, dodging around the traffic. The truck driver was climbing down from his cab, too – a heavily-built Mexican in a red T-shirt and baggy green shorts, and a Dodgers cap screwed on sideways. He stared at me with bulging brown eyes, and said, 'There wasn't a damn thing I could do, man. I stood on everything, but there wasn't a damn thing I could do.'

The passenger door of Jack's Cayenne had been crushed in so far that it had bent the steering wheel. The tangle of metal and plastic was almost incomprehensible, but I could see blonde hair and blood and one of Kylie's hands reaching out from a gap in between the door and the front wheel-arch – unmarked, perfect, with silver rings on every finger – as if she were reaching out for help.

'Kylie!' Jack was begging her. 'Kylie, tell me that you're OK! *Kylie*!'

He climbed up on to the side of the SUV and tried to wrench open the passenger door with his bare hands, but it was wedged in far too tight.

'*Somebody call an ambulance*!' he screamed. '*For Christ's sake, somebody call an ambulance*!'

Of course, somebody already had, and it was only a few minutes before we heard the whooping and scribbling of a distant siren. Jack stayed where he was, leaning against the smashed-in door, pleading with Kylie to still be alive.

'I stood on everything,' the truck driver repeated. 'There wasn't a damn thing I could do.'

'I know,' I said, and gave him a reassuring pat on his big, sweat-soaked shoulder.

Two squad cars arrived, and then an ambulance, and then a fire truck, and the police made all of us spectators shuffle across to the other side of the street. The fire crew started work with cutters and hydraulic spreaders, trying to extricate Kylie from the wreckage. I could see sparks flying and hear the arthritic groaning of metal being bent.

Jack was sitting on the back step of the ambulance, with a shiny metallic blanket around him. A paramedic was standing beside him, with one hand raised, as if he were giving him the benediction.

'I can't afford to lose my license, man,' said the truck driver. 'I got all new carpets to pay for.'

But I wasn't listening. Instead, I was frowning off to my left, further along Olympic. About fifty yards away, I could see Sheba, Jack's Great Dane. She was standing by the side of the road, quite still, more like a statue of a dog than a real dog.

Looking back at the smashed-up Cayenne, I could see then that the rear offside door had burst open in the collision, and that

Sheba must have either been thrown out, or jumped out. I was just about to tell one of the police officers that she was loose when Jack turned around and saw her, too, and sent the paramedic off to bring her back.

Two police officers came over to us. One of them shouted out, 'Anybody here witness this accident? If you did, I want to hear from you.'

I was interviewed twice by two highly disinterested detectives from the Highway Patrol, one of whom should have had a master's degree in nose picking, but after the second visit I received a phone call from my attorney telling me that there was insufficient evidence for a prosecution. Nobody had clearly witnessed what had happened, not even Jack, and the truck driver had been estimated to have been traveling at nearly forty miles an hour in his attempt to beat the traffic signals.

I wrote Jack a letter of condolence, but I think I did it more for my benefit than for his, and I never sent it. Kylie's casket was flown back to Australia, to be interred at the church in Upper Kedron, near Brisbane, where she had been confirmed at the age of thirteen.

Occasionally, friends of mine would tell me that they had run across Jack at medical conventions, or in bars. They all seemed to give me a similar story, that he was 'more distant than he used to be, quieter, like he has his mind on something, but he's pretty much OK.'

Then – in the first week of October – I saw Jack for myself. I was driving home late in the evening down Coldwater Canyon Drive, after attending a bar mitzvah at my friend Jacob Perlman's house in Sherman Oaks. As I came around that wide right-hand bend just before Hidden Valley Road, I saw a jogger running along the road in front of me. My headlights caught the reflectors on his shoes, first of all, and it was just as well that he was wearing them, because his track suit was totally black.

I give him a double-*bip* on my horn to warn him that I was behind him, and I gave him a very wide berth as I drove around him. I wasn't drunk, but I was drunk-ish, and I didn't want to end up with a jogger as a hood ornament.

As I passed him, however, I saw that he wasn't running alone. Six or seven yards ahead of him was a Great Dane, loping at an easy, relaxed pace. I suddenly realized that the Great Dane had to be Sheba, and that the jogger had to be Jack. He lived only about a half-mile away, after all, on Gloaming Drive.

I pulled into the side of the road, and slid to a stop. Maybe I would have kept on going, if I had been sober. But Jack and I had been the Two Musketeers, once upon a time, both for one and one for both, and don't think I hadn't been eaten up by guilt for what I had done to Kylie.

I climbed down from the Jeep and lifted both arms in the air.

'Jack!' I shouted. 'Is that you, Jack? It's me, Bob!'

The jogger immediately ran forward a little way and seized the Great Dane's collar. I still wasn't entirely sure that it *was* Jack, because he and the dog were illuminated only by my near-side tail-light, the offside tail-light having been busted earlier that evening by some overenthusiastic backing-up maneuvers.

'Jack – all I want to do is *talk* to you, man! I need to tell you how sorry I am! *Jack*!'

But Jack (if it was Jack) didn't say a word. Instead, he scrambled down the side of the road, his shoes sliding in the dust, and the Great Dane scrambled after him. They pushed their way through some bushes, and then they were gone.

I could hear them crashing through the undergrowth for a while, but then there was nothing but me and the soft evening wind fluffing in my ears.

'That had to be Jack,' I told myself, as I walked back to my Jeep. 'That had to be Jack and I have to make amends.'

I didn't really care about making amends, to tell you the truth, but I did care about absolution. Like Oscar Wilde said, each man kills the thing he loves, and I may not have done it with a bitter look or a kiss or a flattering word, but I had done it out of jealousy, and maybe that was worse. I needed somebody to forgive me. I needed Jack to forgive me. Most of all, I needed *me* to forgive me.

I took the next left into Gloaming Drive, and drove slowly down it until I came to Jack's house. It was a single-story building, but it was built on several different levels, with glass walls and a wide veranda at the back, with a view over the city. At the front, it was partially shielded from the road by a large yew hedge, and I parked on the opposite side of the street at such an angle that – when he returned from his jog – Jack wouldn't easily be able to see me.

I waited over twenty minutes. Two or three times, I nearly dozed off, and I was beginning to sober up and think that this was a very bad idea, when Jack suddenly appeared in his black track suit, jogging down the road toward me. Sheba was close behind him, running very close to heel.

Jack ran up the front steps of his house, and still jogging on the spot, took out his keys and opened the front door. He and Sheba disappeared inside.

There was a short pause, and then the lights went on.

OK, I thought. What do I do now? Ring the doorbell and say that I want to apologize for killing Kylie? Ring the doorbell and say, here I am, you know you want to hit me, so hit me? Ring the doorbell and burst into tears?

I thought the best thing to do would be to let Jack wind down from his run, give him time to take a shower and pour himself a drink. Maybe he'd be more receptive, when he was relaxed. So I waited another fifteen minutes, even though my muscles were beginning to creak.

Eventually, I eased myself out of the Jeep and closed the door as quietly as I could. I crossed the street until I reached the yew hedge. Looking through the branches, I could see Jack standing in his living room, wearing a tobacco-brown bathrobe, with a cream towel wound around his neck. He was holding what looked like a tumbler of whiskey and he was talking to somebody.

No, this wasn't the right time to ask him for forgiveness, not if he had company. I waited for a while longer and then I skirted my way around to the other side of the yew hedge, to see if I could make out who he was talking to, but I couldn't.

I looked around, to make sure that no nosy neighbors were watching me, and then I quickly crossed the lawn in front of the house and went down the side passage, where the trash bins were stored. It was completely dark here, and I was able to climb up on top of one of the bins, and heave myself over the wooden fence into the back yard.

There were cedar-wood steps leading down from the veranda into the yard. I mounted them cautiously, keeping my head low, until I could peer over the decking into the softly lit living room.

Jack was pacing up and down in front of a large brown leather couch. A woman was sitting in the couch, a blonde, although I couldn't see her face. Her hair was feathery, rather like Kylie's, but it was longer than Kylie's used to be.

The sliding door to the veranda was a few inches ajar. I couldn't distinctly hear what Jack and the blonde were saying to each other, but I stayed on those steps for almost twenty minutes, watching Jack talking and drinking and stalking up and down. He appeared to be angry about something, and frustrated. Maybe he was angry because he had seen me, and frustrated that the law had never punished me for causing Kylie's death.

At one point, however, the blonde woman said something to him, and he stopped, and lowered his head, and nodded, as if he accepted that she was right. He approached the couch and kissed her, and tenderly stroked her hair with the back of his knuckles. If the look in his eyes wasn't the look of love, it was certainly the look of like-you-very-much.

He was halfway through pouring himself a second whiskey when his phone warbled. He picked it up, and paced out of sight, but when he came back he said something to the blonde woman and screwed the top back on the whiskey bottle. Then he disappeared.

I waited, and waited. After about ten minutes Jack reappeared, and now he was dressed in a pale blue shirt and black chinos. He gave the blonde woman another kiss, and then he walked out again. I heard an SUV start up, around the front of the house, and back out of the driveway, and turn northward up Gloaming Drive.

I didn't really know what to do next. The only sensible alternative was to go back home, and try to talk to Jack some other time, although I seriously doubted that he would ever agree to it. I crept crabwise back down the steps, and groped my way back along the side of the house, in the shadows.

But then I thought: what I need here is an intermediary, a go-between, somebody who can speak to Jack on my behalf, and explain how remorseful I feel. And who better to do that than somebody he's obviously very fond of? Who better, in fact, than the blonde woman on the couch?

Women understand about guilt, I reasoned. Women understand about remorse. If I could convince this woman that I was genuinely sorry for what I had done to Kylie, maybe she could persuade Jack to forgive me.

I climbed quietly back up the steps again. I didn't want to

startle her, especially since she might well have had a gun, and I was technically trespassing. I didn't know how fierce Sheba could be, either, if she thought that I was an unwelcome intruder (which, to be honest, I was).

The living room was already in darkness, although the hallway and several other rooms were still lit. I could hear samba music, and water running.

I crossed the veranda and went up to the sliding door. I hesitated, and then I called out, 'Excuse me! Is anybody home?'

This is crazy, I thought. I *know* there's somebody home.

'Excuse me!' I called out, much louder this time. 'This is Bob, I'm an old friend of Jack's!'

Still no answer. I waited and waited, and below me the lights of Los Angeles sparkled and shimmered like the campfires of a vast barbarian army.

I should have gone back down those steps and gone home and forgotten that I had ever seen Jack again. Sometimes we do things for which there is no possible forgiveness, and all we can do is go on living the best way we can.

But I slid the veranda door a little wider, and stepped inside the living room. It was chilly in there, severely air conditioned, and it smelled of dried spices, cinnamon and cloves. I crossed to the center of the room. On the wall there was a strange painting of a pale blue lake, with ritual figures all around it.

I heard the woman singing in one of the bedrooms. '*She walks with a sway when she walks . . . she talks like a witch-lady talks.*' She sounded throaty, to say the least.

'Hallo?' I called, although I was aware that my voice was still too weak for her to hear me. 'This is Bob, I'm a friend of Jack's!'

I heard the clickety-clacking of Sheba's claws on the hardwood floor. I prayed that the next thing I heard wouldn't be '*kill*!'

I glanced down at the brown leather couch where the blonde woman had been sitting. Six or seven scatter cushions were strewn across it, with bright red-and-yellow covers, and fringes. On one of the cushions lay a ski mask, in a brindled mixture of black and brown wool. I picked it up and stared into its empty eye-sockets. There was something about it which really gave me the willies, as if it was a voodoo mask.

'*Put it down*,' said a harsh woman's voice.

'Hey – I'm sorry,' I said, lowering the ski mask, and turning toward the hallway. 'I was just—' It was then that I literally sank to my knees in shock.

It was Sheba, the Great Dane. But Sheba didn't have Sheba's head any more. Sheba had Kylie's head.

She walked toward me and stood in front of me. There was no question about it, it was Kylie. Her face was haggard, with puffed-up lips, and her jaw looked lumpy, as if it had been smashed and rebuilt. But those Hershey-brown eyes were still the same.

'Jesus,' I said. 'Jesus, I'm having a nightmare.'

'You think *you're* having a nightmare?' she croaked.

I struggled to my feet and sat on the couch. Kylie/Sheba stayed where she was, staring at me.

'Christ, Kylie. This is unreal.'

'I wish it was, Bob. But it isn't. How did you get in here?'

'I – just climbed over the fence. What *happened* to you, for Christ's sake?'

'I died, Bob. But I was brought back to life.'

'Like this? This is insane! Was it Jack? Did Jack do this to you?'

Kylie closed her eyes to indicate 'yes.'

'But how could he do it? I mean, *why*?'

Her voice was very strained, but she hadn't lost her Australian accent. 'Jack says that he was so much in love with me, he couldn't bear to lose me. That crash – my entire body was crushed. Legs, pelvis, ribcage, spine. I wouldn't have survived for more than two or three days. So that was when Jack decided to sacrifice Sheba, in order to save me.'

'But how did he get away with it? Doing an operation like that – it must be totally illegal.'

'Jack has his own clinic, remember, and three highly-qualified surgeons. He persuaded them that they would be making medical history. And he paid them all a great deal of money.'

'But how about you? Didn't *you* have any say?'

'I was unconscious, Bob. I didn't know anything about it, until I woke up.'

I have never fainted, ever – not even when my cousin Freddie ripped off three of his fingers with a circular saw. But right then I could feel the blood emptying out of my brain and I was pretty darn close to it. The whole world turned black and white, like a photographic negative, and I felt like I was perspiring ice-water.

'What do you feel about it now?' I asked her. 'How can you manage to *live* like this?'

She gave me a sad, bruised smile. 'I try to treat myself with respect, and I try to treat Sheba with respect. That's why I go out running, to give her body the exercise she needs. We always go out at night, and I always wear that ski mask, so that nobody can see my face and my hair.'

'But you can *talk*. Dogs can't talk.'

'Jack transplanted my vocal chords. I still get breathless, but I don't find talking too difficult.'

She came up closer. I didn't know if I could touch her or not. And if I did, what was I supposed to do? Kiss her? Put my arm around her? Or stroke her? I still couldn't believe that I was looking at a huge brindled dog with a human woman's head.

'Most of all,' she said, 'I try to be Kylie. I try to forget what's happened to me, and live the best life I can.'

I looked her straight in her Hershey-brown eyes. 'You can't bear it, can you?'

'Bob – I *have* to bear it. What else can I do? How does a dog commit suicide? I can't shoot myself. I can't hang myself. I can't open bottles of pills. I can't even get out of the house and run out on to the freeway. I can't turn the door handle and I can't jump over the fences at the sides.'

'But how can Jack say that he loves you when you're suffering like this?'

'He's in total denial. He says he loves me but he's obsessed. He's always bringing me flowers and perfume. He bought me that painting by Sidney Nolan. It must have cost nearly quarter of a million dollars.'

I sat on that couch staring at her, but I simply didn't know what to say. The worst thing was that I was just as responsible for this monstrous thing that had happened to her as Jack was. I had killed her. Jack had given her life. But what a life. It made me question everything I had ever felt about the chronically sick, and the paraplegic, and the catastrophically injured. At what point is a life not worth living any more? And who's to say that it isn't?

For the first time ever, I couldn't think of any wisecracks. I could only think that tears were sliding down my cheeks and there was nothing I could do to stop them.

Kylie said, 'My grandma had a dog she really loved. He was a little fox terrier and his name was Rip. After my grandpa died, Rip was the only companion she had. She used to talk to him like he was human.

She coughed, and took a deep breath.

'Rip got sick. Cancer, I think. As soon as he was diagnosed, my grandma asked the vet to put him down. She held my hand on the day we buried him, and she said that if you truly love someone, whether it's a person or a pet, you never allow them to suffer.'

'What are you saying to me, Kylie?'

She came even closer. I reached out and touched her cheek. She was very cold, but her skin felt just as soft as it had before, when we were lovers.

'Help me, Bob. I'm sure that it was fate that brought you here tonight.'

'Help you?' I knew exactly what she was saying but I had to hear it from her.

'Let me out of here. That's all you have to do. Open the door and let me run away.'

'Oh, great. So that you can throw yourself in front of a truck?'

'You won't ever have to know. Please, Bob. I can't bear living like this any longer.'

I stroked her hair. 'You're asking me to kill you for a second time. I'm not so sure I can do that.'

'Please, Bob.'

I stood up and walked across to the Sidney Nolan painting over the fireplace. 'What does this mean?' I asked her. 'These figures . . . they look kind of Aboriginal.'

'They are. The painting's called *Ritual Lake*. It represents the mystical bond between men and animals.'

I looked down at her. She looked exhausted. 'All right,' I said. 'I'll help you. But I'm damned if I'm going to let you get yourself flattened on the freeway.'

'I don't care what you do. I just want this to be over.'

I led her through the hallway to the front door, and opened it. Just as I did so, Jack's Audi SUV swerved into the drive, its headlights glaring, and stopped.

'*Hurry*!' I said, and began to run down the steps, with Kylie close behind me.

But Jack must have seen that the front door was open and he was quicker than both of us. As we reached the bottom step, he opened the door of his SUV and jumped down in front of us.

'Bob! Bob, my man! What a surprise!'

'Hi, Jack.'

Kylie and I stopped where we were. Jack came up to me and stood only inches in front of me, his eyes unnaturally widened, like those mad people you see in slasher movies. He was holding Kylie's metal-studded leash in his right hand, and slapping it into the palm of his left.

'Taking Kylie for a walk, were you, Bob? I'm amazed she trusts you, after what you did to her.'

'As a matter of fact, Jack, I came round to talk to you.'

'You came round to talk to *me*? What could you possibly have to say to me, Bob, that I would ever want to listen to?'

'Well – maybe the word "remorse" means something to you.'

'"Remorse"? You're feeling remorse? For *what*, Bob? For mutilating the woman I love so severely that *this* was her only chance of survival? Ruining her life, and *my* life, and ending Sheba's life, too?'

'Jack,' said Kylie, in that high, harsh whisper. 'Nothing can change what's happened. All the rage in the world isn't going to bring me back the way I was. I forgive Bob. And if *I* can forgive him, can't you?'

'Get back in the house, Kylie.'

'No, Jack. It's over. I'm going and I'm not coming back.'

'Get back in the house, Kylie! Do as you're damn well told!'

Kylie turned on him. 'I'm not a dog, Jack! I'm not your bitch! I'm a woman, and I'll do whatever I want!'

Jack swung back his arm and lashed her across the face with her leash. She cried out, and cowered back, just like a beaten dog. I grabbed hold of the leash and swung Jack around, trying to pull him off balance, but he punched me very hard on my cheekbone, and I fell backward into the bushes.

'Now, get inside!' Jack snapped at Kylie, and lashed her again.

This time, however, Kylie didn't cringe. She leaped up on her hind legs and pushed Jack with her forepaws. Even though she was a female, she must have weighed at least a hundred and thirty pounds. He collided with the door of his SUV, and then dropped on to the driveway.

'You bitch!' Jack yelled at her, trying to climb to his feet. But she pushed him down again, and then she ducked her head sideways and bit him – first his nose and then his cheek. I saw blood flying all across the front of his pale blue shirt.

'*Get off me*!' Jack screamed. '*Get off me*!'

But now Kylie bit into the side of his neck, viciously hard. He bellowed and snorted, and the heels of his shiny black shoes kicked against the bricks, but she refused to open her jaws.

'Kylie!' I shouted at her. 'For Christ's sake, let him go!'

I clambered to my feet and tried to pull her away from him, but Sheba's body was so smooth haired and muscular that I couldn't even get a proper grip. I took a handful of Kylie's blonde hair, and pulled that instead, even though I was irrationally worried that I might pull her head off. But she kept her teeth buried in Jack's neck until his blood was flooding dark across the driveway, and his shoes gave a last shuddering kick.

Eventually, panting, she raised her head. The lower half of her face was smothered in blood, but her eyes looked triumphant.

'You've killed him,' I said, flatly.

'Yes,' she said. 'That was his punishment for keeping me alive.'

I checked my watch. It was almost a quarter of midnight.

'We'd better get going,' I told her.

We drove west on Sunset, not speaking to each other. There was a full moon right above us, and its white light turned everything to cardboard, so that I felt as if we were driving through a movie set.

We looped around the Will Rogers State Park and then we arrived at the seashore. I parked, and opened the passenger door, so that Kylie could jump out.

I walked out on to the sand, dimpled by a million feet. Kylie followed me, panting. We reached the shoreline and stood together at the water's edge, while the surf tiredly splashed at our feet.

There was a warm breeze blowing from the south-west. I looked down at Kylie and said, 'Here we are, then. Back at the ocean.'

'Thank you,' she said.

'Jesus Christ. I don't know what for.'

'For helping me to end it, that's all.'

She trotted a little way into the water, and then she turned around. 'You're right about boomerangs,' she said. 'They don't really come back. Ever.'

With that, she began to swim away from the seashore. Looking at her then, you would never have known what had happened to her, because all you could see was a blonde girl's head, dipping up and down between the waves.

I stood and watched her swimming away until she was out of sight. Then I threw her leash after her, as hard and as far as I could.

The Scrawler

Peter was standing on the westbound platform of Piccadilly Circus tube station, eating a Mars Bar, when he noticed the words HOW ARE YOU FEELING TODAY, PETER? scratched into a Wonderbra poster on the opposite side of the track.

He glanced right and left, embarrassed, as if everybody else on the crowded platform knew that his name was Peter. But everybody else was talking, or eating, simply staring tiredly at nothing at all. After a minute there was a warm rush of wind and his train arrived, and he stepped aboard. The carriage was jam-packed, but he elbowed his way to the window on the other side of the train so that he could look at the inscription more closely.

The letters were nearly two feet high, irregularly spaced, and they had been gouged so deeply into the poster that they had gone right through to the brick underneath. He couldn't imagine how anybody could have managed to cut them, especially since the poster was more than ten feet above the track, and the track itself carried 650 volts of alternating current.

But there they were: HOW ARE YOU FEELING TODAY, PETER? And he couldn't help feeling that somehow the message was meant for him.

The train pulled away with a jolt, and he staggered into the bosom of a large, middle-aged black lady who didn't complain but gave him a smile and a wink. He said, 'Sorry . . . sorry.' He didn't want her to think that he had done it on purpose.

He got out at West Kensington and walked south on North End Road. It was only five thirty but it was already dark, and the streets were glistening with home-going traffic. As he passed the Seven Stars pub, he noticed that somebody had scrawled a message on its cream-colored tiles, in the same kind of jagged, scratchy lettering that he had seen on the tube. ARE YOU SURE YOU CAN TRUST HER, PETER?

He went back a few paces and stared at it. This was ridiculous.

The message was cut right into the ceramic surface of the tiles, as if it had been inscribed with a narrow-bladed chisel. But it couldn't refer to him, surely. There must be hundreds of Peters in West Kensington. Thousands. But how many of them would have been likely to pass first one message, in Piccadilly, and then a second one, here? And what was the writer trying to say about 'trusting her'?

He turned into Bramber Road, a narrow street of Victorian terraced houses, opposite the scrubby little triangle of Normand Park. It was starting to rain again, and he began to hurry. He reached number nineteen and forced open the wrought-iron gate, which sagged on its hinges, and made it to the shelter of the porch. He took out his key and was just about to insert it in the lock when the lights went on inside the hallway and the door opened. A tall young man with dark curly hair and a leather jacket stepped out, and said, 'Hi. Thanks.'

Peter stood and watched the young man as he went out through the gate and walked down the street, his collar turned up against the rain. He was sure that he recognized him, but he couldn't think why, or how. He stepped into the hallway and closed the door behind him, just as the time switch plunged him into darkness.

He climbed the steep staircase. There was a strong smell of frying onions on the first-floor landing. Mr Chowdery was cooking one of his curries again. He passed Flat Three, where *Neighbours* was playing at top volume on Mrs Wigmore's television. Then he went up to the top floor and let himself into Flat Four.

Peter had lived here for seven months before Gemma had moved in with him, and it still looked like a single man's flat, even though it was cluttered with feminine debris like shopping bags and make up and hairbrushes and discarded bras. The floors were carpeted in plain, oatmeal carpet, and the furniture was mostly Ikea, pale pine and chrome. All of Peter's CDs were neatly arranged in a pine tower, next to his Sony stereo equipment, and all of his paperback books were shelved in alphabetical order.

The only decoration on the walls of the living room was a poster for The Smiths.

Peter went through to the kitchen. It was in darkness, with Gemma's white cotton bodies hanging up in the windows like ghosts. He opened the fridge because all men open the fridge as soon as they come home, but there was nothing in it except for last night's pizza, its cheese turned to yellow plastic and its box spotted with grease.

'Gemma?' he called. He went into the bedroom. The bed was still unmade, the brown durry dragged to one side and the pillows on the floor.

'Gemma?'

'In here,' she called, from the half-open bathroom door. There was a wet towel on the floor and he had to push the door hard to get in. Gemma was standing in the bathtub, behind the green plastic shower-curtain.

'You're early,' she said.

'Yes . . .' he said, bending over to pick up the towel. 'There was a fire alarm so they canceled the last lesson.'

She turned off the water and drew back the curtain. She was a tall, thin girl, almost antelope-like, with a long oval face and enormous brown eyes. Her cheeks were flushed pink and she smelled of Body Shop mint shampoo. 'Hand me that towel, will you?'

'Didn't you go to work?' he asked her.

'No . . . I had a headache. Besides, there's never anything much to do on Fridays.'

She wound the towel around her and went through to the bedroom, where she stood in front of the dressing-table mirror and brushed out her wet hair. He followed her and stood behind her, watching her. ARE YOU SURE YOU CAN TRUST HER, PETER?

'So, what have you been doing all day?'

'Nothing. Sleeping, mostly.'

'I thought we could go for a Chinese tonight.'

'I don't know. I'm not really hungry.'

'Well, I'll get a takeaway then.'

'Whatever.'

He started to straighten the bed. 'Who was that guy I saw downstairs?'

'What guy?'

'He was just coming out when I came in. Tall guy. Dark curly hair.'

'I don't know.'

'It's just that he didn't look like the sort of person that Mr Chowdery would have for a friend. Nor Mrs Wigmore, either.'

Gemma shrugged, with hairgrips in her mouth.

Peter went through to the kitchen again, and this time he switched on the light. Gemma's keys were lying sprawled on the kitchen counter, next to her purse.

'You went out?' he asked her.

'What?'

'I just wondered if you went out at all.'

She came into the kitchen, wearing her knee-length nightshirt. 'No. I told you. I had a headache.'

In the middle of the night, with the amber street light shining across the ceiling, he put his arm around her. She murmured irritably and pushed him away. After that he lay awake for hours, listening to the soft, ceaseless thunder of London at night, feeling as if his world had changed into somewhere that he didn't recognize – somewhere anxious and threatening and insecure.

On Saturday morning they went shopping along the North End Road market. Gemma was unusually distant, as if she had something on her mind, and she hardly ever seemed to look at him, or talk to him, or smile. Peter followed her through the clutter of newspaper and broken tomato boxes, and there was an ache in his throat that couldn't be swallowed away.

At lunchtime they went for a sandwich and a drink at The Colton Arms, and sat in the darkest corner at the back. Gemma was silhouetted against the window, and wreathed in cigarette smoke.

'What do you want to do this afternoon?' Peter asked her. 'I thought we could go to Holland Park.'

'What for?'

'Nothing. Just for a walk.'

'I don't know. I was thinking of going to see Kelley and June.'

'All right, then. We'll go to see Kelley and June.'

'Just me, I was thinking. I feel like a good old girlie natter.'

'All right. What time will you be back?'

'I don't know. I'll call you.'

'What about supper?'

'It's only pork chops, isn't it? I'll do it when I get back.'

Peter didn't know what to say. With the light behind her, he couldn't see her eyes. He laid his hand on top of hers, and although she didn't move it away, he could feel how tense she was. No twining of fingers. Her hand just crouched there, underneath his, rigid, like a small animal waiting for its chance to escape.

'I'm going for a leak,' he told her, taking his hand away.

The gents was cramped, and he had to wait while a white-haired old man with a cigarette in his mouth coughed and peed at the same time, and made an elaborate performance of waggling himself afterward, and grunting while he did up his buttons.

When he stood in front of the urinal, Peter saw letters cut into the wall. They were so large that he couldn't read them at first. They were nearly half an inch deep, and formed in the same scratchy style as the messages he had seen on the tube wall at Piccadilly, and on the side of the Seven Stars.

DON'T YOU THINK SHE'S LYING TO YOU?

He went back into the bar. Gemma was talking on her mobile phone, but as soon as she saw him she said, 'No – I've got to go now. I'll talk to you later,' and quickly flipped it shut.

'Who was that?' he asked her.

'Who was what?'

'Who were you just talking to?'

'Erm, Tricia.'

'Tricia? I thought Tricia was spending the weekend in Wales.'

'She is. It *is* possible to talk on the phone to people in Wales, you know.'

Peter said nothing. He was quite convinced now that the wall messages were meant for him. How anybody could know where he was going to be, and how they could cut the letters so deeply, he had no idea. But what disturbed him most of all was the questions they were asking him.

He picked up his glass and swirled the last of his lager around and around. 'You do still love me?' he said.

'What do you mean? Of course I love you.'

'If there was something wrong, you'd tell me, wouldn't you?'

'Of course I would.'

He looked up at her. He still couldn't see her eyes. DON'T YOU THINK SHE'S LYING TO YOU?

* * *

He was dozing in front of *Eurotrash* when the phone rang on the table beside him. Frowning, he picked it up and pressed the mute button on the TV remote.

'Peter? It's Gemma. I'm sorry I didn't call you earlier but I lost track of the time.'

He peered at his watch. 'It's five past twelve. Where are you?'

'I'm still round at Kelley and June's. I'm sorry. We had a couple of bottles of wine and . . . you know.'

'For Christ's sake, Gemma, you were supposed to come back for supper.'

'Look, I've said I'm sorry, haven't I? It's not like we're married or anything.'

'We're supposed to be engaged, aren't we? Come on, Gemma, think what you'd feel like if I did the same to you.'

'I wouldn't mind if you wanted a night out with the boys. Why should I?'

'So when are you coming back?'

'Tomorrow morning. I'm too pissed to drive.'

'Call a minicab. We can go back and get your car in the morning.'

'I want to stay here. We're having a good time.'

'Gemma—'

But Gemma had hung up, and Peter was left with the dead receiver in his hand, and the flickering image on the TV screen of a Belgian orgy. A young blonde woman with bright red lips was gasping with ecstasy in the arms of a muscular naked man. The man turned around and looked directly into the camera, and gave a long, self-satisfied leer.

Peter switched off the television and went to the bathroom. He saw it as soon as he opened the door, and he stood staring at it with a cold crawling sensation that worked its way slowly up his back and into his scalp.

In the mirror over the washbasin, eight scratchy words had been engraved right into the glass. DON'T YOU THINK SHE DESERVES TO BE PUNISHED?

Peter approached the basin and traced the letters with his fingertips. How could anyone have cut letters as deep as these? They must have used an industrial diamond, or a glass cutter. But who was it, and how had they got in here, and *when* had they done it? He had been sleeping for nearly an hour, but only fitfully, and cutting letters as deep as this would have made an appalling scratching noise.

He looked through the letters at his own face. Thin, beaky nosed, with dark rings under his eyes. A young Pete Townshend, from The Who. *Hope I die before I get old.* He heard a banging noise outside and he gave a silly, girlish jump, knocking his elbow against the washbasin. It was only Mr Chowdery slamming the lid back on his dustbin, but somehow nothing seemed the same any more. If people could walk through locked doors and cut your deepest anxieties into your bathroom mirror, then what else could happen?

Peter slept badly that night. By the time the key turned in the lock at seven thirty-five, and Gemma came in, he was sitting on the couch drinking a large mug of instant coffee and eating a folded-over Kraft cheese sandwich without a plate.

'Oh, you're back, then,' he said.

She walked across the room and drew back the thin cotton curtains. It was a gloomy, gray day, and the window was speckled with rain.

'You look terrible. You're not getting one of your colds, are you?'

'No. I just didn't sleep, that's all.'

'You're not sulking, are you, just because I stayed out?'

'Why should I? Like you keep on telling me, we're not married yet. You can do what you like.'

'Oh God, you *are* sulking.'

She went into the kitchen and put the kettle on. He followed her and stood in the doorway watching her.

'What?' she said.

'You didn't go to see Kelley and June, did you?'

She took down her coffee mug and spooned coffee into it. She was betraying him, he was sure of it. The graffiti was right. She poured boiling water into her mug and stirred it, and he kept on watching her as if she was going to make some insignificant gesture that would give her away.

As she tried to leave the kitchen he barred her way. 'Come on, I want to know the truth. You didn't go to see Kelley and June, did you?'

'Peter, for God's sake.'

'I want to know his name, Gemma. I want to know what the hell you think you're doing to me.'

'I'm not doing anything to you. I just need some space, that's all. You're always *there*. I go into the living room and you're there. I go into the bedroom and you follow me into the bedroom. I can't even go to the toilet without you coming in.'

'We live together, don't we?'

'Yes, but that doesn't mean we can never go more than two inches away from each other. You give me claustrophobia, if you must know.'

He stared at her. He didn't know what to say. In the end she said, '*Excuse* me,' and pushed past him into the living room. He didn't know whether to follow her or not.

At eleven o'clock she went out to the corner shop for milk and cigarettes.

'You can come if you want to,' she said, winding her red woolen scarf around her neck.

'I'm watching the football,' he said. 'Besides, I wouldn't want you to feel more claustrophobic than you do already.'

'Oh, Peter.'

She hadn't been gone longer than three or four minutes when the phone rang. He picked it up and a man's voice said, '*Gem*?'

'Who wants her?'

'*Rick*.'

'Rick who?'

'*Look, man, is she there or not*?'

'She's not, as a matter of fact. Rick who?'

The man put the phone down without answering. Peter sat frowning at the receiver as if he couldn't understand what it was.

As they walked up North End Road toward the tube station, Peter said, 'Who's Rick?'

'Rick?' she said. She thought for a moment and then she shook her head. 'I don't know any Rick.'

'Well, Rick knows you. In fact, Rick knows you well enough to call you "Gem".'

'Oh, *that* Rick. Little bald chap. I met him at one of our promotions at work.'

They crossed the street. On the other side of the road a shop had been converted into a dentist's surgery, its front window painted blue. Below the gilt letters that read I. Wartawa, Dental

Surgeon, somebody had scratched the message YOU DON'T SERIOUSLY BELIEVE HER, DO YOU?

Peter stopped and stared at it, while Gemma kept on walking. He felt so helpless and angry and jealous that he could have smashed the window with his fist. How could she think that he was going to swallow her explanation about Rick being a little bald chap she had met at work? A hundred to one Rick was the curly-headed guy in the leather jacket. A hundred to one.

Somehow, Gemma's betrayal of him must be so terrible that it had actually caused this graffiti to etch itself spontaneously, in the same way that the likenesses of dead people appeared on the walls of the rooms they had died in; or stigmata appeared on the hands and feet of people who experienced spasms of religious ecstasy.

He caught up with her by the entrance to the tube station and she hadn't even noticed that he wasn't walking beside her. 'What?' she asked, as he took hold of her arm.

'I'm all right. I'm fine. So tell me about this Rick.'

'There's nothing to tell,' she said, as he bought their tickets. 'He works for some computer company in Milton Keynes.'

'You gave him your number at home?'

'I don't know. I must have done.'

They went down the stairs to the eastbound platform. West Kensington station was open to the iron-gray afternoon clouds, and the tracks were shining with wet. There were only five or six other people on the platform with them, including a drunk in a torn, brown raincoat who was performing a mesmerizing one-man foxtrot just to stay upright.

'Listen – what you said about space.'

'I didn't mean to upset you, Peter. It's just that I do like to have a few moments on my own, now and again. I'm sorry I called you claustrophobic.'

He looked down at the concrete edging on the platform. There were fourteen letters chiseled into it, jagged and awry. PUNISH HER, PETER.

In the distance, he heard the next train approaching. Soon he could see its headlights gleaming on the rails. He stood close to Gemma and put his arm around her waist. She glanced at him uncomfortably, but after what she had just said, she obviously didn't feel that she could pull herself away.

The train suddenly appeared from underneath the bridge. Peter didn't even hesitate. He shouted out, '*Be careful*!' and at the same time pushed Gemma forward as hard as he could.

Gemma toppled, lost her balance, nearly caught it again, but then Peter pushed her again, gripping her coat collar so that it looked as if he was trying to save her. She tumbled over the edge of the platform right under the train's front wheels.

There was a deafening bang of emergency brakes, followed by a long, hideous screeching, like the grand finale to some cacophonous opera. The train seemed to take forever to come to a stop. Its wheels locked, so that Gemma was dragged almost thirty yards along the track.

Then, for one long moment, there was quiet. Only the traffic from North End Road, and the sound of a 747 rumbling overhead, on its way to Heathrow.

More like a wooden marionette than a man, Peter walked stiff legged to the front of the train. He felt shocked and breathless, but wildly exhilarated, too. The driver was just climbing out of his cab. He had left the rest of the doors closed, so that the train's passengers were trapped inside, staring anxiously out to see what had happened. The drunk had lost his battle to stay upright, and was reclining on the platform on one elbow like a man at a picnic, saying, 'Shit . . . I don't believe it. Shit.'

Peter went up to the driver. He was gray-faced, and his voice shook. 'I've only just gone back to work after the last one,' he blurted. 'I've only just gone back.'

Peter peered down on to the track. Gemma was lying underneath the front platform-side wheel. Her face was covered in red bruises and her dress was soaked in blood. She was staring up at the clouds with an expression of bewilderment, rather than terror. Her right arm had been torn off at the shoulder and the lower part of her right leg was missing.

One of the station staff came running up. 'Ambulance is on its way,' he announced. Then, 'You can't stay here, sir. You'll have to stand well back.'

'That's my fiancée,' said Peter.

'I'm really sorry, sir, but you'll have to stand well back.'

Peter retreated to the bench at the end of the platform while two more station staff appeared and then, at last, an ambulance crew. The power was switched off and they climbed down on to the tracks. Peter began to wish that he hadn't given up smoking.

As he sat on the bench waiting, he saw some words scratched into the side of the train. HAPPY NOW, PETER? And he began to think that, yes, in a way, he was.

It suddenly started to rain very hard.

Later that evening, after he had talked for two hours to a sympathetic, sandy-haired detective, he went back to Bramber Road and let himself into his flat. It was cold and dark, and the first thing he saw when he switched the light on was Gemma's red angora sweater lying on the couch.

'Hallo,' he said, under his breath. 'Anybody home?'

He went into the kitchen. Gemma's white bodies were still hanging in the windows where she had left them yesterday, and he systematically took them down, one after the other, and folded them up. Then he went through to the bedroom and opened the wardrobe. It was crowded with jumpers and skirts and jeans and jackets, and the bottom was heaped with dozens of pairs of shoes from Shelley's and Ravel.

He slid open one of the drawers and picked out a pair of white lacy panties. He pressed them against his face and took a deep breath. They smelled of nothing but Comfort softener. She's gone, he thought. She's really gone. It just goes to show you that you *can* make a difference in your own life, you *can* take control, if you're brave enough. All you have to do is open your eyes, take your blinkers off, and see that the people all around you are screwing you rotten. They may smile and clap you on the back and pretend to be your friends, but they're not. And women are the worst.

He went into the bathroom and stared at his face in the mirror. Ladies and gentlemen of the jury, does this look like a murderer to you? No, it looks like a man who was grievously betrayed by the woman who was supposed to love him, and simply started to ask himself the right questions.

He took off all of his clothes and weighed himself. Then he cleared all of Gemma's cosmetics from the bathroom shelf – her cleansing lotion, her Clearasil, her toothpaste, her shampoo. He put them in a cardboard wine box, along with her make-up and everything else in her dressing-table drawers.

After that, he emptied her wardrobe, stuffing all of her clothes into black plastic dustbin-bags. He even went through the kitchen cupboards, removing her Weight Watchers soups and her sachets of green Japanese tea.

The phone rang. He picked it up and said, 'Who is it?'

'*Rick. Is Gem back yet?*'

'Gemma's never coming back, Rick.'

'*What do you mean? Where can I get in touch with her*?'

'She's dead, Rick. There was an accident.'

'*Oh my God. What happened*?'

'Justice caught up with her, Rick. Justice.'

'*I don't understand what you're talking about.*'

'Of course you do. Fucking her behind my back.'

'*What*?'

'Don't try to pretend that you're innocent, Rick. It was carved in stone, what you two were doing together. Etched in glass, chiseled in brick. You can't get evidence much more concrete than that, can you?'

'*I don't know what on earth you mean. Tell me what happened to her.*'

But Peter hung up, and sat back in his chair, smiling smugly. Let him find out for himself, the bastard. Gemma's death would be in all the papers tomorrow. Then everybody would know that all deceitful women have to pay the price.

A week went past and it rained every day, ceaselessly. The following Saturday morning he went to Gemma's funeral at West London Crematorium. He saw a lot of her friends there – Kelley and June and David and all of the people from work – but he didn't see the tall curly-headed Rick. He had probably had the sense to stay away.

After the ceremony – as he walked back along the puddly asphalt path toward the crematorium gates – a young man with short blond hair and glasses caught up with him.

'We've met before, haven't we?' he said. Then – seeing Peter frown – 'Robin Marshall, we met at Bill and Gillian's party in Kew.'

'Oh, yes. How are you?'

'I've been great, actually. I've just come back from three months in San Francisco. Such a tragedy, Gemma being killed like that. You must be devastated.'

'Yes. Yes, I am.'

'She was such a sweet girl . . . always so *graceful*, I thought. I never saw her do anything awkward or clumsy, ever. I saw her fall off a stepladder once, when she was putting up some Christmas decorations. Somehow she managed to turn it into a *jeté*. Landed on her feet – *ta-da*! – light as a fairy.'

Peter nodded. He was struck by the intense blueness of Robin Marshall's eyes. They were almost unreal, like sapphires. He had good cheekbones, a straight nose, and rather sensual lips. His suntan had faded so that he looked as if he were made up for a television appearance.

'Listen, do you fancy a coffee?' Peter asked. 'I haven't really had anybody to talk to since Gemma.'

'Of course. That'd be nice. There's an Italian restaurant just around the corner. The food's only fit for regurgitation but they do a terrific espresso.'

They sat in the steamed-up window of Florentino's with two large espressos, only two feet away from a hugely fat man in jeans and a squeaky leather jacket who was forking up a bowlful of spaghetti Bolognese.

'You're bound to be feeling disoriented now that Gemma's gone,' said Robin. 'After all, your choice of partner defines who you are. What you see in your partner, that's you.'

'I don't know. It sounds heartless, and I miss her like anything, but I feel relieved, in a way. I don't really think that we were meant for each other. I just wish I could have found out some other way.'

Robin watched him from over the rim of his cup. Those deep blue eyes were almost alien, an Atreides from *Dune*. 'When you say you weren't meant for each other – what do you think was wrong?'

The fat man tore off a piece of bread and pushed it into his mouth to join his churning spaghetti. Peter said, 'She was absolutely beautiful . . . and graceful, like you say. Everybody else used to say that she was gorgeous, and she was. I loved going out with her and showing her off. But when it came down to it . . .'

'When it came down to it, what? What was wrong? What was missing?'

Peter didn't know why he felt able to confide in Robin, but he did. He seemed to be one of those few people who instinctively understand what you're feeling, because they've felt the same way.

'When it came down to it, she didn't – well, she didn't, you know, *excite* me. She didn't turn me on.'

'Hm,' said Robin, and sipped his coffee. 'And why do you think that was?'

Peter shrugged. 'I loved her, as a person. I really did. I was jealous if any other man tried to flirt with her. I mean, like, *burningly* jealous. In the last few days I've been worrying that she was seeing somebody else, and that's been depressing the hell out of me. But I . . . ah—'

'You didn't find her sexually arousing, is that what you're trying to say?'

'I suppose it is, yes. I really don't know why.'

Robin was thoughtfully silent, peering down into his coffee cup. Then he said, 'What about other women? Do you find *any* woman sexually arousing?'

Peter didn't answer, couldn't. He had always liked women, and he had always been curious about women. He had bought jazz mags when he was younger, and masturbated over them. But Robin had come dangerously close to something that he had never dared to ask himself.

'I, er, yes. Some women. Some particular types of women. Not *all* women. But some women.'

Robin still didn't look up from his coffee cup. 'Do you think it would be a good idea if you and I were to meet and discuss this some more? You could come to my flat for supper, if you liked.'

'I'm not sure.'

'The truth is, Peter, I'm on my own at the moment. The reason I came back from San Francisco – well, I've just broken up with somebody who was very close to me. I'd really appreciate some company. You know – just someone to talk to.'

Peter didn't know what to say, but Robin took a business card out of his wallet and said, 'Think about it. My home number's on here, too. Next Thursday would be a good day for me.'

'Thank you,' said Peter. The fat man sniffed yet again, and let out a loud, ripping burp.

He decided to walk home, even though it was nearly three miles and it was raining harder than ever. He needed to think, and he felt that he deserved some punishment, too. He kept his umbrella furled, so that the icy rain lashed against his face, and he couldn't stop thinking about Robin and his Atreides eyes, and those bow-shaped sensual lips.

He reached the junction with Charleville Road. There was a public lavatory in the middle of the traffic island, surrounded by black cast-iron railings. On the side of it, engraved into the brickwork, were the same jagged letters that he had seen before. WHAT ARE YOU, PETER?

He crossed over the busy road and went right up to the wall. Again, the letters were nearly half an inch deep. He pressed his hand against the wet bricks and wondered if he was suffering the first symptoms of schizophrenia. But schizophrenic people hear voices. They don't see messages chiseled into solid stone.

He wiped his dripping nose with the back of his hand. He needed a pee so he walked around to the steps that led down to the Gents. As he went down them, a gray-haired man in a damp-shouldered raincoat passed him on the way up, and gave him a wink.

The toilet was smelly and the floor was wet. A thin young man in a threadbare overcoat was washing his hair in one of the basins, while a painfully ribby Jack Russell stood shivering beside him. 'Spare some change, mate?' he asked, huskily, his hair still soapy and his head still immersed.

Peter was about to open one of the cubicle doors. He found three pounds in his trouser pocket and put it down on the counter next to the young man's dirty green plastic comb. The young man didn't thank him so Peter simply said, 'There, buy yourself a cup of tea or something,' and went back to the cubicle.

He locked the door behind him. There was no seat on the lavatory and somebody had unraveled all of the toilet paper on to the floor. The walls were covered in drawings and poems and telephone numbers. *If you want the suck of your life meet me here 7:30 Tues 9. I like young black boys with really tight holes. O seasons, O castles! What soul is without fault? Spurs are crap.* There were crude felt-tip drawings of naked women and dozens of disembodied penises with semen flying out of them like machine-gun fire. And then – as Peter looked higher up the wall – he felt a cold, crawling sensation around the back of his neck.

Hacked into the tiles was the message WHY DON'T YOU TRY IT, PETER?

He finished and flushed the toilet. He stood in the cubicle for a long time with his hand pressed over his mouth, thinking. Robin had disturbed him deeply, and he had been tempted to say yes when he had asked him around for supper. But he wasn't at all sure of himself yet. Supposing he wasn't really gay at all? Supposing he was grieving for Gemma more than he consciously realized, and was simply looking for help and sympathy and a shoulder to cry on? Supposing – for all of her grace and all of her beauty – Gemma simply hadn't been his type of woman?

He would need to be sure before he saw Robin again. It would be too embarrassing to accept Robin's invitation and then discover that he had made a terrible mistake.

He stayed in the cubicle for three or four minutes, not knowing what to do. But finally he opened the door and stepped outside. The young man in the shabby overcoat was still bent over the basin, almost as if he had been waiting for Peter to emerge. The dog yawned and shook itself.

Peter went up to the young man and stood close behind him.

'I – ah – I don't suppose you need any more money?'

The young man stopped rinsing his tousled hair, but said nothing.

'It's just that – well, I've never done anything like this before. Just come up to a total stranger and asked him if he's interested. So I'm not sure if this is the way to go about it.'

Still the stranger said nothing, and remained with his head bent over the gray, soapy water.

'If you're not interested, just say the word and I'll go.'

At last the young man stood up straight, his shoulders bony under his coat. Peter couldn't see his face properly because the mirror was all steamed up.

'Well?' said Peter. He was growing anxious and impatient, and he was right on the edge of turning around and leaving.

'You ask far too many questions,' said the boy, in a dry, whispery voice.

'What? What do you mean?'

'Exactly that. You never stop doubting yourself. You never stop doubting other people. You don't have any faith.'

'Faith? What does faith have to do with it?'

'Faith has everything to do with it,' the young man replied. He lifted his right hand, which was very thin and very long-fingered, and unfolded it. To Peter's horror, he had curved gray fingernails that were almost three inches long.

He reached up to the mirror, and used the nail of his index finger to scratch the glass. With a gritty scraping noise that set Peter's teeth on edge, he scrawled NO FAITH, NO FUTURE. Then he turned around.

To Peter's shock, he wasn't a young man at all. His face was leathery and deeply-wrinkled, and his eyes were as black and glittery as beetles. His mouth was almost lipless, as if somebody had made a deep horizontal cut with a very sharp knife.

Peter took one step back, and then another.

'Where are you going, Peter?' the man asked him, in the same whispery voice. 'You can't run away from your own lack of faith.'

'Who are you?' said Peter.

'They used to call me the Scrawler, in the East End, during the Blitz, when they were hiding in the tube stations. I used to scratch their worst nightmares on the tunnel walls. HALLO, SIDNEY, EVER WONDERED WHAT YOUR WIFE'S UP TO? That used to put the wind up them!'

'Get away from me. I don't know what the hell you're talking about, and I don't want to know, either.'

'You can't get away from me, Peter. Once I've sniffed you out, there's no getting away from me. I've been living in London for longer than you can even imagine, mate. I've been scrawling and scratching my way through the East End slums, and the sex clubs of Soho, and Holborn, and Notting Hill, and Brixton. I have a very keen nose for fear, Peter. I can smell it on people, like body odor. Toffs, drunks, newspaper reporters, bank clerks.' He closed his eyes for a moment and took a deep, appreciative breath.

'Who the hell are you? Leave me alone.'

The Scrawler's eyes popped open again. 'How can I leave you alone when you won't leave *me* alone? You're always doubting yourself, that's your trouble. You're always afraid that you're going to be alone. You thought it was your mind that carved all of those questions, didn't you? Or maybe some holy miracle. But it wasn't you and it wasn't a miracle. It was me.'

'Get away from me, will you?'

'Every city holds the same terrors, Peter. And what's the greatest terror of all? The terror of not being loved. The terror of living amongst millions and millions of people and having nobody.

'That's who I am, mate, and that's *what* I am. I'm nothing more than the terror of loneliness, come to life. And if you ask me where I come from, and how I came to be wandering the streets sniffing out people's insecurity, then all I can say is, I've always been here. You look at Rowlandson's etchings, my friend. You look at *Punch* engravings of the London mob. You look at photographs of Piccadilly in the nineteen twenties. That fellow by the gin-house door; that fellow sitting on the top deck of the open omnibus; that face in the crowd on Waterloo Bridge. That's me, Peter, looking for people like you.'

'You're mad. You're just mad. Get away from me.'

'I can't do that, Peter. So long as you doubt yourself, mate, I will follow you everywhere, wherever you go, and I will never, ever, ever give you peace.'

Peter stared at the Scrawler for a very long time, his chest rising and falling like a man who's been running. He *did* have faith. He *did* believe in himself. But what did he really believe in? And why did he always feel that he never fitted in? At work, he suspected that his colleagues didn't like him, and that they talked about him behind his back. And he couldn't even walk along the street without thinking that people were staring at him, and thinking what a misfit he was. He had never been able to believe that Gemma had really loved him and really wanted to marry him, and maybe that was why he had never been able to trust her.

But if he could get rid of his doubt – if he could stop asking himself so many questions – if he could *kill* his lack of faith—

He lifted his umbrella and struck the Scrawler on the shoulder. The Scrawler instantly snatched the umbrella and hurled it across to the other side of the toilet. Peter struck him with his fist, but he felt as if he had nothing beneath that flapping raincoat but a cage of bare bones. Without a word, the Scrawler opened out the index fingernails of both hands and slashed Peter across his face, first one cheek, then the other. The nails cut right through to his tongue, leaving his cheeks wide open, like extra mouths.

Blood sprayed everywhere, all over the basins, halfway up the walls.

Peter tried to seize the Scrawler's neck. He was too shocked to speak, and in any case he couldn't feel his tongue, but he let out a fierce and bloody *hhhuurrrhhhhhhh*! and hit the Scrawler's head against the mirror, cracking it in half.

'Now you've fucking done it,' the Scrawler breathed into his ear. He locked his left arm around Peter's neck and pushed the hard, sharp nail of his right up against Peter's groin. He grunted, and pushed even harder, and his nail pierced Peter's black funeral trousers, punctured his shirt tail and his underpants, and then plunged deep into subcutaneous fat, puncturing his body cavity with an audible exhalation of gases. Peter felt the fingernail slide inside him, right inside, and it was the most indecent invasion of his body that he could have imagined, a single long fingernail cutting through intestines and muscle and connective tissue.

He didn't utter a sound as the Scrawler slowly dragged his hand further and further up, so that its fingernail cut into his stomach, right up to his breastbone. His shirt front was suddenly soaked with blood. The Scrawler stepped back, breathing harsh and hard. Peter swayed and coughed and then sank slowly to the wet tiled floor, pressing his forehead against it like a religious penitent.

Right in front of his eyes, he saw the words HOW ARE YOU FEELING TODAY, PETER? They were cut deep into the ceramic, and they were slowly filling up with blood.

A month later, on a cold, brilliant day, Robin Marshall was called to the inquest at West London Coroner's Court, so that he could give evidence about Peter's apparent state of mind on the day that he died.

He stood in the witness box with the mid-morning sun shining on his blond hair. 'I had the impression that Peter was confused.'

'Confused about what?' asked the coroner.

'He had just attended his fiancée's funeral. I think he had very mixed feelings about her.'

'In what way?'

'He felt guilty that he may not have loved her as much as he ought to have done.'

'Can you elaborate?'

Robin looked serious. 'I think he felt uncertain about his sexual orientation, apart from other things.'

'I see. Anything else?'

'Even though he said that his fiancée hadn't really – well, excited him – he was still very jealous if he thought that she was seeing other men.'

'Did he think that she *was* seeing other men?'

Robin nodded. 'He said that it was making him very depressed. And of course he was very depressed about her death, too; and still in shock, if you ask me.'

Richard Morton, a thirty-five-year-old computer salesman from Milton Keynes, gave evidence that he had talked to Peter on the telephone just after Gemma's accident, and that Peter had seemed to believe that he and Gemma had been having an affair. 'He was beside himself with rage. I simply couldn't understand why.'

Dr George Protter, Peter's GP, said that Peter had been reasonably healthy, although he had suffered from several mild allergies, and had once consulted him after an anxiety attack at work. 'As far as the matter of his late fiancée seeing other men is concerned, this was more than likely a figment of his imagination. She was a patient of my colleague Dr Carpenter, and three weeks before she died he had diagnosed a lump in her left breast. Under the circumstances it would hardly have been surprising if she had acted toward the deceased in a preoccupied manner. As Dr Carpenter will testify at *her* inquest next week, the evening before she fell beneath the train at West Kensington Station he had been to make a house call to tell her that she would have to have exploratory surgery.'

Dr Vikram Pathanda, the senior pathologist at Hammersmith Hospital, then described how Peter had died. 'There were two deep diagonal wounds, one to each cheek, that went right through to the mouth cavity. There was a deep penetrative wound to the lower abdomen, followed by an invasive section of the abdomen, in an upward direction, right up to the sternum. The injuries were such that death would have occurred within two or three minutes.

'The wounds were caused by a specially sharpened, quarter-inch stonemason's chisel which was found at the trauma scene. There is no question at all in my mind that they were self-inflicted.'

The coroner took off his glasses. 'Thank you, Dr Pathanda. And now, I think, we could all adjourn for a spot of lunch.'

Robin Marshall sat on the top deck of the number fifteen bus, one hand raised to shield his eyes from the late-afternoon sun. Next to him, a black boy in enormous cargo pants was listening to rap on his stereo and joining in the beat with an occasional, '*unh-a-unh-a.*'

The bus stopped outside Paddington Station. As it did so, another bus drew alongside. Robin looked at a handsome young Asian sitting near the front of the bus. Then he looked down at the side, where there was a large advertisement for Pepsi Cola.

Somebody had scratched letters in the side of the bus – high, jagged letters that went right through the paint and exposed the bare aluminum. They said, HOW ARE YOU FEELING TODAY, ROBIN?

Sepsis

'What have you got there?' she asked him, her eyes shining.

'Nothing – it's a surprise,' he said, keeping the lapels of his overcoat drawn tightly together.

'What *is* it?' she demanded. 'I can't bear surprises!'

'It's something I bought specially for you, because I love you so much.'

'Show me!'

She tried to circle around him and peer down the front of his coat, but he backed away from her. 'Before I show you, you're going to have to make me a promise. You must promise to love this just as much as you love me.'

'How can I, when I don't know what it is?'

'Because it's all of my love for you, all of it, all wrapped up in one little bundle.'

'Show me!'

'Come on,' he coaxed her. 'If you don't promise, I'll take it back, and you'll never find out what it was.'

'*Show* me!'

'Promise first!'

She took a deep breath. 'All-right-whatever-is-in-your-coat-I-promise-to-love-it-just-as-much-as-I-love-you.'

'Cross your heart and hope to die?'

'Cross my heart and hope to die.'

Gently, he reached inside his coat and lifted out a tiny tortoiseshell kitten, with big green eyes. It gave a diminutive mew, and clung on to his lapel with its brambly little claws.

'Oh, it's a *darling*!' she said. 'Oh, it's absolutely *perfect*!'

'What did I tell you? All of my love, all wrapped up in one little bundle. What are you going to call her?'

She took the kitten and cupped her in her hands, stroking the top of her head with her finger. 'I don't know yet. But something romantic. Something really, really romantic.'

She made a mewing noise, and the kitten mewed back. She did it again, and again the kitten copied her.

'There! I'll call her Echo.'

'*Echo*? What's that? Sounds more like a newspaper than a cat.'

'No, silly, it's Greek mythology.'

'If you say so.'

'Echo was a beautiful, beautiful nymph, the most beautiful nymph that ever was.'

'Oh, yeah? So what happened to her?'

'Everybody loved Echo but Zeus' grumpy old wife Hera got mad at her because she kept Hera talking while Zeus had hanky-panky with another goddess. Hera cursed her so that she could never speak her own words ever again – only the last words that were spoken to her by somebody else.'

He shook his head in admiration. 'Do you know something, I think I love your brain as much as your body. Well, *almost* as much. Unfortunately . . . your brain doesn't have breasts.'

She threw a cushion at him.

His name was David Stavanger and her name was Melanie Angela Thomas. They were both twenty-four years old, although David was a Capricorn and Melanie was an Aries. Their star charts said that they should always be quarreling, but nobody who knew them had ever seen two people so much in love with each other. They lived and breathed each other, sharing everything from wine to whispers, and when they were together they radiated an almost palpable aura.

Some evenings they did nothing but gaze at each other in awed silence, as if neither of them could believe that God had brought them another human being so desirable. And they *were* desirable, both of them. David was six foot ten inches tall with cropped blond hair and a strong, straight-nosed Nordic face that he had inherited from his grandfather. He was broad-shouldered, fit, and one of the most impressive wide receivers that the Green Bay Packers had fielded for over a decade. Melanie was small and slim, with glossy brunette hair that almost reached the small of her back. She had the dreamy, heavy-lidded beauty of a girl in a Pre-Raphaelite painting, as if she passed her time wandering through fields of poppies in poppy-colored velvet. She had graduated with a first-class English degree from the

University of Wisconsin in Green Bay and now she was working as a contributing editor for *MidWest* magazine.

They had met when Melanie was sent to interview pro football players about their private lives. Her first question had been, 'What kind of girls appeal to you the most?' and without blinking David had answered, 'You.'

David and Melanie shared a ground-floor apartment in a large, white-painted house in a street in Ashwaubenon lined with sugar maples. David drove a blue Dodge pickup and Melanie had a new silver Volkswagen Beetle. The evening after David brought Echo home, Melanie was sitting on the front veranda on the swing seat, with Echo in her lap, while David went jogging.

It was one of those evenings in late August when the moths patter against the lamps and the chilly dew begins to settle on the lawn and you can feel that somewhere in the far north-west, Mr Winter is already sharpening his cutlery.

Mr Kasabian came down from the first-floor apartment to put out the trash. He looked like Gepetto, the puppet-maker who had carved Pinocchio, with a yard-brush moustache and circular eyeglasses and a black shiny vest. When he saw Echo dancing in Melanie's lap he climbed up on to the veranda to take a closer look.

'Cute little fellow.'

'Girl, actually. David brought her home yesterday.'

'Reminds me of my Wilma,' said Mr Kasabian, wistfully. 'My Wilma used to love her cats.'

'You must miss her so bad.'

Mr Kasabian nodded. 'It'll be three years this November twelfth, but believe me it's still a shock when I wake up in the morning and I put out my hand and find that she's not there any more.'

'I don't know what I'd do if I lost David.'

'With the grace of God you won't have to think about that until you've both lived a long and happy life.'

Mr Kasabian went back inside, and just then David appeared around the corner in his green-and-white tracksuit, his Nikes slapping on the sidewalk. 'Thirty-one minutes eighteen seconds!' he gasped, triumphantly. He came up on to the veranda and gave her a kiss.

'You're so *sweaty*!' she said.

'Sorry – I'll hit the shower. Do you want to get me a beer?'

'No,' she said, and clung on to his tracksuit. 'Come here, I *love* you all sweaty.'

He kissed her again and she licked his lips and his cheeks and then she ran her fingers into his hair and pulled him closer so that she could lick the sweat from his forehead.

'Hey – beats the shower,' said David, kissing her again and again.

She tugged open his zipper and buried her face inside his tracksuit, licking his glistening chest.

'Come on inside,' she said, picking up Echo and taking hold of his hand.

In the living room, she pulled off his tracksuit top and licked his shoulders and his back and his stomach. 'I love the taste of you,' she said. 'You taste like salt and honey, mixed.'

He closed his eyes. His chest was still rising and falling from his running.

She guided him over to the couch so that he could sit down. She unlaced his Nikes and peeled off his sports socks. Kneeling in front of him she licked the soles of his feet and slithered her tongue in between his toes, like a pink seal sliding amongst the rocks. Then she untied the cord around his waistband and pulled down his pants, followed by his white boxer shorts.

While he lay back on the couch she licked him everywhere, all around his sweaty scrotum and deep into the crevice of his buttocks. She wanted every flavor of him, the riper the better. She wanted to own the taste of him, completely.

And that was how it started.

Every night after that they would tongue-bathe each other all over, and then lie in each other's arms, breathing each other's breath, their skins sticky with drying saliva. Every night he would bury his face between her thighs, licking her and drinking her, and she would suck his glans so hard that he yelped in pain. When he did that, Echo would mew, too.

One night, eleven days later, he lifted his head and his chin was bearded in scarlet. He kissed her, and she licked it off his face, and then he dipped his head down for more.

* * *

Melanie's parents took them out for dinner at MacKenzie's Steak and Seafood. They sat close to each other, their fingers twisted together, staring at each other in the candlelight.

Her father looked at her mother after a while and raised one eyebrow. He was a lean, quiet-spoken man with brushed-back silver hair and a large, hawklike nose. Her mother looked almost exactly like Melanie, except her hair was bobbed short and high-lighted blonde and her figure was fuller. She was wearing a bright turquoise dress, while Melanie was all in black.

'So . . . do you two lovebirds have any plans to get married yet?' asked Mr Thomas. 'Or is that me being old-fashioned?'

'I think we're past getting married,' said Melanie, still smiling at David.

'*Past* getting married? What does that mean?'

'It means that we're much, much closer than any wedding ceremony could make us.'

'I'm sorry, I don't get it.'

Melanie turned to her father and touched his hand. 'You and Mom were so lucky to find each other . . . But sometimes two people can fall in love so much that they're both the same person . . . they don't just share each other, they *are* each other.'

Her father shook his head. 'That's a little beyond me, I'm afraid. I was just wondering if you'd considered the financial advantages of being married.' He grunted, trying to make a joke of it. 'Huh – I don't exactly know what tax breaks you two can expect from being the same person.'

Their meals arrived. They had all chosen steak and lobster, apart from Melanie, who had ordered a seared-tuna salad. Their conversation turned to the football season, and then to the latest John Grisham novel that Melanie's father had been reading, and then to one of Melanie's friends from *MidWest* magazine, who had been diagnosed with cervical cancer at the age of twenty-six.

'She wants her ashes spread on her vegetable patch, would you believe, so that her boyfriend will actually eat her.'

'I think that's so morbid,' said Melanie's mother.

'I don't. I think it's beautiful.'

David poured her another glass of white wine. 'How's your tuna?'

'It's gorgeous. Do you want to try some?'

'No, that's OK.'

'No, go on, try some.'

With that, she leaned across and kissed him, ostentatiously pushing a half-masticated wad of fish into his open mouth. David took it, and chewed it, and said, 'Good. Yes, you're right.'

Melanie's parents stared at them in disbelief. David turned to them unabashed. 'It's really good,' he confirmed, and swallowed.

The next day Melanie's mother phoned her at work.

'I'm worried about you.'

'Why? I'm fine. I've never been so happy in my life.'

'It's just that your relationship with David – well, it seems so *intense*.'

'That's because it *is* intense.'

'But the way you act together . . . I don't know how to say this, really. All this kissing and canoodling and sharing your food. Apart from anything else, it's embarrassing for other people.'

'Mom, we love each other. And like I said to Dad, we're not just partners, we're the same person.'

'I know. But everybody needs a little space in their lives . . . a little time to be themselves. I adore your father, but I always enjoy it when he goes off for a game of golf. For a few hours, I can listen to the music I want to listen to, or arrange flowers, or talk to my friends on the phone. I can just be *me*.'

'But David *is* me. The same way that I'm David.'

'It worries me, that's all. I don't think it's healthy.'

'Mother! You make it sound like a disease, not a relationship.'

October came. David started to miss practice at Lambeau Field and Melanie began to take afternoons off work, simply so that they could lie naked on the bed together in the wintry half-darkness and lick each other and stare into each other's eyes. Their greed for each other was insatiable. When they were out walking in the cold, and Melanie's nose started to run, David licked it for her. In the privacy of their own bedroom and bathroom, there was nothing that they wouldn't kiss or suck or drink from each other.

They visited their parents and their friends less and less. When they did, they were no company at all, because they spent the whole time caressing each other, deaf and blind to everybody and everything else.

One afternoon when it was beginning to snow, the Packers' assistant head coach Jim Pulaski came around to their apartment. He was a squat man with bristly gray hair and a broad Polish-looking face, deeply lined by years of standing on the touchline. He sat on the couch in his sheepskin coat and warned David that if he missed one more practice he was off the team. 'You're a star, David, no question. But the cheeseheads are more important than the stars, and every time you don't show up for practice you're letting the cheeseheads down.' 'Cheeseheads' was the nickname that the Packers gave their supporters.

Without taking his eyes off Melanie, David said, 'Sorry, coach? What did you say?'

'Nothing,' said Mr Pulaski, and after a long while he stood up, tugged on his fur-lined hat, and let himself out of the front door. As he crunched across the icy driveway out he met Mr Kasabian struggling in with his shopping bags. He took one of them and helped him up the porch steps.

'Thanks,' said Mr Kasabian, his breath smoking in the cold. 'I'm always afraid of falling. At my age, you fall, you break your hip, they take you to hospital, you die.'

'You live upstairs?'

'That's right. Twenty-seven years this Christmas.'

'You see much of David and Melanie?'

'I used to.'

'Used to?'

'Not these days. These days, *pfff*, they make me feel like the Invisible Man.'

'You and everybody else.'

Mr Kasabian nodded toward the green Toyota parked at the curb with *Green Bay Packers* lettered on the side. 'David's in trouble?'

'You could say that. We're going to have to can him unless he gets his act together. Even when he *does* show up for practice he's got his head up his ass.'

'Mister, I don't know what to tell you. I was in love with my wife for thirty-eight years but I never saw two people like this before. This isn't just smooching, this is like some kind of hypnotized hypnosis. If you ask me, this is all going to turn out very, very bad.'

Mr Kasabian stood in the whirling snow and watched as the coach drove away. Then he looked back at the light in the downstairs window and shook his head.

Three days before Christmas, Echo went missing. Melanie searched for her everywhere: in the cupboards, behind the couch, under the cushions, down in the cellar. She even went outside and called for her under the crawl space, even though Echo hated the cold. No Echo. Only the echo of her own voice in the white, wintry street. 'Echo! *Echo*!'

When David came back from the store she was sitting in her rocking chair in tears, with the drapes half-drawn.

'I can't find Echo.'

'She has to be someplace,' he said, picking up cushions and newspapers as if he expected to find her crouching underneath.

'I haven't seen her all day. She must be so hungry.'

'Maybe she went out to do her business and one of the neighbors picked her up.'

They knocked on every door on both sides of the street, all wrapped up in their coats and scarves. The world was frigid and silent.

'You haven't seen a tortoiseshell kitten, have you?'

Regretful shaking of heads.

Right at the end of the street, they were answered by an elderly woman with little black darting eyes and a face the color of liverwurst.

'If I hev, den vot?'

'You've seen her? She's only about this big and her name's Echo.'

'There's a reward,' David put in.

'Revord?'

'Fifty dollars to anybody who brings her back safe.'

'I never sin such a kitten.'

'You're sure?'

'She's of . . . great sentimental value,' Melanie explained. 'Great *emotional* value. She represents – well, she represents my partner and me. Our love for each other. That's why we have to have her back.'

'A hundred dollars,' said David.

'Vy you say hundert dollar?'

'Because – if you've seen her – if you *have* her—'

'Vot I say? I tell you I never sin such a kitten. Vot does it matter, fifty dollar, hundert dollar? You tell me I lie?'

'Of course not. I didn't mean that at all. I just wanted to show you how much we'd appreciate it if you *did* have her. Which, of course, you don't.'

The woman pointed her finger at them. 'Bad luck to you to sink such a bad sing. Bad luck, bad luck, bad luck.'

With that, she closed the door and they were left on the porch with snow falling silently on their shoulders.

'Well, *she* was neighborly,' said David.

They searched until eleven o'clock at night, and one by one the houses in the neighborhood blinked into darkness. At last they had to admit that there was no hope of them finding Echo until morning.

'I'll make some posters,' said Melanie, lying on her stomach with her nightshirt drawn to her armpits, while David steadily licked her back.

'That's a great idea . . . we could use one of those pictures that we took of her on the veranda.'

'Oh, I feel so sorry for her, David . . . she's probably feeling so cold and lost.'

'She'll come back,' said David. 'She's our love together, isn't she? That's what she is. And our love's going to last for ever.'

He continued to lick around her buttocks and the backs of her thighs, while she lay on the pillow with tears steadily dripping down the side of her nose. After he had licked the soles of her feet, he came up the bed again and licked her face.

'Salt,' he said.

'Sorrow,' she whispered.

The next morning the sky was as dark as slate and it was snowing again. Melanie designed a poster on her PC and printed out over a hundred copies. *Lost, tortoiseshell kitten, only three months old, answers to the name of Echo. Embodies owners' undying love so substantial reward for finder.*

David went from street to street, tacking the posters on to trees and palings. The streets were almost deserted, except for a few 4x4s silently rolling through the snow, like mysterious hearses.

He came back just before twelve. Melanie said, 'The head coach called. He wants you to call him back. He didn't sound very happy.'

David held her close and kissed her forehead. His lips were cold and her forehead was warm. 'It's not important any more, is it? The world outside.'

'Aren't you going to call him?'

'Why should I? What does it matter if *he's* happy or not? So long as we are. The most important thing is to find Echo.'

More days went by. The phone rang constantly but unless it was somebody calling about Echo they simply hung up without saying any more and after a while it hardly ever rang at all. The mailman went past every day but they never went to the mailbox to collect their letters.

One of Melanie's editors called around in a black beret and a long black fur coat and rang the doorbell for over quarter of an hour, but eventually she went away. David and Melanie lay in each other's arms, sometimes naked, sometimes half dressed, while the snow continued to fall as if it were never going to stop. They ate well and drank well, but as the days went by their faces took on an unhealthy transparency, as if the loss of Echo had weakened their emotional immune systems, and infected their very souls.

Early one Thursday morning, before it grew light, David was woken up by Melanie shaking him.

'David! David! It's *freezing*!'

He sat up. She was right. The bedroom was so cold that there were starry ice-crystals on the inside of the windows where their breath had frozen in the night.

'Jesus, the boiler must have broken down.'

He climbed out of bed while Melanie bundled herself even more tightly in the quilt. He took his blue toweling bathrobe from the back of the chair, shuffled into his slippers, and went shivering along the corridor to the cellar door. Their landlady Mrs Gustaffson had promised to have the boiler serviced before winter set in, but Mrs Gustaffson had a tendency to forget anything which involved spending money.

David switched on the light and went down the cellar stairs. The cellar was crowded mostly with Mrs Gustaffson's junk: a broken couch, a treadle sewing-machine, various assorted pieces of timber and tools and picture frames and hosepipes and bits of bicycle. Dried teazles hung from the ceiling beams, as well as oil lamps and butcher hooks.

The huge, old, oil-fired boiler which stood against the far wall was silent and stone cold. It looked like a Wurlitzer jukebox built out of rusty cast-iron. It couldn't have run out of oil – Green Bay Heating had filled the tank up only three weeks ago. More likely the burners were clogged, or else the outside temperature had dropped so far that the oil in the pipes had solidified. That would mean going out into the yard with a blowtorch to get it moving again.

David checked the valves and the stopcocks, and as he was leaning around the back of the boiler he became aware of a sweet, cloying smell. He sniffed, and sniffed again, and leaned around the side of the boiler so that he could look behind it. It was too dark for him to see anything, so he went back upstairs to the kitchen and came back with his flashlight.

He pointed the beam diagonally downward between the pipes, and saw a few black-and-gray tufts of fur. 'Oh, shit,' he breathed, and knelt down on the floor as close to the boiler as he could. He managed to work his right arm in between the body of the boiler and the brick wall, but his forearm was too thick and muscular and he couldn't reach far enough.

Back in the bedroom Melanie was still invisibly wrapped up in the quilt and a sickly yellow sunshine was beginning to glitter on the ice crystals on the windows.

'Is it fixed yet?' she asked him. 'It's like an igloo in here.'

'I'm – ah – I've found something.'

When he didn't say anything else, she drew down the quilt from her face and stared at him. There were tears in his eyes and he was opening and closing his fists.

'You've found something? What?'

'It's Echo.'

'You found Echo! That's wonderful! Where is she?'

'She's dead, Mel. She must have gone behind the boiler to keep warm, and gotten trapped or something.'

'Oh, no, say it isn't true. Please, David, say it isn't true.'

'I'm sorry, Mel.' David sat down on the edge of the bed and took hold of her hand.

'It was that woman, that woman putting a curse on us! She wished us bad luck, didn't she, and now Echo's dead, and Echo's your *love*, David, all in one bundle.'

'I still love you, Mel. You know that.'

'But I promised to love her as much as I love you. I promised. I swore to you.'

'There's nothing we can do.'

Melanie sat up. 'Where is she? Did you bring her upstairs?'

'I can't get her out. I tried but the gap behind the boiler's too tight.'

'Then I'll have to do it.'

'Mel, you don't have to. I can ask Mr Kasabian to do it. He used to be a vet, remember.'

'Mr Kasabian isn't here. He went to see his daughter in Sheboygan yesterday. No, David. Echo is mine and *I'll* do it.'

He stood beside her, feeling helpless, while she knelt down beside the boiler and reached into the narrow crevice at the back. At last, with her cheek pressed right against the cold iron casing, she said, 'Got her . . . I can feel her.' She tugged, and tugged again, and then she drew her hand out, holding nothing but a small furry leg.

'Oh my God, she's fallen apart.' She dropped the leg and quickly stood up, her hand clamped over her mouth, retching. David put his arms around her and said, 'Leave it, just leave it. I'll get the handyman to do it.'

Melanie took three deep breaths, and then she said, 'No . . . I have to get her out. She's mine, she's the love you gave me. It has to be me.'

She knelt down and slid her hand in behind the boiler again. David looked into her eyes while she struggled to extricate Echo's body. She kept swallowing with disgust, but she wouldn't give up. At last, very slowly, she managed to lift the dead kitten up from the floor, so that she could reach over the pipes with her other hand and grasp it by the scruff of its neck.

Quaking with effort and revulsion, she stood up and cradled the body in her hands. The ripe stench of rotten kitten-flesh was almost unbearable. It was impossible for them to know exactly how long Echo had been trapped, but it must have been more than two weeks, and during that time she had been cooked by the heat of the boiler during the day, and then cooled by night, and then cooked again the following day, until her fur was scorched and bedraggled and her flesh was little more than blackened slime.

Echo's head lay in the palm of Melanie's right hand, staring up at David with eyes as white and blind as the eyes of a boiled codfish, her mouth half-open so that he could see her green glistening tongue.

'We can bury her,' said David. 'Look – there's an old toolbox there. We can use it as a casket. We can bury her in the yard so that she can rest in peace.'

Melanie shook her head. 'She's *us*, David. We can't bury her. She's you and me. She's all of your love, all wrapped up in one bundle, and all of my love, too, because you and me, we're the same person, and Echo was us, too.'

David gently stroked the matted fur on Echo's upturned stomach. Inside, he heard a sticky, thick, glutinous sound, which came from Echo's putrescent intestines. 'You're right,' he said, his voice hoarse with emotion. 'But if we don't bury her, what are we going to do?'

They sat facing each other on opposite sides of the scrubbed-pine kitchen table. The kitchen was even colder than the rest of the apartment, because the wind was blowing in through the ventilator hood over the hob. They had both put their duffel coats on, and Melanie was even wearing red woolen mittens.

'This is your love,' said Melanie. In front of her, on a large blue dinner-plate, lay Echo, resting on her side. 'If it becomes part of me, then it can never, ever die . . . not as long as *I'm* alive, anyhow.'

'I love you,' David whispered. He looked years older, and whiter, almost like his own grandfather.

With both hands, Melanie grasped the fur around Echo's throat, and pulled it hard. She had to twist it this way and that, but at last she managed to break the skin apart She inserted two fingers, then four, and wrenched open the kitten's stomach inch by inch, with a sound like tearing linen. Echo's ribcage was exposed, with her lungs pale yellow and slimy, and then her intestines, in coils so green that they were luminous.

David stared at Melanie and he was shivering. The look on Melanie's face was extraordinary, beatific, St Melanie of the Sacred Consumption. She scooped her mittened hand into Echo's abdominal cavity and lifted out her stomach and strings of bowel and connective tissue. Then she bent her head forward and crammed them into her mouth. She slowly chewed, her eyes still open, and as she chewed the kitten's viscera hung down her chin in loops, and the duodenum was still connected to the animal's body by a thin, trembling web.

Melanie swallowed, and swallowed again. Then she pulled off one of Echo's hind legs, and bit into it, tearing off the fur and the flesh with her teeth, and chewing both of them. She did the same with her other leg, even though the thigh meat was so decomposed that it was more like black molasses than flesh, and it made the fur stick around Melanie's lips like a beard.

It took her almost an hour to eat Echo's body, although she gagged when she pushed the cat's spongy lungs into her mouth, and David had to bring her a glass of water. During all of this time, neither of them spoke, but they never took their eyes off each other. This was a ritual of transubstantiation, in which love had become flesh, and flesh was being devoured so that it could become love again.

At last, hardly anything remained of Echo but her head, her bones, and a thin bedraggled tail. David reached across the kitchen table and gripped Melanie's hands.

'I don't know where we go from here,' he shivered.

'But we've done it. We're really one person. We can go anyplace we like. We can do anything we want.'

'I'm frightened of us.'

'You don't have to be. Nothing can touch us now.'

David lowered his head, still gripping her fingers very tight. 'I'd better . . . I'd better call the handyman.'

'Not yet. Let's go back to bed first.'

'I'm cold, Melanie. I never felt so cold in my life. Even when we were playing in Chicago and the temperature was minus thirteen.'

'I'll warm you up.'

He stood up, but as he turned around Melanie suddenly let out a terrible cackling retch. She pressed her hand over her mouth, but her shoulders hunched in an agonizing terrible spasm and she vomited all over the table – skin, fur, bones and slippery lumps of rotten flesh. David held her close, but she couldn't stop herself from regurgitating everything that she had crammed down her throat.

She sat back, white-faced, sweating, sobbing.

'I'm sorry, I'm so sorry. I tried to keep it down. I tried so hard. It doesn't mean I don't love you. Please, David, it doesn't mean I don't love you.'

David kissed her hair and licked the perspiration from her forehead and sucked the sour saliva from her lips. 'It doesn't matter, Mel. You're right . . . we can do anything. We're one, that's all that counts. Look.'

He picked up a handful of fur and intestine from the table and pushed it into his mouth. He swallowed it, and picked up another handful, and swallowed that, too.

'You know what this tastes like? This tastes like *we're* going to taste, when we die.'

They lay in each other's arms all day and all night, buried in the quilt. The temperature dropped and dropped like a stone down a well. By mid-afternoon the following day, David had started to shake uncontrollably, and as it grew dark he began to moan and sweat and thrash from side to side.

'David . . . I should call the doctor.'

'Anything we want – *anything*—'

'I could call Jim Pulaski, he could help.'

David suddenly sat up rigid. 'We're one! *We're one*! Don't let them take the offensive! Don't let them get past the fifty-yard line! We're one!'

She woke a few minutes after midnight and he was silent and still and cold as the air around them. The sheets were freezing, too, and when she lifted the quilt she discovered that his bowels and his bladder had opened and soaked the mattress. She kissed him and stroked his hair and whispered his name again and again, but she knew that he was gone. When morning came she cleaned him all over in the way that they had always cleaned each other, with her tongue, and then she laid him on the quilt naked with his eyes wide open and his arms outspread. She thought that she had never seen any man look so perfect.

It was midwinter, of course, one of the coldest winters since 1965, and Mr Kasabian's sense of smell wasn't the most acute. But when he returned home on Friday morning he was immediately struck not only by the chill but by the thick, sour smell in the hallway. He knocked on David and Melanie's door and called out, 'Melanie? David? You there?'

There was no answer, so he knocked again. 'Melanie? David? Are you OK?'

He was worried now. Both of their automobiles were still in the driveway, covered with snow, and there were no footprints on their veranda, so they must be home. He tried to force open the door with his shoulder, but it was far too solidly-built and his shoulder was far too bony.

In the end he went upstairs and called Mrs Gustaffson.

'I think something bad has happened to Melanie and David.'

'Bad like what? I have to be in Manitowoc in an hour.'

'I don't know, Mrs Gustaffson. But I think it's something very, very bad.'

Mrs Gustaffson arrived twenty minutes later, in her old black Buick. She was a large woman with colorless eyes and wiry gray hair and a double chin that wobbled whenever she shook her head, which was often. Mrs Gustaffson didn't like to say 'yes' to anything.

She let herself in. Mr Kasabian was sitting on the stairs with a maroon shawl around his shoulders.

'Why is it so cold in here?' she demanded. 'And what in God's name is that *smell*?'

'That's why I call you. I knock and I knock and I shout out, but nobody don't answer.'

'Well, let's see what's going on, shall we?' said Mrs Gustaffson. She took out her keys, sorted through them until she found the key to David and Melanie's apartment. When she unlocked the door, however, she found that it was wedged from the other side, and she couldn't open it more than two or three inches.

'Mr Stavanger! Ms Thomas! This is Mrs Gustaffson! Will you please open the door for me?'

There was still no reply, but a chilly draft blew out of the apartment with a hollow, sorrowful moaning, and it carried with it a stench like nothing that Mrs Gustaffson had ever smelled before. She pressed her hand over her nose and mouth and took a step back.

'Do you think they're dead?' asked Mr Kasabian. 'We should call the cops, I think so.'

'I agree,' said Mrs Gustaffson. She opened her large black crocodile purse and took out her cellphone. Just as she flipped it open, however, they heard a bumping sound from inside the apartment, and then a clang, as if somebody had dropped a saucepan on the kitchen floor.

'They're inside,' said Mrs Gustaffson. 'They're hiding for some reason. Mr Stavanger! Do you hear me! Ms Thomas! Open the door! I have to talk to you!'

No response. Mrs Gustaffson knocked and rattled the door handle, but she couldn't open the door any wider and even if David and Melanie were inside the apartment, they obviously had no intention of answering.

Mrs Gustaffson went along the hallway to the back of the house, closely followed by Mr Kasabian. She unlocked the back door and carefully climbed down the icy steps outside. 'I told you to put salt on these steps, Mr Kasabian, didn't I? Somebody could have a very nasty accident.'

'I did, last week only. Then it snow again and freeze over again.'

Mrs Gustaffson made her way along the back of the house. There were no lights in any of the downstairs windows, and a long icicle hung from the bathroom overflow pipe, which showed that the bathroom hadn't been used for days.

At last she reached the kitchen window. The sill was too high for her to reach, so Mr Kasabian dragged over a small wooden trough in which he usually planted herbs, so that she could climb up on it. She wiped the frosty window with her glove, and peered inside.

At first she could see nothing but shadows, and the faint whiteness of the icebox door. But then something moved across the kitchen, very slowly. Something bulky, with arms that swung limply at its side, and a strangely small head. Mrs Gustaffson stared at it for one baffled moment, and then she stepped down.

'Somebody's in there,' she said, and her usually strident voice was like the croak of a child who has seen something in the darkness of her bedroom that is far too frightening to put into words.

'They're dead?' asked Mrs Kasabian.

'No, not dead. I don't know what.'

'We should call the cops.'

'I have to see what that is.'

'That's not a good idea, Mrs Gustaffson. Who knows who that is? Maybe it's a murdering murderer.'

'I have to know what I saw. Come with me.'

'Mrs Gustaffson, I'm an old man.'

'And I'm an old woman. What difference does that make?'

She climbed back up the steps to the back door, gripping the handrail. She went back inside and Mr Kasabian followed her to David and Melanie's door. She put her shoulder against it and pushed, and it began to give a little. Mr Kasabian pushed, too. It felt as if the couch had been wedged against the door, but as they kept on pushing they managed to inch it further and further away. At last the door was open wide enough for them to step into the living room.

'This is dead smell, no question,' said Mr Kasabian. The living room was dark and bitterly cold, and there were books and magazines and clothes strewn everywhere. There were marks on the wallpaper, too, like handprints.

'I think seriously this is time for cops.'

They were halfway across the living room when they heard another bump, and a shuffling sound.

'Oh holy Jesus what is that?' whispered Mr Kasabian.

Mrs Gustaffson said nothing, but took two or three more steps toward the kitchen door, which was slightly ajar.

Together they approached the kitchen until they were standing right outside the door. Mrs Gustaffson cocked her head to one side and said, 'I can hear – what is that? – *crying*?'

But it was more like somebody struggling for breath, as if they were carrying a very heavy weight.

'Mr Stavanger?' called Mrs Gustaffson, with as much authority as she could manage. 'I need to talk to you, Mr Stavanger.'

She pushed the kitchen door open a little further, and then she pushed it wide. Mr Kasabian let out an involuntary mewl of dread.

There *was* a figure standing in the kitchen. It was silhouetted against the window, an extraordinary bulky creature with a small head and massive shoulders, and arms that swung uselessly down at its sides. As Mrs Gustaffson stepped into the room, it staggered as if it were almost on the point of collapse. Mr Kasabian switched on the light.

The stripped-pine kitchen looked like an abattoir. There were wild smears of dried blood all across the floor, bloody handprints on every work surface, and the sink was heaped with black and clotted lumps of flesh. The smell was so acrid that Mrs Gustaffson's eyes filled with tears.

The bulky figure that swayed in front of them *was* David . . . but a David who was long dead. His skin was white, and tinged in places with green. His arms hung down and his legs buckled at the knees, so that his feet trailed on the linoleum. He had no head, but out of his neck cavity rose Melanie's head, her hair caked with dried blood, her eyes staring.

It took Mrs Gustaffson and Mr Kasabian ten long heartbeats to understand what they were looking at. Melanie had opened up David's body, from his chest to his groin, and emptied it of most of his viscera. Then she had cut off his head and widened his throat, so that she could climb inside his ribcage and force her own head through. She was actually *wearing* David's body like a heavy, decaying cloak.

She had made up David's severed head with foundation and lipstick, and decorated his hair with dried chrysanthemums. Then she had put it into a string bag along with Echo's head, and hung the two of them around her neck. She had inserted Echo's bedraggled tail into her vagina, so that it hung down between her thighs.

'Melanie,' said Mr Kasabian, in total shock. 'Melanie, what happened?'

Melanie tried to take a step forward, but David's body was far too heavy for her, and all she could manage was a sideways lurch.

'We're one person,' she said, and there was such joy and excitement in her voice that Mrs Gustaffson had to cover her ears. 'We're one person!'

Camelot

Jack was scraping finely chopped garlic into the skillet when he heard somebody banging at the restaurant door.

'Shit,' he breathed. He took the skillet off the gas and wiped his hands on his apron. The banging was repeated, more forcefully this time, and the door handle was rattled.

'OK, OK! I hear you!'

He wove his way between the circular tables and the bentwood chairs. The yellow linen blinds were drawn right down over the windows, so that all he could see were two shadows. The early-morning sun distorted them, hunched them up and gave them pointed ears, so that they looked like wolves.

He shot the bolts and unlocked the door. Two men in putty-colored raincoats were standing outside. One was dark and unshaven, with greased-back hair and a broken nose. The other was sandy and overweight, with clear beads of perspiration on his upper lip.

'Yes?'

The dark man held out a gilded badge. 'Sergeant Eli Waxman, San Francisco Police Department. Are you Mr Jack Keller?'

'That's me. Is anything wrong?'

Sergeant Waxman flipped open his notebook and peered at it as if he couldn't read his own handwriting. 'You live at three-six-six-three Heliograph Street, apartment two?'

'Yes, I do. For Christ's sake, tell me what's happened.'

'Your partner is Ms Jacqueline Fronsart, twenty-four, a student in Baltic singing at The Institute of Baltic Singing?'

'That's right.'

Sergeant Waxman closed his notebook. 'I'm sorry to tell you, Mr Keller, but Ms Fronsart has been mirrorized.'

'What?'

'Your neighbors heard her screaming round about nine thirty this morning. One of them broke into your apartment and found her. They tried to get her out but there was nothing they could do.'

'Oh, God.' Jack couldn't believe what he was hearing. 'Which – what – which mirror was it?'

'Big tilting mirror, in the bedroom.'

'Oh, God. Where is it now? It didn't get broken, did it?'

'No, it's still intact. We left it where it was. The coroner can remove it for you, if that's what you want. It's entirely up to you.'

Jack covered his eyes with his hand and kept them covered. Maybe, if he blacked out the world for long enough, the detectives would vanish and this wouldn't have happened. But even in the darkness behind his fingers he could hear their raincoats rustling, and their shoes shifting uncomfortably on the polished wood floor. Eventually he looked up at them and said, 'I bought that mirror about six months ago. The owner swore to me that it was docile.'

'You want to tell me where you got it?'

'Loculus Antiques, in Sonoma. I have their card someplace.'

'Don't worry, we can find it if we need to. I'll be straight with you, though – I don't hold out much hope of any restitution.'

'Jesus. I'm not interested in restitution. I just want—'

He thought of Jacqueline, standing on his balcony, naked except for a large straw hat piled ridiculously high with peaches and pears and bananas. He could see her turning her face toward him in slo-mo. Those liquid brown eyes, so wide apart that she looked more like a beautiful salmon than a woman. Those brown shoulders, patterned with henna. Those enormous breasts, with nipples that shone like plums.

'*Desire, I can see it in your every looking*,' she had whispered. She always whispered, to save her larynx for her Baltic singing.

She had pushed him back on to the violently patterned durry, and knelt astride his chest. Then she had displayed herself to him, her smooth hairless vulva, and she had pulled open her lips with her fingers to show him the green canary-feather that she had inserted into her urethra.

'*The plumage of vanity*,' she had whispered.

Sergeant Waxman took hold of Jack's upper arm and gave him a comforting squeeze. 'I'm real sorry for your loss, Mr Keller. I saw her myself and – well, she was something, wasn't she?'

'What am I supposed to do?' asked Jack. For the first time in his life he felt totally detached, and adrift, like a man in a rowboat with only one oar, circling around and around, out of reach of anybody.

'Different people make different decisions, sir,' said the sandy-haired detective.

'Decisions? Decisions about what?'

'About their mirrors, sir. Some folks store them away in their basements, or their attics, hoping that a time is going to come when we know how to get their loved ones back out of them. Some folks – well, they bury them, and have proper funerals.'

'They *bury* them? I didn't know that.'

'It's unusual, sir, but not unknown. Other folks just cover up their mirrors with sheets or blankets, and leave them where they are, but some doctors think this could amount to cruelty, on account of the person in the mirror still being able to hear what's going on and everything.'

'Oh, God,' said Jack.

The sandy-haired detective took out a folded handkerchief and dabbed his forehead 'Most folks, though—'

'Most folks *what*?'

'Most folks *break* their mirrors, sooner or later. I guess it's like taking their loved ones off life support.'

Jack stared at him. 'But if you break a mirror – what about the person inside it? Are they still trapped in some kind of mirror-world? Or do they get broken, too?'

Sergeant Waxman said, solemnly, 'We don't know the answer to that, Mr Keller, and I very much doubt if we ever will.'

When the detectives had left, Jack locked the restaurant door and stood with his back against it, with tears streaming down his cheeks, as warm and sticky as if he had poked his eyes out. 'Jacqueline,' he moaned. 'Jacqueline, why *you*? Why you, of all people? Why you?'

He knelt down on the waxed oak floor, doubled-up with the physical pain of losing her, and sobbed between gritted teeth. 'Why you, Jacqueline? Why you? You're so beautiful, why you?'

He cried for almost ten minutes and then he couldn't cry any more. He stood up, wiped his eyes on one of the table napkins, and blew his nose. He looked around at all the empty tables. He doubted if he would ever be able to open again. Keller's Far-Flung Food would become a memory, just like Jacqueline.

God, he thought. Every morning you wake up, and you climb out of bed, but you never know when life is going to punch you straight in the face.

He went back into the kitchen, turned off all the hobs and ovens, and hung up his apron. There were half a dozen Inuit moccasins lying on the chopping board, ready for unstitching and marinating; and yew branches for yew branch soup. He picked up a fresh, furry moose antler. That was supposed to be today's special. He put it down again, his throat so tight that he could hardly breathe.

He was almost ready to leave when the back door was flung open, and Punipuni Puu-suke appeared, in his black Richard Nixon T-shirt and his flappy white linen pants. Jack didn't know exactly how old Punipuni was, but his crew-cut hair looked like one of those wire brushes you use for getting rust off the fenders of 1963 pick-up trucks, and his eyes were so pouchy that Jack could never tell if they were open or not. All the same, he was one of the most experienced bone chefs in San Francisco, as well as being an acknowledged Oriental philosopher. He had written a slim, papery book called *Do Not Ask A Fish The Way Across the Desert*.

Punipuni took off his red leather shoulder bag and then he looked around the kitchen. 'Mr German-cellar?' (He always believed that people should acknowledge the ethnic origins of their names, but translate them into English so that others could share their meaning.) 'Mr German-cellar, is something wrong?'

'I'm sorry, Pu, I didn't have time to call you. I'm not opening today. In fact I think I'm closing for good. Jacqueline was mirrorized.'

Punipuni came across the kitchen and took hold of his hands. 'Mr German-cellar, my heart is inside your chest. When did this tragedy occur?'

'This morning. Just now. The police were here. I have to go home and see what I can do.'

'She was so wonderful, Mr German-cellar. I don't know what I can say to console you.'

Jack shook his head. 'There's nothing. Not yet. You can go home if you like.'

'Maybe I come along too. Sometimes a shoulder to weep on is better than money discovered in a sycamore tree.'

'OK. I'd appreciate it.'

He lived up on Russian Hill, in a small pink Victorian house in the English Quarter. It was so steep here that he had to park his Ford Peacock with its front wheels cramped against the curb, and its gearbox in reverse. It was a sunny day, and far below them the Bay was sparkling like shattered glass; but there was a thin cold breeze blowing which smelled of a fisherman's dying breath.

'Jack!'

A maroon-faced man with white whiskers was trudging up the hill with a bull mastiff on a short choke-chain. He was dressed in yellowish-brown tweeds, with the cuffs of his pants tucked into his stockings.

'I say, Jack!' he repeated, and raised his arm in salute.

'Major,' Jack acknowledged him, and then looked up to his second-story apartment. Somebody had left the windows wide open, Jacqueline probably, and the white drapes were curling in the breeze.

'Dreadfully sorry to hear what happened, old boy! The Nemesis and I are awfully cut up about it. Such a splendid young girl!'

'Thank you,' said Jack.

'Buggers, some of these mirrors, aren't they? Can't trust them an inch.'

'I thought this one was safe.'

'Well, *none* of them are safe, are they, when it comes down to it? Same as these perishing dogs. They behave themselves perfectly, for years, and then suddenly, for no reason that you can think of, *snap*! They bite some kiddie's nose off, or some such. The Nemesis won't have a mirror in the house. Just as well, I suppose. With a dial like hers, she'd crack it as soon as look at it – what!'

Jack tried to smile, but all he could manage was a painful smirk. He let himself into the front door and climbed the narrow stairs, closely followed by Punipuni. Inside, the hallway was very quiet, and smelled of overripe melons. Halfway up the stairs there was a stained-glass window with a picture of a blindfolded woman on it, and a distant castle with thick black smoke pouring out of it, and rooks circling.

Punipuni caught hold of his sleeve. 'Your God does not require you to do this, Mr German-cellar.'

'No,' said Jack. 'But my heart does. Do you think I'm just going to hire some removal guy and have her carted away? I love her, Pu. I always will. Forever.'

'Forever is not a straight line,' said Punipuni. 'Remember that your favorite carpet store may not always be visible from your front doorstep.'

They reached the upstairs landing. Jack went across to his front door and took out his key. His heart was thumping like an Irish drum and he wasn't at all sure that he was going to be able to do this. But there was a brass ankh on the door, where Jacqueline had nailed it, and he could see her kissing her fingertips and pressing it against the ankh, and saying, 'This is the symbol of life everlasting that will never die.'

She had been naked at the time, except for a deerstalker hat like Sherlock Holmes. She loved Sherlock Holmes, and she often called Jack 'Watson'. Without warning she would take out her violin and play a few scraping notes of Cajun music on it and proclaim, 'The game is afoot!'

He opened the door and pushed it wide. The apartment was silent, except for the noise of the traffic outside. There was a narrow hallway, with a coat stand that was clustered with twenty or thirty hats – skimmers and derbies and shapeless old fedoras – and the floor was heaped with smelly, discarded shoes – brown Oxfords and gilded ballet-pumps and $350 Guevara trainers.

Jack climbed over the shoes into the living room. It was furnished with heavy red-leather chairs and couches, and glass-fronted bookcases crammed with leather-bound books. Over the cast-iron fireplace hung a large colored lithograph. It depicted a voluptuous naked woman riding a bicycle over a hurrying carpet of living mice, crushing them under her tires. Only on very close examination could it be seen that instead of a saddle the bicycle was fitted with a thick purple dildo, complete with bulging testicles. The caption read '*The Second Most Pleasurable Way To Exterminate Rodents – Pestifex Powder*.'

The bedroom door was ajar but he hardly dared to go inside. At last Punipuni nudged him and said, 'Go on, Jack. You have to. You cannot mend a broken ginger-jar by refusing to look at it.'

'Yes, you're right.' Jack crossed the living room and pushed open the bedroom door. The pine four-poster bed was still unmade, with its durry dragged across it diagonally, and its pillows still scattered. On the opposite side of the room, between the two open windows, stood Jacqueline's dressing table, with all of her Debussy perfumes and her Seurat face-powders, and dozens of paintbrushes in a white ceramic jar.

In the corner stood the cheval mirror, oval, and almost six feet high on its swiveling base. It was made out of dark, highly polished mahogany, with grapevines carved all around it, and the face of a mocking cherub at the crest of the frame. Jack walked around the bed and confronted it. All he could see was himself, and the quilt, and Punipuni standing in the doorway behind him.

He looked terrible. His hair was still disheveled from taking off his apron, and he was wearing a crumpled blue shirt with paint spots on it and a pair of baggy Levis with ripped-out knees. There were plum-colored circles under his eyes.

He reached out and touched the dusty surface of the mirror with his fingertips. 'Jacqueline,' he said. 'Jacqueline – are you there?'

'Maybe there was mix-up,' said Punipuni, trying to sound optimistic. 'Maybe she just went out to buy lipstick.'

But Jack knew that there had been no mistake. In the mirror, Jacqueline's white silken robe was lying on the floor at the end of the bed. But when he looked around, it wasn't there, not in the real world.

He leaned close to the mirror. 'Jacqueline!' he called out, hoarsely. 'Jacqueline, sweetheart, it's Jack!'

'Maybe she hides,' Punipuni suggested. 'Maybe she doesn't want you to see her suffer.'

But at that moment, Jacqueline appeared in the mirror, and came walking slowly across the room toward him, like a woman in a dream. She was naked apart from very high black stiletto shoes with black silk chrysanthemums on them, and a huge black funeral hat, bobbing with ostrich plumes. She was wearing upswept dark glasses and dangly jet earrings, and her lips were painted glossy black.

Jack gripped the frame of the mirror in anguish. 'Jacqueline! Oh God, Jacqueline!'

Her mirror image came up to his mirror image and wrapped

her arms around it. He could see her clearly in the mirror, but he could neither see nor feel her *here*, in the bedroom.

'Jack . . .' she whispered, and even though he couldn't see her eyes behind her dark glasses, her voice was quaking with panic. 'You have to get me out of here. Please.'

'I don't know *how*, sweetheart. Nobody knows how.'

'All I was doing . . . I was plucking my eyebrows. I leaned forward toward the mirror . . . the next thing I knew I lost my balance. It was like falling through ice. Jack, I *hate* it here. I'm so frightened. You have to get me out.'

Jack didn't know what to say. He could see Jacqueline kissing him and stroking his hair and pressing her breasts against his chest, but it was all an illusion.

Punipuni gave an uncomfortable cough. 'Maybe I leave now, Mr German-cellar. You know my number. You call if you want my help. A real friend waits like a rook on the gatepost.'

Jack said, 'Thanks, Pu. I'll catch you later.' He didn't turn around. He didn't want Punipuni to see the welter of tears in his eyes.

After Punipuni had left, Jack knelt in front of the mirror and Jacqueline knelt down inside it, facing him, although he could see himself kneeling behind her.

'You have to find a way to get me out,' said Jacqueline. 'It's so unfriendly here . . . the people won't speak to me. I ask them how to get back through the mirror but all they do is smile. And it's so *silent*. No traffic. All you can hear is the wind.'

'Listen,' Jack told her. 'I'll go back to Sonoma, where we bought the mirror. Maybe the guy in the antiques store can help us.'

Jacqueline lowered her head so that all he could see was the feathery brim of her funeral hat. 'I miss you so much, Jack. I just want to be back in bed with you.'

Jack didn't know what to say. But Jacqueline lifted her head again, and said, 'Take off your clothes.'

'What?'

'Please, take off your clothes.'

Slowly, like a man with aching knees and elbows, he unbuttoned his shirt and his jeans, and pulled them off. He took off his red-and-white striped boxer shorts, too, and stood naked in front of the mirror, his penis half erect. The early-afternoon sun shone in his pubic hairs so that they looked like electric filaments.

'Come to the mirror,' said Jacqueline. She approached its surface from the inside, so that her hands were pressed flat against the glass. Her breasts were squashed against the glass, too, so that her nipples looked like large dried fruits.

Jack took his penis in his hand and held the swollen purple glans against the mirror. Jacqueline stuck out her tongue and licked the other side of the glass, again and again. Jack couldn't feel anything, but the sight of her tongue against his glans gave him an extraordinary sensation of frustration and arousal. He began to rub his penis up and down, gripping it tighter and tighter, while Jacqueline licked even faster.

She reached down between her thighs and parted her vulva with her fingers. With her long middle finger she began to flick her clitoris, and the reflected sunlight from the wooden floor showed Jack that she was glistening with juice.

He rubbed himself harder and harder until he knew that he couldn't stop himself from climaxing.

'Oh, God,' he said, and sperm shot in loops all over the mirror, all over Jacqueline's reflected tongue, and on her reflected nose, and even in her reflected hair. She licked at it greedily, even though she could neither touch it nor taste it. Watching her, Jack pressed his forehead against the mirror in utter despair.

He stayed there, feeling drained, while she lay back on the floor, opened her legs wide, and slowly massaged herself, playing with her clitoris and sliding her long black-polished fingernails into her slippery pink hole. After a while, she closed her legs tightly, and shivered. He wasn't sure if she was having an orgasm or not, but she lay on the floor motionless for over a minute, the plumes of her hat stirring in the breeze from the wide-open window.

Mr Santorini, in the downstairs apartment, was playing *Carry Me To Heaven With Candy-Colored Ribbons* on his wind-up gramophone. Jack could hear the scratchy tenor voice like a message from long ago and far away.

San Francisco folk wisdom says that for every ten miles you drive away from the city, it grows ten degrees Fahrenheit hotter.

It was so hot by the time that Jack reached Sonoma that afternoon that the air was like liquid honey. He turned left off East Spain Street and there was Loculus Antiques, a single-story conservatory shaded by eucalyptus trees. He parked his Peacock and climbed out, but Punipuni stayed where he was, listening to Cambodian jazz on the radio. *That Old Fish Hook Fandango*, by Samlor Chapheck and the South East Asian Swingers.

Jack opened the door of Loculus Antiques and a bell jangled. Inside, the conservatory was stacked with antique sofas and dining chairs and plaster busts of Aristotle, and it smelled of dried-out horsehair and failed attempts to make money. There was a strange light in there, too, like a mortuary, because the glass roof had been painted over green. A man appeared from the back of the store wearing what looked like white linen pajamas. He looked about fifty-five, with a skull-like head and fraying white hair and thick-rimmed spectacles. His top front teeth stuck out like a horse.

'May I show you something?' he drawled. His accent wasn't Northern California. More like Marblehead, Massachusetts.

'You probably don't remember me, but you sold me a mirror about six months ago. Jack Keller.'

'A mirraw, hmm? Well, I sell an awful lot of mirraws. All guaranteed safe, of course.'

'This one wasn't. I lost my partner this morning. I was just starting work when the police came around and told me she'd been mirrorized.'

The man slowly took off his spectacles and stared at Jack with bulging pale blue eyes. 'You're absolutely sure it was one of mine? I don't see how it could have been. I'm *very* careful, you know. I lost my own pet Pomeranian that way. It was only a little hand-mirraw, too. One second she was chasing her squeaky bone. The next . . . gone!

He put his spectacles back on. 'I had to—' And he made a smacking gesture with his hands, to indicate that he had broken the mirror to put his dog down. 'That endless pathetic barking . . . I couldn't bear it.'

'The same thing's happened to my partner,' said Jack, trying to control his anger. 'And it was one of *your* mirrors, I still have the receipt. A cheval mirror, with a mahogany frame, with grapevines carved all around it.'

The man's face drained of color. '*That* mirraw. Oh, dear.'

'Oh, dear? Is that all you can say? I've lost the only woman I've ever loved. A beautiful, vibrant young woman with all of her life still in front of her.'

'I *am* sorry. My Pom was a pedigree, you know . . . but this is *much* worse, isn't it?'

Jack went right up to him. 'I want to know how to get her out. And if I can't get her out, I'm going to come back here and I'm going to tear your head off with my bare hands.'

'Well! There's no need to be so *aggressive*.'

'Believe me, pal, you don't even know the meaning of the word aggressive. But you will do, if you don't tell me how to get my partner out of that goddamned mirror.'

'Please,' said the man, lifting both hands as if he were admitting liability. 'I only sold it to you because I thought that it *had* to be a fake.'

'What are you talking about?'

'I bought it cheap from a dealer in Sacramento. He wouldn't say why he was selling it at such a knock-down price. It has a story attached to it, but if the story's true . . . well, even if it's only *half*-true . . .'

'What story?' Jack demanded.

'Believe me, I wouldn't have sold it to you if I thought there was any risk attached, especially after that last outbreak of silver plunge. I'm always so careful with mirraws.'

He went over to his desk, which was cluttered with papers and books and a framed photograph of Madame Chiang Kai-Shek, with the handwritten message, *To Timmy, What A Night*!

He pulled open his desk drawers, one after the other. 'I put it down to vanity, you know. If people stare into the mirraw long enough, it's bound to set off *some* reaction. I mean, it happens with *people*, doesn't it? If you stare at somebody long enough, they're bound to say "who do you think *you're* looking at?", aren't they?'

He couldn't find what he was looking for in his drawers, so he pulled down a steady shower of pamphlets and invoices and pieces of paper from the shelves behind his desk. At last he said, 'Here we are! We're in luck!'

He unfolded a worn-out sheet of typing paper and smoothed it with the edge of his hand. 'The Camelot Looking-Glass. Made circa 1842, as a gift from an admiring nation to Alfred Lord Tennyson on publication of the revised version of his great poem *The Lady of Shalott.*'

'What does that mean?' said Jack, impatiently. 'I don't understand.'

'The mirraw was specially commissioned by The Arthurian Society in England as a token of esteem for *The Lady of Shalott*. You do *know* about *The Lady of Shalott*?'

Jack shook his head. 'What does this have to do with my getting Jacqueline back?'

'It could have *everything* to do with it. Or, on the other hand, nothing at all, if the mirraw's a fake.'

'Go on.'

The man pulled up a bentwood chair and sat down. 'Some literary experts think that *The Lady of Shalott* was a poetic description of silver plunge.'

'I think I'm losing my patience here,' said Jack.

'No! No! Listen! *The Lady of Shalott* is about a beautiful woman who is condemned to spend all of her days in a tower, weaving tapestries of whatever she sees through her window. She weaves tapestries of all the passing seasons. She weaves courtships, weddings, funerals. The catch is, though, that she is under a spell. She is only allowed to look at the world by means of her mirraw. Otherwise, she will die.

'Let's see if I can remember some of it.

> *'There she weaves by night and day*
> *A magic web with colors gay.*
> *She has heard a whisper say,*
> *A curse is on her if she stay*
> *To look down to Camelot . . .*
>
> *'And moving thro' a mirraw clear*
> *That hangs before her all the year,*
> *Shadows of the world appear.*
> *There she sees the highway near*
> *Winding down to Camelot . . .'*

'Yes, great, very poetic,' Jack interrupted. 'But I still don't see how this can help Jacqueline.'

'Please – just let me finish. One day, Sir Lancelot comes riding past the tower. He looks magnificent. He has a shining saddle and jingling bridle-bells and his helmet feather burns like a flame. The Lady of Shalott sees him in her mirraw, and she can't resist turning around to look at him directly.

'She left the web, she left the loom
She made three paces thro' the room
She saw the water-lily bloom,
She saw the helmet and the plume
She look'd down to Camelot.
Out flew the web and floated wide;
The mirraw crack'd from side to side;
'The curse is come upon me,' cried
The Lady of Shalott.'

'She knows that she is doomed. She leaves the tower. She finds a boat in the river and paints her name on it, *The Lady of Shalott*. Then she lies down in it and floats to Camelot, singing her last sad song. The reapers in the fields beside the river can hear this lament, as her blood slowly freezes and her eyes grow dark. By the time her boat reaches the jetty at Camelot, she's dead.

'Sir Lancelot comes down to the wharf with the rest of the crowds. He sees her lying in the boat and thinks how beautiful she is, and he asks God to give her grace. That's what Tennyson wrote in the poem, anyhow. But listen to what it says on this piece of paper.

'"Several other stories suggest that Sir Lancelot visited the Lady of Shalott in her tower many times and become so entranced by her beauty that he became her lover, even though she could not look at him directly when they made love because of the curse that was on her. One day however he gave her ecstasy so intense that she turned to look at him. She vanished into her mirraw and was never seen again.

'"The mirraw presented to Alfred, Lord Tennyson, is reputed to be the original mirraw in which The Lady of Shalott disappeared, with a new decorative frame paid for by public subscription. When Lord Tennyson died in 1892, the mirraw was taken from his house at Aldworth, near Haslemere, in southern England, and sold to a New York company of auctioneers."'

Jack snatched the paper out of his hand and read it for himself. 'You knew that this mirror had swallowed this Shalott woman and yet you sold it to us without any warning?'

'Because the Lady of Shalott is only a poem, and Sir Lancelot is only a myth, and Camelot never existed! I never thought that it could happen for real! Even Lord Tennyson thought that the mirraw was a phoney, and that some poor idiot from The Arthurian Society had been bamboozled into paying a fortune for an ordinary looking-glass!'

'For Christ's sake!' Jack shouted at him. 'Even ordinary mirrors can be dangerous, you know that! Look what happened to your dog!'

The man ran his hand through his straggling white hair. 'The dealer in Sacramento said that it had never given anybody any trouble, not in thirty years. I inspected for silver plunge, but of course it's not always easy to tell if a mirraw's been infected or not.'

Jack took two or three deep breaths to calm himself down. At that moment, Punipuni appeared in the doorway of the antiques store, and the bell jangled.

'Everything is OK, Mr German-cellar?'

'No, Pu, it isn't.'

The man jerked his head toward Punipuni and said, 'Who's this?'

'A friend. His name is Punipuni Puu-suke.'

The man held out his hand. 'Pleased to know you. My name's Davis Culbut.'

'Pleased to know you, too, Mr French-somersault.'

'I beg your pardon?'

'That is what your name derives from, sir. The French word for head over heels. Topsy-turvy maybe.'

'I see,' said Davis Culbut, plainly mystified. He turned back to Jack and held up the typewritten sheet of paper. 'It says here that Sir Lancelot grieved for the Lady of Shalott so much that he consulted Merlin, the magician, to see how he might get her back. But Merlin told him that the curse is irreversible. The only way for him to be reunited with her would be for him to pass through the mirraw, too.'

'You mean—?'

'Yes, I'm afraid I do. You *can* have your lady-friend back, but only if you join her. Even so . . . this is only a legend, like Camelot, and I can't give you any guarantees.'

'Mr German-cellar!' said Punipuni, emphatically. 'You cannot go to live in the world of reflection!'

Jack said nothing. After a lengthy silence, Davis Culbut folded the sheet of paper and handed it to him. 'I can only tell you that I'm very sorry for your loss, Mr Keller. I'm afraid there's nothing else that I can do.'

They sat by the window in Steiner's Bar on First Street West and ordered two cold William Randolph Hearsts. Their waitress was a llama, with her hair braided and tied with red-and-white ribbons, and a brass bell around her neck.

'You want to see a menu?' she asked them, in a high, rasping voice that came right from the back of the throat. 'The special today is saddle of saddle, with maraschinos.'

Jack shook his head. 'No, thank you. Just the beers.'

The waitress stared at him with her slitted golden eyes. 'You look kind of down, my friend, if you don't mind my saying so.'

'Mirror trouble,' said Punipuni.

'Oh, I'm sorry. My nephew had mirror trouble, too. He lost his two daughters.'

Jack looked up at her. 'Did he ever try to get them back?'

The waitress shook her head so that her bell jangled. 'What can you do? Once they're gone, they're gone.'

'Did he ever think of going after them?'

'I don't follow you.'

'Did he ever think of going into the mirror himself, to see if he could rescue them?'

The waitress shook her head again. 'He has five other children, and a wife to take care of.'

'So what did he do?'

'He broke the mirror, in the end. He couldn't bear to hear his little girls crying.'

When she had gone, Jack and Punipuni sat and drank their beers in silence. At last, though, Punipuni wiped his mouth with the back of his hand and said, 'You're thinking of trying it, aren't you?'

'What else can I do, Pu? I love her. I can't just leave her there.'

'Even supposing you manage to get into the mirror, what's going to happen if you can't get back out?'

'Then I'll just have to make my life *there*, instead of here.'

Punipuni took hold of Jack's hands and gripped them tight. 'If your loved one falls from a high tower, even the flamingos cannot save her, and they can fly.'

That night, Jack sat on the end of the bed staring at himself in the cheval mirror, like a fortune teller confronted by his own mischance. Outside, the city glittered on the ocean's edge, like Camelot.

'*Jacqueline*?' he said, as quietly as he could, as if he didn't really want to disturb her.

He thought of the day when he first met her. She was riding side-saddle on a white cow through a field of sunflowers, under a sky the color of polished brass. She was wearing a broken wedding cake on her head, and a white damask tablecloth, wound around and around her and trailing to the ground.

He stopped and shaded his eyes. He had been visiting his friend Osmond at the Mumm's Winery in Napa, and he had drunk two very cold bottles of Cuvée Napa *méthode champenoise*. He had taken the wrong turning while looking for the parking lot, and he had lost his way.

'Excuse me!' he shouted, even though she was less than ten feet away from him. 'Can you direct me to Yountville?'

The cow replied first. 'I'm sorry,' she sighed, with a distinctive French accent. 'I've never been there.' She slowly rolled her shining black eyes from side to side, taking in the sunflower field. 'To tell you the truth, I've never been *anywhere*.'

But Jacqueline laughed and said, '*I* can show you, don't worry!' She slithered down from the cow and walked up to him, so that she was disturbingly close. The tablecloth had slipped and he could see that, underneath it, her breasts were bare.

'You're not really interested in going to Yountville, are you?' she asked him. She was wearing a very strong perfume, like a mixture of lilies and vertigo. 'Not any more.'

'Have I drunk too much wine or is that a wedding cake on your head?'

'Yes . . . I was supposed to get married today, but I decided against it.'

Jack swayed, and blinked, and looked around the sunflower

field. Sunflowers, as far as the eye could see, nodding like busybodies.

'Hold this,' Jacqueline had told him.

Jacqueline had given him one end of the tablecloth, and then she had proceeded to turn around and around, both arms uplifted, unwinding herself. Soon she had been completely naked, except for the wedding cake on her head and tiny, white stiletto-heeled boots, with white laces. Jack was sure that he must be hallucinating. Too much heat, too much *méthode champenoise*.

Jacqueline had an extraordinary figure, almost distorted, like a fantasy. Wide shoulders, enormous breasts, the narrowest of waists, and narrow hips, too. Her skin had been tanned the color of melted caramel and it was shiny with lotion. The warm breeze that made the sunflowers nod had made her nipples knurl and stiffen, too.

'I was supposed to consummate my marriage today,' she told him. 'But since I don't have a groom any longer . . .'

'Who were you supposed to be marrying?'

'A Frenchman. But I decided against it.'

Jack licked his lips. They were rough from sunburn and too much alcohol. Jacqueline rested one hand lightly on his shoulder and said, 'You don't mind doing the honors, though?'

'The honors?'

She turned around and bent over, reaching behind her with both hands and pulling apart the cheeks of her bottom. He found himself staring at her tightly-wrinkled anus and her bare, pouting vulva. Her labia were open so that he could see right inside her, pink and glistening and glutinous.

'Well?' she asked him, after a moment. 'What are you waiting for?'

'I, ah—'

The cow stopped munching sunflowers for a moment. '*Si vous ne trouvez pas agréables, monsieur, vous trouverez de moins des choses nouvelles*,' she quoted, with yellow petals falling from her mottled lips. 'If you do not find anything you like, sir, at least you will find something new.'

Jack stripped off his shirt and unbuckled his belt, undressing as rapidly as he used to, when he was a boy, on the banks of his grandpa's swimming hole. His penis was already hard, and when he tugged off his white boxer shorts it bobbed up eagerly.

He approached Jacqueline from behind, his penis in his hand, and moistened his glans against her shining labia.

'With this cock, you consummate our union,' Jacqueline recited.

He pushed himself into her, as slowly as he could. She was very wet inside, and hot, as if she were running a temperature. His penis disappeared into her vagina as far as it would go, and for a long, long moment he stood in the sunflower field, buried inside her, his eyes closed, feeling the sun and the wind on his naked body. He felt as if a moment as perfect as this was beyond sin, beyond morality, beyond all explanation.

With his eyes still closed, he heard a light buzzing noise. He felt something settle on his shoulder, and when he opened his eyes he saw that it was a small honey-bee. He tried to flick it off, but it stayed where it was, crawling toward his neck. He twitched his shoulder, and then he blew on it, but the honey bee kept its footing.

He heard another buzzing noise, and then another. Two more honey bees spiraled out of the breeze and settled on his back. Jacqueline groped between her legs until she found his scrotum, and she dug her fingernails into his tightly-wrinkled skin and pulled at it. 'Harder!' she demanded. 'Harder! I want this union to be thoroughly consummated! Harder!'

Jack withdrew his penis a little way and then pushed it into her deeper. She let out a high ululation of pleasure: *tirra-lirra-lirra*! He pushed his penis in again, and again, but each time he did so more and more honey bees settled on his shoulders. They seemed to come from all directions, pattering out of the wind like hail-stones. Soon his whole back was covered in a black glittering cape of honey bees. They crawled into his hair, too, and on to his face. They even tried to crawl into his nostrils, and into his mouth.

'Harder, sir knight!' Jacqueline screamed at him. He gripped her hips in both hands and began to ram his penis into her so hard that he tugged her two or three inches into the air with every thrust. But now the honey bees were gathering between his legs, covering his balls and crawling up the crack of his buttocks. One of them stung him, and then another. He felt a burning sensation in his scrotum, and all around the base of his penis. His balls began to swell up until he was sure that they were twice their normal size.

A honey bee crept into his anus, and stung him two or three inches inside his rectum. This explorer was followed by another, and another, and then by dozens more, until he felt as if a blazing thorn-bush had been forced deep into his bottom. Yet Jacqueline kept screaming at him, her breasts jiggling like two huge Jell-Os with every thrust, and in spite of the pain he felt a rising ecstasy that made him feel that his penis was a volcano, and that his sperm was molten lava, and that he was right on the brink of eruption.

Jacqueline began to quake. 'Oh con-*sume*-AAAAAAAation!' she cried out, as if she were singing the last verse in a tragic opera. She dropped on to her knees on the dry-baked earth, between the sunflower stalks, and as she did so, Jack, in his suit of living bees, spurted semen on to her lower back, and her anus, and her gaping cunt.

He pitched sideways on to the earth beside her, stunned by his ejaculation, and as he did so, the bees rose up from him, almost as one, and buzzed away. Only a few remained, dazedly crawling out of his asshole, as if they were potholers who had survived a whole week underground. They preened their wings for a while, and then they flew away, too.

'You've been stung,' said Jacqueline, touching Jack's swollen lips. His body was covered all over with red lumps and his eyes were so puffy he was almost blind. His penis was gigantic, even now that his erection had died away.

Jack stroked the line of her finely plucked cheekbones. He had never seen a girl with eyes this color. They were so green that they shone like traffic signals on a wet August night in Savannah.

'Who are you?' he asked her.

'Jacqueline Fronsart. I live in Yountville. I can show you the way.'

They lay amongst the sunflowers for almost a half hour, naked. Jacqueline stretched out the skin of Jack's scrotum so that it glowed scarlet against the sunlight, like a medieval parchment, and then she licked it with her tongue to cool the swelling. In return he sucked her nipples against the roof of his mouth until she moaned at him in Mandarin to stop.

Eventually the cow coughed and said, 'They'll be wondering where I am. And anyway, my udder's beginning to feel full.'

'You shouldn't eat sunflowers,' Jacqueline admonished her.

'You shouldn't eat forbidden fruit,' the cow retorted.

* * *

But now Jacqueline was gone and the mirror showed nothing but his own reversed image, and the bed, and the dying sunlight inching down the bedroom wall. Dim, jerky, far away, he heard a boat hooting in the Bay and it reminded him of the old dentist from Graham Greene's *The Power and the Glory*. Still waiting there, the last boat whistling in the last harbor.

'What's going to happen if you can't get back out?' Punipuni had asked him.

He didn't know. He couldn't see much of the world in the mirror. Only the bedroom, and part of the hallway, and it all looked the same as this world, except that it was horizontally transversed. Medieval painters invented a device with three mirrors which enabled you to see your face the way it really was. Frightening, in a way. Your own face, staring at you, as if your head had been cut off.

He stood up and pulled his dark blue cotton sweater over his head. He had never felt so alone. He unfastened his belt and stepped out of his stone-colored chinos. He folded his chinos and laid them on the bed. At last he took off his shorts and stood naked in front of the mirror.

'Jacqueline?' he called. Even if he couldn't penetrate the mirror, he needed to see her, to know that she was still there. *Who hath seen her wave her hand? Or at the casement seen her stand? The Lady of Shalott.*

'Jacqueline?' he repeated. 'Jacqueline, I'll come join you. I don't care what it's like in the mirror world. I just can't stand to live without you.'

The phone rang, beside the bed. He ignored it, to begin with, but it rang on and on and in the end he had to pick it up.

'Mr German-cellar? It is I Punipuni Puu-suke.'

'What do you want, Pu?'

'I have decided that it is in the interests of both of us for me to open the restaurant this evening. I will be serving boiled pens in their own ink.'

Jack didn't take his eyes off the mirror. He was sure that he had seen the mirror curtains stir, even though the windows were closed.

'Pu . . . if that's what you want to do.'

'We cannot afford to be closed, Mr German-cellar. The fierceness of the competition does not allow us.' He paused for a moment, and then he said, 'What are you contemplating, Mr German-cellar?'

'Nothing. Nothing at all.'

'You are not reconsidering a plunge into the mirror, sir? You know that it is better to rub margarine on your head than to run after a wig in a hurricane.'

'Pu—'

'Mr German-cellar, I do not wish for throat-constricting goodbyes. I wish for you to remain on this side of the reflective divide.'

'Pu, I'll be fine. Just open the restaurant.'

'You must promise me, Mr German-cellar, that you will not do anything maniacal.'

Jack put the phone down. He couldn't make any promises to anyone. You can only make a promise if you understand how the world works, and after Jacqueleine's disappearance he had discovered that life is not arranged in any kind of pattern, but incomprehensible. Nothing follows. Nothing fits together.

He returned to the mirror and stood facing it. As he did so, the door in the reflection slowly swung open and Jacqueline slowly walked in. Her face was very pale, and her hair was elaborately curled and braided. She was wearing a royal-blue military jacket, with gold epaulets and frogging, and black riding-boots which came right up over her knees, but nothing else. Her heels rapped on the bedroom floor as she approached him.

Jack pressed the palms of his hands against the mirror. 'Jacqueline . . . what's going on? Why are you dressed like that?'

She pressed her palms against his, although all he could feel was cold glass. Her eyes looked unfocused, as if she were very tired, or drugged.

'It's a parade,' she told him, as if that explained everything.

'Parade? What parade? You're practically naked.'

She gave him a blurred and regretful smile. 'It's all different here, Jack.'

He felt a tear creeping down his left cheek. 'I've decided to join you. I've thought about it . . . and there isn't any other way.'

'You can't. Not unless the mirror wants you.'

'Then tell me how.'

'You *can't*, Jack. It doesn't work that way. It's all to do with vanity.'

'I don't understand. I just want us to be together, it doesn't matter where.'

Jacqueline said, 'I walked down to the Embarcadero yesterday afternoon. The band was playing. The bears were dancing. And there it was, waiting for me. A rowboat, with my name on it.'

'What?'

She looked at him dreamily. 'Jack . . . there's always a boat waiting for all of us. The last boat whistling in the last harbor. One day we all have to close the book and close the door behind us and walk down the hill.'

'*Tell me how I can get into the mirror*!'

'You can't, Jack.'

Jack took a step back. He was breathing so heavily that his heart was thumping and his head was swimming. Jacqueline was less than three feet away from him, with those salmon eyes and those enormous breasts and that vulva like a brimming peach. All of the days and nights they had spent together flickered through his head like pictures in a zoetrope.

Jacqueline said, 'Jack – you *have* to understand. It's not that everything changes. Don't you get it? *Everything was back to front to begin with*.'

He took another step back, and then another, and then another. When he reached the bed, he stepped to one side. Jacqueline stood with her hands pressed flat against the mirror, like a child staring into a toy-store window.

'Jack, whatever you're thinking, don't.'

He didn't hesitate. He ran toward the mirror, and on his last step he stretched out both of his hands ahead of him like a diver and plunged straight into the glass. It burst apart, with a crack like lightning, and he hurtled through the mahogany frame and on to the floor, with Jacqueline lying underneath him.

But this wasn't the soft, warm Jacqueline who had wriggled next to him in bed. This was a brilliant, sharp, shining Jacqueline – a woman made out of thousands of shards of dazzling glass. Her face was made of broken facets in which he could see his own face reflected again and again. Her breasts were nothing more than crushed and crackling heaps of splinters, and her legs were like scimitars.

But Jack was overwhelmed with grief and lust and he wanted

her still, however broken she was. He pushed his stiffened penis into her shattered vagina, and he thrust, and thrust, and grunted, and thrust, even though the glass cut slices from his glans, and stripped his skin to bloody ribbons. With each thrust the glass sliced deeper and deeper, into the spongy blood-filled tissue of his penile shaft, into his veins, into his nerve endings. Yet he could no longer distinguish between agony and pleasure, between need and self-mutilation.

He held Jacqueline as tightly as he could, and kissed her. The tip of his tongue was sliced off, and his face was criss-crossed with gaping cuts.

'We're together,' he panted, with blood bubbling out of his mouth. 'We're together!'

He squeezed her breasts with both hands and three of his fingers were cut down to the bone. His left index finger flapped loosely on a thread of skin, and nothing else. But he kept on pushing his hips against her, even though his penis was in tatters, and his scrotum was sliced open so that his bloodied testicles hung out on tubes.

'We're together . . . we're together. I don't mind where I live, so long as I have you.'

At last he had lost so much blood that he had to stop pushing, and lie on top of her, panting. He was beginning to feel cold, but he didn't mind, because he had Jacqueline. He tried to shift himself a little, to make himself more comfortable, but Jacqueline crackled underneath him, as if she were made of nothing but broken glass.

The afternoon seemed to pass like a dream, or a poem. The sun reached the floor and sparkled on the fragments of bloodied mirror. Jack could see his own reflection in a piece of Jacqueline's cheek, and he thought to himself, *now I know what she means about the last boat whistling in the last harbor.*

Eventually it began to grow dark, and the bedroom filled with shadows.

For often thro' the silent nights
A funeral, with plumes and lights
And music, went to Camelot.
Or when the moon was overhead
Came two young lovers lately wed;

'I am half-sick of shadows,' said
The Lady of Shalott.

Punipuni knocked on Jack's door at midnight. He made three paces through the room; then stopped.

'Oh, Mr German-cellar,' he said. He pressed his hand over his mouth to stop himself from sobbing out loud, although nobody would have heard him. 'Oh, Mr German-cellar.'

He wrapped Jack's body in the multicolored durry from the bed, and carried him down to the street. He stowed him into the trunk of his ageing brown Kamikaze, and drove him to the Embarcadero. The night was very clear, and the stars were so bright that it was difficult to tell which was city and which was sky.

He found a leaky abandoned rowboat beside one of the piers. He lifted Jack into it, and laid him on his back, so that his bloodied face was looking up at Cassiopeia. Then he untied the rope, and gave the rowboat a push, so that it slowly floated away. The reflected lights of Camelot glittered all around it, red and yellow and green.

Punipuni stood and watched it with his hands in his pockets. 'Men should never go looking for darkness, Mr German-cellar. You can only find darkness in a closed cupboard.'

During the night, as the tide ebbed, the rowboat drifted out toward the ocean, under the Golden Gate bridge.

As the tide began to turn, another rowboat appeared from the opposite direction, and in this rowboat lay a naked woman in sunglasses, lying on a bed of dried brown chrysanthemums. The two rowboats knocked against each other with a hollow sound, like coffins; and then they drifted away, their prows locked together as if there were only one rowboat, reflected in a mirror.

Reflection of Evil

It was raining so hard that Mark stayed in the Range Rover, drinking cold espresso straight from the flask and listening to a play on the radio about a widow who compulsively knitted cardigans for her recently dead husband.

'It took me ages to find this shade of gray. Shale, they call it. It matches his eyes.'

'He's dead, Maureen. He's never going to wear it.'

'Don't be silly. *Nobody* dies, so long as you remember what they looked like.'

He was thinking about calling it a day when he saw Katie trudging across the field toward him, in her bright red raincoat, with the pointy hood. As she approached he let down the window, tipping out the last of his coffee. The rain spattered icy-cold against his cheek.

'You look *drowned*!' he called out. 'Why don't you pack it in?'

'We've found something really exciting, that's why.'

She came up to the Range Rover and pulled back her hood. Her curly blonde hair was stuck to her forehead and there was a drip on the end of her nose. She had always put him in mind of a poor bedraggled fairy, even when she was dry, and today she looked as if she had fallen out of her traveler's joy bush and into a puddle.

'Where's Nigel?' he asked her.

'He's still there, digging.'

'I told him to survey the ditches. What the hell's he digging for?'

'Mark, we think we might have found Shalott.'

'What? What are you talking about?'

Katie wiped the rain from her face with the back of her hand. 'Those ditches aren't ditches, they used to be a stream, and there's an *island* in the middle. And those lumps we thought were Iron Age sheep pens, they're stones, all cut and dressed, like the stones for building a wall.'

'Oh, I *see*,' said Mark. 'And you and Nigel, being you and Nigel, you immediately thought "Shalott"!'

'Why not? It's in the right location, isn't it, upstream from Cadbury?'

Mark shook his head. 'Come on, Katie, I know that you and Nigel think that Camelot was all true. If you dug up an old tomato-ketchup bottle you'd probably persuade yourselves that it came from the Round Table.'

'It's not just the stones, Mark. We've found some kind of metal frame. It's mostly buried, but Nigel's trying to get it out.'

'A *frame*?'

Katie stretched her arms as wide as she could. 'It's big, and it's very tarnished. Nigel thinks it could be a mirror.'

'I get it . . . island, Camelot, mirror. *Must* be Shalott!'

'Come and have a look anyway. I mean, it might just be scrap, but you never know.'

Mark checked his watch. 'Let's leave it till tomorrow. We can't do anything sensible in this weather.'

'I don't think we can just *leave* it there. Supposing somebody else comes along and decides to finish digging it up? It could be valuable. If we *have* found Shalott, and it if *is* a mirror—'

'Katie, read my lips, Shalott is a myth. Whatever it is you've dug up, can't you just cover it up again and leave it till tomorrow? It's going to be pitch dark in half an hour.'

Katie put on one of those faces that meant she was going to go on nagging about this until she got her own way. They weren't having any kind of relationship, but ever since Katie had joined the company, six weeks ago, they had been mildly flirting with each other, and Mark wouldn't have minded if it went a little further. He let his head drop down in surrender, and said, 'OK . . . if I *must*.'

The widow in the radio play was still fretting about her latest sweater. 'He's not so very keen on raglan sleeves . . . he thinks they make him look round-shouldered.'

'He's dead, Maureen. He probably doesn't *have* any shoulders.'

Katie turned around and started back up the hill. Mark climbed down from the Range Rover, slammed the door, and trudged through the long grass behind her. The skies were hung with filthy gray curtains, and the wind was blowing directly from the north-east, so that his wet raincoat collar kept petulantly slapping his face. He wouldn't have come out here at all, not today, but the weather had put him eleven days behind schedule, and the county council were starting to grow impatient.

'*We're* going to be bloody popular!' he shouted. 'If this *is* bloody Shalott!'

Katie spun around as she walked, her hands thrust deep in her duffel-coat pockets. 'But it could be! A castle, on an island, right in the heart of King Arthur country!'

Mark caught up with her. 'Forget it, Katie. It's all stories – especially the Lady of Shalott. Burne-Jones, Tennyson, the Victorians loved that kind of thing. A cursèd woman in a castle, dying of unrequited love. Sounds like my ex, come to think of it.'

They topped the ridge. Through the misty swathes of rain, they could just about make out the thickly wooded hills that half encircled the valley on the eastern side. Below them lay a wide, boggy meadow. A straggling line of knobbly topped willows crossed the meadow diagonally from south-east to north-west, like a procession of medieval monks, marking the course of an ancient ditch. They could see Nigel about a quarter of a mile away, in his fluorescent yellow jacket and his white plastic helmet, digging.

Mark clasped his hands together and raised his eyes toward the overbearing clouds. 'Dear Lord, if You're up there, please let Nigel be digging up a bit of old bedstead.'

'But if this *is* Shalott—' Katie persisted.

'It *isn't* Shalott, Katie. There is no Shalott, and there never was. Even if it *is* – which it isn't – it's situated slap bang in the middle of the proposed route for the Woolston relief road, which is already three and a half years late and six point nine million pounds over budget. Which means that the county council will have to rethink their entire highways-building plan, and we won't get paid until the whole mess has gone through a full-scale public enquiry, which probably means in fifteen years' time.'

'But think of it!' said Katie. 'There – where Nigel's digging – that could be the island where the castle used to stand, where the Lady of Shalott wove her tapestries. And these were the fields where the reapers heard her singing! And that ditch was the river, where she floated down to Camelot in her boat, singing her last lament before she died!'

'If any of that is true, sweetheart, then *this* is the hill where you and I and Historic Site Assessment Plc went instantly bankrupt.'

'But we'd be *famous,* wouldn't we?'

'No, we wouldn't. You don't think for one moment that *we'd* be allowed to dig it up, do you? Every medieval archeologist from every university in the western hemisphere would be crawling all over this site like bluebottles over a dead hedgehog.'

'We're perfectly well qualified.'

'No, darling, we're not, and I think you're forgetting what we do. We don't get paid to find sites of outstanding archeological significance interest, we get paid *not* to find them. Bronze Age buckle? Shove it in your pocket and rediscover it five miles away, well away from the proposed new supermarket site. An Iron Age sheep pen, fine. We can call in a JCB and have it shifted to the Ancient Britain display at Frome. But not Shalott, Katie. Shalott would bloody sink us.'

They struggled down the hill and across the meadow. The rain began to ease off, but the wind was still blustery. As they clambered down the ditch, and up the other side, Nigel stood up and took off his helmet. He was very tall, Nigel, with tight curly hair, a large complicated nose, and a hesitant, disconnected way of walking and talking. But Mark hadn't employed him for his looks or his physical coordination or his people skills. He had employed him because of his MA Hist. and his Dip. Arch. & Landscape, which were prominently displayed on the top of the company notepaper.

'Nigel! How's it going? Katie tells me you've found Shalott.'

'Well – *no* – Mark! I don't like to jump to – you know – *hah*! – hasty conclusions! Not when we could be dealing with – *pff*! I don't know! – the most exciting archeological find *ever*! But these *stones*, look!'

Mark turned to Katie and rolled up his eyes in exaggerated weariness. But Katie said, 'Go on, Mark. *Look*.'

Nigel was circling around the rough grassy tussocks, flapping his hands. 'I've cut back some of the turf, d'you see – and – underneath – well, *see*?' He had already exposed six or seven rectangular stones, the color of well-matured Cheddar cheese. Every stone bore a dense pattern of chisel marks, as if it had been gnawed by a giant stone-eating rat.

'*Bath* stone,' said Nigel. 'Quarried from Hazlebury most likely, and look at that jadding . . . late thirteenth century, in my humble opinion. Certainly not cut by the old method.'

Mark peered at the stones and couldn't really see anything but stones. 'The old method?'

Nigel let out a honk of laughter. 'Silly, isn't it? The *old* method is what quarrymen used to call the *new* method – cutting the stone with saws, instead of breaking it away with bars.'

'What wags they were. But what makes you think this could be Shalott?'

Nigel shielded his eyes with his hand and looked around the meadow, blinking. 'The *location* suggests it, more than anything else. You can see by the way these foundation stones are arranged that there was certainly a tower here. You don't use stones five feet thick to build a single-story pigsty, do you? But then you have to ask yourself *why* would you build a tower here?'

'Do you? Oh yes, I suppose you do.'

'You wouldn't have picked the middle of a valley to build a fort,' said Nigel. 'You would only build a tower here as a folly, or to keep somebody imprisoned, perhaps.'

'Like the Lady of Shalott?'

'Well, exactly.'

'So, if there was a tower here, where's the rest of it?'

'Oh, pilfered, most likely. As soon its owners left it empty, most of the stones would have been carried off by local small-holders, for building walls and stables and farmhouses. I'll bet you could still find them if you went looking for them.'

'Well, I'll bet you could,' said Mark, blowing his nose. 'Pity they didn't take the lot.'

Nigel blinked at him through rain-speckled glasses. 'If they'd done that – *hah*! – we never would have known that this was Shalott, would we?'

'Precisely.'

Nigel said, 'I don't think the tower was standing here for very long. At a very rough estimate it was built just before twelve seventy-five, and most likely abandoned during the Black Death, around thirteen forty.'

'Oh, yes?' Mark was already trying to work out what equipment they were going to need to shift these stones and where they could dump them. Back at Hazelbury quarry, maybe, where they originally came from. Nobody would ever find them there. Or maybe they could sell them as garden benches. He had a friend in Chelsea who ran a profitable sideline in ancient stones and eighteenth-century garden ornaments, for wealthy customers who weren't too fussy where they came from.

Nigel took hold of Mark's sleeve and pointed to a stone that was still half buried in grass. There were some deep marks chiseled into it. 'Look – you can just make out a cross, and part of a skull, and the letters DSPM. That's an acronym for medieval Latin, meaning "*God save us from the pestilence within these walls*".'

'So whoever lived in this tower was infected with the Black Death?'

'That's the most obvious assumption, yes.'

Mark nodded. 'OK, then . . .' he said, and kept on nodding.

'This is very, very exciting,' said Nigel. 'I mean, it's – well! – it could be *stupefying*, when you come to think of it!'

'Yes,' said Mark. He looked around the site, still nodding. 'Katie told me you'd found some metal thing.'

'Well! *Hah*! That's the clincher, so far as I'm concerned! At least it *will* be, if it turns out to be what I think it is!'

He strode back to the place where he had been digging, and Mark reluctantly followed him. Barely visible in the mud was a length of blackened metal, about a meter and a half long and curved at both ends.

'It's a fireguard, isn't it?' said Mark. Nigel had cleaned a part of it, and he could see that there were flowers embossed on it, and bunches of grapes, and vine tendrils. In the center of it was a lump that looked like a human face, although it was so encrusted with mud that it was impossible to tell if it was a man or a woman.

Mark peered at it closely. 'An old Victorian fireguard, that's all.'

'I don't think so,' said Nigel. 'I think it's the top edge of a mirror. And a thirteenth century mirror, at that.'

'Nigel . . . a *mirror*, as big as that, in twelve seventy-five? They didn't have glass mirrors in those days, remember. This would have to be solid silver, or silver-plated, at least.'

'Exactly!' said Nigel. 'A solid silver mirror – five feet across.'

'That's practically unheard of.'

'Not if *The Lady of Shalott* was true. She had a mirror, didn't she, not for looking at *herself*, but for looking at the world outside, so that she could weave a tapestry of life in Camelot, without having to look at it directly!

'There she weaves by night and day
A magic web with colors gay.
She has heard a whisper say
A curse is on her if she stay
To look down to Camelot.

'But moving through a mirror clear
That hangs before her all the year,
Shadows of the world appear . . .'

Katie joined in:

'And in her web she still delights
To weave the mirror's magic sights
For often thro' the silent nights
A funeral, with plumes and lights
And music, went to Camelot.'

'Top of the class,' said Mark. 'Now, how long do you think it's going to take to dig this out?'

'Oh . . . several weeks,' said Nigel. 'Months, even.'

'I hope that's one of your University of Essex jokes.'

'No, well, it has to be excavated properly. We don't want to damage it, do we? And there could well be other valuable artifacts hidden in the soil all around it. Combs, buttons, necklaces, who knows? We need to fence this area off, don't we, and inform the police, and the British Museum?'

Mark said, 'No, Nigel, we don't.'

Nigel slowly stood up, blinking with perplexity. 'Mark – we *have* to! This tower, this mirror – they could change the entire concept of Arthurian legend! They're archeological proof that the Lady of Shalott wasn't just a story, and that Camelot was really here!'

'Nigel, that's a wonderful notion, but it's not going to pay off our overdraft, is it?'

Katie said, 'I don't understand. If this *is* the Lady of Shalott's mirror, and it's genuine, it could be worth *millions*!'

'It could, yes. But not to us. Treasure trove belongs to Her Majesty's Government. Not only that, this isn't our land, and we're working under contract for the county council. So our chances of getting a share of it are just about zero.'

'So what are you suggesting?' said Nigel. 'You want us to *bury* it again, and forget we ever found it? We can't do that!'

'Oh, no,' Mark told him, 'I'm not suggesting that for a moment.' He pointed to the perforated vines in the top of the frame. 'We could run a couple of chains through here, though, couldn't we, and use the Range Rover to pull it out?'

'What? That could cause *irreparable* damage!'

'Nigel – everything that happens in this world causes irreparable damage. That's the whole definition of history.'

The rain had stopped completely now and Katie pushed back her hood. 'I hate to say it, Mark, but I think you're right. *We* found this tower, *we* found this mirror. If we report it, we'll get nothing at all. No money, no credit. Not even a mention in the papers.'

Nigel stood over the metal frame for a long time, his hand thoughtfully covering the lower part of his face.

'Well?' Mark asked him, at last. It was already growing dark, and a chilly mist was rising between the knobbly topped willow-trees.

'All right, then, bugger it,' said Nigel. 'Let's pull the bugger out.'

Mark drove the Range Rover down the hill and jostled along the banks of the ditch until he reached the island of Shalott. He switched on all the floodlights, front and rear, and then he and Nigel fastened towing chains to the metal frame, wrapping them in torn T-shirts to protect the mouldings as much as they could. Mark slowly revved the Range Rover forward, its tires spinning in the fibrous brown mud. Nigel screamed, '*Steady*! *Steady*!'

At first the metal frame wouldn't move, but Mark tried pulling it, and then easing off the throttle, and then pulling it again. Gradually, it began to emerge from the peaty soil which covered it, and even before it was halfway out, he could see that Nigel was right, and that it was a mirror – or a large sheet of metal, anyway. He pulled it completely free, and Nigel screamed, '*Stop*!'

They hunkered down beside it and shone their flashlights on it. The decorative vine-tendrils had been badly bent by the towing chains, but there was no other obvious damage. The surface of the mirror was black and mottled, like a serious bruise, but otherwise it seemed to have survived its seven hundred years with very little corrosion. It was over an inch thick and it was so heavy that they could barely lift it.

'What do we do now?' asked Katie.

'We take it back to the house, we clean it up, and we try to check out its provenance – where it was made, who made it, and what its history was. We have it assayed. Then we talk to one or two dealers who are interested in this kind of thing, and see how much we can get for it.'

'And what about Shalott?' asked Nigel. In the upward beam of his flashlight, his face had become a theatrical mask.

'You can finish off your survey, Nigel. I think you ought to. But give me two versions. One for the county council, and one for posterity. As soon as you're done, I'll arrange for somebody to take all the stones away, and store them. Don't worry. You'll be able to publish your story in five or ten years' time, and you'll probably make a fortune out of it.'

'But the island – it's all going to be lost.'

'That's the story of Britain, Nigel. Nothing *you* can do can change it.'

They heaved the mirror into the back of the Range Rover and drove back into Wincanton. Mark had rented a small end-of-terrace house on the outskirts, because it was much cheaper than staying in a hotel for seven weeks. The house was plain, flat fronted, with a scrubby front garden and a dilapidated wooden garage. In the back garden stood a single naked cherry tree. Inside, the ground-level rooms had been knocked together to make a living room with a dining area at one end. The carpet was yellow with green Paisley swirls on it, and the furniture was reproduction, all chintz and dark varnish.

Between them, grunting, they maneuvered the mirror into the living room and propped it against the wall. Katie folded up two bath towels and they wedged it underneath the frame to stop it from marking the carpet.

'I feel like a criminal,' said Nigel.

Mark lit the gas fire and briskly chafed his hands. 'You shouldn't. You should feel like an Englishman, protecting his heritage.'

Katie said, 'I still don't know if we've done the right thing. I mean, there's still time to declare it as a treasure trove.'

'Well, go ahead, if you want Historical Site Assessment to go out of business and you don't want a third share of whatever we can sell it for.'

Katie went up to the mirror, licked the tip of her finger and cleaned some of the mud off it. As she did so, she suddenly recoiled, as if she had been stung. '*Ow*,' she said, and stared at her fingertip. 'It gave me a shock.'

'A shock? What kind of a shock?'

'Like static, you know, when you get out of a car.'

Mark approached the mirror and touched it with all five fingers of his left hand. 'I can't feel anything.' He licked his fingers and tried again, and this time he lifted his hand away and said, 'Ouch! You're right! It's like it's *charged*.'

'Silver's *very* conductive,' said Nigel, as if that explained everything. 'Sir John Raseburne wore a silver helmet at Agincourt, and he was struck by lightning. He was thrown so far into the air that the French thought he could fly.'

He touched the mirror himself. After a while, he said, 'No, nothing. You must have earthed it, you two.'

Mark looked at the black, diseased surface of the mirror and said nothing.

That evening, Mark ordered a takeaway curry from the Wincanton Tandoori in the High Street, and they ate chicken Madras and mushroom bhaji while they took it in turns to clean away seven centuries of tarnish.

Neil played *The Best of Matt Monro* on his CD player. 'I'm sorry . . . I didn't bring any of my madrigals.'

'Don't apologize. This is *almost* medieval.'

First of all, they washed down the mirror with warm, soapy water and cellulose car sponges, until all of the peaty soil was sluiced off it. Katie stood on a kitchen chair and cleaned all of the decorative detail at the top of the frame with a toothbrush and Q-tips. As she worried the mud out of the human head in the center of the mirror, it gradually emerged as a woman, with high cheekbones and slanted eyes and her hair looped up in elaborate braids. Underneath her chin there was a scroll with the single word *Lamia*.

'Lamia?' said Mark. 'Is that Latin, or what?'

'No, no, *Greek*,' said Nigel. 'It's the Greek name for Lilith, who was Adam's first companion, before Eve. She insisted on having the same rights as Adam and so God threw her out of Eden. She married a demon and became the queen of demons.

He stepped closer to the mirror and touched the woman's faintly smiling lips. 'Lamia was supposed to be the most incredibly beautiful woman you could imagine. She had white skin and black eyes and breasts that no man could resist fondling. Just one night with Lamia and *pfff*! – you would never look at a human woman again.'

'What was the catch?'

'She sucked all of the blood out of you, that's all.'

'You're talking about my ex again.'

Katie said, 'I seem to remember that John Keats wrote a poem called *Lamia*, didn't he?'

'That's right,' said Nigel. A chap called Lycius met Lamia and fell madly in love with her. The trouble is, he didn't realize that she was a bloodsucker and that she was cursed by God.'

'Cursed?' said Katie.

'Yes, God had condemned her for her disobedience for ever. "Some penanced lady-elf . . . some demon's mistress, or the demon's self."'

'Like the Lady of Shalott.'

'Well, I supposc so, yes.'

'Perhaps they were one and the same person . . . Lamia, and the Lady of Shalott.'

They all looked at the woman's face on top of the mirror. There was no question that she was beautiful; and even though the casting had a simplified, medieval style, the sculptor had managed to convey a sense of slyness, and of secrecy.

'She was a bit of a mystery, really,' said Nigel. 'She was supposed to be a virgin, d'you see, "yet in the lore of love deep learnèd to the red heart's core." She was a bloodsucking enchantress, but at the same time she was capable of deep and genuine love. Men couldn't resist her. Lycius said she gave him "a hundred thirsts".'

'Just like this bloody Madras chicken,' said Mark. 'Is there any more beer in the fridge?'

Katie carried on cleaning the mirror long after Mark and Nigel had grown tired of it. They sat in two reproduction armchairs drinking Stella Artois and eating cheese and onion crisps and heckling *Question Time*, while Katie applied 3M's Tarni-Shield with a soft blue cloth and gradually exposed a circle of shining silver, large enough to see her own face.

'There,' she said. 'I reckon we can have it all cleaned up by tomorrow.'

'I'll give my friend a call,' said Mark. 'Maybe he can send somebody down to look at it.'

'It's amazing, isn't it, to think that the last person to look into this mirror could have been the Lady of Shalott?'

'You blithering idiot,' said Nigel.

'I beg your pardon?'

Nigel waved his can of lager at the television screen. 'Not you. Him. He thinks that single mothers should get two votes.'

They didn't go to bed until well past one a.m. Mark had the main bedroom because he was the boss, even though it wasn't exactly luxurious. The double bed was lumpy and the white Regency-style wardrobe was crowded with wire hangers. Katie had the smaller bedroom at the back, with teddy-bear wallpaper, while Nigel had to sleep on the sofa in the living room.

Mark slept badly that night. He dreamed that he was walking at the rear of a long funeral procession, with a horse-drawn hearse, and black-dyed ostrich plumes nodding in the wind. A woman's voice was calling him from very far away, and he stopped, while the funeral procession carried on. For some reason he felt infinitely sad and lonely, the same way that he had felt when he was five, when his mother died.

'Mark!' she kept calling him. '*Mark*!'

He woke up with a harsh intake of breath. It was still dark, although his travel clock said seven twenty-six a.m.

'Mark!' she repeated, and it wasn't his mother, but Katie, and she was calling him from downstairs.

He climbed out of bed, still stunned from sleeping. He dragged his toweling bathrobe from the hook on the back of the door and stumbled down the narrow staircase. In the living room the curtains were drawn back, although the gray November day was still dismal and dark, and it was raining. Katie was standing in the middle of the room in a pink cotton nightshirt, her hair all messed up, her forearms raised like the figure in *The Scream*.

'Katie! What the hell's going on?'

'It's Nigel. Look at him, Mark, he's dead.'

'What?' Mark switched the ceiling light on. Nigel was lying on his back on the chintz-upholstered couch, wearing nothing but green woolen socks and a brown plaid shirt, which was pulled right up to his chin. His bony white chest had a crucifix of dark hair across it. His penis looked like a dead fledgling.

But it was the expression on his face that horrified Mark the most. He was staring up at the ceiling, wide-eyed, his mouth stretched wide open, as if he were shouting at somebody. There was no doubt that he was dead. His throat had been torn open, in a stringy red mess of tendons and cartilage, and the cushion beneath his head was soaked black with blood.

'Jesus,' said Mark. He took three or four very deep breaths. 'Jesus.'

Katie was almost as white as Nigel. 'What could have *done* that? It looks like he was bitten by a *dog*.'

Mark went through to the kitchen and rattled the back door handle. 'Locked,' he said, coming back into the living room. 'There's no dog anywhere.'

'Then what—?' Katie promptly sat down, and lowered her head. 'Oh God, I think I'm going to faint.'

'I'll have to call the police,' said Mark. He couldn't stop staring at Nigel's face. Nigel didn't look terrified. In fact, he looked almost exultant, as if having his throat ripped out had been the most thrilling experience of his whole life.

'But what did it?' asked Katie. '*We* didn't do it, and Nigel couldn't have done it himself.'

Mark frowned down at the yellow swirly carpet. He could make out a blotchy trail of footprints leading from the side of the couch to the center of the room. He thought at first that they must be Nigel's, but on closer examination they seemed to be far too small, and there was no blood on Nigel's socks. Close to the coffee table the footprints formed a pattern like a huge, petal-shedding rose, and then, much fainter, they made their toward the mirror. Where they stopped.

'Look,' he said. 'What do you make of that?'

Katie approached the mirror and peered into the shiny circle that she had cleaned yesterday evening. 'It's almost as if . . . no.'

'It's almost as if *what*?'

'It's almost as if somebody killed Nigel and then walked straight into the mirror.'

'That's insane. People can't walk into mirrors.'

'But these footprints . . . they don't go anywhere else.'

'It's impossible. Whoever it was, they must have done it to trick us.'

They both looked up at the face of Lamia. She looked back at them, secret and serene. Her smile seemed to say *wouldn't you like to know*?

'They built a tower, didn't they?' said Katie. She was trembling with shock. 'They built a tower for the express purpose of keeping the Lady of Shalott locked up. If she was Lamia, then they locked her up because she seduced men and drank their blood.'

'Katie, for Christ's sake. That was seven hundred years ago. That's if it really happened at all.'

Katie pointed to Nigel's body on the couch. 'Nigel's dead, Mark! *That* really happened! But *nobody* could have entered this room last night, could they? Not without breaking the door down and waking us up. *Nobody* could have entered this room unless they stepped right out of this mirror!'

'So what do you suggest? We call the police?'

'We *have* to!'

'Oh, yes? And what do we tell them? "Well, officer, it was like this. We took a thirteenth-century mirror that didn't belong to us and The Lady of Shalott came out of it in the middle of the night and tore Nigel's throat out?" They'll send us to Broadmoor, Katie! They'll put us in the funny farm for life!'

'Mark, listen, this is real.'

'It's only a story, Katie. It's only a legend.'

'But think of the poem, *The Lady of Shalott*. Think of what it says. "*Moving thro' a mirror clear, that hangs before her all the year, shadows of the world appear*." Don't you get it? Tennyson specifically wrote *through* a mirror, not *in* it. The Lady of Shalott wasn't looking *at* her mirror, she was *inside* it, looking out!'

'This gets better.'

'But it all fits together. She was Lamia. A bloodsucker, a vampire! Like all vampires, she could only come out at night. But she didn't hide inside a coffin all day . . . she hid inside a mirror! Daylight can't penetrate a mirror, any more than it can penetrate a closed coffin!'

'I don't know much about vampires, Katie, but I do know that you can't see them in mirrors.'

'Of course not. And this is the reason why! Lamia and her reflection are one and the same. When she steps out of the mirror, she's no longer inside it, so she doesn't appear to have a reflection. And the curse on her must be that she can only come out of the mirror at night, like *all* vampires.'

'Katie, for Christ's sake . . . you're getting completely carried away.'

'But it's the only answer that makes any sense! Why did they lock up The Lady of Shalott on an island, in a stream? Because vampires can't cross running water. Why did they carve a crucifix and a skull on the stones outside? The words said, *God save us from the pestilence within these walls*. They didn't mean the Black Death . . . they meant *her*! The Lady of Shalott, Lamia, *she* was the pestilence!'

Mark sat down. He looked at Nigel and then he looked away again. He had never seen a dead body before, but the dead were so totally dead that you could quickly lose interest in them, after a while. They didn't talk. They didn't even breathe. He could understand why morticians were so blasé.

'So?' he asked Katie, at last. 'What do you think we ought to do?'

'Let's draw the curtains,' she said. 'Let's shut out all the daylight. If you sit here, perhaps she'll be tempted to come out again. After all, she's been seven hundred years without fresh blood, hasn't she? She must be thirsty.'

Mark stared at her. 'You're having a laugh, aren't you? You want me to sit here in the dark, hoping that some mythical woman is going to step out of a dirty old mirror and try to suck all the blood out of me?'

He was trying to show Katie that he wasn't afraid, and that her vampire idea was nonsense, but all the time Nigel was lying on the couch, silently shouting at the ceiling. And there was so much blood, and so many footprints. What else could have happened in this room last night?

Katie said, 'It's up to you. If you think I'm being ridiculous, let's forget it. Let's call the police and tell them exactly what happened. I'm sure that forensics will prove that we didn't kill him.'

'I wouldn't count on it, myself.'

Mark stood up again and went over to the mirror. He peered into the polished circle, but all he could see was his own face, dimly haloed.

'All right, then,' he said. 'Let's give it a try, just to put your mind at rest. *Then* we call the police.'

Katie drew the brown velvet curtains and tucked them in at the bottom to keep out the tiniest chink of daylight. It was well past eight o'clock now, but it was still pouring with rain outside and the morning was so gloomy that she need hardly have bothered. Mark pulled one of the armchairs up in front of the mirror and sat facing it.

'I feel like one of those goats they tie up, to catch tigers.'

'Well, I wouldn't worry. I'm probably wrong.'

Mark took out a crumpled Kleenex and blew his nose, and then sniffed. '*Phwoaff*!' he protested. 'Nigel's smelling already. Rotten chicken, or what?'

'That's the blood,' said Katie. Adding, after a moment, 'My uncle used to be a butcher. He always said that bad blood is the worst smell in the world.'

They sat in silence for a while. The smell of blood seemed to be growing thicker, and riper, and it was all Mark could do not to gag. His throat was dry, too, and he wished he had drunk some orange juice before starting this vigil.

'You couldn't fetch me a drink, could you?' he asked Katie.

'Shh,' said Katie. 'I think I can see something.'

'What? Where?'

'Look at the mirror, in the middle. Like a very faint light.'

Mark stared toward the mirror in the darkness. At first he couldn't see anything but overwhelming blackness. But then he saw a flicker, like somebody waving a white scarf, and then another.

Very gradually, a *face* began to appear in the polished circle. Mark felt a slow crawling sensation down his back, and his lower jaw began to judder so much that he had to clench his teeth to stop it. The face was pale and bland but strangely beautiful, and it was staring straight at him, unblinking, and smiling. It looked more like the face of a marble statue than a human being. Mark tried to look away, but he couldn't. Every time he turned his head toward Katie he was compelled to turn back again.

The darkened living room seemed to grow even more airless and suffocating, and when he said, '*Katie . . . can you see what I see*?' his voice sounded muffled, as if he had a pillow over his face.

Soundlessly, the pale woman took one step out of the surface of the mirror. She was naked, and her skin was the color of the moon. The black tarnish clung to her for a moment, like oily cobwebs, but as she took another step forward they slid away from her, leaving her luminous and pristine.

Mark could do nothing but stare at her. She came closer and closer, until he could have reached up and touched her. She had a high forehead, and her hair was braided in strange, elaborate loops. She had no eyebrows, which made her face expressionless. But her eyes were extraordinary. Her eyes were like looking at death.

She raised her right hand and lightly kissed her fingertips. He could feel her aura, both electrical and freezing cold, as if somebody had left a fridge door wide open. She whispered something, but it sounded more French than English – very soft and elided – and he could only understand a few words of it.

'*My sweet love*,' she said. '*Come to me, give me your very life*.'

There were dried runnels of blood on her breasts and down her slightly bulging stomach, and down her thighs. Her feet were spattered in blood, too. Mark looked up at her, and he couldn't think what to say or what to do. He felt as if all of the energy had drained out of him, and he couldn't even speak.

We all have to die one day, he thought. *But to die now, today, in this naked woman's arms . . . what an adventure that would be.*

'Mark!' shouted Katie. 'Grab her, Mark! Hold on to her!'

The woman twisted around and hissed at Katie, as furiously as a snake. Mark heaved himself out of his chair and tried to seize the woman's arm, but she was cold and slippery, like half-melted ice, and her wrist slithered out of his grasp.

'*Now*, Katie!' he yelled at her.

Katie threw herself at the curtains, and dragged them down, the curtain hooks popping like firecrackers. The woman went for her, and she had almost reached the window when the last curtain-hook popped and the living room was drowned with gray, drained daylight. She whipped around again and stared at Mark, and the expression on her face almost stopped his heart.

'*Of all men*,' she whispered. '*You have been the most faithless, and you will be punished*.'

Katie was on her knees, struggling to free herself from the curtains. The woman seized Katie's curls, lifted her up, and bit into her neck, with an audible crunch. Katie didn't even scream.

She stared at Mark in mute desperation and fell sideways on to the carpet, with blood jetting out of her neck and spraying across the furniture.

The woman came slowly toward him, and Mark took one step back, and then another, shifting the armchair so that it stood between them. But she stopped. Her skin was already shining, as if it were melting, and she closed her eyes. Mark waited, holding his breath. Katie was convulsing, one foot jerking against the leg of the coffee table, so that the empty beer cans rattled together.

The woman opened her eyes, and gave Mark one last unreadable look. Then she turned back toward the mirror. She took three paces, and it swallowed her, like an oil-streaked pool of water.

Mark waited, and waited, not moving. Outside the window, the rain began to clear, and he heard the whine of a milk float going past.

After a while, he sat down. He thought of calling the police, but what could he tell them? Then he thought of tying the bodies to the mirror, and dropping them into a rhyne, where they would never be found. But the police would come anyway, wouldn't they, asking questions?

The day slowly went by. Just after two o'clock the clouds cleared for a moment, and the naked apple tree in the back garden sparkled with sunlight. At half past three, a loud clatter in the hallway made him jump, but it was only an old woman with a shopping trolley pushing a copy of the *Wincanton Advertiser* through the letterbox.

And so the darkness gradually gathered, and Mark sat in his armchair in front of the mirror, waiting.

'I am half-sick of shadows, said
The Lady of Shalott.'

Neighbors from Hell

You hear about these people, how they've experienced something so terrible that they totally blank it out, and don't remember that it ever happened at all. Like, they see their sister crushed in an auto accident, and when you ask them about it a couple of years later they stare at you and say, 'What sister?'

I never personally believed that people could do that. I was convinced that if something really truly terrible happened to me, I'd be sweating about it every waking moment for the rest of my natural life.

But . . .

It was pretty horrible the way my grandmother died. I was working in The Blue Turtle Bar in Fort Lauderdale last summer when the phone rang and it was Mr Szponder, the super in my mother's apartment building. He said in his rusty old voice that she'd tumbled into a bath of scalding water and that she was now in intensive care at St Philomena's.

'Oh, God. How bad is it?'

'Bad. Thirty percent third-degree burns, that's what they told me. They don't expect her to make it. Not at her age.'

'I'll catch the next flight, OK?'

I asked Eugene for the rest of the week off. Eugene had greasy black curls right down to the collar of his red-and-yellow Hawaiian shirt and a face like somebody had been using a pumpkin for a dartboard. He hefted his big hairy arm around my shoulders and said, 'Jimmy . . . you take as long as you like.'

'Thanks, Eugene.'

'In fact, why don't you take forever?'

'What do you mean? You're *canning* me? This is my grandmother I'm talking about here. This is the woman who raised me.'

'This is also the middle of the season and if it's a choice between profit and compassion . . . well, let's just say that there isn't a Cadillac dealership in town which takes compassion in exchange for late-model Sevilles.'

I could see by the look in his pebbly little eyes that he wasn't going to give way and it wasn't even worth saying, 'Screw you, Eugene.' It just wasn't.

I went back to the tattily furnished house I was sharing on Broward Street with three inarticulate musicians from Boise, Idaho, and a wide-eyed brunette called Wendiii who thought that the capital of Florida was 'F.'

'Hey, you leaving us, man?' asked the lead guitarist, peering at me through curtains of straggly, sun-bleached hair.

'My grandma's had an accident. They think she's probably going to die.'

'Bummer.'

'Yeah. She practically raised me single-handed after my mom died.'

'You coming back?'

I looked around at the bare-boarded living room with its broken blinds and its rucked-up rug and every available surface crowded with empty Coors cans. Somehow it seemed as if all the romance had gone out of the Fort Lauderdale lifestyle, as if the sun had gone behind a cloud and a chilly breeze had suddenly started to blow.

'Maybe,' I said.

Wendiii came out of the john, buttoning up her tiny denim shorts. 'You take care, you hear?' she told me, and gave me long, wet, open-mouthed kiss. 'It's such a pity that you and me never got it on.'

Now she tells me, I thought. But my taxi had drawn up outside, and it was time to go. She lifted her elbows and took a little silver crucifix from around her neck and gave it to me.

'I can't take this.'

'Then borrow it, and bring it back safe.'

In Chicago the sky was dark and the rain came clattering down like bucketfuls of nails. I hurried across the sidewalk outside St Philomena's with a copy of *Newsweek* on top of my head but it didn't stop water from pouring down the back of my neck. The hospital lobby was lit like a migraine and the corridors were crowded with gurneys and wheelchairs and people arguing and old folks staring into space and nodding as if they absolutely definitely agreed that life wasn't worth living.

A tall black nurse led me up to intensive care, loping along in front of me with all the loopy grace of a giraffe. My grandmother lay in greenish gloom, her head and her hands wrapped in bandages. Her face was waxy and blotched and her cheeks had collapsed so that you could see the skull underneath. She looked as if she were dead already.

I sat down beside her. 'Grandma? It's me, Jimmy.'

It was a long time before her eyes flickered open, and when they did I had a chilly feeling of dread. All the blue seemed to have drained from her irises and it was obvious that she knew that death was only hours away.

'Jimmy . . .'

'Mr Szponder told me what happened, grandma. Oh, Jesus, what can I say?'

'They're keeping me comfortable, Jimmy, don't you worry.' She gave a feeble, sticky cough. 'Plenty of morphine to stop me from hurting.'

'Grandma . . . you should have had somebody looking after you. How many times did I tell you that?'

'I never needed anybody to look after me, Jimmy. I was always the looker-afterer.'

'Well, you sure looked after me good. Nobody could have raised me better.'

Grandma coughed again. 'Promise me one thing, Jimmy. You will promise me, won't you?'

'Anything. Just say the word.'

She tried to raise her head, but the effort and the pain were too much for her. 'Promise me you won't think bad of your mother.'

I frowned at her and shook my head. 'Why should I think bad of her? It wasn't her fault that she died.'

'Try to understand, that's all I'm saying.'

'Grandma, I don't get it. Try to understand *what*?'

She looked at me for a long time but she didn't say anything else. After a while she closed her eyes and I left her to sleep.

I met her gingery-haired doctor on the way out.

'What chances does she have?' I asked him.

He took off his eyeglasses and gave me a shrug. 'There are

times when I have to say that patients would be better off if they could come to some conclusion.'

'*Conclusion*? She's a human being, not a fucking book.'

I took a taxi over to her apartment building on the South Side, in one of the few surviving streets of narrow, four-story Victorian houses, overshadowed by the Dan Ryan Expressway. It was still raining and the expressway traffic was deafening.

I opened the scabby front door and went inside, carrying a brown paper shopping sack with six cans of Heineken and a turkey sandwich. The hallway was dark, with a brown linoleum floor and an old-fashioned umbrella stand. There was a strong smell of lavender floor polish and frying garlic. Somewhere a television was playing at top volume, and a baby was crying. It was hard to believe that I used to think of this building as home.

A door opened and Mr Szponder came out, with his rounded face and his saggy gray cardigan. His gray hair was swept back so that he looked like a porcupine.

'Jimmy . . . what can I say?' He held me in his arms and slapped my back as if he were trying to bring up my wind. 'I always tried to look out for your grandma, you know . . . but she was such a proud lady.'

'Thanks, Mr Szponder.'

'You can call me Wladislaw. What do you like? Tea? Vodka?'

'Nothing, thanks. I could use a little sleep, that's all.'

'OK, but anything you need.'

He gave me a final rib-crushing squeeze and breathed onions into my face.

Up on the fourth floor, grandma's apartment was silent and gloomy and damp. It seemed so much more cramped than it had when I was young, but very little had changed. The sagging brown velvet couch was still taking up too much space in front of the hearth, and the stuffed owl still stared at me from the mantelpiece as if it wanted to peck out my eyes. A framed photograph of a sad-looking seven-year-old boy stood next to the owl and that was me. I went through to the narrow kitchen and opened the tiny icebox. I was almost brought to tears by grandma's pathetic little collection of leftovers, all on saucers and neatly covered with cling wrap.

I popped open a can of beer and went back to the living room. So many memories were here. So many voices from the past. Grandpa singing at Christmas; grandma telling me stories about children who got lost in the deep dark forest, and could only find their way out by leaving trails of breadcrumbs. They looked after me as if I were some kind of little prince, those two, and when grandpa died in 1989 he left me a letter which said, '*There aren't any ghosts, Jimmy. Always remember that the past can't hurt you.*' To be honest, I never knew what the hell he was trying to tell me.

I tried to eat my turkey sandwich but it tasted like brown velvet couch and lavender polish and after two or three bites I wrapped it up again and threw it in the trash. I switched on the huge old Zenith television and watched this movie about a woman who thinks that her children are possessed. The rain spattered against the window and the traffic streamed along the Dan Ryan Expressway with an endless swishing noise, and out on the lake a steamer sounded its horn like the saddest creature you ever heard.

I woke up with a jolt. It was dark outside, and the apartment was illuminated only by the flickering light of *Wheel of Fortune*. The audience were screaming with laughter, but I was sure that I had heard somebody else screaming, too. There's a difference between a roller-coaster scream of hilarity and a scream of absolute terror.

I turned the volume down and listened. Nothing at first, except the traffic, and the muffled sound of a television from downstairs. I waited and waited and there was still nothing. But then I heard it again. It was a child screaming, a little boy, and when I say screaming this was a total freezing fear-of-death scream. I felt as if I had dropped into cold water right up to my neck.

I stood up, trying to work out where the screaming was coming from. It wasn't underneath me. It wasn't the next-door apartment, either. And this was the top story, so there was nobody living above.

Suddenly I heard it again, and this time I could make out part of what the child was screaming. '*Mommy*! *Mommy*! *No mommy you can't*! *Mommy you can't, you can't*, *you can't*! NO MOMMY YOU CAN'T!'

I went quickly through to grandma's bedroom, where the covers were still turned neatly back, and grandma's nightdress was still lying ready on the quilt. The screaming went on and on, and I could tell now that it was coming from the top-story apartment of the house next door. I thumped on the wall with my fist and yelled out, '*What's happening*? *What the hell are you doing*?'

The screaming stopped for a second, but then the child let out a high, shrill shriek, almost inhuman, more like a bird than a child. I hurried out of the apartment and ran downstairs, three and four stairs at a time. When I got to the hallway I banged on Mr Szponder's door.

'Mr Szponder! Mr Szponder!'

He opened his door in his vest and suspenders with a half-eaten submarine sandwich in his hand. 'Jimmy? Whatsa matter?'

'Call the cops! It's next door, that side, there's some mother who's hurting a kid! Tell them to hurry, it sounds like she's practically killing him! Top floor!'

'Hunh?' said Mr Szponder. 'What do you mean, killing?'

'Just dial nine one one and do it now! I'm going up there!'

'OK, OK.' Mr Szponder dithered for a moment, uncertain of what to do with his sandwich. In the end he put it down on the seat of a chair and went off to find his telephone.

I ran down the front steps into the rain. The house next door was different from the house in which my grandma had lived. It was narrower, with a hooded porch, and dark, rain-soaked rendering. I bounded up to the front door and pressed the top floor bell-push. Then I hammered on the knocker and shouted out, 'Open up! Open up! I've called the cops! Open the fucking door!'

Nobody answered, so I pressed every single bell push, and there were at least a dozen of them. After a long while, a man's voice came over the intercom. '*Who is this*?'

'I live next door. You have to let me in. There's a kid screaming on the top floor. Can't you hear him?'

'*What do you mean, kid*?'

'There's a kid screaming for help. Sounds like his mother's hurting him. For Christ's sake open the door, will you?'

'*I don't hear no screaming*.'

'Well, maybe he's stopped but he was screaming before. He could be hurt.'

'*So what's it got to do with me*?'

'It doesn't have to have anything to do with you. Just open the goddamned door, will you? That's all I'm asking you to do.'

'*I don't even know who you are. You sound like a maniac*.'

'Listen to me – if you don't let me in and that kid dies, then it's going to be your fault. Got it?'

There was a lengthy silence.

'Hallo?' I called, and pressed every bell push all over again. 'Hallo? Can anybody hear me?'

I was still pushing the bells and banging on the door when a police cruiser arrived with its lights flashing. Two cops climbed out, a man and a woman, and came up the steps. The man was tall and thin but the woman looked as if she could have gone nine rounds with Jesse Ventura. The raindrops sparkled on their transparent plastic cap-covers.

'What's the problem?'

'I was next door – staying in my grandmother's place. I heard a kid screaming. I think it's the top floor apartment.'

The woman cop pressed all the buttons again, and eventually the same man answered. '*Look – I told you – I didn't hear no screaming and this is nothing to do with me so stop ringing my bell or else I'm going to call the cops*.'

'I am the cops, sir. Open the door.'

Immediately, there was a dull buzz and the door swung open. The cops stepped inside and I tried to follow them but the woman cop stopped me. 'You wait here, sir. We'll deal with this.'

They disappeared up the rickety stairs and I was left standing in the hallway. There was a mottled mirror on the hallstand opposite me and it made me look like a ghost. Pale face, sticking-up hair, skinny shoulders like a wire coat hanger. Just like the seven-year-old boy on grandma's mantelpiece.

It was strange, but there was something vaguely familiar about this hallway. Maybe it was the beige-and-white diamond-patterned tiles on the floor, or the waist-high wooden paneling. There must have been tens of thousands of old town houses that were decorated like that. Yet it wasn't just the decor. There was something about the *smell*, too. Not damp and garlicky like next door, but dry and herby, like potpourri that has almost lost its scent.

I waited for almost ten minutes while the police officers went from floor to floor, knocking on every door. I could hear them talking and people complaining. Eventually they came back down again.

'Well?' I said.

'There's no kid in this building, sir.'

'What? I heard him with my own ears.'

'Nobody has a kid in this building, sir. We've been through every apartment.'

'It was the top floor. I swear to God. He was screaming something like, "mommy, mommy, you can't" – over and over.'

'The top floor apartment is vacant, sir. Has been for years. The landlord uses it for storage, that's all.'

'You're sure?'

'Absolutely. We're going to check the two buildings either side, just to make sure, but I seriously think you must have been mistaken. Probably somebody's television turned up too loud. You know what these old folks are like. Deaf as ducks.'

I followed them down the steps. Mr Szponder stood in his open doorway watching me.

'Well, what's happening?' he asked me, as the cops started ringing bells next door.

'They looked through the house from top to bottom. No kid.'

'Maybe your imagination, Jimmy.'

'Yeah, maybe.'

'Better your imagination than some kid *really* getting hurt. Think about it.'

I nodded. I couldn't think of anything to say.

The next morning, while I was washing my teeth, the telephone rang. It was the gingery-haired doctor from St Philomena's.

'I'm sorry to tell you that your grandmother reached her conclusion just a few minutes ago. She didn't suffer.'

'I see,' I said, with a mouthful of minty foam.

I called a couple of my cousins to tell them what had happened, but none of them seemed to be very upset. Cousin Dick lived in Milwaukee and could easily have come to Chicago to meet me but he said he had a 'gonad-cruncher' of a business meeting with Wisconsin Cuneo Press. Cousin Erwin sounded, quite frankly, as if he were stoned out of his brain. He kept saying, '*there you are, Jimmy . . . another milestone bites the dust*.'

Cousin Frances was more sympathetic. I had always liked

Cousin Frances. She was about the same age as me and worked for Bloomingdales in New York. When I called her she was on her lunch break and she was so upset that she started to cough and couldn't stop coughing.

'Listen,' she said, 'when are you going back to Florida?'

'I'm not in any hurry. I was fired for taking time off.'

'Why don't you stop over in New York (*cough*)? I'd love to see you again.'

'I don't know. Have a drink of water.'

Pause. More coughing. Then, 'Just call me when you get to La Guardia.'

Cousin Frances lived in a terraced brownstone on East Seventeenth Street in the Village. The street itself was pretty crummy and rundown but her loft was airy and beautifully decorated as you'd expect from somebody who made a living designing window displays. Three walls were plastered and painted magnolia, the fourth wall had been stripped back to its natural brick, with all kinds of strange artifacts on it, like driftwood antlers from the Hamptons and a Native American medicine stick from Wyoming.

Cousin Frances herself was very thin and highly groomed, with a shining blonde bob and a line in silky blouses and slinky pajama-like pants. She was the youngest daughter of my mother's sister Irene, and in a certain light she looked very much like my mother, or at least the two or three photographs that I still had of my mother. High forehead, wide-apart eyes, distinctive cheekbones, but a rather lipless mouth, which made her look colder than she actually was.

She poured me a cold glass of Stag's Leap Chardonnay and elegantly unfolded herself on the maroon leather couch. 'It's been so long. How long has it been? But you haven't changed a bit. You don't look a day over twenty-two.'

'I don't know whether that's a compliment or not.'

'Of course! Are you still working on that novel of yours?'

'Now and then. More then than now.'

'Writer's block?' I could smell her perfume now, Issey Miyaki.

I shrugged. 'I think you have to have a sense of direction to write a novel. A sense that you're going someplace . . . developing, changing, growing up.'

'And you don't feel that?'

'I don't know. I feel like everybody else got on the train but I dropped my ticket and when I looked up the train was already leaving the station. So here I am, still standing on the platform. Suitcase all packed but not a train in sight.'

She looked at me for a long time with those wide-apart eyes. In the end, she said, 'She didn't suffer, did she?'

'Grandma? I hope not. The last time I saw her she was sleeping.'

'I would have come to the funeral, but—'

'It doesn't matter. We had a few of her friends there. The super from her building. An Italian guy from the grocery store on the corner. It was OK. Very quiet. Very . . .'

'Lonely?' she suggested.

'Yes,' I said. 'Lonely.' But I wasn't sure who she was really talking about.

She had a date to go out later that evening to some drinks party, but all the same she made us some supper. She stood in the small designer kitchen and mixed up *conchiglie alla puttanesca* in a blue earthenware bowl. 'Tomatoes, capers, black Gaeta olives, crushed red chilies, anchovies, all mixed up with extra-virgin olive oil and pasta . . . they call it "harlot's sauce".'

I forked a few pasta shells out of the bowl and tasted them. 'That's good. My compliments to the harlot.'

'Do you cook, Jimmy?'

'Me? No, never.'

'*Never*? Not even meatballs?'

'I have a thing about ovens.'

She shook her head in bewilderment. 'I've heard of people being afraid of heights, or cats, or water. But *ovens*? That must be a first.'

'Stove-o-phobia, I guess. Don't ask me why.'

We ate together at the kitchen counter and talked about grandma and about the sisters who had been our mothers. Mine had died suddenly when I was five. Frances' mother had contracted breast cancer at the age of thirty-seven and died an appalling lingering death that went on for months and months.

'So, we're orphans now, you and me,' said Frances, and laid her hand on top of mine.

* * *

Just after nine o'clock the doorbell rang. It was a wiry-haired guy in a black velvet coat and a black silk shirt. 'Frances? You ready?' he said, eyeing me suspiciously.

'Almost, just got to put my shoes on. Nick – meet my cousin Jimmy. Jimmy, this is Nick. He's the inspirational half of Inspirational Plaster Moldings, Inc.'

'Good to know you,' I said. 'Glad you're not the plastered half.'

'You're welcome to come along,' Frances told me. 'They usually have organic wine and rice cakes, and all kinds of malicious gossip about dados and suspended ceilings.'

'Think I'll pass, if it's all the same to you.'

After Frances and Nick had gone, I undressed and went for a long, hot shower. It had taken a lot out of me, emotionally, seeing grandma die. When I shampooed my hair and closed my eyes I could still see her sitting on the end of my bed, her head a little tilted to one side, smiling at me.

'Grandma, why did mommy die?'

'God wanted her back, that's all, to help in heaven.'

'Didn't she love me?'

'Of course she loved you. You'll never know how much. But when God calls you, you have to go, whoever you are, and no matter how much you like living on earth.'

I was still soaping myself when I thought I heard a cry. I guessed it was probably a pair of copulating cats in the yard outside, and so I didn't pay it much attention. But then I heard it again, much louder, and this time it didn't sound like cats at all. It sounded like a child, calling for help.

Immediately I shut off the faucets and listened. There was silence for almost half a minute, apart from the honking of the traffic outside and the steady dripping of water on to the shower tray. No, I must have imagined it. I stepped out of the shower and wrapped a towel around my waist.

Then, my God, the child was screaming and screaming and I ran into the living area and it seemed like it was all around me. '*Mommy*! *Mommy*! *You can't*! *Stop it mommy you can't, you can't*! STOP IT MOMMY YOU CAN'T!'

I tugged on my jeans, my wet legs sticking to the denim. Then I dragged on my sweater and shoved my feet into my shoes, squashing the backs down because I didn't have time to loosen the laces. I opened the loft door and wedged a book into the gap so that it wouldn't swing shut behind me. On the landing, I pressed the button for the elevator and it seemed to take forever before I heard the motor click and bang, and the car come slowly whining upward.

I ran out into the street. The wind was up and it was wild, with newspapers and cardboard boxes and paper cups whirling in the air. I hurried up the steps of the next-door house and started jabbing at the doorbells. I was so frantic that it took me sixteen or seventeen heartbeats before I realized that these were the same doorbells that I had been pressing in Chicago.

I stopped. I took a step back. I couldn't believe what I was looking at. Not only was I pressing the same doorbells, but I was standing in front of the same house. It had the same black-painted front door, the same hooded porch, the same damp-stained rendering.

I felt a kind of *compressed* sensation inside of my head, as if the whole world was collapsing, and I was the center of gravity.

How could it be the exact same house? How could that happen? Chicago was nearly a thousand miles away, and what were the chances that I was staying right next door to a house that looked identical to the one that was next door to grandma's?

For a moment I didn't know what to do. Then a man's voice came over the intercom. '*Who's there*?' I couldn't tell if it was the same voice that I had heard in Chicago.

'I – ah – do you think could you open the door for me, please?'

'*Who is this*?'

'Listen, I think there's a child in trouble on the top floor.'

'*What child? The top floor's empty. No children live here.*'

'Do you mind if I just take a look. I work for the ASPCC.'

'*The what*?'

'Child cruelty prevention officer.'

'*I told you. No children live here.*'

I was unnerved, but I didn't want to give up. Even if I couldn't work out how this building was the same building from Chicago, I still wanted to know what all that screaming was. 'Just open the door, OK?'

Silence.

'Just open the fucking door, OK?'

Still silence.

I waited for a while, wondering what to do, and then I held on to the porch railing and gave the door a hefty kick. The frame cracked, so I kicked it again, and again, and again, and then a large piece of wood around the lock gave way and the door juddered open.

I went inside. The hallway was dark but I managed to find the light switch. The walls were paneled in darkly varnished wood, waist high, and the floor was patterned in beige-and-white diamonds. There was a hall stand with a blotchy mirror in it, and there was a dry, barely perceptible smell of dead roses.

I climbed the stairs. They were creaky but thickly covered in heavy-duty hessian carpet. Chinks of light shone from almost every door, and I could hear televisions and people talking and arguing and scraping dishes. A woman said, '*There should be a law against it . . . haven't I always said that*?' and a man replied, '*What are you talking about*? *How can you have a law against body odor*?'

I reached the second story and looked up toward the third. Without warning the lights clicked off and left me in darkness, and it took me quite a few moments of fumbling before I found the time switch. When the lights came on again, there was a man standing at the top of the stairs. It was impossible to see his face, because there was a bare light bulb hanging right behind him, but I could see that he was bulky and bald and wearing a thick sweater.

'Who are you?' he demanded.

'Child cruelty prevention officer.'

'That was you I was talking to before?'

'That's right.'

'Don't you hear good? There's no children live here. Now get out before I throw you out.'

'You didn't hear any screaming? A little boy, screaming?'

He didn't answer.

'Listen,' I insisted, 'I'm going to call the police and if they find out you've been abusing some kid—'

'Go,' he interrupted me. 'Just turn around and go.'

'I heard a boy screaming I swear to God.'

'*Go*. There are some things in life you don't want to go looking for.'

'If you think that I'm going to—'

'Go, Jimmy. Let it lie.'

I shielded my eyes with my hand, trying to see the man's face, but I couldn't. How the hell did he know my name? What was he trying to say to me? Let it lie? Let *what* lie? But he stayed where he was, guarding the top of the third-story stairs, and I knew that I wasn't going to get past him and I wasn't sure that I really wanted to.

I lowered my hand and said, 'OK, OK,' and backed off along the landing. Out in the street, I stood in the wind wondering what to do. A squad car drove slowly past me, but I didn't try to hail it. I realized by then that this wasn't a matter for the cops. This was a matter of madness, or metaphysics, or who the hell knew what.

'What do you know about your neighbors?' I asked Cousin Frances, over breakfast.

'Nothing. Why?'

'Ever give you any trouble? You know – parties, noise, that kind of thing?'

She frowned at me as she nibbled the corner of her croissant. 'Never. I mean like there's nobody there. Only the picture-framing store. I think they use the upstairs as a workshop.'

'No, no. I mean your neighbors that way.'

'That's right.'

Without a word I put down my cup of espresso, walked out of the apartment and pressed the button to summon the elevator. Cousin Frances called after me, 'What? What did I say?' I didn't answer, couldn't, not until I saw for myself. But when I got out into the street I saw that she was right. The building next door housed a picture-framing gallery called A Sense of Gilt. No narrow house with a hooded porch; no peeling black door; no doorbells.

I came back to my coffee. 'I'm sorry. I think I need to go back to Florida.'

There were thunderstorms all the way down the Atlantic coast from Norfolk to Savannah and my flight was delayed for over six hours. I tried to sleep on a bench next to the benign and watchful bust of Fiorello La Guardia but I couldn't get that screaming out of my mind, nor that narrow house with its damp-stained rendering.

What were the options? None, really, except that I was suffering from grief. Houses can't move from one city to another. My grandmother's death must have triggered some kind of breakdown which caused me to have hallucinations, or hyper-realistic dreams. But why was I hallucinating about a child screaming, and what significance did the house have? There was something faintly familiar about it, but nothing that I could put my finger on.

We were supposed to fly directly into Fort Lauderdale but the storms were so severe that we were diverted to Charleston. We didn't get there till one thirty-five a.m., and the weather was still rising, so United Airlines bussed us into the city to put us up for the night. The woman sitting next to me kept sniffing and wiping her eyes. 'I was supposed to see my son today. I haven't seen my son in fifteen years.' Rain quivered on the windows, and turned the street lights to stars.

When we reached the Radisson Hotel on Lockwood Drive, I found over a hundred exhausted passengers crowded around the reception desk. I wearily joined the back of the line, nudging my battered old bag along with my foot. Jesus. It was nearly two thirty in the morning and there were still about seventy people in front of me.

It was then that a woman in a black dress came walking across the lobby. I don't know why I noticed her. She was, what, thirty-two or thirty-three. Her brunette hair was cut in a kind of dated Jackie Kennedy look, and her dress came just below her knee. She was wearing gloves, too, black gloves. She came right up to me and said, 'You don't want to wait here. I'll show you where to stay.'

'Excuse me?'

She said, 'Come on. You're tired, aren't you?'

I thought: *hallo – hooker*. But she didn't actually *look* like a hooker. She was dressed too plainly, and what hooker wears little pearl earrings and a little pearl brooch on her dress? She looked more like somebody's mother.

I picked up my bag and followed her out of the Radisson and on to Lockwood. Although it was stormy, the night was still warm, and I could smell the ocean and that distinctive subtropical aroma of moss and mold. In the distance, lightning was crackling like electric hair.

The woman led me quickly along the street, walking two or three steps in front of me.

'I don't know what I owe the honor of this to,' I said.

She half turned her head. 'It's easy to get lost. It's not so easy to find out where you're supposed to be going. Sometimes you need somebody to help you.'

'OK,' I said. I was totally baffled, but I was too damned tired to argue.

After about five minutes' walking we reached the corner of Broad Street, in the city's historic district. She pointed across the street at a row of old terraced houses, their stucco painted in faded pinks and primrose yellows and powder-blues, with the shadows of yucca trees dancing across the front of them. 'That one,' she said. 'Mrs Woodward's house. She takes in guests.'

'That's very nice of you, thank you.'

She hesitated, looking at me narrowly, as if she always wanted to remember me. Then she turned and started to walk away.

'Hey!' I called. 'What can I do to thank you?'

She didn't turn around. She walked into the shadows at the end of the next block and then she wasn't there at all.

Mrs Woodward answered the door in hairpins and no make up and a flowery robe and I could tell that she wasn't entirely thrilled about being woken up at nearly three a.m. by a tired and sweaty guy wanting a bed and a shower.

'You were highly recommended,' I said, trying to make her feel better.

'Oh, yes? Well, you'd better come in, I suppose. But I've only the attic room remaining.'

'I need someplace comfortable to sleep, that's all.'

'All right. You can sign the register in the morning.'

The house dated from the eighteenth century and was crowded with mahogany antiques and heavy, suffocating tapestries. In the hallway hung a gloomy oil portrait of a pointy-nosed man in a colonial navy uniform with a telescope under his arm. Mrs Woodward led me up three flights of tilting stairs and into a small bedroom with a sloping ceiling and a twinkling view of Charleston through the skylight.

I dropped my bag on the mat and sat down on the quilted bed.

'This is great. I'd still be waiting to check into the Radisson if I hadn't found this place.'

'You want a cup of hot chocolate?'

'No, no thanks. Don't go to any trouble.'

'Bathroom's on the floor below. I'd appreciate it if you'd wait until the morning before you took a shower. The plumbing's a little thunderous.'

I washed myself in the tiny basin under the eaves, and dried myself with a towel the size of a Kleenex while I looked out over the city. Although it was clear, the wind had risen almost to hurricane force and the draft seethed in through the crevices all around my window.

Eventually, ass-weary, I climbed into bed. There was a guide to the National Maritime Museum on the nightstand, and I tried to read it, but my left eye kept drooping. I switched off the light, bundled myself up in the quilt, and fell asleep.

'Mommy, you can't! Mommy, you can't! Please, mommy, you can't! NO MOMMY YOU CAN'T!'

I jerked up in bed and I was slathered in sweat. For a second I couldn't think where I was, but then I heard the storm shuddering across the roof and the city lights of Charleston through the window. Jesus. Dreaming again. Dreaming about screaming. I eased myself out of bed and went to fill my toothbrush glass with water. Jesus.

I was filling up my glass a second time when I heard the child screaming again. 'No, mommy, don't! No mommy you can't! PLEASE NO MOMMY PLEASE!'

I switched on the light. There was a small antique mirror on the bureau, so small that I could only see my eyes in it. The boy was screaming, I could hear him. This wasn't any dream. This wasn't any hallucination. I could hear him, and he was screaming from the house next door. Either this was real, or else I was suffering from schizophrenia, which is when you can genuinely hear people talking and screaming on the other side of walls. But when you're suffering from schizophrenia, you don't think, 'I could be suffering from schizophrenia.' You believe it's real. And the difference was, I *knew* this was real.

'*Mommy no mommy no mommy you can't please don't please don't please.*'

I dressed, and he was still screaming and pleading while I laced up my shoes. Very carefully, I opened the door of my attic bedroom and started to creep downstairs. Those stairs sounded like the Hallelujah chorus, every one of them creaking and squeaking in harmony. At last I reached the hall, where a long-case clock was ticking our lives away beat by beat.

Outside, on Broad Street, the wind was buffeting and blustering and there was nobody around. I made my way to the house next door, and there it was, with its hooded porch and its damp-stained rendering, narrow and dark and telling me nothing.

I stood and stared at it, my hair lifted by the wind. This time I wasn't going to try ringing the doorbells, and I wasn't going to try to force my way inside. This house had a secret and the secret was meant especially for me, even if it didn't want me to know it.

I went back to Mrs Woodward's, locking the street door behind me. As quickly and as quietly as I could, I climbed the stairs to my attic bedroom. I thought at first that the boy might have stopped screaming, but as I went to the window I heard a piercing shriek.

The window frame was old and rotten and it was badly swollen with the rain and the subtropical humidity. I tried to push it open with my hand but in the end I had to take my shoulder to it, and two of the panes snapped. All the same I managed to swing it wide open and latch it, and then I climbed up on to the bureau and carefully maneuvered myself on to the roof. Christ, not as young as I used to be. The wind was so strong that I was almost swept off, especially since it came in violent, unexpected gusts. The chimney stacks were howling and the TV antenna was having an epileptic fit.

I edged my way along the parapet to the roof of the house next door. There was no doubt that it was the same house, the hooded-porch house, because it was covered with nineteenth-century slates and it didn't have a colonial-style parapet. I didn't even question the logic of how it had come to be here, in the center of historic Charleston. I was too concerned with not falling seventy-five feet into the garden. The noise of the storm was deafening, and lightning was still crackling in the distance, over toward Charles Towne Landing, but the boy kept on screaming and begging and now I knew that I was very close.

There was a skylight in the center of the next-door roof, and it was brightly lit. I wedged my right foot into the rain gutter, then my left, and crawled crabwise toward it, keeping myself pressed close to the slates in case a sudden whirlwind lifted me away.

'Mommy you can't! Please mommy no! NO MOMMY YOU CAN'T YOU CAN'T!'

Grunting with effort, I reached the skylight. I wiped the rain away with my hand and peered down into the room below.

It was a kitchen, with a green linoleum floor and a cream-and-green painted hutch. On the right-hand side stood a heavy 1950s-style gas range, and just below me there were tables and chairs, also painted cream and green. Two of the chairs had been knocked over, as well as a child's high-chair.

At first there was nobody in sight, in spite of the screaming, but then a young boy suddenly appeared. He was about five or six years old, wearing faded blue pajamas, and his face was scarlet with crying and distress. A second later, a woman in a cheap pink dress came into view, her hair in wild disarray, carrying a struggling child in her arms. The child was no more than eighteen months old, a girl, and she was naked and bruised.

The woman was shouting something, very harshly. The boy in the blue pajamas danced around her, still screaming and catching at her dress.

'*No, mommy*! *You can't*! *You can't*! *No mommy you can't*!'

His voice rose to a shriek, and he jumped up and tried to pull the little girl out of his mother's arms. But the woman swung her arm and slapped him so hard that he tumbled over one of the fallen chairs and knocked his head against the table.

Now the mother opened the oven door. Even from where I was clinging on to the roof I could see that the gas was lit. She knelt down in front of the oven and held the screaming, thrashing child toward it.

'*No*!' I shouted, thumping on the skylight. '*No you can't do that*! *No*!'

The woman didn't hear me, or didn't want to hear me. She hesitated for a long moment, and then she forced the little girl into the oven. The little girl thrashed and screamed, but the woman crammed her arms and legs inside and slammed the door.

I was in total shock. I couldn't believe what I had seen. The woman stood up, staggered, and backed away from the range, running one hand distractedly through her hair. The boy got up, too, and stood beside her. He had stopped screaming now. He just stared at the oven door, shivering, his face as white as paper.

'*Open the oven*!' I yelled. '*Open the oven*! *For God's sake, open it*!'

The woman still took no notice but the boy looked up at me as if he couldn't understand where all the shouting and thumping was coming from.

As soon as he looked up, I recognized him. He was the boy in the photograph that had stood on my grandmother's mantelpiece.

He was me.

I don't know how I managed to get down from that roof without killing myself. It took me almost five minutes of sweating and grunting, and at one point I felt the guttering start to give way. In the end, however, I managed to get back to the comparative safety of Mrs Woodward's parapet, and climb back in through my attic window.

I limped downstairs and into the street, but I guess I knew all along what I would find there. The house next door was a flat-fronted, three-story dwelling, painted yellow, with a white door and the date 1784 over the lintel. The house with the hooded porch had gone, although God alone knew where, or how.

Three weeks later, when I was back in Fort Lauderdale, working at The Scorpion Lounge, I received a package of photographs and letters from my grandmother's attorneys.

'Your late grandmother's legacy will be settled within the next three months. Meanwhile we thought you would like to have her various papers.'

I opened them up that evening, on the veranda of my rented cottage on Sunview Street. Most of the letters were routine – thank-you notes from children and cousins, bills from plumbers and carpet fitters. But then I came across a letter from my dad, dated twenty-six years ago, and handwritten, which was very unusual for him.

Dear Margaret,

It's very difficult for me to write to you this way because Ellie is your daughter and obviously you feel protective toward her. I know you don't think much of me for walking out on her and the kids but believe me I didn't know what else to do.

I talked to her on the phone last night and I'm *very* concerned about her state of mind. She's talking about little Janie being sent from hell to make her life a misery by crying and crying and never stopping and always wetting the bed. I don't think the Ellie I know would hurt her children intentionally but she doesn't sound like herself at all.

Please can I ask you to call around and talk to her and make sure that everything's OK. I wouldn't ask you this in the normal way of things as you know but I am very anxious.

All the best,

Travers.

Fastened to this letter by a paper clip was a yellowed cutting from the *Chicago Sun-Times*, dated eleven days later. MOTHER ROASTS BABY. Underneath the banner headline there was a photograph of the house with the hooded porch, and another photograph of the woman who had pushed her child into the oven. It was the same woman who had guided me from the Radisson Hotel to Mrs Woodward's lodging house. It was my mother.

There was also a cutting from the *Tribune*, with another photograph of my mother, with me standing beside her, and a little curly-headed girl sitting on her lap. 'Eleanor Parker with baby Jane and son five-year-old son James, who witnessed the tragedy.'

Finally, there was a neatly typed letter to my grandparents from Dr Abraham Lowenstein, head of the Psychiatric Department at St Vincent's Memorial Hospital. It read:

Dear Mr and Mrs Harman,

We have concluded our psychiatric examination of your grandson James. All of our specialists are of the same opinion: that the shock he suffered from witnessing the death of his sister has caused him to suffer selective amnesia, which is likely to last for the rest of his life.

> 'In lay terms, selective amnesia is a way in which the mind protects itself from experiences that are too damaging to be coped with by the usual processes of grieving and emotional closure. It is our belief that further treatment will be of little practical effect and will only expose James to unnecessary anxiety and stress.

So it was true. People *can* forget terrible experiences, totally, as if they never happened at all. But what Dr Lowenstein couldn't explain was how the experience itself could come looking for the person who had forgotten it – trying to remind them of what had happened – as if it *needed* to be remembered.

Or why I shall never give Wendiii her crucifix back, because I still wake up in the night, hearing a young boy screaming, '*No, mommy, you can't*! *No, mommy, please, you can't*! NO MOMMY YOU CAN'T!' And I have to have something to hold on to.

Son of Beast

Helen dropped her pink toweling bathrobe on to the floor and was just about to step into the shower when her cellphone played *I Say A Little Prayer.*

She said, 'Shit.' She was tired and aching after sitting in her car all night on the corner of Grear Alley, waiting for a rape suspect who had never appeared. But the tune played over and over and she knew that the caller wasn't going to leave her alone until she answered. She picked up the cellphone from the top of the laundry basket and said, wearily, 'Foxley.'

'Did I wake you?' asked Klaus.

'Wake me? I haven't even managed to crawl into bed yet.'

'Sorry, but Melville wants you down here asap. Hausman's All-Day Diner on East Eighth Street. It looks like Son of Beast has been at it again.'

'Oh, shit.'

'Yeah. My feelings exactly.'

She parked her red metallic Pontiac Sunfire on the opposite side of East Eighth Street and crossed the road through the whirling snow. It was bitterly cold and she wished that she had remembered her gloves. As she approached the diner, she shook down the hood of her dark blue duffel-coat so that the two cops in the doorway could see who she was.

Klaus Geiger was already there, talking to the owner. Klaus was big and wide shouldered, so that he looked more like a linebacker for the Bengals, rather than a detective. His dirty-blond hair was all mussed up, and there were plum-colored circles under his eyes, as if he hadn't slept, either.

'You look like you haven't slept either,' said Helen.

'I didn't. Greta's cutting two new teeth.'

'The joys of parenthood, right?'

Klaus turned to the owner and said, 'Mr Hausman, this is Detective Foxley, from the Personal Crimes Unit. Mr Hausman came to open up this morning about a quarter of six and found the back door had been forced.'

The owner took off his eyeglasses and rubbed them with a crumpled paper napkin. He was balding, mid-fifties, with skin the color of liverwurst and a large mole on the left side of his chin. 'I don't know how anybody could do a thing like that. It's like killing two people both at once. It's terrible.'

Without a word, Helen went over to the young woman's body. She was lying on her back with her head between two bar stools. Her black woolen dress had been dragged right up to her armpits and although she was still wearing a black lacey bra, her panties were missing. Her head had been wrapped around with several layers of cling wrap, so that her eyes stared out like a koi carp just beneath the surface of a frozen pond.

Like all of the nine previous victims, she was heavily pregnant – seven or eight months. A photographer was taking pictures of her from every angle, while a crime-scenes specialist in a white Tyvek suit was kneeling down beside her. He almost looked as if he were praying, but he was using a cotton bud to take fluid samples.

The intermittent flashing of the camera made the young woman's body appear to jump, as if she were still alive. Helen bent over her. As far as she could tell without unwrapping her head, she was young, and quite pretty, with freckles and short brunette hair.

'Do we know who she was?' asked Helen.

'Karen Marie Dozier,' Klaus told her. 'Age twenty-four. Her library card gives her address as Indian Hills Avenue, St Bernard.'

There was no need to ask if the young woman had been sexually assaulted. There were purple finger-bruises all over her thighs, and her swollen vagina was overflowing with blood-streaked semen.

Klaus said, 'Same MO as all the others. And the same damn calling-card.'

He held up a plastic evidence envelope. Inside was a ticket for Son of Beast, the huge wooden roller-coaster at King's Island pleasure park, over two hundred feet high and seven thousand feet long, with passenger cars that traveled at nearly eighty miles an hour. Helen had tried it only once, and she had felt as sick to her stomach as she did this morning.

* * *

'That's nine,' said Colonel Melville. 'Nine pregnant women raped and suffocated in sixteenth months. *Nine*.

He paused, and he was breathing so furiously that he was whistling through his left nostril.

'The perpetrator has left us dozens of finger impressions. He's so damn lavish with his DNA that we could clone the bastard, if we had the technology. He always leaves a ticket for the roller-coaster ride. Yet we don't have a motive, we don't have a single credible witness, and we don't have a single constructive lead.'

He held up a copy of the *Cincinnati Enquirer*, with the banner headline: *Ninth Mom-To-Be Murder: Cops Still Clueless.*

Colonel Melville was short and thickset with prickly white hair and a head that looked as if it was on the point of explosion, even when he was calm. Today he was so frustrated and angry that all he could do was twist the newspaper like a chicken's neck.

'This guy is making us look like assholes. Not only that, no pregnant woman can feel safe in this city, and that's an ongoing humiliation for this Investigations Bureau and for the Cincinnati Police Department as a whole.'

'Maybe we could try another decoy,' suggested Klaus. He was referring to three efforts they had made during the summer to lure Son of Beast into the open, by having a policewoman walk through downtown late in the evening wearing a prosthetic bump.

Helen shook her head. 'It didn't work before and I don't think it's going to work now. Somehow, Son of Beast has a way of distinguishing a genuinely pregnant woman from a fake.'

'So how the hell does he do that?' asked Detective Rylance. 'Do you think he's maybe a gynecologist?'

Klaus said, 'Maybe he's a gynecologist who was reported by one of his patients for malpractice, and wants to take his revenge on pregnant women in general.'

'I don't think so,' said Helen. 'Not even a gynecologist could have told that those decoys weren't really pregnant, not without going right up to them and physically squeezing their stomachs. But if Son of Beast knows for sure which women are pregnant and which ones aren't, maybe he has access to medical records.'

'Only two of the victims attended the same maternity clinic,' Klaus reminded her. 'It wouldn't have been easy for him to access the medical records of seven different clinics – three of which were private, remember, and one of which was in Covington.'

'Not easy,' Helen agreed. 'But not impossible.'

'OK, not impossible. But we still don't have a motive.'

Helen picked up her Styrofoam cup of latte, but it had gone cold now, and there was wrinkly skin on top of it. 'Maybe we should be asking ourselves why he always leaves a Son of Beast ticket behind.'

'He's taunting us,' said Detective Rylance. 'He's saying, here I am, I'm going to take you on the scariest roller-coaster ride you've ever experienced. I'm going to fling you this way and that. You're helpless.'

'I'm not sure I agree with you,' said Helen. 'I think there could be more to it than that.'

'Well, look into it, Detective,' said Colonel Melville. 'And – Geiger – you go back to every one of those maternity clinics and double-check everybody who has access to their records. I want some real brainstorming from all of you. I want fresh angles. I want fresh evidence. I want you to find me some witnesses who actually saw something. I want this son of a bitch hunted down, and nailed to the floor by his balls.'

Helen went back to her apartment at three thirty p.m. that afternoon, undressed, showered, and threw herself into bed. It was dark outside, and the snow was falling across Walnut Street thicker than ever, so that the sound of the traffic was muffled, but she still couldn't sleep. She kept thinking of Karen Dozier, staring up at her through all those layers of cling wrap, the way she must have stared up at the man who was raping her.

She thought she heard a child crying out, and the slow clanking of a roller-coaster car, as it was cranked up to the top of the very first summit. But the child's cry was only the yowling of a cat, and the clanking noise was only the elevator, at the other end of the hallway.

She switched on her bedside lamp. It was seven thirty-five p.m. For the first time in a long time she missed having Tony lying beside her. They had split up at the end of September, for all kinds of reasons, mostly the antisocial hours she had to work, and her reluctance to make love after she had witnessed some particularly vicious sex crime. She had found it almost impossible to feel aroused when she had spent the day comforting a ten-year-old boy whose scrotum had been burned by cigarettes, or a seventeen-year-old girl who had been forcibly sodomized with a wine bottle.

She went into the kitchen and switched on the kettle to make a cup of herbal tea. In the darkness of the window, she saw herself reflected, a slim young woman of thirty-one years and seven months, with scruffy, short-cropped hair, and a kind of pale, watery prettiness that always deceived men into thinking that she was helpless and weak. She decided that she needed some new nightwear. The white knee-length sleep-T that she was wearing made her look like a mental patient.

The kettle started to whistle, piercingly. At the same time, her phone began to play *I Say A Little Prayer*. She took off the kettle and picked up the phone and said, 'Foxley.'

'I didn't wake you, did I?' said Klaus.

'What's this? *Déjà vu* all over again? No, you didn't wake me. I'm way too tired to sleep.'

'I've just had some old guy walk in from the street, says he can help us with You-Know-Who.'

'You have him with you now?' She had picked up on the fact that Klaus had deliberately refrained from saying 'Son of Beast.' The Investigations Bureau had never released the information that the Moms-To-Be Murderer had left roller-coaster tickets at every crime scene, nor what they called him.

'Sure. He's still here. He says he needs to speak to you personally.'

'*Me*? Why does he need to talk to me?'

'He says you're the only person who can do it.'

'I don't understand. The only person who can do *what*?'

'He won't give me any specific details. Look –' he lowered his voice – 'he's probably a screwball. But we're really clutching at straws, right, and if he can give us any kind of a lead . . .'

Helen tugged at her hair. Her reflection in the kitchen window tugged at *her* hair, too, although Helen thought that her reflection did it more hesitantly than she did. 'OK,' she said. 'I'll be cross-town in twenty minutes. Buy your screwball a cup of coffee or something. Keep him talking.'

* * *

She drove across to Cincinnati Police headquarters on Ezzard Charles Drive with her windshield wipers flapping to clear the snow. Klaus was on the fourth floor, sitting on the edge of his desk and talking to an elderly man in a very long black overcoat. The man had a shock of wiry gray hair and rimless eyeglasses. His face was criss-crossed with thousands of wrinkles, like very soft leather that has been folded and refolded countless times. An old-fashioned black homburg hat was resting in his lap, and his hands, in black leather gloves, were neatly folded on top of it.

Klaus stood up as Helen came into the office. 'This is Detective Foxley, sir. Foxley, this is Mr . . .'

'Hochheimer,' said the elderly man, rising to his feet and taking off his right glove. 'Joachim Hochheimer. I read about the murder of the pregnant woman in the *Post* this evening.'

Helen didn't take off her coat. 'And you think you can help us in some way?'

'I think it's possible. But as I have already said to your associate here, it will require a considerable sacrifice.'

'OK, then. What kind of considerable sacrifice are we talking about?'

'Do you mind if I sit down again? My hip, well, I'm waiting to have it replaced.'

'Sure, go ahead. Klaus – you couldn't buy me a coffee, could you? I think I'm beginning to hallucinate.'

'Sure thing.'

When Klaus had left the office, the elderly man said, 'Young lady – you may find it very difficult to believe what I am going to tell you. There is a risk that you will dismiss me as senile, or mad. If that turns out to be your opinion, then what can I do?'

'Mr Hochheimer, we're investigating a series of very brutal homicides here. We welcome any suggestions, no matter how loony they might seem to be. Well – sorry – I'm not saying that *your* suggestions are loony. I don't even know what they are yet. But I'm trying to tell you that we appreciate your coming in, whatever you have to tell us.'

Mr Hochheimer nodded, very gravely. 'Of course. I consider it an honor that you are even prepared to listen to me.'

'So,' said Helen, sitting down next to him. 'What's this all about?'

He cleared his throat. 'As you know, hundreds of German

immigrants flooded into Cincinnati in the middle of the nineteenth century, to work in the Ohio River docks and pork packing factories. Among these immigrants was a family originally from Reuthingen, deep in the forests of the Swabian Jura. They were refugees not from poverty, but from prejudice and relentless persecution.'

'They were Jews?'

'Oh, no, not Jews. They were a different sort of people altogether. Different from you, different from me. Different from the rest of humanity.'

'How – different?'

'Their bloodline came originally from Leipzig, from the university, which is one of the oldest universities in the world. In the fifteenth century, several physicians at the university were carrying out secret genealogical experiments to see if they could endow human beings with some of the attributes of animals, or fish, or insects.

'For example, they tried to inseminate women with the semen from salmon, to see if they could produce a human being who was capable of swimming underwater without having to breathe. They tried similar experiments with dogs, and horses, and even spiders.

'Today we think such experiments are nonsense, but we should remind ourselves that in fourteen hundred and thirty, people were still convinced that a pregnant woman who was frightened by a rabbit would give birth to a child with a hare lip, or that an albino baby was the result of its expectant mother drinking too much milk.'

'Go on,' said Helen.

'Almost all of the experiments failed, naturally. But one experiment – just one – was what you might call a qualified success. A young serving-girl called Mathilde Festa was impregnated with sperm from a horseleech. The idea was that her child, when it was grown, could be trained as a physician, and suck infected blood from its patients' wounds itself, without the necessity for leeches.'

What a nutjob, thought Helen. *To think I got out of bed and drove all the way across town to listen to this.*

'Forgive me,' she said, trying to sound interested. 'I thought that leeches were hermaphrodites, like oysters.'

'They are, but they still produce semen. Some species of leech have up to eighty testes.'

'Eighty? Really? That's a whole lot of balls.'

Mr Hochheimer closed his eyes for a moment, as if he were trying to be very patient with her.

'I'm sorry,' said Helen. 'I'm kind of frazzled, that's all. I haven't slept in thirty-seven hours. And I'm beginning to wonder what point you're trying to make to me here.'

Mr Hochheimer opened his eyes again and smiled at her. 'I understand your skepticism. I told you that this wouldn't be easy to believe. But the fact is that Mathilde Festa gave birth to what appeared to be a normal-looking baby, except that his skin was slightly *mottled* in appearance. He was also born with four teeth, which were rough and serrated, like those of a leech.

'After his birth the physicians at Leipzig kept him concealed, because the university authorities and the church would have been outraged if they had discovered the nature of their experiments. But when he was four years old, the boy managed to escape from the walled garden in which he was playing.

'The physicians found him two days later, in the attic of an abandoned house close by, in a deep coma. Beside him was the body of another small boy, so white and so *collapsed* in appearance that they couldn't believe that he was human. Mathilde Festa's son had bitten this small boy, and had sucked out of him every last milliliter of blood and bodily fluid and bone marrow, until the unfortunate child was nothing more than an empty sack of dry skin and desiccated ribs.

'What was even more remarkable, though, was that Mathilde Festa's son had grown to nearly twice his size. He had been only four years old when he escaped from the garden. Now he looked like a boy of eight.'

'This is beginning to sound like something by the Brothers Grimm,' said Helen.

'A fairy story, yes. I agree. If they had strangled Mathilde Festa's son there and then, as they should have done, that would have been an end to it, and nobody would ever have believed that it really happened.'

'But they didn't strangle him?'

'No – at least two of the physicians were determined that their life's work should not be lost. They believed that the death of one small boy was a small price to pay for successfully inter-breeding one of God's species with another. They smuggled Mathilde Festa and her boy to Munich, and from Munich they took him to Reuthingen, deep in the forest, where he grew up as a normal child. Or as normal as any child could be, if he were half human and half leech. Mathilde Festa christened him Friedrich.'

'I hate to push you, Mr Hochheimer, but it's getting kind of late and I'm very tired. How exactly is any of this relevant to the Moms-to-Be Murderer?'

Joachim Hochheimer raised one hand, to indicate that Helen should be patient. 'When Friedrich was grown to manhood, he took a wife, a very simple-minded farmer's daughter who hadn't been able to find any other man to marry her. They were very happy together, by all accounts, but they were persecuted by other people in Reuthingen, because of the strangeness of Friedrich's appearance and also because of his wife's backward-ness. Children tossed rocks at their cottage, and whenever they went out people shook their fists at them and spat.

'One day, when she was walking home from the village, a gang of young men attacked Friedrich's wife. She was pregnant at the time with Friedrich's first child, almost full term. The young men dragged her into a barn and one of them raped her. Or *tried* to rape her.'

He hesitated, and squeezed his hands together as if he couldn't decide if he ought to continue. His leather gloves made a soft creaking sound.

'Go on,' said Helen. 'I deal with sex crimes every day, Mr Hochheimer. I've heard it all before.'

'This, young lady, I don't think that you *have* heard before. As the young man forced his way into Friedrich's struggling wife, her waters broke. Her womb opened and the baby inside her seized her attacker's penis with his teeth.

'The young man was screaming. His friends helped him to pull himself out. But the baby came out, too, its teeth still buried in his penis, and even when his friends battered the baby with sticks, it refused to release him. He fainted and his friends ran away.

'The next morning, Friedrich found his wife lying in the barn, desperately weak, but still alive. Close beside her, sleeping, lay a young man, naked, almost fully-grown. Beside him, amongst the bales of straw, lay something that was described as looking like a crumpled nightshirt, except that it had a face on it, a face without eyes, and tufts of hair.'

Helen sat back. 'Well, Mr Hochheimer, that's quite a story.'

'A description of what happened was written in great detail by one of the physicians from Leipzig, and his account is still lodged in the university library. I have seen it for myself.'

'You think it's true?'

'I assure you, it is completely true. The descendants of the family of which I spoke are still here in Cincinnati.'

'Well, it's a very interesting story, sir. But how can it help us to solve these murders?'

'It said in the *Post* that you have been unable to track down your suspect in spite of a wealth of evidence. It said that you have even tried decoys pretending to be pregnant, but your suspect seems to know that they are not genuine.'

'That's correct.'

'Supposing a decoy *were* to be genuine.'

'That's impossible,' said Helen. 'We can't possibly ask a pregnant woman to expose herself to a serial killer. What if something went wrong? The police department would be crucified.'

'Ah! But what if the pregnant woman were quite capable of defending herself? What if her unborn child were quite capable of protecting her?'

Helen suddenly understood what Joachim Hochheimer was suggesting. It made her feel as if she had scores of cicadas crawling inside her clothes. At that moment, Klaus came back with a cup of coffee in each hand.

'*Foxley*?' he frowned. 'Are you OK? You look like shit.'

She ignored him. Instead, she said to Joachim Hochheimer, 'You're seriously suggesting that some woman gets herself pregnant with one of these – leech babies? And allows the Moms-to-Be Murderer to rape her . . . so that it . . .?'

She imitated a biting gesture with her fingers.

Joachim Hochheimer shrugged. 'There would be no escape for him. Perhaps you think of it as summary justice, but what choice do you have? To allow him to continue his killings? To allow even more innocent young women and their unborn babies to be slaughtered?'

'Jesus,' said Helen.

Klaus put down the coffee cups. 'You want to explain to me what's going on here? What's a goddamned leech-baby when it's at home?'

Again, Helen ignored him. 'Why me?' she asked Joachim Hochheimer. 'Why did you come to see me?'

'I read an interview with you, the last time a young pregnant woman was murdered. You are young, you are unattached, you have an award for bravery. I don't know. I suppose I just looked at your picture and thought, this could be the one.'

'And how were you proposing that I should get pregnant?'

'The Vuldus family have a son who is only two years younger than you. Richard Vuldus.'

Helen stared at him. The desk lamp was shining on his eyeglasses so that he looked as if he were blind.

'It's impossible,' she said. 'Even if I believed you – which I don't – it's totally out of the question.'

Joachim Hochheimer stayed where he was for a while, nodding. Then he stood up and said, 'At least you know about it now. At least you have the option to try it, if you change your mind. Here – take my card. You can usually reach me at this number during the night.'

He put on his homburg hat and left the office. When he had gone, Klaus said, 'What the hell was *that* all about?'

'You were right,' said Helen. 'He *was* a screwball. One hundred and ten percent unadulterated FDA-rated screwball.'

She spent the next four and a half days checking every single mention of the roller-coaster Son of Beast since its official opening on May twenty-sixth, 2000 – on the Internet, in newspaper cuttings, in transcripts of TV and radio news reports.

When it had opened, Son of Beast had broken all kinds of records for wood-constructed roller-coasters. The tallest, the fastest, the only woodie with loops. It had cost millions of dollars to construct and used up 1.65 million board feet of timber.

She had almost given up when she came across an article from the *Cincinnati Enquirer* from April twenty-fifth two years previously. *"Son of Beast Killed Our Baby" Man Loses Lawsuit.*

'A judge yesterday threw out a $3.5 million lawsuit by a Norwood man who claimed that a "violent and hair-raising" ride on the newly opened Son of Beast roller-coaster caused his pregnant girlfriend to miscarry their baby.

'After his girlfriend confessed to the court that the roller-coaster ride had not been responsible for her losing the child, Judge David Davis told Henry Clarke, thirty-five, a realtor from Smith Road, Norwood, that he was dismissing the action against Paramount Entertainment.

'Jennifer Prescott, thirty-three, admitted that she had booked in advance to have her pregnancy terminated at a private clinic in Covington, KY, and had used their ride on the King's Island attraction to conceal what she had done from Mr Clarke.

'Mrs Prescott is estranged from her husband Robert Prescott, also of Norwood. She told the court that she started an affair with Mr Clarke in November last year believing him to be a "kind and considerate person".

'But he became increasingly possessive and physically abusive, and she had already decided to leave him before she discovered that she was expecting his baby.

'She invented the roller-coaster story because she was terrified of what Mr Clarke would do to her if he discovered that she had deliberately ended her pregnancy.'

Helen printed out a copy of the news story and took it into Colonel Melville's office.

'What do you think?' she asked him.

Colonel Melville read the article, took out his handkerchief and loudly blew his nose. 'Mr Clarke has a pretty good résumé, doesn't he? A history of domestic violence. A motive for attacking pregnant women. And a reason for using the name Son of Beast. Let's pick this joker up, shall we, and see what he has to say for himself?'

But there was no trace of Henry Clarke anywhere in Cincinnati or its surrounding suburbs. He had left his job at Friedmann, Kite Realty Inc only two weeks after he had lost his court action against Paramount. He had left his house in Norwood, too, leaving all of his furniture behind. His parents hadn't heard from him, not even a phone call, and he had told none of his friends where he was going.

He had sold his Ford Explorer to a used-car dealership in Bridgetown, to the west of the city center, but he had taken cash for it and not exchanged it for another vehicle.

'I have such a feeling about this guy,' said Helen, the week before Christmas, when she and Klaus were sitting in the office eating sugared donuts and drinking coffee. 'He's vanished, but he hasn't gone.'

The sky outside the office window was dark green, and it was snowing again. People with black umbrellas were struggling along the sidewalks like a scene out of a Dickens novel.

Helen went to the window and looked down at them. 'That could be him, under any one of those umbrellas.'

'Don't let your imagination run away with you,' said Klaus. 'Do you want this last donut?'

Helen wasn't letting her imagination run away with her. On Christmas morning the body of a young pregnant woman was discovered underneath the Riverfront Stadium. Her head had been wound round with four layers of Saran Wrap, and she had been raped. Her name was Clare Jefferson and she was twenty-three years old.

Helen stood underneath the gloomy concrete supports of the stadium, her hands in her pockets, watching the crime scene specialists at work. Klaus came up to her and said, 'Happy Christmas. Did you open your presents yet?'

The red flashing lights on top of the squad cars were a lurid parody of Christmas-tree lights. Helen said, '*Ten*. Shit. Isn't he ever going to stop?'

One of the crime scene specialists came over, holding up a roller-coaster ticket. 'Thought you'd want to see this.'

She couldn't sleep that night. She took two sleeping pills and watched TV until two thirty a.m., but her brain wouldn't stop churning over and her eyes refused to close. She had arranged to see her parents tomorrow in Indian Hills Village, to make up for missing Christmas lunch, but she knew already that she wasn't going to go.

How could she eat turkey and pull crackers when that young girl was lying in the mortuary, with her dead baby still inside her? Son of Beast had raped and suffocated ten women, but altogether he had murdered twenty innocent souls.

She switched on the light and went across to her dressing table. Tucked into the side of the mirror was Joachim Hochheimer's visiting card. She took it out and looked at it for a long time.

He was a lunatic, right? If sixteenth-century physicians had managed to cross a woman and a horseleech, surely it would have been common medical knowledge by now. At the very least it would have been mentioned in *Ripley's Believe It Or Not*.

And even if it really *had* happened, and Mathilde Festa really *had* managed to give birth to generations of descendants, surely the leech genes would have been bred out of them by now?

And even if they hadn't been bred out of them, and it was still genetically possible for a woman to become pregnant with a creature like that, could any woman bring herself to do it?

She sat down on the end of her rumpled bed. She thought: *if this is the only way that Son of Beast can be stopped from murdering more women and unborn babies, I'm going to have to find the courage to do it myself. I can't ask anybody else*. Not only that, it was the twenty-sixth day of the month, and she was ovulating. If there was any time to conceive a Vuldus baby, it was now.

She picked up her phone and punched out Joachim Hochheimer's number.

He opened the door for her. The hallway was so gloomy that she could hardly see his face, only the reflection from his eyeglasses.

'Come in. We thought that you might have changed your mind.'

'I very nearly did.'

Inside, the apartment was overheated and stuffy and smelled of stale *potpourri*, cinnamon and cloves. It was furnished in a heavy Germanic style, with dusty brocade drapes and huge armchairs and mahogany cabinets filled with Eastern European china – plates and fruit bowls and figurines of fan dancers. It was on the top floor of a nineteenth-century commercial building overlooking Fountain Square, right in the heart of the city. Helen went to the window and looked out, and she could see the Tyler Davidson fountain, with the Genius of Water standing on top of it, with curtains of ice suspended from her outstretched hands. All around it, dozens of children were sliding on the slippery pavement.

'The Vuldus family rented this apartment from the shipping insurance company who used to occupy the lower floors,' said Joachim Hochheimer. 'That was in 1871, and they have lived here ever since.'

He came up her and held out his hand. 'May I take your coat?'

'Listen,' she said, 'I'm really not so sure I want to go through with this.'

He nodded. 'It is a step into the totally unknown, isn't it, which not many of us ever have the courage to take. If you feel you cannot do it, then of course you must go home and forget that I ever suggested it.'

'Is he here?' asked Helen. 'Richard Vuldus?'

'Yes, he's in the bedroom. He's waiting for you.'

'Maybe you can give him my apologies.'

'Of course.'

For a long moment, neither of them moved. But then Helen's cellphone played *I Say A Little Prayer For You*. She said, 'Excuse me, Mr Hochheimer,' and opened it up.

It was Klaus. 'Foxley?' he demanded. 'Where the hell are you?'

'I had an errand to run. I'm free now. What do you want?'

'We just had a first report from the ME. Clare Jefferson was two hundred seventy-one days pregnant. About three days away from giving birth.'

'Oh, God.'

'Not only that, Foxley. She was expecting twins.'

Helen closed her eyes, but inside her mind she could clearly see Clare Jefferson lying on her back in the dark concrete recess underneath the Riverfront Stadium, her head swaddled in plastic wrap, her smock pulled up right over her breasts, and the red emergency lights flashing. Inside her swollen stomach, two dead babies had been cuddling each other.

'Helen? You there?'

'I'm here.'

'Are you coming into headquarters?'

She cleared her throat. 'Give me a little time, Klaus. Maybe an hour or so.'

'OK. But we really need you here, soon as you can.'

Helen closed her cellphone and dropped it back into her coat pocket. Joachim Hochheimer was watching her intently and he could obviously sense that something had changed.

Helen said, quietly, and as calmly as she could, 'Maybe you can introduce me to Richard.'

* * *

The bedroom was furnished in the same grandiose style as the rest of the apartment, with a huge four-poster bed with a green-and-crimson quilt, impenetrable crimson drapes, and a bow-fronted armoire with elaborate gilded handles. On either side of the bed hung oil paintings of naked nymphs dancing in the woods, their heads thrown back in lust and hilarity.

Richard Vuldus was standing by the window looking down at Fountain Square, wearing a long black cotton robe with very wide sleeves, as if he were a stage magician. He was tall, with long black curly hair that almost reached his shoulders. Helen saw a diamond sparkle in his left ear-lobe.

'Richard,' said Joachim Hochheimer. 'Richard, this is the young lady I was telling you about.'

Richard Vuldus turned around. Helen couldn't stop herself from taking a small, sharp intake of breath, almost like a hiccup. He was extraordinarily handsome, but in a strange, unsettling way that Helen had never seen before. His face was long and oval and very pale, and his eyebrows were arched, almost like a woman's. His nose was thin and straight, and his lips were thin but gracefully curved, as if he had just made a deeply lewd suggestion, but said it in such a way that no woman could have resisted it.

He came up to Helen with his robes softly billowing. The cotton was deep black, but very fine, so that with the bedside lamp behind him, she could see the outline of his muscular body, and his half-tumescent penis.

'Joachim!' he smiled, holding out his hand to her. 'You didn't warn me that she was beautiful!' His eyes were mesmerizing: his irises were completely black, and they glistened like polished jet. His voice had a slight European accent, so that 'beautiful' came out with five syllables, 'bee-aye-*oo*-ti-fool.'

'I'm Helen,' said Helen. Her heart was beating so hard against her ribcage that it actually hurt.

'I know,' said Richard Vuldus. 'And I know that this cannot be easy for you, in any way. But I assure you that I will do my best to make you feel at ease. Even if what we are doing today is not out of love for each other, it is out of love for innocent people, yes, and unborn babies who do not deserve to die?'

'I – ah – I guess we could put it that way.'

'Perhaps you would like a drink?' Joachim Hochheimer asked her. 'A glass of champagne?'

'I have to go on duty later. Besides . . . if we're going to do this, I'd rather just get it over with.'

'Of course,' said Richard Vuldus. He came closer to her and now she could see what Joachim Hochheimer had meant by *mottled*. There were faint dark-gray patches around his temples, and across his cheekbones, and down the sides of his neck. He had a smell about him, too. Not unpleasant – in fact it was quite attractive – but different from any other man she had ever known. Musky, but metallic, like overheated iron.

'I'll leave you alone now,' said Joachim Hochheimer. 'If there's anything you need – if you have any more questions—'

'There is just one thing,' said Helen. 'What do *you* get out of this? Don't tell me you're just being public-spirited.'

Joachim Hochheimer looked surprised. 'I thought that was obvious, dear lady. What *we* get out of it is a new member of the Vuldus family – one with new blood. We have been trying for generation after generation to breed ourselves back to purity, and we are not too far away from that now. They cursed us, those physicians, all those centuries ago, by interbreeding us. But the time will eventually come when all of the monstrosity is bred out of us.'

Richard Vuldus took hold of her hand. His fingers were very cold, but they were strong, too. 'You will be doing our family a great service, Helen, and we thank you and admire you for it.'

Helen nearly lost her nerve. Not only would she have to make love to this strange young man, she would have to carry his baby, and when she was nearly ready to give birth she would have to risk her own life and her baby's life to trap Son of Beast. Even if she succeeded she would be faced with a nightmare. She would have to find a way of explaining to what had happened to Son of Beast, and a way of making sure that her new child escaped, and was safely returned to the Vuldus family.

It was madness. It was all madness. She was just about to turn around and ask for her coat back when Richard Vuldus laid both of his hands on her shoulders, and held her firmly, and looked directly into her eyes. His eyes were so black it was like looking into space.

'The day we take no more risks, Helen, that is the day we lie down and die.'

She didn't know what to say to him. Behind her, Joachim Hochheimer quietly closed the bedroom door.

'Come,' said Richard Vuldus. He led her over to the side of the bed, closer to the bedside lamp. He touched her hair, and her cheek. 'Do you know what I see in you? I see a woman of such complexity. A woman who needs to show what she can do, but has not yet discovered a way to do it. Maybe this will be the way.'

He drew her soft blue-gray sweater over her head, so that for a moment she was blinded. When she emerged, he gently teased up her hair with his fingertips.

'You should grow your hair,' he told her. 'You would look like a dryad with long hair. Free and wild. A child of nature.'

'Can we just—?'

'Of course.'

He tugged down the zipper at the side of her skirt, and unfastened the hook and eye. She stepped out of it, so that she was standing in front of him in nothing but her blue lacy bra and black pantyhose. He kissed her forehead, although she didn't want kisses, in the same way that prostitutes never wanted kisses. This was business, not love. At least she supposed it was business. She began to feel light-headed and disoriented, as if she hadn't eaten for two days.

With his long, chilly fingers, Richard Vuldus released the catch of her bra. Her breasts were small and rounded and high – drum majorettes' breasts, Tony used to call them. Richard Vuldus touched her nipples and they crinkled and stiffened.

'You should imagine now that we have been friends for a very long time,' he murmured. 'Maybe we knew each other at college. We were never lovers, but looked at each other from time to time and knew that if things had turned out differently, we might have been. Now, tonight, many years later, we have met again by accident.'

He slipped his fingers inside the waistband of her pantyhose and gently tugged them down to her thighs. He cupped the cheeks of her bottom in both hands, and then he let his left hand stray round to her vulva. One long middle finger slipped between her lips, touching her clitoris so lightly that she barely felt it, but it was so cold that she became aware of her own wetness. She shivered – but against all of her instincts, she was aroused.

He lowered her into a sitting position on the bed. Then he knelt down in front of her, and drew her pantyhose all the way down and off her feet. As he did so, he took hold of each foot and kissed it in turn, his fingers working their way between her toes, his thumb pressing deep her insteps. She had gone to a reflexologist once, to relieve her tension, but she had never had her feet massaged like this before. Every time the ball of his thumb rolled around the bottom of her foot, she felt as if he were kneading her perineum, between her vagina and her anus, and the sensation was almost unbearably erotic. She began to feel delirious with pleasure.

He stood up, and leaned over her, and kissed her forehead. She found herself tilting her head back so that she could kiss his neck, and then his chin, and then his lips.

'There is such darkness in the world,' he whispered. 'There is darkness so deep that sometimes we have despaired of ever finding our way out of it. But tonight you and I will light a light, no matter how small, and everything will gradually brighten, and we will see again.'

'Kiss me,' she said, and as he kissed her, she plunged her hands into the soft blackness of his robes, and felt his body underneath, his hard muscles, his ribs, his hips.

He straightened up, and drew the robes over his head like the great black shadow of a raven flying overhead. The robes fell softly on to the floor and he was naked in the lamplight. He was wide-shouldered, but his stomach was very flat, and Helen could see the definition of every pectoral and deltoid and biceps as if he were a living diagram of the human body. He was completely hairless – no chest hair, no underarm hair, no pubic hair – and his skin was smooth and faintly luminous, with a pattern of those darker patches down his sides and around his thighs.

His penis was fully erect now, and it was enormous, with a gaping plum-colored glans, already glistening with fluid. Helen reached out and took hold of the shaft, and gripped it tight, and his distended veins felt like the twisted creepers around a tree trunk.

She lifted her head, so that she could kiss his penis, but he gripped her shoulder and pressed her back. 'Not that way,' he said. 'We must conserve everything we can.'

She said, 'You're incredible. I never met a man like you before. Ever.'

He climbed on to the bed next to her. He said nothing, but firmly turned her over on to her stomach. Then he knelt behind her and took hold of her hips and lifted her into a crouching position.

'I am the father of your child,' he said. 'I am nothing more than that.'

With that, he parted the cheeks of her bottom with his thumbs, and positioned the head of his penis between the lips of her vulva. Helen lowered her head. She felt as if the pattern on the quilt were alive, and that its swirls and curlicues were crawling underneath her like green-and-crimson centipedes.

Richard Vuldus slowly pushed his erection inside her, and it felt so large that she couldn't help herself from gasping. He drew himself out again, hesitated for a second, and then pushed himself inside her a second time, so deeply that she could feel his naked testicles against her lips.

God, she had never had sex like this before, ever, with anybody. She almost felt as if she were going mad. The blood pumped through her head so hard that she could hear it, and she started to tremble. Not only was her body completely naked, but her soul, too. She felt subjugated, dominated, but lusted-after, and needed. She pressed her head down against the pillow and reached behind her with both hands, spreading the cheeks of her bottom even wider so that Richard Vuldus could penetrate her deeper. There was a brutal urgency in Richard Vuldus' love-making, and he forced his penis into her faster and faster. She was so wet that they were both smothered in slippery juice.

Helen could feel an orgasm beginning to rise between her legs, and her thighs started to quiver. She squeezed her eyes shut and gritted her teeth and gripped the quilt tight. All the same, it hit her before she expected it, like a huge black locomotive coming out of the darkness with its headlight glaring and its whistle screaming.

'*Ahhhh*!' she shouted. '*Ohmygod ohymygod aaahhhhhh*!'

As Helen quaked and jumped, Richard Vuldus climaxed too. She actually felt the glans of his penis bulging, and the first spurt of sperm. He pumped again, and again, and again, as if he had been storing up this semen for years, and could at last release it, every drop of it, and find relief.

He continued to kneel behind her for a few seconds, his hands grasping her hips, but then he slowly rolled over and lay on his back. Helen rolled over, too, and lay close beside him.

'You, Richard Vuldus, are simply amazing.' She reached out to touch his lips with her fingertip.

He took hold of her wrist and moved her hand away, gently but firmly. 'This was not for love, Helen. Not my love for you, nor your love for me. This was for justice, and revenge.'

She stared at him, and then she sat up. 'You mean to tell me that meant *nothing* to you?'

'It meant everything. More than you can know.'

She hesitated for a moment. Then she climbed off the bed and retrieved her clothes from the floor.

'Thank you, Helen,' he said, softly.

She pulled her sweater over her head. 'Don't mention it. I'll let you know if you've succeeded in knocking me up.'

When she left the apartment, Joachim Hochheimer took hold of her hand, and tried to raise it to his lips, but Helen pulled herself away.

'Thank you, *gnädige Fraulein*,' he said. 'We are forever in your debt.'

Toward the end of January, she began to feel tired, and her breasts began to feel swollen, but she was still not convinced that Richard Vuldus had succeeded in making her pregnant. He had made love to her only once, after all; and besides that, she was beginning to convince herself that she had dreamed the whole incident. She had gone back to Fountain Square several times during the evening, and she had seen no lights in the Vuldus apartment. She had called Joachim Hochheimer, too, but nobody had picked up.

'What's bugging you?' Klaus asked her, as they sat in First Watch café one morning, eating bacado omelets and drinking horseshoe coffee.

'Please?'

'I said, what's bugging you? You haven't heard a word I've been saying.'

'I don't know. Sorry. I feel weird.'

They had driven only a few blocks down Walnut Street before she tugged at his coat and said, 'Stop the car! Stop the car, please!'

She just managed to open the door and lean over the gutter before she was sick – half-chewed bacon and avocado and eggs, in a steaming gravy of hot coffee.

That evening, she took a home pregnancy test, and yes, it was positive. She stood staring at herself in her bathroom mirror. My God, what have I done? What kind of a baby is growing inside me?

She went back into the bedroom and sat on the edge of the bed. At that moment the phone rang.

'Detective Foxley? Helen? This is Joachim Hochheimer speaking.'

'Oh, yes?'

'Everything is well, yes?'

'It depends on your point of view, Mr Hochheimer.'

'You are expecting Richard's child, is what I mean.'

'Yes, Mr Hochheimer.'

'Thank you, dear lady, from the bottom of my heart.'

She put the phone down. Almost immediately, it rang again.

'Foxley? It's Klaus. S.O.B. has done it again.'

'Where?'

'The Serpentine Wall, Yeatman's Cove. Do you want to meet me down there?'

'On my way.'

She pulled on her sweater and took her duffel coat out of the closet. She was just about to leave the apartment when her stomach tightened and she felt a rising surge of nausea. She hurried into the bathroom, knelt down in front of the toilet, and brought up a fountain of chili and Cheddar cheese.

Klaus said, 'You're *pregnant*? You're kidding me? By whom? You didn't tell me you had a new boyfriend.'

'It's nobody I've ever talked about.'

'So what are you going to do? You're not going to *have* the kid, surely? How are you going to be a single mom and a detective at the same time? I mean – I'm assuming that the guy isn't going to marry you. Maybe he is.'

'No, he's not going to marry me.'

Klaus swirled the remains of his beer around his glass and shook his head. 'You're full of surprises, Foxley. I have to give you that.'

'I surprise myself, most of the time.'

'Well,' said Klaus, 'just make sure that you check with me before you choose your maternity clinic.'

'Why's that?'

He took a roughly scrawled diagram out of his inside pocket. 'I may be wrong, but I've been looking into the records of the various clinics which were attended by Son of Beast's victims. There's nothing in any of them to suggest that Son of Beast could have hacked into any medical records. But today I realized that his eighth victim was a patient at the same clinic as his first victim, and his ninth victim was a patient at the same clinic as his second victim, and so on. It appears to me that he has a list of seven clinics and that he's picking his victims from each clinic in rotation. I could be wrong, but it's beginning to look like a pattern.'

Helen took the diagram and frowned at it. 'So he wouldn't necessarily need any access to medical records. He simply goes to the next clinic on his list and follows his victim out of the building when she leaves.'

'It's beginning to look that way.'

'But why should he do that? That means that we can predict which clinic he's going to pick his next victim from, and we can stake it out.'

'That's right. And the next one is . . . The Christ Hospital on Auburn.'

But when winter melted away, so did Son of Beast. After the killing of a thirty-one-year-old mother-to-be at Yeatman's Cove, there were no more Moms-to-Be murders for seven months, and they began to wonder if he had given up, or left Cincinnati for good.

Eventually, Colonel Melville decided that the stake-out at The Christ Hospital was no longer cost-effective, and assigned the surveillance team to other duties.

For Helen, that summer seemed to last for ever, one sweltering day after another, week after week, month after month. The city was suffocating, and this year there was a teeming plague of cicadas, sawing away noisily day and night, and penetrating every crevice of every building, cramming themselves into office ventilation systems, and tangling themselves in people's hair. The windshield of Helen's Pontiac was permanently smeared with cicada guts.

Meanwhile, the baby inside her grew and grew. Her sickness passed, but she still felt exhausted, especially when the baby started to wriggle and heave inside her all night. Every Thursday afternoon she went to The Christ Hospital, waited for fifteen minutes in the ladies' room, reading a book, and then left. If Son of Beast were still in the city, watching and waiting for his next opportunity, she wanted to make sure that she gave him a victim with regular patterns of behavior.

She didn't actually attend the maternity clinic. This birth had to be off the books, unregistered. All the same, she bought books on pregnancy and made sure that she took plenty of vitamins and kept her blood pressure down. She developed a desperate craving for five-way chili – spaghetti, chili, cheese, kidney beans and onions – and she found it a daily struggle to keep her weight down.

It was a lonely time. She kept away from her friends and her family because she wanted as few of them as possible to know that she was expecting a baby. And as the months went by, and Son of Beast failed to reappear, it seemed to be increasingly likely that she had suffered this pregnancy for no purpose.

Only Klaus came round regularly to see her, and each time he brought her flowers, or a box of candies. In August, when she was eight months' pregnant, he brought her a little blue-and-white knitted suit, with a hood.

'How do you know it's going to be a boy?' she asked him.

'Because I can't imagine you having a girl.'

On a thundery afternoon in the first week of September she drove up to The Christ Hospital as usual and parked her car. It was only four thirty p.m. but the sky was black, and lightning was flickering over the hills. She was walking toward the hospital entrance when she noticed a man in a gray raincoat standing under the trees. She made a point of not looking at him directly, but when she went through the revolving doors into the hospital lobby, she quickly turned her head, and she could see that he had been watching her.

She went to the ladies' room and sat in one of the cubicles. Baby was being hyperactive today, churning and turning inside her. There was no reason to suppose that the man in the gray raincoat was Son of Beast, but somehow she felt that the time had arrived, that the cogs of her destiny were all beginning to click into place. Baby turned over again, and she began to feel deeply apprehensive.

She waited for twenty minutes. Then she left the ladies' room and walked across the lobby and out of the revolving door. It was raining, hard, so that the asphalt driveway in front of the hospital was dancing with spray. There was no sign of the man in the gray raincoat.

She pulled up her hood and hurried toward the parking lot as fast as she could. Lightning crackled, almost directly overhead, followed by a deafening barrage of thunder. She reached her car and unlocked the door, and was just about to climb in when somebody's arm wrapped itself around her neck and lifted her upward and backward, throttling her.

'You're going to do what I tell you!' said a thick, sinus-blocked voice.

'I gah – my baby – *gah* – can't—!'

'You're going to come around to the back of the car and you're going to open the trunk and you're going to climb in. You got that?'

'I can't – breathe – can't—!'

With his right hand, the man reached around and twisted her car keys away from her. 'If you don't do what I say, I'm going to cut your belly right open, here and now. Give me your cell.'

'Please – I – *gah*—'

'Are you going to do what I tell you? Give me your cell!'

The man was compressing her larynx so hard that Helen could see nothing but scarlet, and stars. She fumbled in her pocket and took out her cellphone, and handed it to him.

'You're going to do what I tell you, right? And you're not going to scream, and you're not going to try to run away?'

She nodded.

The man shuffled her round to the back of the car, as if they were a clumsy pair of dancing partners.

'Open the trunk. Go on, open the trunk. Now get in there. Hurry it up, before somebody sees you. And don't try anything stupid.'

Awkwardly, she lifted one foot into the trunk. As she did so, however, she twisted around and yanked her gun out from under her coat.

'*Freeze*!' she screamed. But the man was too close to her, and far too quick. He grabbed her wrist with both hands and twisted it around so hard that it ripped her tendons, and the gun clattered on to the ground.

'You're a *cop*?' he shouted at her. 'You're a fucking *cop*?'

He pushed her violently into the trunk, next to the spare wheel, and shoved her head down.

'You've been trying to trap me? Is that it? You got yourself pregnant on purpose, just to trap me?'

Helen tried to lift her head but he jammed it down again. Then he slammed the trunk lid and she was left in darkness.

She heard him climb into the driver's seat and start the engine. Then he pulled out of the hospital parking-lot and made his way toward Auburn Avenue. As he drove, Helen was swung right and left and jostled up and down. She tried to work out which direction he was taking, and how far they had driven, but after a while she gave up.

He seemed to drive her for hours, and for miles. But at last he slowed down, almost to a crawl, and she could hear traffic, and sirens, and people's footsteps. He must have taken her downtown, to the city center.

He turned, and turned again, and then she felt a bump, and the car drove slowly down a steep, winding gradient. An underground parking facility, she guessed.

At last the car stopped, and she heard the man climbing out. The trunk opened, and he was standing there, looking down at her, a fortyish man with gray hair and a heavy gray moustache. He had a broad face which reminded Helen of one of her uncles, but he had piggy little eyes and thick, purplish lips, as if he had been eating too many blueberries.

He had brought her down to what looked like the lower level of an office building. It was gloomy and cold, with dripping concrete walls and a single fluorescent light that kept flickering and buzzing as if it were just about to burn out.

'All right,' the man ordered her. 'Out.'

'You're not going to hurt my baby?'

'What do you care?'

'You can do whatever you like, but please don't hurt my baby.'

'Oh, my heart bleeds. When did any woman ever really care about her baby? Now – *out*.'

Helen climbed out of the trunk. The man reached up to pull down the lid, and as he did so, Helen dodged to the left, and started to run. Almost immediately, however, he caught up with her, and seized her arm, and tripped her up. She fell on to her back on the rough concrete floor, her head narrowly missing the rear bumper of a parked Toyota.

She twisted and struggled, but the man clambered astride her and pressed her down against the floor, with his knees on her upper arms. He was very heavy and strong, and even though she had graduated best in her class in unarmed combat, she found it impossible to throw him off.

'Women—' he panted. 'You conceive babies, don't you, but you only give birth to them so long as it suits you. You don't give a shit about human life. All that matters to you is your own convenience. In fact – *you* – you're worse. You've used your baby to try to trap me. You don't even care that your baby is going to die, when you die. How fucking sick is that?'

'Please—' Helen begged him.

But the man lifted her head and banged it hard against the concrete. Then he banged it again, and again, until she was half concussed and she could feel the wetness of blood in her hair.

He took a roll of Saran Wrap out of his coat pocket, and he pulled it out and stretched it over her face. She was so stunned that she couldn't stop him. She tried to take a breath, but all she managed to do was suck the cling wrap tighter.

The man wrapped her head around and around. Helen couldn't move and she couldn't breathe and she could barely see. The man loomed over her as if he were in a fog.

In spite of her training, she panicked. She thrashed her head from side to side and kicked her legs. But the man opened her coat, and dragged up her blue corduroy maternity dress, and then he pulled her pantyhose down around her ankles. Her blood was thumping in her ears, and all she could hear was a deep, distorted echo, as if she were lying at the bottom of a swimming pool.

She couldn't see the man unbutton his own coat, but she felt him lever her thighs apart. He pushed his way inside her with three grunting thrusts, until he was buried deep. Then he leaned forward and stared at her through the cling wrap, his face only an inch away from hers. He looked triumphant.

Suddenly, she felt a warm gush of wetness between her thighs. At the same time, there was turmoil inside her stomach, as if the baby were rolling right over. The man screamed like a girl and pushed against her chest.

'*Aaagghhh*! Christ! Let go of me! Let go of me! *For Christ's sake you witch let go of me*!'

Helen felt an agonizing spasm, and then another, and then another. The man kept on screaming and cursing and trying to pull himself out of her. Helen tore at the Saran Wrap covering her face, and managed to rip most of it away. She took a deep swallow of air, but then she started screaming, too. The pain in her back was more than she could bear. She felt as if she were being cracked in half.

There was a moment when she and the man were locked together in purgatory, both of them shrieking at each other. But then suddenly the man managed to heave himself backward, and Helen felt her baby slither out of her. The man fell on to his side, crying and whimpering, his heels kicking against the concrete.

Helen sat up. She was so stunned that everything looked jumbled and unfocused, but she could see that the man was fighting to pull something away from him.

'*Get it off me*! *Get it off me*! *Get it off me*!'

She held on to the Toyota's bumper and tried to pull herself up. Gradually, her vision began to clear, and what she saw made her slowly sit back down, quaking with horror.

Between the man's legs, biting his penis right down to the root, was a black bladder-like creature with glistening skin. It was the same size as a newborn baby, but it wasn't human at all.

The man was slapping it and pulling it, but it was obviously too slippery for him to get any grip, and the thing was stretching and contracting as if it were sucking at him.

'*Christ, get this off me*!' the man screamed, and it was more of a prayer than a cry for help.

In front of Helen's eyes the black bladder-like creature swelled larger and larger, and as it did so, the man's struggling became weaker and jerkier. After only a few minutes he gave an epileptic shudder and his head dropped back, with his neck bulging. But the creature wasn't finished with him yet. It continued its stretching and contracting for almost twenty minutes more, its formless body growing more and more distended, until it was nearly the same size as he was. Then it rolled off him with a wallowing sound like a waterbed and lay beside him, unmoving.

Helen felt another twinge of pain, and another, but after a third contraction her afterbirth slithered out. It was black, and warty, unlike any afterbirth she had ever seen before. She kicked it away, underneath a car. If there had been anything in her stomach, she would have vomited.

After what seemed like hours, she managed to stand up. She crept over to the man and looked down at him. He looked like a parody of a man, made out of pale brown paper, like a broken hornet's nest. Even his eyeballs had been drained of all their fluid, so that they were flat.

She sat down again, resting her back against a pillar. What the hell was she going to do now? She could retrieve her cell from the dead man's body and call Klaus. But how was she going to explain what had happened here?

She looked at the creature. She doubted if it was going to lie there for very much longer, digesting the fluids that it had sucked from its prey. What was she going to do with it if it started moving again?

She heard the sound of a vehicle driving down the ramp. A black panel-van came around the corner, its tires squealing, and stopped a few yards away from her, with its headlights full on. The doors opened and Joachim Hochheimer appeared, closely followed by Richard Vuldus, both wearing long black coats.

'My dear lady,' said Joachim Hochheimer, reaching out his hand to help Helen to her feet. 'How are you feeling?'

'How did you know that I was here?' she croaked. Her throat was so dry that she could barely speak.

'We have been following you every day, ever since you became pregnant.'

'I never saw you.'

'Well, let us say that after all of these centuries of persecution, we have learned how not to be noticed.'

Richard Vuldus went straight over to the creature and hunkered down beside it, laying his hand on it with pride and awe.

'We have done it, Joachim! At last we have purified the genes.'

Helen took Joachim Hochheimer's elbow, for support. 'What *is* that disgusting thing?' she asked him. 'I thought I was carrying a baby all that time . . . not a thing like that. I feel sick to my stomach.'

'You shouldn't be revolted, Detective. It is not a baby, no, but a horseleech, *hirudo medicinalis*. The Vuldus family have been trying for generations to return to their original form, and with your help they have achieved their aim at last. This horseleech will now breed others, with the size and intelligence of humans, but all the qualities of a leech.'

'But how is it going to survive? Where is it going to live?'

'Caesar Creek lake. It covers two thousand eight hundred acres, and there are dozens of inlets where it can conceal itself, and flourish. Richard, you must help me lift it into the van, before its skin dries out too much.'

'And what about *him*?' asked Helen, nodding at the flattened body of Son of Beast.

'Don't worry . . . we will dispose of him for you. He will vanish as if he had never been born.'

Joachim Hochheimer helped Helen to climb into her car, while Richard Vuldus retrieved her keys and her cell from Son of Beast's coat. He gave her his wallet, too. Helen opened it and found six tickets for the roller-coaster ride, and a Kentucky driver's license in the name of Ronald M. Breen. But there was no doubt that the man in the ID photograph was Henry Clarke, one-time realtor of Smith Road, Norwood.

'You have our deepest gratitude,' said Richard Vuldus.

'Sure,' said Helen. She started the engine and backed up. Richard Vuldus raised one hand to her, in salute, but she didn't wave back. She drove up the ramp, out of the parking lot, and into the afternoon rain.

She drove slowly back home to Walnut Street, trembling, with tears streaming down her cheeks.

GIRL WAS 'SUCKED DRY' SAYS CORONER

A seventeen-year-old girl Waynesville girl whose body was recovered from Caesar Creek Lake early yesterday was said by the Hamilton County Coroner to have been completely drained of all her blood and all bodily fluids.

Dr Kenneth Deane was at a loss to explain what had happened to her, but said there was evidence that she had been bitten by a 'very large aquatic creature with serrated teeth.'

Cincinnati Post, March 17.

Anti-Claus

It was the bitterest October for eleven years. An ice storm swept down from Canada across northern Minnesota and didn't let up for nine days and nine nights, which meant that Jerry and I had no choice but to book a couple of rooms at the Sturgeon Motel in Roseau, population 2,633, and wait until the weather cleared.

We spent most of the time in the North Star Bar, talking to the locals and listening to country songs about miserable trappers and women who wouldn't stay faithful. Outside the world was being blasted with ice, so that power lines snapped and trucks got stranded because their fuel had turned into wax and people went temporarily blind because their eyeballs froze over.

Jerry was as placid as a fireside dog and didn't seem to care if he spent the rest of his life in the North Star Bar, but I started to get cabin fever after only two days. I just wanted to get on with the job and get back to my family in St Paul. I called Jenny twice a day, and talked to the kids, too, Tracey and Mikey, but their voices sounded so tiny and far away that it only made the isolation seem sharper.

Most of the time we talked to the barmaid, Alma Lindenmuth. She had piled-up bleached-blonde hair with the roots showing and a thick, cigarette-smoke voice. She wore a studded denim shirt which showed a lot of cleavage and she smelled of Tommy Girl and something else, sex I guess, like burying your face in the sheets the morning after.

'You guys shouldn't of come up here in the fall, you should of come in August when it's real warm and beautiful and you can fish and everything.'

'Well, we didn't come to enjoy ourselves. We're doing a survey for the Minnesota Forestry Department.'

'Can't you enjoy yourselves just a little bit?'

'Oh, *I* can,' said Jerry, with one eye closed against his dangling cigarette. 'But Jack here, he's married, with two young kids. Enjoyment *verboten*.'

Alma leaned forward on the bar, provocatively squashing her mole-spattered breasts together. 'Do you know how to merengue?' she asked Jerry.

'Sure, I can cook anything.'

We also talked to an old guy who sat at the far end of the bar knocking back Jack Daniel's one shot glass after the other, one shot every ten minutes, give or take. He wore a wild, high-combed gray hairpiece which looked older than he was, and had a skinny, emaciated face with white prickles of stubble where he couldn't shave into the creases. He was dressed entirely in black, and his eyes were black, too, like excavations to the center of the earth.

'So you've come up here to do what?' he wanted to know, without even looking at us.

'A survey, that's all. The Forestry Department wants to cut down a few thousand acres of jack pine and pitch pine and replace them with white pine and Austrian pine.'

'Why do they want to do that for?'

'Because white pine and Austrian pine are much more commercially profitable.'

'Ah, money. Might have guessed it. And so where are you doing this survey of yours, precisely?'

'Up in the Lost River Forest, mainly, between here and the border.'

'Up near Saint Nicholas?'

'That's right. Saint Nicholas and Pineroad.'

The old man gave a dry sniff and pushed his shot glass forward for a refill. 'Know why they called it Saint Nicholas?'

'I don't have any idea.'

'They called it Saint Nicholas because that's where Santa Claus originated from.'

'Oh, really? I thought Santa Claus came from Lapland or someplace like that.'

'North Pole, isn't it?' put in Jerry, and gave his distinctive little whoop.

The old man turned to me and there was something in his expression that was deeply unsettling. I had only seen that look once before in my life, when a farmer drove up to me in his Jeep when I was carrying out a survey in Lac qui Parle, and came toward me with a pump-action shotgun like he really intended to use it. He said, hoarsely, 'There's Santa Claus the story and then there's the real Santa Claus. The real Santa Claus lived on his own in a cabin on the Sad Dog River.'

'Oh, sure,' said Jerry. 'So how come he turns up every year at Dayton's department store?'

The old man knocked back his refill and pushed over his shot glass for another. 'You want to learn something or don't you?'

'Go on, then,' I encouraged him, and gave Jerry a quick shake of my head to indicate that he should keep his smart remarks to himself.

The old man said, 'This was just before the turn of the century when there was only five or six hundred people living in Roseau. Life was pretty much touch and go in those days, and in 1898 the spring wheat harvest failed and some of the farm families were pretty close to starvation. But this guy turned up one day, just like out of nowhere, and said that he could change their fortunes if they agreed to give him ten percent off the top.

'Of course they didn't believe him but he went out into the fields and he performed this kind of ritual on every farm, with bones and smoke and circles drawn in the dirt. He did this every week for the whole season, until the farmers came to accept him like they would the veterinary surgeon or the milk-collection man.

'He set up home in a shack, deep in the tangly woods by the Sad Dog oxbow, and he painted that shack as black as night, and nobody knew what tricks he got up to, when he was alone, but some people say they heard screaming and shouting and roaring coming from out of that shack like all the demons in hell. The local preacher said that he was an emissary of Satan, and that no good would come of all of his rituals, and behind his back that was what the people of Roseau started to call him, Satan, even though they carried on allowing him to visit their farms with his bones and his smoke because they was superstitious as well as religious and if he really could make their wheat grow, then they wasn't going to act prejudicial toward him.

'Well, the upshot was that the winter harvest was the very best ever, and they brought in more than forty thousand bushels of hard red wheat. They rang the church bell and they gave their thanks to the Lord. But that was when Satan came around asking for his ten per cent off the top.

'Of course none of the farmers would give him nothing. They said that bones and smoke and patterns in the dirt was jiggery-pokery, that was all, and that God had provided, God and good fortune, and a long warm summer. So Satan said OK, if you won't give me my due, then I'll take it. I can't walk off with four thousand bushels of wheat, so I'll help myself to whatever takes my fancy.'

Alma Lindenmuth came up and filled the old man's glass again. 'This one's on me,' I told her.

'John Shooks, you're not spinning that old Santa story, is he? He tells it to everybody who's too polite to shut him up.'

'Hey, it's a very entertaining story,' said Jerry.

'I could entertain you better than that.'

'I'll bet you could. But we're not pressed for time, are we?'

'That's what the people of Roseau thought,' the old man remarked. 'But they had no time left at all.'

'So what did he do, this Satan?' I asked him.

'On the night of December tenth, 1898, he went from one farm to the next, five farms in all, and he was riding on a black sled drawn by eight black dogs and he was carrying a sack. Several people saw him but nobody guessed what he was up to. All but one of the farms had locked their doors and windows, which was pretty much unheard of in those days, but mostly everybody in Roseau had taken Satan's threat to heart and they wanted to make sure that he didn't lay hands on any of their hard-earned property.

'But it wasn't property he was looking for, and he didn't take no notice of their locks. He climbed on to their rooftops and he broke a hole through the shingles and he climbed down into their children's bedrooms. Remember they had big families in those days, and in one house alone there was seven kids. He cut their heads off with a sickle, all of them, regardless of age, and he stowed the heads in his sack and off he went to his next destination.

'Nobody knows how he managed to break into those houses without anybody hearing him, or how he killed so many kids without waking up the others. But he murdered twenty-seven in all, and took all of their heads. Worst of all, he was never caught. Of course they sent out a sheriff's posse to hunt him down, and for a few miles they could follow his tracks in the snow. But right on the edge of the woods the tracks petered out, and the dogs lost his scent, and the sheriff had to admit that Satan had gotten clean away. The posse went to his shack and they ransacked it and then they burned it down to the ground, but that was all they could do. Satan was never seen again and neither was the children's heads.'

'You won't read about that night in any of the local history books, and you can understand why. But when it's Christmas time, parents in Roseau still tell their children that they'd better be good, and that they'd better pay up what they owe, whether it's money or favors, because Satan will come through the ceiling with his sickle looking for his ten percent off the top.'

'Well, that's some yarn,' I admitted.

'You think it's a yarn and you don't believe it, but Santa is only Satan spelled wrong, and two Decembers back we had some professor up here from Washington, DC, because the FBI was investigating nine children who had their heads whopped off in Iowa someplace and she said that the mode-ass operandy was exactly the same as the Sad Dog Satan.'

'That *is* interesting.'

'Sure it's interesting, but I'll tell you what the clincher is. This professor said the same mode-ass operandy has been used for hundreds of years even further back than Saint Nicholas himself, which is why I say that the Sad Dog Satan is the real Santa and not your bearded fat guy with the reindeers and the bright red suit, although you can see why the story got changed so that kids wouldn't be scared shitless. The real Santa comes at night and he climbs through your roof and takes your kids' heads off and carries them away in his sack, and that's not mythology, that's the truth.'

Jerry lifted his empty glass to show Alma Lindenmuth that he was ready for another. Alma Lindenmuth said, 'Same old story, over and over.'

'It's a great story. And that never occurred to me before, you know, Santa being a palindrome of Satan.'

'It's an anagram,' I corrected him. 'Not a palindrome. A palindrome is the same backward as it is forward.'

Jerry winked at Alma Lindenmuth and said, 'You're forward, Alma. How about doing it backward?'

* * *

On the tenth night the storm cleared and by morning the sun was shining on the ice and there was even a drip on the nose of Roseau's founder, Martin Braaten, standing in the town square with one of those pioneering looks on his face.

Jerry and I said goodbye to Alma Lindenmuth and John Shooks and we drove northward on 310 into the Lost River Forest. It was a brilliant, sparkling day and we had two flasks of hot coffee and fresh-baked donuts and everything seemed pretty good with the world. Jerry seemed particularly pleased with himself and I guessed that Alma Lindenmuth had paid him a farewell visit last night at the Sturgeon Hotel.

Saint Nicholas wasn't much of a place, only five houses and a gas station, but it did have an airfield. We had rented a helicopter from Lost River Air Services so that we could take a look at the forests from the air, and make some outline recommendations to the Forestry Department about the prime sites for felling and replanting. Mostly we were looking for sheltered southern slopes where the young saplings would be protected from the north-west winds, giving us quicker growth and a quicker return on the state's investment.

The blue-and-white helicopter was waiting for us with its rotors idly turning. Jerry parked the Cherokee and we walked across the airfield with our eyes watering and our noses running and the dry snow whipping around our ankles.

The pilot was a morose old veteran with a wrinkly leather jacket and a wrinkly leather face. 'You can call me Bub,' he announced.

'That's great,' said Jerry. 'I'm Bob and this is my pal Bib.'

The pilot eyed him narrowly. 'You pulling my chain, son?'

'No sir, Bub.'

We climbed into the helicopter and buckled up and Bub took us up almost immediately, while Jerry unfolded the maps. 'We want to fly west-north-west to the Roseau River and then south-south-west to Pierce's Peak.'

We triangulated the Lost River Forest for over three and a half hours, taking photographs and videos and shading in our maps with thick green crayons. At last I said, 'That's it, Bub. I think we're just about done for today. Are you OK for tomorrow, though, just in case we need to double-check anything?'

'So long as the weather holds off.'

We were heading back toward Saint Nicholas when Jerry suddenly touched me on the shoulder and pointed downward off our starboard side. 'See that? The Sad Dog River oxbow. That's where Satan had his shack.'

I turned to Bub and shouted, 'Can you take us down lower?'

'You're paying.'

The land was flat and scrubby here, and the Sad Dog River squiggled its way across the plain before dividing itself into an oxbow. In the middle of the oxbow, I could make out the ruins of an old shack, with only its stone chimney left standing. The river ran on either side of it, shining in the two o'clock sunlight like two streams of molten metal.

'Let's take a look!' I yelled.

'You want to land?'

'Sure, just for a couple of minutes.'

'Bib's thinking of buying this place for a summer home,' put in Jerry.

Bub angled the helicopter around the trees and landed only fifty feet away from the shack. Jerry and I climbed out and approached the shack with our coat collars turned up. It had been burned right down to the floorboards, so it was impossible to tell if it had ever been painted black, but because most of the timbers had been reduced to charcoal they hadn't rotted. The roof had fallen in, and there was nothing left of the door but a corroded metal catch, but there was still a wheelback chair beside the fireplace, burned but intact, as if it were still waiting for its owner to return home.

'What are you actually looking for?' asked Jerry, clapping himself with his arms to keep himself warm.

'I don't know . . . I just wanted to see the place, that's all. I mean, if the stable where Jesus was born was still standing, you'd want to take a look at that, too, wouldn't you?'

'This place gives me the creeps.'

I looked around and I had to admit that the Sad Dog River oxbow was a pretty desolate location. Bub had shut off the helicopter's engine and the quietness was overwhelming. The Sad Dog River itself was so shallow that it barely gurgled, and there were no birds singing in the trees. All I could hear was the fluffing of the wind in my ears. A crow fluttered down and perched on the back of the wheelback chair, staring at us with its head on one side, but it didn't croak, and after a while it flapped off again.

I had the unsettling feeling that somebody had walked up behind me, and was standing very close to me, staring at me.

'Come on,' said Jerry. 'I'm in serious need of a drink.'

We were walking back to the helicopter when Jerry stumbled. 'You got it wrong again,' I told him. 'It's drink first, *then* fall over.'

'Goddamned tripped on something.'

He went back and kicked at the tufty grass. Then suddenly he hunkered down, and took out his clasp knife, and started to dig.

'What have you got there?'

'Some kind of a handle.'

He kept on digging out chunks of turf and at last he exposed a rectangular metal box with a rusted metal handle. He tugged it, and tugged it again, and at last he managed to wrench it free.

'The lost treasure of the Sad Dog River Satan,' he announced.

'OK . . . let's see what it is.'

The box was locked, and the lock was thickly rusted, but Bub found a long screwdriver and after considerable cursing and grunting we managed to pry the lid open. Inside was a soft gray cloth, in which a collection of bones were carefully wrapped; and seven glass jars containing some kind of powder; and five blackened sleigh-bells. Jerry lifted up one of the glass jars and peered at the handwritten label. 'Human Dust'.

Bub said, 'What is it, magic-making stuff?'

'It looks like it. Did you ever hear of the Satan of Sad Dog River?'

Bub shook his head. 'Wasn't brung up in these parts. Came from Sweet Home, Oregon, me.'

'He was supposed to have lived in that shack. Killed twenty-seven children by cutting their heads off.'

'No shit.'

Jerry closed the box and said, 'Let's go find that drink. I reckon this could be worth something. You know, maybe the Roseau town museum might be interested in buying it.'

'You think so? They don't even want to *talk* about what happened that night, let alone commemorate it.'

We took the rusty old box back to Roseau and showed it to John Shooks.

'There,' he said, picking over its contents with undisguised triumph. 'Told you it wasn't mythology.'

Alma Lindenmuth puckered up her nose in disgust. 'It all looks horrible. What are you going to do with it?'

'Sell it, most likely,' said Jerry.

'Not in Roseau you won't,' said John Shooks. 'That'd be like trying to sell bits of airplane wreck to the people in New York.'

'I think maybe we should find out exactly what all of this is,' I suggested. 'I mean, if the Sad Dog River Satan used it to make the wheat crop grow, how did it work?'

Jerry said, 'He was lucky with the weather, that's all. You don't seriously think that human dust and old bones can give you a bumper cereal crop?'

'I'd just be interested to know what kind of a ritual he was carrying out. And don't be so dismissive. I saw a TV documentary about a Modoc wonder-worker once, and *he* used bones and powders and circles in the dirt. He brought on a rainstorm in under an hour, and it went on raining for three weeks solid.'

'Oh, please. What was that, the Discovery Channel?'

'OK, but I still think we ought to look into it. Suppose it can help us to make pines grow quicker?'

'Good soil, good light, regular rainfall, that's what makes pines grow quicker.' Jerry lifted out the jars of powder one by one. 'Not Crushed Mirror, Rowan Ash, Medlar Flower, Houndstongue, Sulfur Salt and Dry Frog Blood.'

'Well, sure, you're probably right,' I told him. But I still couldn't shake off the feeling that had crept over me by that burned-out shack on the Sad Dog River, like somebody coming up close behind me and breathing on my neck.

We were called back to St Paul the following afternoon. Since there seemed to be no prospect of making any ready cash out of Satan's box, Jerry let me have it. I wrapped it up in a copy of the *Roseau Times-Region* and packed it in my suitcase along with my cable-knit sweaters.

Even in the city it was minus five and when I drove back out to Maplewood my neighbors were clearing a fresh fall of snow from their driveways. We lived in a small development close to Maplewood golf course, just six houses in a private loop. I parked outside and Jenny opened the door wearing jeans and a red reindeer sweater, her blonde hair shining in the winter sun. Tracey and Mikey came running out after her, and it was just like one of those family reunions you used to see on the cover of *The Saturday Evening Post*.

My neighbor Ben Kellerman raised his woolly hat to me to reveal his bald dome and called out, 'Go back to your woods, Jack!' It was joke between us, based on some Robbie Robertson song about a hick trying to make it big in the city.

There was chicken pot-pie that night, and candied yams, and the house was warm and cozy. I took Tracey and Mikey upstairs at seven o'clock and sat on the end of Mikey's bed and read them a story about Santa Claus. Not the Santa Claus that John Shooks had told me about, but the jolly fat guy with the big white beard.

'When it's Christmas, I'm going to stay awake all night so that I can see Santa coming down the chimney,' said Mikey. He was seven and a half, with sticky-out ears. He was a whirlwind of energy during the day, but he could never keep his eyes open later than a quarter of nine.

'*I'm* going to bake him a Christmas cake,' said Tracey, sedately. She was such a pretty thing, skinny and small like her mother, with big gray eyes and wrists so thin that you could close your hand around them.

When the kids were tucked up in bed, Jenny and I sat in front of the fire with a bottle of red wine and talked. I told her all about Satan from Sad Dog River, and she shuddered. 'That's a *terrible* story.'

'Yes, but there must be some truth in it. After all, we found Satan's box of tricks, so even if he wasn't responsible for making the crops grow, he existed, at least.'

'I don't know why you brought the box back with you. It's *ghoulish*.'

'It's only a musty old collection of different powders, and bones.'

'What kind of bones?'

'How should I know? Dog's, probably.'

'Well, I don't want it in the house.'

'All right, I'll put it in the garage.'

'I don't know why you don't just throw it in the trash.'

'I want to find out more about it. I want to know what this Satan was actually trying to do.'

'Well, I don't. I think it's horrible.'

* * *

I put the box on my workbench at the back of the garage. I stood looking at it for a while before I switched off the light. It's difficult to explain, but it definitely had a *tension* about it, like the wheelback chair, as if it were waiting for its owner to come back and open it.

I locked the garage door and went up to bed. Jenny was waiting for me and she looked so fresh and she smelled so good. There's nothing to compare to a homecoming when you've been away for two weeks looking at trees and more trees.

When she fell asleep I lay awake next to her. A hazy moon was shining, and just after one o'clock in the morning it started to snow. I turned over and tried to sleep, but for some reason I couldn't, as tired as I was, as contented as I was.

Just after two o'clock I heard a rattling noise, somewhere downstairs. I sat up and listened, with my ears straining. Another rattle, and then another, and then silence. It sounded like somebody shaking dice.

I must have fallen asleep around three, but I dreamed that I could hear the rattling again, and so I climbed out of bed and made my way downstairs. The rattling was coming from the garage, no question about it. I pressed my ear against the door, listening and listening. I was just about to turn the key when the door was flung wide open, and a white-faced man was standing in the doorway, screaming at me.

I sat up in bed, sweating. The moon had passed the window and it had stopped snowing. I drank half a glass of water, and then I dragged the covers over me and tried to get back to sleep again. There was no more rattling, no more screaming, but I felt as if the house had been visited that night, although I couldn't understand by whom, or by *what*.

The next morning Jenny took the kids shopping at Marshall Field's, which gave me a chance to go into my study in my blue-striped robe and my rundown slippers and do some research on the Internet. I sipped hot black coffee while my PC looked for Santa and Satan and fertility rituals and crop circles.

I was surprised to find out how recently our modern idea of 'Santa Claus' was developed. Up until Clement Clark Moore published his poem *The Night Before Christmas*, Santa was almost always portrayed as a haggard, old Father Time figure, with an hourglass and a scythe – deeply threatening, rather than merry – the pall-bearer of the dying year. But Moore described him as 'chubby and plump, a right jolly old elf', and in the 1870s the illustrator Thomas Nast drew him as a white-bearded figure in a red suit with white fur trim. In the 1930s and 1940s, Haddon H. Sundblom, an advertising illustrator for Coca Cola, painted dozens of pictures of the grandfatherly Santa as we think of him today, with his red cap and his heavy belt and boots and his round, rosy cheeks. The gaunt, doomy Father Christmas – the *real* Father Christmas – was forgotten.

Much more cheerful, I guess, to tell your kids that Christmas is the time for lots of toys and candies and singing, rather than remind them that they're one year nearer their graves.

After I had checked out Santa, I went searching for any rituals involving Human Dust and Crushed Mirrors. It took me over an hour, but at last I turned up details of a ceremony that dated way back to the days of Nectanebo I, the last native ruler of Ancient Egypt, in 380 BC. Apparently, good king Nectanebo had an entourage of black magicians, who were employed to do deals with the gods. They were said to have derived their powers of sorcery from a god called Set, a dark and sinister being who is historically associated with Satan. It was Set who murdered the fertility god, Osiris, in order to steal his powers, and Set who blinded Horus, the Egyptian war god, which led to the invasion of Egypt by Assyria and Persia and other foreign invaders.

In the *Les Véritables Clavicules de Satan,* a fourteenth-century book of demonology which was banned by Pope Innocent VI, I found an account which said, 'Satan walks abroad, offering his assistance to those in the direst need. When cattle give no milk, he will work his magic to restore their flow. When crops die, he will ensure that they flourish. He will appear to be a savior and a friend to all, but woe betide any who do not pay him what he demands, for he will surely take more than they can bear to give him.'

The ritual for reviving crops was recounted in detail. It involved lighting five fires, and sprinkling seven spoonfuls of powder into each of them, and inscribing a five-pointed star in the soil. The sorcerer would then tap five bones together and repeat the words of the Satanic invocation five times. '*I summon thee, O Prince of Darkness, O Spirit of the Pit . . .*' and so on.

I made a few notes and then I sat back and had a long think. This sounded like total mumbo-jumbo, but if it didn't work at all, why had it survived for more than twenty-three centuries? And what had *really* happened in Roseau, when the wheat harvest had failed?

While Jenny and the kids were out, I decided to try an experiment. I pulled on my boots and my thick plaid coat and I took Satan's box out into the snow-covered yard. I lit five fires out of kindling, and drew a five-pointed star with a sharp stick, and then I walked around each of the fires in turn, spooning in powder from Satan's screw-top jars. To finish up, I unwrapped the bones, and held them between my fingers, and rattled them together while I read out the Satanic invocation.

'*I adjure thee to grant my will and my pleasure. I adjure thee to make my crop grow tall and strong. Venite O Satan, amen.*'

It was then that Ben Kellerman looked over the fence with his duck-hunting cap on. 'Christ, Jack, what the hell are you doing out here? Cooking a chicken with the feathers still on it?'

'Sorry, Ben. Just trying something out.'

'Well next time you want to try something out, make sure the wind's blowing in the opposite direction.'

I had to admit that Ben was right. As the powders crackled in the fires, they gave off swirls of thick, pungent smoke, and the smoke smelled of incinerated flesh, and hair, and scorched wool. It was what witches must have smelled like, when they were burned at the stake.

After I had finished the invocation, I packed the bones and the powders back into the box and went back inside. I watched the fires for a while, in the gathering gloom of a winter's afternoon, but eventually the wind began to rise, and scatter the yard with sparks and ashes.

I had to go to Portland, Oregon, that weekend, to attend a convention of wood pulpers. As you can imagine, wood pulpers are not the most scintillating people you'll ever meet. They're very rich, most of them, I'll grant you that. They're deeply concerned about the environment, too – mainly because of the eye-watering fines they're likely to incur if they don't replant the acres of forest that they've turned into cardboard boxes. But when I wasn't discussing the comparative profitability of different species of fir, or the joys of corrugated packaging, I retreated to my hotel room with the latest Michael Crichton novel and a large glass of Canadian Club.

On the third evening, when I returned to my room, the red light on the phone was blinking. It was Jenny, and she had left me a voice message. 'Something so weird has happened . . . it's in the back yard. There's *grass* growing, right up through the snow.'

And so there was. By the time I got home, mid-morning on Monday, there were hundreds of thin green spears of grass rising at least three inches clear of the snow, all over the yard, and a few weeds, too. I knelt down and brushed the palm of my hand across them.

'Grass doesn't usually grow in November, does it?' asked Jenny. 'Not like this.'

'No, not usually.'

'There isn't any grass growing in anybody else's yard, only ours.'

I stood up. 'I know. I know there isn't.'

So it worked. The ritual performed by the Sad Dog River Satan actually worked. He *had* revived their wheat crop. He *had* been responsible for giving them a bumper harvest, and saving them all from starvation. Of course there was no rational scientific explanation for it. None of the powders had been sprinkled on the ground in sufficient quantity to act as a growth accelerant, even if any of them had been components of any recognized fertilizer, which they weren't. You can't make your cabbages grow bigger by showering them with crushed mirrors and frogs' blood.

I went back into the house, but I couldn't resist looking out of the window from time to time, and each time I looked it seemed as if the grass was even taller, and even thicker.

If this ritual worked, then I was going to be rich. No two ways about it. I could sell my services to every farm and forestry department in the country. Think of it. They would never risk losing a crop to drought or storms or diseases. They wouldn't need nitrogen, phosphorous and potassium any more, only me. I would save them billions of dollars, and I could charge them millions.

'You're very quiet,' said Jenny, over our spaghetti supper.

I smiled at her, and nodded. 'I was thinking about Christmas, that's all. I think it might have come early this year.'

During November the grass in our yard continued to grow thick and lush, and I had to cut it with a sickle every weekend. I took two weeks off work, and I sat down with my accountant George Nevis and mapped out a business plan, although I didn't tell George exactly what my product was. 'Just take a look out of the window, George. It's the middle of winter, in St Paul, and I can make the grass grow. This is my very first test, but I believe I can do the same thing for every cash crop in the world.'

George blinked at me through his thick-lensed eyeglasses. 'Jack, you're talking very serious profit here. But not just profit. This has huge political implications, too. Like, *huge*. Even the President can't make the grass grow in the middle of winter.'

I patted him on the back. 'It's a new era, George, and it belongs to me.'

Two days before Christmas, Jenny came into my study and said, 'There's somebody to see you. He wouldn't give his name.'

I was having a headache working out a franchise scheme for Miracle Crop Services. Obviously it was going to be impossible for me to visit every potential customer in person, so I would have to employ people to tour the country and perform the ritual for me. The principal problem was that – once I had told them how it was done, and given them the wherewithal to do it – they could go out and do it on their own and tell me to stick my franchise where you don't need Ray-Bans.

'Sorry – whoever it is, tell him I'm busy.'

But Jenny came back a few moments later and said, 'He says he really has to see you. It's about the grass.'

'OK, OK.' I left my desk and went to the front door. A tall, thin man was standing in the porch, one side of his face illuminated scarlet by the sunshine that came through the stained-glass window, the other side yellow. He wore a black wide-brimmed hat and a long black coat and his hair was almost shoulder length, dry and gray. He had a large nose, but otherwise his face was strangely unmemorable, as if he had moved his head while his photograph was being taken.

'Hallo, Jack,' he said, but he didn't extend his hand.

'Yes? I'm very busy, I'm afraid.'

'Well, I've come to relieve you of all of that.'

'Excuse me?'

'I believe that you have something that belongs to me. In fact, I only had to look over into your back yard to *know* that you have something that belongs to me.'

'I don't know what you're talking about. I think you'd better get off my property before I call the cops.'

'My box, Jack. My trusty old box, with all of my powders and my bones and my –' and here he held up his finger and thumb and made a little shaking gesture – '*jingle*, *jingle*, sleigh bells.'

'I don't have anything that belongs to you. I don't even know who the hell you are.'

The man gave the faintest of smiles. 'I think you know exactly who I am, Jack. I'm the kind of man who can wait a very long time to get what he wants. I'm the kind of man who follows you right to the ends of the earth. You have my trusty old box, Jack. I went back for it and it wasn't there and it sure took some sniffing around to find out what had happened to it.'

'It was abandoned. It was lying in the dirt. Who's to say it's yours?'

'It's mine because it's mine, Jack, and I want it back.'

'Well, forget it. OK? You understand English? That box is mine now and you don't have any way of proving different.'

'So what are you going to do with it, Jack? Apart from making your back yard look like Kentucky?'

'I don't have to tell you what I'm going to do with it.'

The man smiled even more widely, his eyes glittering in his red-and-yellow harlequin face. 'I know. You think you're going to make your fortune, don't you? You think you're going to be rich beyond the dreams of men. But it doesn't work that way, Jack. Never has. The ritual works once and only once. It gives you a helping hand when you're lower than low and you don't know what else to do. And it always carries its price, and one way or another, you have to pay that price, in full.'

'OK, you've had your say. Now I'm calling the cops.'

'You still don't get it, do you? The ritual isn't an act of kindness. I'm not in the charity business, Jack, never have been. The ritual is temptation. The ritual is what you turn to when the Lord thy God appears to have abandoned you. Why do you think I come at Christmas-time? Is there anything more satisfying than having somebody deny their faith on the very eve of the Virgin Birth?'

'You're crazy. Get out of here.'

'I want my trusty old box, Jack, I'm warning you, and if I don't get my trusty old box, you're going to have to pay me recompense.'

I slammed the door in his face. He waited outside for a while: I could see his face through the hammered-glass porthole. Then he turned and went away, closing the screen door very carefully so that it didn't make a sound.

Tracey and Mikey came scuttling down the stairs and Mikey said, 'Daddy banged the door!'

'The wind caught it,' I told him, tousling his hair.

Jenny came out of the kitchen looking worried. 'Who was that man? What did he want?'

'Nothing. Just a bum, looking for a handout.'

'You were angry with him. I heard you.'

'I told you, it's nothing.'

I tried to go back into my study but Jenny caught my arm. 'There's something wrong, isn't there? Ever since you came home from Roseau, you've been acting so strange.'

'There's nothing wrong. In fact everything's one hundred and ninety percent right. This year we're going to have a Christmas we'll remember for the rest of our lives.'

It snowed on Christmas Eve and carol singers came around from house to house, carrying lanterns. Tracey and Mikey knelt up on the window seat looking out at the street and their faces were lit up by the Christmas lights. Jenny squeezed my hand and said, 'Mikey's so excited I think he's going to be sick.'

We had supper together, and then the children put out Tracey's Christmas cake and a glass of Canadian Club for Santa. The cake was lopsided but I assured Tracey that Santa wouldn't mind, in fact Lopsided Cake was his favorite. I hugged them both before they went to bed and believe me there is no smell like the smell of your own children at Christmas. You don't need spices or mulled wine.

As we sat together that evening, Jenny said, 'I wish you'd tell me what's really going on.'

'Nothing at all. I'm planning to go into crop management, that's all. I've had enough years of experience, growing things.'

'But that man. He wasn't just a bum, was he? He said he wanted to talk to you about the grass.'

'He was being nosey, that's all.'

She frowned at me. 'It isn't just a freak of nature, is it, that grass?'

'What else could it be?'

'You tell me. There's some sort of connection, isn't there, between the grass growing like that and you wanting to start up a new business? Why can't you tell me what it is?'

'You wouldn't understand it even if I told you. It's too technical.'

She suddenly sat up straight. 'You used the things in that box, didn't you, like that man in Roseau?' God, women and their intuition. 'You did the same ritual, and it worked.'

'Jenny – don't be ridiculous. You can't make grass grow by burning fires and sprinkling powder on it.'

'There were ashes on the snow, I saw them. You did it, didn't you, and it worked?'

I took a deep breath. 'All right, yes. I did it and it worked. And if it works for the grass and it works for wheat it's going to work for corn and broccoli and potatoes and rutabaga. God knows, it may even work for sheep and cows. That's why this is going to be the best Christmas ever. This is the Christmas when we start getting very, very rich.'

'So what did that man want?'

'I told you. He was sticking his nose in where it wasn't wanted. He saw the grass and wondered how I'd managed to grow it.'

'And you slammed the door on him?'

'Jenny—'

'Jack, I have a very bad feeling about this. I mean it. Using the things in that box – that's like making a deal with the devil.'

'It's folk magic, that's all. It's perfectly harmless.'

At that moment the phone rang. Jenny answered it but it was Jerry, wanting to talk to me.

'Listen, Jack, I don't want to spoil your Christmas Eve, but something's happened.'

'What is it? You sound terrible. Do you have a cold?'

'I called Alma. You remember Alma from the North Star Bar?'

'Of course I remember Alma. What about her?'

'I called her. I was going to invite her down to St Paul for New Year's.'

'So? Is she coming?'

'She's dead, Jack. They found her this morning. She and John Shooks, both. It seems like a guy came into the bar two nights ago asking about a tin box. He talked to Alma and he talked to John Shooks and it seems like they wouldn't tell him nothing, and there was some kind of an argument.

'It was Alma's day off yesterday, but when she didn't show up this morning the manager went to look for her. He broke into her room and there she was in bed with her head cut off. Tortured, too, all of her fingernails and toenails pulled out. The cops went round to John Shooks' place and the same thing had happened to him. Jesus – they haven't even found their heads yet.'

I talked to Jerry a while longer, just to calm him down, but then I had to put the phone down, because I was starting to shake. That was how the man in the black hat had discovered where I lived. And if he could do that to Alma Lindenmuth and John Shooks just to find me, what was he going to do to *me*?

'*If I don't get my trusty old box, you're going to have to pay me recompense*.'

We went to bed late that night, well after midnight. All I told Jenny about Jerry was that two of his friends had been killed in an accident. I didn't want *her* to start worrying, too. We tippy-toed into the children's room and filled the pillowcases they had left out for Santa – a Bratz doll and a hairbrush set for Tracey and a collection of Harry Potter figures for Mikey, as well as candies and oranges and nuts.

I left their doorway a couple of inches ajar and then I followed Jenny to the bedroom. 'You're so *tense*,' she said. 'What's the matter?'

'Nothing, really.'

'Jack – what I said about making a deal with the devil – I didn't really mean it.'

'Well, maybe it was a pretty stupid thing for me to do.'

'If you think it's really going to make us rich—'

I took hold of her hands and kissed her on the forehead. 'I don't know. Sometimes you can stop and take a look at yourself and it hits you – my God, is this really *me*, behaving like this?'

'You're a good man, Jack.'

'I used to think so. Now I'm not so sure.'

We went to bed but this was another night when I couldn't sleep. The hours ticked by and the clock in the hallway chimed each hour. At three o'clock, after the chimes had died away, I was sure that I could hear a faint jingling. Just an echo, probably. I had a brief fight with my pillow and tried to get comfortable, but the covers were all twisted and I didn't want to pull them too hard in case I woke Jenny.

As I settled down, I heard the jingling again. It was slightly louder this time, and closer. I lay in the darkness, waiting and listening. Then I heard a hollow knocking sound, right outside our bedroom window, as if something had struck the fascia boards around the guttering. I eased myself out of bed and looked outside.

It was steadily snowing, and the street was glistening white. There, in our driveway, was a long black sleigh, with eight shaggy black dogs harnessed in it, panting patiently. The sleigh was empty, except for a heap of black sacks. I suddenly realized what the knocking sound had been – a long ladder, placed against the house.

'Jenny!' I shouted at her, shaking her shoulder. 'Jenny, wake up! Call the police!

She sat up and stared at me blurrily.

'Call nine one one! Do it now!'

But right above us, I heard footsteps crossing the roof, and then the creak of shingles being torn out. The children, for God's sake. He was trying to get to the children.

I hurtled along the landing to the children's room, but as I reached the door it slammed shut, and I heard the key turn. I pummeled against the paneling with my fists, and I threw my shoulder against it, but it wouldn't budge.

'Tracey! Mikey! Wake up! Open the door! Open the door and get out of there, quick!'

I heard more creaks as nails were dragged out of the roof. I hammered on the door again and shouted, 'Tracey! Mikey! Wake up! You have to get out of there!'

Now I heard Mikey crying, and Tracey calling, 'What is it? What is it? The ceiling's breaking!'

'The door's locked! Turn the key and get out of there, quick as you can!'

Jenny came hurrying along the landing, her hair wild. 'The police are coming right now. Five minutes, they said. What's happening?'

'Open the door Tracey goddamnit! Open the door!'

'I can't!' wailed Tracey. 'The key won't turn!'

'What's happening?' Jenny screamed at me. 'What's happening? Why can't you open the door?'

'It's him,' I told her. 'It's the man who came this afternoon. It's Satan.'

'What? What have you done? Get my children out of there! Get my children out of there!'

I held on to the banister and kicked at the door with my bare feet, but it was too solid to budge. Inside, Tracey and Mikey were shrieking hysterically.

'Daddy! Somebody's coming through the ceiling! Daddy, open the door! It's a man and he's coming through the ceiling!'

Oh shit, I thought. Oh shit oh shit. Jenny was totally panicking now and beating at the door so hard that she was breaking all her nails and spattering the paintwork with blood.

God there was only one thing to do and I hoped it wasn't too late. I ran along the landing and down the stairs, three at a time. Jenny called after me, 'Where are you going? Jack! We have to open the door!'

'Mommy! Mommy! I can see his legs! Open the door, mommy!'

I careered through the kitchen and opened the door that led to the garage. I seized the metal box from my workbench and went running back upstairs with it.

'What good will that do?' Jenny screamed at me. 'You could have brought your ax!'

But I went up close to the door and shouted out, 'Listen to me! I have it! Your box! If you let my children alone and open the door you can have it back right now!'

I heard a crack-*thump* as the man broke through the last of the plaster and dropped down on to the floor. Tracey moaned and Mikey gave that little yelp that he always gives when he's really, seriously scared.

'Can you hear me?' I asked him. 'I have it right here in my hand. You can have it back, no questions asked, no charges brought, nothing. Just open the door and take the box and we'll let you leave.'

There was a long, long silence. I could still hear Mikey mewling so the man couldn't have hurt them yet.

'Please,' I said. 'Those are our children.'

Jenny stood close beside me, clenching and unclenching her bloodied fists. Then she suddenly screeched out, '*Open the door you bastard*! *Open the door*!'

Another silence, and then the key was turned. The door swung open by itself.

Tracey and Mikey were cowering down behind Mikey's bed. The man was standing in the middle of their bedroom, his black clothes covered in plaster dust. He had torn a hole in the ceiling three feet across and snow was whirling into the bedroom, and melting as it touched the carpet. He was holding a large curved sickle, with a black handle and an oily blade.

I stepped forward, lifting the box in my left hand. 'Here,' I said. 'Everything's in there, except for the powder I used on the grass.'

He smiled at me, and hooked his sickle into his belt, and took the box in both hands.

'I'm sorry I took it,' I told him. 'I didn't realize that it was yours . . . that you were still alive after all those years.'

Jenny skirted around behind me, took hold of Tracey and Mikey, and hurried them out of the bedroom. The man raised one eyebrow and said, 'Beautiful children. You were wise.'

'No . . . I was just what you said I was. Greedy. Wanting something for nothing. And I almost lost my family because of it.'

'Oh, I shouldn't be too hard on yourself, Jack. We all make mistakes.'

His mistake was to put the box down on the floor and open it up, just to make sure that everything was there. He should have trusted me. While he was bent over it, I swung myself around like a baseball pitcher and lifted the sickle that I was holding in my right hand. He sensed my movement and began to raise his eyes but it was then that I hit him across the back of the neck and the sickle chopped right through his dry gray hair and right through his vertebrae and halfway through his throat. His head dropped forward on to his chest as if it were attached by a hinge, and blood jumped out of his neck and into the box. He looked at me – he actually looked at me, upside-down, from under his arm, and that look would give me nightmares for countless Christmases to come. Then he fell sideways on to the carpet.

I didn't want to do it, but somehow I knew that I had to. I turned him over and hacked at his neck twice more, until his head was completely severed. After that I didn't have the strength to do anything else, but kneel beside him with gloves made of gradually-drying blood, while the snow fell on to my shoulders, and a police siren warbled closer and closer.

It was Christmas Day, and Santa had been.

Sarcophagus

'Are you sure this is safe?' asked Maureen. The evening sun had suddenly entered her dorm room, so she had to lift one podgy hand to shield her eyes.

'Of course it's safe,' Myron told her. 'The ancient Egyptians did it, in the reign of King Seti, thirteenth century BC. If the king complained that one of his concubines was growing too chubby, his eunuch used to find a sarcophagus beetle, and insert it under her skin. Then he let it roam around inside her for a couple of hours.

'They eat subcutaneous fat, that's all these suckers eat. It's natural liposuction.'

Maureen looked at the small brown-and-yellow beetle that was struggling to climb up the side of the Perspex box. It looked harmless enough, like a ladybug.

Myron took off his glasses and polished them on his Albert Einstein T-shirt. 'It's your decision. Sure, your fifty bucks will help me to buy some more rare insect specimens, but you're very pretty as you are. A little *zaftig,* maybe.'

It was *zaftig* that decided her. 'I'll do it,' said Maureen. She heaved herself back on the bed and lifted up her XXL sweatshirt. Myron sat next to her, took a scalpel out of a sterilized wrapper, and pinched three inches of flesh from the left side of her stomach.

'This will hurt just a tad,' he told her, and cut a quarter-inch slit, right into her underlying fat. Blood ran into her panty elastic.

Carefully, Myron opened the Perspex box. He used a drinking straw to suck out the beetle, and to drop it over Maureen's open cut. It immediately burrowed beneath her skin.

'It feels like a spider crawling all over me,' said Maureen. 'But *inside.*'

Myron checked his watch. 'I'll be back in two hours exactly. By that time you should look like Gwyneth Paltrow.'

As he stepped outside the dorm, Myron collided with a tall, slim, dark-haired girl in skintight jeans.

'Ellie? Ellie Newman? Well, look at you!'

Ellie grinned. 'Atkins Diet. I lost forty-eight pounds.'

'You look *great*! Do you have time for a drink?'

Walking Ellie back to her dorm, Myron heard the campus clock strike eleven.

'Shit,' he said, clapping his hand to his mouth. 'Maureen.'

'What about Maureen?'

He pushed open the door. Maureen's room was in darkness. He switched on the light. Maureen was still lying on her bed. Her face was a glittery-eyed skull, and her skin hung from her shoulders like heavy folds of drapery.

'Myron,' she croaked. 'Am I thin, Myron?'

As he approached her, Myron heard scratching coming from the bathroom, followed by a wallowing sound. Cautiously, he peered inside.

Underneath the basin was a huge, distended bag. It was translucent, so Myron could see that it was filled with thick lumps of white fat. It was only when he looked closer that he could see its tiny black head, and its minuscule legs.

'Yes, Maureen, you're thin,' he said. 'You don't have an ounce of fat on you.'